To Minda,

Louise

The Longing of the Day

A Tale of
Bittersweet Love
and Savage
Challenges in
Wyoming Territory

Louise Lenahan Wallace

by Louise Lenahan Wallace

OGDEN PUBLICATIONS INC.
Topeka, Kansas

ISBN 0-941678-65-2
First printing, August 2000; second printing October 2000.
Printed and bound in the United States of America

Fireside Library

Other books by OGDEN PUBLICATIONS

These Lonesome Hills	Letha Boyer
Home in the Hills	Letha Boyer
Of These Contented Hills	Letha Boyer
The Talking Hills	Letha Boyer
Born Tall	Garnet Tien
The Turning Wheel	Garnet Tien
The Farm	LaNelle Dickinson Kearney
The Family	LaNelle Dickinson Kearney
Lizzy Ida's Luxury	Zoe Rexroad
Lizzy Ida's Mail Order Grandma	Zoe Rexroad
Mandy to the Rescue	Zoe Rexroad
Carpenter's Cabin	Cleoral Lovell
Quest for the Shepherd's Son	Juanita Killough Urbach
Martin's Nest	Ellie Watson McMasters
Third Time for Charm	Mabel Killian
To Marry a Stranger	Glenda McRae
Pledges in the West	Glenda McRae
Sod Schoolhouse	Courtner King and Bonnie Bess Worline
Texas Wildflower	Debra Hall
River Run to Texas	George Chaffee
Aurora	Marie Kramer
Home on the Trail	Mona Exinger
Horseshoe Creek	C.P. Sargent
Dr. Julie's Apprentice	Don White

For more information about Ogden Publications titles,
or to place an order, please call:
(800) 678-4883

Dedication

To my Mom,
Della Ladd Lenahan,
with love.
— Louise

The Longing of the Day

By Louise Lenahan Wallace

Come to me in my dreams, and then
By day I shall be well again!
For then the night will more than pay
The hopeless longing of the day.
— From *Longing*
by Matthew Arnold

Prologue
1865

The night was sultry that early summer evening. It was also still. Too still. No breeze rustled the cottonwood leaves. No bellow of frog nor chirp of cricket nor beat of insect wing disturbed the hush. Even the creek, sunk summer-dry shallow in its rocky bed, slunk muted on its mysterious journey to the river.

The log cabin, too, hulked, a silent presence in the night. No smoke drifted from the chimney, and not even the faintest spark of light escaped the tightly bound shutters and door.

The moon had not yet risen as though it, too, had been caught up in the silence. The deafening silence. The waiting silence.

When movement came, it was so stealthy the stillness was not disturbed. The cabin door inched open. A shrouded figure emerged and blended with the night even before the door swung swiftly shut.

Hidden in black-cloak folds, the man turned at once toward the creek. A few swift strides, and he had gained the water's edge. Bending low, he opened his cape and pulled it away from the small boy desperately clinging to him.

1

The Longing of the Day

Gently, but firmly, the man sought to disengage the trembling arms from around his neck, speaking in a bare whisper as he did so. "Let go, Matt, so you can take Catty."

For another instant the clenched fists clung in a strangling hug, then obediently slid away. The man waited until Matt hunched down in the shelter of a weedy bush before he handed the child the blanket-wrapped bundle he had been carrying in his other arm.

"Take care of Catty, son. Your Ma and me are dependin' on you to stay here and be quiet. You must be a big boy and remember what we told you."

Matt's gray eyes, wide with uncertainty and pleading, fastened on his father's haggard face. Finding no trace of relenting, no hope of reprieve in those stern features, he gulped and nodded.

The father reached out and let his hand linger against his son's tousled black hair. His eyes — the same campfire smoke gray as Matt's — softened. But only for an instant before they steeled again. He enfolded the two children in a swift hug, glanced around, and rose to glide noiselessly back to the cabin. The door opened a crack. He slipped inside, and the night was left to wait in shrouded silence once more.

Alone in the darkness, Matt peered about fearfully. In all his 3 years he had never been outside at night by himself. Faint pricklings of starlight transformed rocks and weeds into weird shapes. He could hear his own loud breathing and feel his heart thumping fiercely and noisily against his shirt.

Night odors rose around him. The dankness of creek water and rotting weeds along the bank. The plains grass heavy with dew and the acrid, crushed leaves of the bush

2

under which he huddled.

His arms were cramping, hanging on to Catty, but he dared not put her down. Papa said to hold her, and he'd be furious if he came back and found Matt had disobeyed. Still all too vivid in his memory was the strapping he'd received when Mama told him to watch Catty, and he had gone instead to the creek for a drink because the water bucket was empty. Thus, from his earliest days, his parents exacted instant and absolute obedience from him. So he sat and clutched his sister and watched the night shadows flicker, never leaving the fragile shelter of the bush.

Not even when calls and cries and hideous screams shattered the silence or when living shadows leaped, withdrew and leaped again. He huddled, too terrified to cry, head bowed over the baby. He didn't know why the black night glowed so red around him; he was only aware that, suddenly, it had become very quiet again, and he wondered why Papa didn't come.

Cold and cramped, he hunched under the bush, waiting. At last he slept from sheer exhaustion, and the baby quietly slept, too.

He stirred, frowning, cold because his dog Rascal had pulled all the covers off the bed. Smoke from Mama's breakfast fire stung heavy against his nose, and Catty whimpered close by his ear. Old Sage's hooves, thumping as Papa rode up to the door, brought Matt to blinking wakefulness.

For another slow second, actuality and imagination teetered before reality bit deep into his belly with cruel fangs. The creek at his feet. Catty's whimpers changing to high-pitched cries. And memory of a stern command they must make no noise.

The Longing of the Day

Out of a night of events he didn't understand, his mind gripped the one clear fact of his father's warning even as his arms gripped his sister. But as he desperately tried to hush her, she only wailed harder for the milk he could not give her.

"Shut up, Catty," he pleaded. "Please!"

So frantic were his efforts to shush her, he didn't notice the boots that stopped in front of him until he looked up, far up past homespun pants and plaid shirt, into grief-stricken eyes. Papa's friend.

But Matt's first relief that adult help had come at last fled. The man looked so angry. Instinctively, Matt tried to dodge the big hands that reached down to draw Catty from him, but he quickly found struggling was no use against the man's iron strength.

He and Catty were seized in a fierce-squeezing embrace, his face pushed against the prickly plaid shirt. Familiar odors of leather and shaving soap filled his nose. Eagerly he raised his head to look for Papa but couldn't find him. He looked back in blinking confusion to the grim face above him.

He was miserably cold and hungry — and wet. Catty had made a huge soggy spot in the back of the blanket she was wrapped in, and it had seeped through onto his own pants. *Why didn't Mama come?* He wanted his Mama. But this man holding him, who smelled just like Papa, was saying he would take Matt and Catty to his home.

Matt didn't understand at all. He had crouched under the bush just like he was told. He had hung onto Catty. And he had kept as quiet as he could.

Boosted firmly up onto the front of a horse so tall it made him dizzy to watch the ground slide backward beneath the galloping hooves, he hugged Catty to his small chest. Feeling the man's rough shirt sleeve scratching against his cheek, bewilderment overwhelmed Matt. Mama and Papa must be awful mad at him. But he hadn't meant to be bad. He couldn't even remember what he'd done wrong.

He had not cried throughout all those past terrible hours. Now, riding away, leaving behind all he knew of home, he bent his head over his baby sister. Tears — huge, silent, hopeless — began to slide slowly down his cheeks.

1886

"Ma, Ma! Buttermilk's calving!" Eighteen-year-old Eve burst into the kitchen where her mother was ironing, causing Anne Clayton to jump a foot and swat her hand against the just reheated iron.

"Eve!" she sputtered. "You scared me half to death!"

"Sorry, but Ma, I really think she's calving! You better come look."

Praying it was not so, knowing it was too soon, Anne rushed to the barn. A hasty check of the cow's eyes and breathing proved Buttermilk was, indeed, calving. By the end of the hour, she had dropped a heifer.

"Ma, she's so small." Eve's blue eyes were wide with apprehension. "Will she be all right?"

"She looks well formed," Anne said cautiously. "If we can get her on her feet and sucking, she might make it."

Even as she spoke, the calf gave a sudden, violent sneeze and flailed out with her still-soft hooves. The two women dodged backward and watched the miracle. The baby calf shook herself and began the process of standing. She was hampered by the fact her front legs wanted to go north and

The Longing of the Day

her back ones south. Stumbling to her knees, she emitted a miniature blat. At the sound, Buttermilk stepped over to her and began washing the tiny face. The baby flipped her ears, tried again and succeeded in getting all her legs under her facing one way. She sneezed again and nuzzled her mother. Buttermilk responded by lowing softly and proceeding with a more vigorous washing, which almost knocked the calf over.

"We did it, Ma." Eve's voice held awe.

Watching the calf now suckling eagerly, Anne nodded. "I think she might just make it." They cleaned the stall, gave Buttermilk a generous mash and made certain she had plenty of fresh water nearby before they returned to the house. The kitchen, with bright braided rugs on the floor and daisy yellow curtains at the window over the sink, was Anne's favorite room. Once there, she wanted nothing so much as to collapse in a chair and never move again. Eyeing Eve, however, she was forced to laugh. "If I look as much a wreck as you, I'll disown myself!"

Eve chuckled. "You'd better not look in a mirror then. I just hope Reverend Wardley doesn't pick this morning for a pastoral visit. He'd really get his back up, wouldn't he?"

"Don't be disrespectful," Anne warned sternly.

Only after a chastened Eve had started for her bedroom to get cleaned up did Anne allow herself to contemplate the proper minister's probable reaction to their appearance. Her sudden fit of choking laughter caused Eve to call out in alarm, "Ma, are you all right?"

"Of course," Anne gasped. "I just swallowed when I shouldn't have." *And that*, she thought wryly, *is certainly swift vengeance for uncharitable thoughts. Will I never*

8

learn? Probably not, sighed a small voice from her interior as a new wave of amusement welled.

In her own room, heedless of her stained dress, Anne sank onto the edge of the neatly made bed. All the starch had gone out of her. She would just rest a moment and then get back to ...

"Ma, do you have any extra hairpins?" Eve asked from the doorway. "A couple of mine must have slipped out."

Startled by her daughter's plaintive tone, Anne glanced up and chuckled before she could stop herself. "You do look a tad lopsided," she admitted with kindly understatement, surveying Eve's red-gold braids. The right one remained sedately looped across the top of her head. The left one, still partially pinned, adorned her nose. "As a fashion trend, I think it needs a bit of reworking," Anne teased. "The pins are in the box on the dresser. Help yourself."

"Thanks, Ma." Eve tucked in a final pin and inspected her reflection critically. "That's much better. When I leaned over to fasten my shoe, the whole thing just plopped into my face, sudden as a bronc buster eatin' the dust, pride first."

Her blue eyes twinkled so mischievously Anne hadn't the heart to chide her. Her sometimes too-precisely descriptive language came from tagging behind three older and vocal brothers from the time she could walk. *It's a wonder she came out civilized at all,* Anne acknowledged ruefully. She allowed herself to smile only after Eve returned to her own bedroom.

Alone again, Anne glanced in the mirror over the dressing table, her fingers instinctively reaching to jiggle the bun at the back of her head. Her hair, once as rich and copper

The Longing of the Day

gleaming as Eve's, was now faded and gray streaked. It still caught her off guard, sometimes, when she looked in the mirror. *When did my hair become my mother's?* Satisfied it wasn't about to imitate the walls of Jericho and come tumbling down, she peeked over her shoulder to make certain Eve hadn't come back. Reassured by a lilting voice from her daughter's room singing about scarlet ribbons, she permitted herself the luxury of scowling hideously at her reflection before she became practical again, of necessity losing the wistfulness in the thought that she might have to buy more pins the next time she was in town. Lifting the lid of her odds-and-ends box, she stirred the small pile experimentally. Yes, she would have to add pins to her list.

As she was about to close the lid, her glance fell on the gold pocket watch lying in the box. After a moment's hesitation, she reached to lift it out. Turning it over, she closed her eyes and smoothed her work-worn fingers over the words etched on the back.

Amanda to Stephen — 1860

The watch rightfully belonged to Matthew and Catherine Jamison. Ben had found it in 3-year-old Matt's pocket after the Indian raid that killed the children's parents.

For the thousandth time, her mind skidded back two decades to that night, five months after her own child's death, when Ben had brought Matt and Catty home.

Those had been called the Bloody Years and with good reason. Between 1862 and 1868, hundreds of soldiers and settlers in Wyoming had been massacred in Indian raids. On a summer night in 1865, it had been Stephen and Amanda Jamison, the Claytons' nearest neighbors.

After Ben could talk about it to her, he told of finding the children by the edge of the creek. How Matt, huddled in the high grass, cradling his baby sister, tried to soothe her cries while their home burned to nothing behind them.

When Ben tried to take Catty from Matt, the little boy protested fiercely that he couldn't give her to anyone else because his Ma and Pa had told him to take care of her. Without a word, Ben folded the little boy, still clutching the baby, into his own arms and held them close to his chest on the horse. Pain-mute, he carried them together to Anne — Anne, still so grief-numbed for baby Elizabeth, who had lived only a few short hours. Anne — so ice-locked in pain that she had shut her heart to her husband, to her sons, to the world. But something, a tiny spark, ignited Anne as she saw Matt, so fiercely protective of his baby sister, too young for the burden thrust upon him. Matt stared at Anne a long moment. Two bleeding hearts connected. "Ma and Pa said f'r me to take care of Catty. Will you help me?"

After five wretched months, the helplessness of those two little ones thawed the frozen numbness of her anguished yearning for her dead baby. Pierced it and gave her back her life, her sanity — her self.

For the first time in all those awful weeks, tears welled in her eyes. As she opened her arms, Matt carefully handed the baby to her. She gathered Catty into one arm and Matt into the other and both of them into her heart. She felt Matt begin to shudder against her. Rubbing her cheek against his, she looked up to see Ben watching, tears trickling unheeded

The Longing of the Day

down his cheeks. She had never seen him cry before.

Now, 21 years later, her fingers closed around the watch. Ben wouldn't hear of Anne's giving it to Matt and Catty. "The time ain't right," he kept insisting. "Matt and Catty know the truth. We made certain of that a long time ago. But we've raised 'em. They're ours now, just as sure as Jason or Luke or Eve. So why stir ever'thin' up?"

She tried so hard to explain, patiently pointing out the watch was all Matt and Catty had of their birth parents. "They have a right to be able to keep it themselves."

But Ben shook his head, and the stark pain in his eyes pierced her heart. "They gave you back to me when I thought I'd lost you," he said slowly. "C'n you forget that? I can't."

So seldom did Ben show his deepest emotions by pleading with her. But he had been pleading then. "When the time is right, we'll give it to 'em," he promised, "but not yet."

Anne sighed and laid the watch gently back in the box. In 21 years, the time had never been right.

With effort, Anne pushed the old doubt to the back of her mind. With Ben and Matt gone on spring roundup, there was so much to do both in the house and out. She had little time to give thought to a worry that wasn't immediately pressing. Returning to the kitchen, she glared at the pile of ironing waiting for her. The pile, not the least intimidated into shrinking, merely glared back.

She sighed, built up the fire and put her flatirons back on the stove to heat. Her weary, cross mood wasn't in the least eased when her daughter came bouncing into the room, chipper as a cricket on the hearth. "Know what I feel like doing?" Eve asked brightly. "Making a pumpkin pie."

Anne, feeling as wrung out as yesterday's dish rag from the morning in the barn, did not say, "What on earth for?" She did not look at her daughter as though Eve had taken leave of her senses. She did, however, take a deep, steadying breath before allowing herself to speak. "You and I couldn't possibly eat a whole pie before it spoils," she pointed out — most reasonably, she thought.

Eve's laughter bubbled up. "I know, Ma, but I have a feeling Pa and Matt will come home today. A pumpkin pie would be a real treat for them after all that range food."

Anne took a firmer grip on her reasonableness. "But they can't possibly be back for another two or three days — or even a week. It's much too early."

"I know it seems early, but I just have a feeling. And if I make one and they don't come today, we can always take it over to Luke and Hannah's. For certain, it won't go to waste there with the four boys. Or even over to Aaron and Catty's. We haven't seen her for almost a week." Sensing Anne was weakening a bit, Eve added, temptingly, "It'd be a good excuse. You were saying just last night you've been meaning to go over."

When Anne still held out, mostly because she loathed to admit she didn't have her daughter's energy for tackling such a project, Eve added the final, cunning offer. "I'll make the pie. It'll only take a minute to get one in the oven. While it's baking, you can have a hot cup of tea, and I'll finish the ironing."

Anne's lips twitched with poorly suppressed amusement. "You ever think of taking up horse trading? You've bought yourself a pumpkin pie and an iron. I still say they

13

The Longing of the Day

won't be back for at least a week. But it would be nice for them to get back early. I wonder what they're doing right now?" It was an old game she and Eve played, trying to put themselves on the roundup at any given time.

"Honestly, Ma," Eve burst out, "wouldn't you like to trade places with them just once, so you'd know what it's really like out there? Instead of having to stay home year after year and guess, and then have them come and tell about all the exciting things they've been doing." Anne obediently considered the image of Ben scrubbing the kitchen floor on his hands and knees, and herself wrestling a calf to the branding fire. No, she simply could not picture barrel-chested, muscular Ben in a ruffled pink apron.

"I bet they're all cozy in camp right now, drinking coffee, swapping stories and just taking it so-o-o easy, while we're here, doing all this back-breaking work," Eve said indignantly, knowing perfectly well her suspicions were exaggerated, but fortunately, not knowing how completely wide of the post her guess had looped.

Springtime on the Wyoming plains! How good to be alive on a day such as this, Matt thought, *to be riding over the newly green grasses with the wind catching the scent of a thousand fragrances.*

"Hey, Matt, you hear that?"

Twenty-four-year-old Matt Jamison pulled his sorrel to a halt beside Will Braden's gray. To the east, wind whispered through the willows. From above, a band of crows hurled insults. And north ...

"Sounds like he's tanglin' with a wildcat f'r sure!" Matt said.

"If noise ever lost a go-to, he's in deep trouble."

Urging their mounts to a lope, the young cowmen rounded an up-thrusting rock slab and found themselves staring down a sheer, seemingly bottomless drop-off. They exchanged knowing glances. And groaned.

Without doubt, the protesting bleats issued from below.

Dismounting, Matt and Will took a few steps toward the edge. It disappeared in a sudden downward crumbling of earth and stones, and they jumped back barely in time to avoid pitching into the chasm. Dropping to his belly, Matt wriggled forward. "I c'n see him! He's on a ledge about a rod down. Here's where he went over."

Will crept to his side. "Ground's still soft from the snow. He just got too inquisitive and the bank caved."

Matt nodded agreement, although the problem was not how the calf got down, but how they were going to get him back up in one piece. "I'll go down and tie him off. You c'n pull him back up."

"You better be careful."

"About the bank? No fret. I'll be down and up again in no time!"

"Wasn't talkin' about the bank. That feller's Mama is somewhere around, you c'n bet. She ain't goin' to like you messin' with her immortality."

"Her immortality's goin' to be steaks on a plate before long," Matt scoffed.

"Yeah, but she don't know that. Would you care to mention

The Longing of the Day

it to her? Here she comes!"

Will was near enough to his horse to make a flying mount as the enraged mother charged around the outcropping. Matt dived sideways and felt the bank disintegrate beneath him. Clutching frantically at dirt and rocks, finding nothing to break his descent, he seemed to fall forever.

He landed with a rib-wrenching thud.

Cautiously, he opened his eyes.

Blue sky overhead. Red earth piled over him.

And two mournful brown eyes, not three inches from his own gray ones, staring at him.

"Maaa?"

If Matt had followed his first instinct, he would have been back up that cliff in one effortless leap.

"Maaa?" The baby nuzzled his face with an extremely rough — and wet — tongue.

"I ain't your Ma," Matt mumbled, trying to keep his mouth shut. Careful not to startle the calf, he worked his way to his feet, his various parts sending up yells of protest from a dozen scraped and battered places.

The gangling, out-at-elbows-and-knees growth of adolescence had finally lost its playful grip and endowed him with a height of 6 feet in a world where most cowmen were inches shorter. As he unwound to his full height, the calf snorted in fear and backed away. Dirt and pebbles trickled into the chasm below as the calf's retreat unwittingly drew him too near the lip of the precipice. Matt hunkered down again and held out his fingers. Reassured, the animal edged forward and nuzzled him eagerly.

Matt spoke softly, distracting the calf as he waited for Will.

"Matt, you all right?" Craning his neck, he caught sight of Will's unruly mop of black hair, his face strangely pale under its beginning tan. His coal-dark, anxious eyes peered over the ledge nearly 20 feet above Matt's head. Unable to trust his weight to the treacherous rim, he had bellied up to it, not knowing whether he'd find his friend alive or dead. Will grinned. "Couldn't you find an easier way to get down there?"

"Easier, but not near so quick!"

Will tossed Matt's rope wrapped around his bed blanket. Painfully aware the only thing between him and death was a narrow, slippery ledge, Matt stroked the calf's face to gain its confidence, and then subtly slipped his bandanna over the calf's eyes. Fashioning the blanket into a rough sling, he heaved the calf onto it, tying him so he couldn't slip out. "OK, Will, pull him up."

The animal struggled at first, but Matt stroked and spoke softly to him, glad the baby calf was unable to comprehend his journey. Will hauled him over the top.

After what seemed a week but couldn't have been more than two or three days, Will tossed the rope down again. Catching the dangling end, Matt knotted it securely about his waist. Signaling once more to his friend, he began his own agonizing ascent. Sweating, struggling, adding to the scrapes and bruises he had already acquired, he finally reached the top. Will grasped his arms and hauled him over like a sack of meal.

Completely spent, they collapsed on the grass and tried to catch their breath. But an outraged bellow informed them the mother cow was doing her best to break loose from Will's rope. Hauling themselves to their feet, they set about

The Longing of the Day

the task of freeing 700 pounds of maternal wrath while staying alive. They removed the blindfold from the calf. He struggled, wavered, then rose from his knees. Flinging up his tail in an unmistakable gesture, he trotted over to his mother and began sniffing her curiously.

The two men studied her.

"Which one of us gets to do it?" Will asked, finally.

Matt cuffed back his hat. "I will. You tied her up, so I reckon it's my turn to have a talk with her." Handing his reins to Will, he leaned on his heels and eased over to the cow, who watched his every move, with murder in her eyes. "Will, you got these ropes tied tighter'n my Aunt Fannie's corset."

Unperturbed, the other man drawled, "If I didn't, there'd have been two of us on that ledge. You was already claimin' squatter's rights, so I didn't think I'd be much welcome."

Matt's reply was indistinct. It was also notably short. Will grinned.

Matt stood and slowly stepped back. "Now!" When Will tossed him the sorrel's reins, he made a flying scramble into the saddle, uncoiled the last of the rope and waited.

At realization of freedom, the cow heaved to her feet with gun-crack speed and fury. She stood blinking, head lowered, ready to charge. But finding her adversaries now mounted, her enthusiasm waned. A man afoot was one thing. She knew, however, from past bitter experience, she could only lose in a battle with these four-footed creatures. Snorting her disgust at their low tactics, she turned to her calf and began washing all human taint off him.

Pushing the cow and calf ahead of them, Matt and Will continued their sweep across the plains. Collecting several more strays, but without any of the difficulty or excitement, of their earlier encounter, they arrived back at the herd.

Nodding a farewell to Will, Matt pulled in his horse at the top of a rise and sat, reins slacked easy and saddle creaking as he shifted to take in the view from all sides. His features taken separately, he was not especially handsome. But his face showed a steadfastness, a quiet self-assurance of which, all unknowing in that carefree moment, he would need every fragment in the months to come.

He surveyed the milling, bawling cattle loosely bunched below. Spring roundup and branding was hot, dirty, tiring work, and Matt thoroughly enjoyed it. As with this morning, it provided challenge and variety in a job that for most of the year was dull routine.

His sorrel blew as Ben rode up beside him. Ben Clayton had spent most of his 57 years outdoors in the saddle. As a consequence, his features were deeply weathered. A host of fine lines creased the skin around his eyes, the result of all those years of squinting into sun, wind and snow. His once-brown hair showed mostly gray now, but his eyes had remained a deep, clear blue. As he reined in, he caught sight of Matt's battered face and his jaw dropped. "You look like you been drug through a knothole backwards!"

Matt smiled crookedly. "Bet you didn't know knothole crawlin' is my favorite off-time activity." Briefly, he explained the rescue of the calf and shrugged off Ben's concern.

Sharing his dislike of emotional displays, Ben nevertheless warned, "You better heal fast, before your Ma sees you. She'll have your hide, you takin' a chance like that. And prob'ly mine, too," he added ruefully.

The Longing of the Day

The subject tacitly closed between them, Ben took off his hat and sleeved sweat from his forehead. "We're doin' just fine, son." His gaze swept the plains. "We should be done by mid-afternoon. Looks like it's goin' to be our best gather yet."

At this final announcement, a typical understatement by Ben, Matt's blood quickened. "That's great, Pa," he said casually enough in his turn. But he couldn't keep his grin down. Ben saw it and grinned in return, both of them looking like young ones who had just been handed the Christmas present of their dreams.

"What do you think Ma'll say when we get back and tell about it bein' our best gather ever?"

"Same as she always does when we come home, I'll wager. 'I'm glad you're home!' Then she'll say, 'Are you hungry?' A practical woman, your Ma." The sudden lighting in Ben's eyes belied his casual tone. As if to hide foolish emotion, he cleared his throat. "We best be gettin' on with the work at hand." He started his buckskin down the slope.

Matt followed, but he continued thinking of the two women they had left behind. Anne, bustling and energetic, her heart as big as her physical frame was small. And Eve — Eve. Unable to give words to the knowledge his heart carried, he understood only too well Ben's "foolish" emotion. It would, indeed, be good to get home, to the weathered gray ranch house and to the two women awaiting their return.

Ben and Matt whooped into the ranch yard in a whirling

cloud of dust. Anne and Eve, hearing the racket, hurried out to greet them. As always after an absence, Matt found himself discovering with some amazement details he normally took for granted: Anne's small, finely boned stature and her bright brown eyes; Eve's delicateness, so like her mother's. But Eve's eyes were Ben's, wide and deeply blue. The sun glinted from her red-gold hair coiled neatly about her head in two thick braids.

Ben dismounted, picked up Anne and whirled her jubilantly around. He kissed her heartily before he finally set her on her feet again. When she caught her breath, she exclaimed, "You're home. We're so glad! Are you hungry?"

"Yes, my Anne, we're home, and have we got news f'r you!"

"Hi, big brother," Eve put in to Matt around Ben's exuberance. "What happened to you?" she added in dismay, staring at his still-livid bruises.

His eyes crinkled mischievously. "Hello, lil' sis. This is nothin'. You should see the other fella!"

Her anxious questioning was cut off as Ben slipped his arm around Anne's waist and announced, "You bet we're hungry! Hungrier than two hawks in a chickenyard. Got anythin' we c'n eat?"

Anne conceded they might be able to come up with something. Once inside the house, she presided over the stove while Eve set out dishes and silverware. As they entered, Matt's ever-alert nose sniffed out an appetizing odor that made his mouth water. He caught sight of the freshly baked pumpkin pie sitting on the worktable and started over to it.

The Longing of the Day

"Oh, no you don't." Eve had read his intention only too clearly. "Not until you've had some stew."

Matt and Ben exchanged a stealthy glance. Anne caught the look and said apologetically, "We weren't really expecting you back this soon; we were going to finish up the stew for our supper. I was thinking it'd heat up quick for now, but you don't have to eat it. Go cut a piece of bacon," she told her daughter. "We'll fix something else."

Eve started off, but Ben said quickly, "Never mind. Hungry as we are, even stew'll taste good."

And Matt added, with angelic innocence, "Sure, Ma, it'll be fine. We haven't had any stew since supper last night. Or was it breakfast this mornin'? And anyway, it didn't taste a bit like yours. Ol' Toothpick out there must use different ingredients than you do."

"I get the message," Anne said dryly. "And from the looks of you, you complained to him one too many times. Whatever have you been doing?"

"Chicken and dumplin's would be right good f'r supper," Ben cut in.

"And," Matt added hopefully, "that pie smells good right now!"

Effectively distracted, Anne glanced over at the worktable. "Eve made that. She said she wanted to bake one just in case you came back early. I tried to tell her you wouldn't be back for a couple days, but she said she had a feeling." Anne shook her head at her daughter. "Nothing's worse than a know-it-all young one!"

"I don't know how I knew," Eve said, blushing. "I just did."

"I'm glad," Matt assured her. "Pumpkin pie's my favorite."

"Or mince or rhubarb," Eve returned wickedly. "I think maybe we can spare a small piece after you finish your stew."

"You're so generous, Coppertop," Matt said. It was a telling shot, for Eve hated the color of her hair. Behind Anne's back, Eve stuck her tongue out at him.

Fortunately for Eve, Anne failed to see her saucy answer. If she had, she would have dealt out a swift response of her own. Mercifully unaware, she ladled the stew into bowls and told her husband, "We're dying to hear what happened. Go ahead and eat so you can tell us."

"This news is too good to wait," Ben spoke eagerly as he took the pot from her and set it on the table. Catching her hands, he pulled her down onto his lap, unmindful of Matt and Eve watching.

"It was a good gather. The best we've ever had. The cattle came through the winter in excellent shape and with quite an increase. Now we're havin' a good spring on top of that. Plenty of rain, but not so much we're bein' drowned. Just enough to make all this good green grass f'r the critters to get fat on. With such a fine spring, we'll likely have a good summer. And the way the market is, if we have a good summer ... well, when we ship our beef this fall ..." Ben's hands tightened on Anne's as his voice vibrated with excitement. "We may just find this is the year we've been waitin' f'r all this time!"

Silence hung in the air as Anne and Eve stared at him, wide-eyed. Eve breathlessly voiced their common thought. "Pa, you mean we'll be rich?"

"Ben," Anne whispered. He could feel her trembling. He

The Longing of the Day

hated to throw cold water, but he had to finish.

"Just remember, it's a long trail between here and autumn. An awful lot c'n happen. You know that as well as I do." He let his gaze touch each of their now solemn faces. "But, to answer your question, Little Bit," and his smile once more spread across his face, "if ever'thin' goes right, yes. We shall be, let us say, quite well off."

Unable to absorb the momentous news, they stared at him in total silence. But before they could break into excited discussion, Anne suggested quietly, "I think we should give thanks, don't you?" She stood and touched his shoulder.

Ben looked up at her and slowly nodded. He didn't feel comfortable talking out loud to the Almighty in front of the others. Not even after so many years of doing it. It wasn't the prayers that fretted him. Well able to speak his mind at other times, he just felt so stumble-footed and tongue-tied when he tried to express any emotion out loud. But maintaining a close relationship of their family to God had been one of only two conditions Anne had set down against their coming to Wyoming when churches had been scarce as hen's teeth. And how could he refuse her?

He had promised then, and had kept his word through many a mumbled Bible reading and evening prayer. Even after a minister moved to town a few years back, they had kept up their family prayers. He figured personal discomfort was a mighty poor excuse f'r not givin' thanks when they were due. *As in this case where they sure enough were*, he thought as he bowed his head.

Success. It had been such a long time comin'...

After supper that night, Eve and Matt sat on the back steps. "It's just so hard to believe. To think we'll be able to buy anything we want! If you had your choice of anything in the world, what would you want the most?"

Stretching out his long legs, Matt studied the waxing moon and said with offhanded casualness, "Guess I don't know. When you think 'bout it, we have so much here, right now. What more could we ask f'r?"

"Spoilsport!" she protested. "There has to be something you want. Everyone has to have one big, secret wish."

Even as his heart whispered its own answer, he doggedly concentrated on the star-filled heavens. No rain tonight. "A ranch of my own, I guess. What would you choose if you could have anythin' you wanted?"

She clasped her arms about her knees, her voice dreamy. "Something I want more than anything else in the world."

When she didn't continue, he risked a glance at her and caught her embarrassed expression. "Go on," he prompted.

"Maybe I shouldn't say it. You might laugh."

"Prob'ly. But how will you know if you don't try me?"

She still hesitated. "It's just that maybe it's kind of a silly thing to want."

"You've never wanted more than one or two 'silly' things in your life. You've got more common sense than any-body I know. Except Pa and Ma."

"Such flattery, brother! You just leave me speechless."

He smiled wickedly. "So what's your secret wish out of all the world?"

The Longing of the Day

Her eyes grew wistful again, and she clasped her hands in her lap. "I would so much like to have a locket. Not a big one," she amended hastily, "just a small one, but in the shape of a heart. I read about one in that book you brought me from the drive four years ago. She was such a beautiful lady and she always wore a heart-shaped locket around her neck. It was her greatest treasure."

"I didn't know you had even read that book."

"Oh, yes! I've just about memorized it. But I still like reading it."

"Always knew I had excellent taste."

Her voice grew solemn. "But she lost it. She leaned over a pool one day, looking at her reflection, and the chain broke. The locket fell into the water. She was heartbroken. It had been a gift from her dead lover. And even though her husband got her another one, it just wasn't the same as having that first one. Can you imagine? She had two lockets. She was so lucky."

Matt considered the story with proper gravity. "And what would you do if you had one and lost it in the water?"

"I wouldn't lose it! I'd hang onto it if I was ever wearing it and looked into a pool of water."

She spoke so seriously he didn't dare laugh. Temper was part of her — and so was her trust in him. But in spite of all his efforts, he could feel a chuckle edging dangerously close to the surface. He said hastily, "Just be sure you don't get so busy holdin' it with one hand and doin' your female fussin' with the other that you lean too far over and fall in yourself."

He demonstrated his idea of female fussin' complete with simpering expressions, as he spoke. Surprise, hurt that he had failed to take seriously something so important to her, flickered in her eyes. But the sight of him, so big and masculine and imitating a primping woman, was so ludicrous, she couldn't help chuckling. In a burst of relief, he let his own laughter explode.

"Eve, it's time to come in."

They stood at Anne's call from the kitchen. "All teasin' aside, Eve, maybe someday your wish will come true."

"I don't care if it doesn't, I guess. After all, if it does, what will I have to wish for?"

"I guess there's always somethin' to wish f'r, somethin' we know we'll never have," he said quietly.

"I suppose. 'Night, brother." She smiled affectionately.

He watched her go up the steps to the kitchen. He waited until she extinguished the lamp inside. Then, "Good night, Eve," he whispered and turned toward the bunkhouse.

The great promise of that spring was not to be realized. After the wealth of rains that had marked the early part of 1886, Nature became shrewish and withheld the showers that signaled her favor. The winds, blowing hot and dry over Wyoming, across all the cattle country, seemed to leave no place untouched for beast or human being to escape their parching breath. With water supplies dwindling to nothing, and the grass shriveling on its roots, the suffering of the cattle had become intense.

Morning after morning, Ben stepped to the kitchen doorway and silently studied the skyline. Morning after morning, following his fruitless search for a break-in-the-weather sign, the lines across his forehead showed a little deeper as he joined Matt at the barn for chores.

On a Sunday morning in late May, Ben and Matt returned to the kitchen after completing the barn work. Ben thumped his milk pail onto the bench so hard the contents sloshed. Anne started to protest the mess and waste, but Ben cut across her indignation. "Not a rain cloud or even the hope of one in sight. And it's goin' to be another scorcher."

29

The Longing of the Day

Glaring at his sloppiness, Anne fetched a damp cloth to wipe up the spill as Ben thrust his head under the pump at the sink. Sputtering and dripping, he reached for the flour sack towel, his words muffled. "Don't know how much longer it c'n go on. Heat's one thing, but this is really over-doin' it." He raked the comb through his hair. "I tell you ..." He glanced out the window, composedly unaware he was in Anne's way as she tried to get to the sink. "Say, now, there's Chase Aubrey comin' to take you to church. He's at least an hour early. And he looks right solemn, too. You two ain't had a fight, have you, Eve, that he's comin' to make up?"

"Oh, Pa." Eve's blush was his reward, but Matt, watching her sharply, saw her eyes brighten. His own narrowed as Ben went on, unheeding.

"Yessir, hair slicked back, Sunday boots pinchin' 'cause they're too small, he's got all the earmarks of a man come a courtin'. I remember with your Ma what a miserable time it was."

"Ben." Anne's voice was her most no-nonsense.

He looked sheepish and grinned as Chase's boots pounded on the porch. He flung open the door before the young freighter could knock, but the teasing remark about courting died at sight of Chase's face. "What's happened?" he snapped.

Chase's glance took in their expressions. Eve smiling, her cheeks still suspiciously pink. Anne, motherly indulgent. Matt sulking. Chase hated what he was about to do to them. "Bad news," he blurted and saw them stiffen to receive it. "The Lindermans up on Blue Creek. They've been burned out. Ehren Linderman and his son Frederic are dead. Miz Linderman and Verena are missin'." He heard Anne's moan and saw Eve grip her hands tightly in front of her. The Lindermans had become friends after moving to Blue Creek a year ago. Before Ben could put his question into words, Chase nodded.

"They figure it's Black Snake. He's always been a mean 'un, and he took off from the reservation three days ago with six others. The Army's been called in. They've already started after 'em."

Ben loosed a curse, but for once Anne seemed not to have heard her husband. She stared at Chase as though pleading that he be wrong. Eve gripped her hands together so tightly her knuckles showed white. Ben's voice grated. "They positive it was Black Snake?"

"There's no doubt. He started a fire in the grass. When they went out to fight it, that's when he got 'em."

Ben cursed again and slammed his fist down on the table. The violence seemed to release the family from their shock. Anne pressed the back of her hand hard against her mouth, and instinctively her eyes searched out Matt. *Dear God, was it to begin all over again?*

Ben paced up and down, muttering. Eve and Matt stared at Chase as though they had never seen him before. The younger Lindermans had been their friends, too.

Chase would have allowed them their moment of grief, but Ben harshly demanded more answers. "The Army's after 'em?" Chase nodded. "By God, I hope they get 'em this time." And Anne knew that Ben, too, was remembering.

Chase looked at Eve. She was just about Verena Linderman's age. *What if it had been her?* His fists clenched his hat, crushing it between his hands. "They'll get 'em."

31

The Longing of the Day

And it, too, was an oath.

Anne drew a sharp breath. "Jason and Luke, and Catty ..."

Chase turned to her. "I'll tell 'em. That's what I'm doin', warnin' everybody in this section to stick close to home today. Other men from town are warnin' everyone else before they start f'r church. I've got to go, but I'll let you know as soon as we hear anythin'." His last word hung in the air even after the door slammed behind him.

Eve jumped at the thud. "Chase, be careful," she cried and ran out after him.

Anne didn't see her daughter's departure; she saw only Mathilda Linderman's face, careworn, full of hope, telling her goodbye the day she and Ehren left with their son and daughter-in-law to move up to Blue Creek.

Matt moved numbly to the window in time to see Chase embrace Eve before he swung into his buggy and lurched away. Ben's voice issuing hasty orders brought him back to the familiar kitchen as Eve, still ashen and dazed, came in again. Matt wanted to comfort her. All he could do was turn away.

"Thou shalt not be afraid for the terror by night ..." Anne, head bowed, tears running down her cheeks in spite of her tightly shut eyelids, was reciting the 91st Psalm.

"... Nor for the arrow that flieth by day." One by one the others joined in. When Anne's voice faltered, Ben reached to grip her hand fiercely in his own. "For he shall give his angels charge over thee to keep thee in all thy ways ..."

The news came five days later — the news they prayed not to hear, which, in their hearts, they knew would come anyway. The mutilated bodies of Mathilda and Verena Linderman had been found miles away from their burned-out ranch home.

"Why?" Eve demanded of Matt. "Why the Lindermans? Will it be our turn next?"

Matt had never seen her so bitter, and it shook him badly. She, like Anne, had always taken quiet strength from her faith. Without a loud showing, her trust was simply there. He couldn't have told how her own steady belief sustained him. Like Ben, he'd never been much of one to speak his feelings. For him, God was in the outdoors, a part of the animal life with which he worked daily.

He knew, of course, as well as Eve did, all the phrases of solace for heartache like this. He would have given anything for a magic formula with which to comfort her, but there was no magic, only their deep-rooted trust in God and the slow healing of time.

The next weeks dragged by in a heat-shimmering haze. All of them grieved. The import of menace put deeper lines by Ben's mouth and sharpened Anne's and Eve's awareness of danger they had come to accept as an everyday part of life on the plains. Matt retreated into himself and became more quiet as he made the daily rounds of work with Ben.

Black Snake and his band had been captured and rumors flew until no one knew what to believe. Black Snake vowed

The Longing of the Day

he would burn out the white man to the last settler, and said if they killed him, others would carry out his vengeance. For days after that, every sun-started fire was blamed on "a horde of Injuns tryin' to wipe us out."

Ben held long discussions airing different actions and their possible consequences with his sons, Jason and Luke, and Catty's husband, Aaron Grandler, as well as Matt. Jason was tall, dark and strongly built like his father. He and his wife Becky had been married 11 years and had four children. Each passing year molded him a little closer to Ben's image in both appearance and manner, except he lacked a certain brazenness, a tendency to loud laughter that marked his father's character.

Luke, of the fiery red hair and beard — and temper — was five years younger than Jason. What his older brother lacked in brashness and brassiness, Luke more than made up the deficit. No one could do anything quite as well as he could. No one knew quite as much about anything as he did. If a body had any doubts about Luke's prowess, all he had to do was ask Luke — he'd tell him. Weren't his wife, Hannah, and his four little boys extensions of that proof?

Aaron Grandler, blond, lean and reticent, had learned to hold his own in arguments with his father-in-law since joining the family three years before. If there was anything Ben liked, it was a good, strong argument with this younger generation, pitting his knowledge and years against their newer, untried ideas for raising cattle successfully.

Except for Matt, each one had a home ranch on land bordering Ben and Anne's Arrow A. Each ranch was run independently of the others. Ben and Anne held firmly to the idea their sons and daughters should manage their own lives and families. But in rough times the family could and did band together for the good of all, whether it was a matter of sharing food, ideas or courage.

All the men, of course, belonged to the Wyoming Stock Growers Association, formed to set up ground rules for such matters as water rights, brands and boundary lines. Ben wouldn't hear a word against this organization, although Jason had, on occasion, been known to mutter to Aaron and Matt that they still hadn't found a way to control minor details like the weather, even if the association was composed of God's own right-hand men.

Aaron, because he didn't want to create in-law problems, and Matt, because he still ate at Ben's table, dared not be as outspoken as Jason, although, in their eyes, he had full justification for his impertinence.

Ben's favorite argument was a body had only to look at the record of the past several years to see the cattle business in Wyoming was coming into its own. "We're becomin' a beef-eatin' nation. Investors have been pourin' money into cattle, and they say a beef bonanza is on the way. If you don't put out a little money now, how c'n you expect to make any profit later?"

To which logic Jason replied contemptuously, "And where are these *investors* from? Outside the country. How c'n these velvet britchers possibly know what's really happenin' when they're not here workin' the herds day by day, sweatin' and strainin' with the rest of us?"

"You don't have to be everywhere at once," Ben countered. "Look at Chester Arthur, our good Republican president until

The Longing of the Day

last year." Ben tended to ignore the accomplishments of incumbent Democratic President Cleveland. "Arthur couldn't be everywhere at the same time, but he had a grip on the facts, better'n some as were on the spot."

Jason shook his head, refusing to be led down that path. In Ben's estimation, arguing government politics ran a close second to arguing the cattle question, both of which controversies he could carry on for hours, with or without opposition.

So they discussed and argued their mutual problems. Although there was no clear-cut solution, there was easing in the airing of opinions. There was so little anyone could do, except face each day as it came, and pray for rain.

Ben scoffed at the "burn-out" rumors even as he, along with everyone else, took every precaution possible. The way Ben figured it, the biggest rumor in the world couldn't actually start a fire, and he wasn't 'bout to start seein' the whole Indian nation behind every bush and blade of grass. Besides which, the trouble was up north, not down in the southern part of the Territory where they were.

But Black Snake and his men couldn't have chosen a more potent weapon — terror. Fire was the greatest enemy of the ranchers, an enemy greater than sickness or drought and more feared. A grass fire, sweeping along through the already tinder-dry growth, with nothing to stop it and no water with which to fight it, could strike fear into the heart of the most hardened cowman.

Monday, June 14, dawned heavy and sultry. No sound of

bird or insect or breeze, only a hushed, frightened expectancy hovered in the too-still air.

The men, checking their ticking pocket watches against the ascending sun, patrolled the range, waiting. Wide firebreaks plowed around the perimeter of the main ranch buildings spoke mutely of their hope that should a fire reach close to home, it would have nothing upon which to feed. Ben had ordered the cattle to be held on the southeast range, close to the creek — the creek bed itself was Nature's already-plowed firebreak.

And so the men, having done all they could, checked their pocket watches once again against the rising sun and patrolled the range, waiting ... waiting.

At the house, in uncharacteristic silence, Anne and Eve finished up the noon dishes and stole covert glances at the Seth Thomas clock as it calmly, unhurriedly, ticked their lives away.

Dishwater swished as Anne's hands cut through it with grim, determined purpose, rattling silverware against the pan bottom and crashing plate against plate.

A plate slipped from Eve's suddenly nerveless grasp and crashed to the floor.

Anne continued silently rattling silverware and plate against plate.

Anne and Eve worked in silence, stealing glances at each other periodically. Tick-tock, tick-tock, tick-tock.

"Oh, dear God," Anne breathed, as a ringing sound assailed her ears.

"It's not our bell!" Eve's pinched voice cracked as she and Anne stared at each other for one instant of mutual thanks, then of fright. Not theirs, indeed, tolling its fire message

The Longing of the Day

across the plains. But whose? Jason and Becky? Catty and Aaron? Luke and Hannah? *Whose?*

They ran for the barn.

Ben, grim-faced, was already directing the men coming for instructions. Eve saw Anne dart a questioning look at him. He shook his head. "Near as we c'n tell, it started natural, but we're not takin' no chances." His grip on the 12-gauge shotgun in his right hand tightened even as he spoke.

With fascinated horror Eve realized the other men were armed, too, with all the guns they could lay hands to. All the fear she had felt before was only a shadow in the face of the knowledge gripping her now.

But even so, there was no time for thought other than of the fire itself. The men were piling into the wagons among the ropes and shovels and burlap sacks. "Get to the north ridge," Ben ordered. "Matt will direct you from there."

The fire was not threatening their immediate family, but the Corleys, their neighbors to the north. But if it got past the Corley place, the Arrow A stood next in line in the path of destruction. And Matt was already in the midst of it. Eve's heart leaped with a sudden stab of pure terror.

"Eve, come *on!*" Anne, apron flying, sped past her to the wagon. After one paralyzing second, she obeyed. Anne's face was set. Eve knew, in spite of the heart-thumping fear her mother was pushing down, Anne would fight as hard and as well as any man on the place, and Eve was determined she, too, would do no less.

Smoke enveloped them even before they topped the ridge and saw the flames. It was a sight none of them would ever forget. The red-orange tongues were still a considerable distance away, but licking closer. Dense black smoke, rolling upward, blotted out the sky. The grit and ashes that had been only a haze in the air at the house were a sullen, suffocating cloud. Anne and Eve began coughing violently as the mad specter of heat rushed to greet them.

Jason, Luke and Aaron had come with all their men. Owen Corley was there, too, directing his cowhands. The wagon jolted to a stop, and Eve glimpsed Matt at the center of a knot of men. She scrambled to the ground. The knot broke, and the cowhands jostled past her to their positions, Matt's calm decisiveness exerting its control even beneath all the shouting and dashing about. Only when he saw Anne and Eve purposefully approach him did he falter, allowing a flicker of fear to cross his face.

In response to his unspoken protest, Anne only said in a grim voice, "We're here, Matt. Tell us what to do."

His eyes flicked from her determined face to Eve, who jutted her chin out. "We're staying, Matt. Just like Ma says."

Something she couldn't read flashed in his eyes before he spoke. "I got no time to argue with you. Take those gunny sacks and spread out along the line. Just try to keep the flames back as best you c'n."

Anne grabbed a sack. Matt caught Eve's arm as she turned to follow her mother. "Watch your skirts don't drag against the flames," he said crossly, that look again flicking in his eyes too rapidly for her to read.

"We'll watch."

The Longing of the Day

"Eve ..." But Aaron shook his arm, and he turned away. "You better bring up some of the cattle," she heard Matt say as she edged into place along the line. She knew what the cattle would be used for. They would be shot and half the carcass skinned out. Dirt and rocks would be piled onto the empty half and the carcass used as a "drag." Two men would pull it behind their horses along the edge of the fire to smother the flames. They would have to change sides frequently or else the horse on the near side of the fire would have its hooves charred. The drag was not a pretty sight, but it was effective. Some of the time. As Eve began to swing her sack, she prayed it would work now.

They seemed to have been fighting for days instead of just one afternoon. Eve knew they were losing the battle. It seemed impossible to go on as they were forced back, inch by inch, almost to the ridge behind the ranch. *If the fire tops that slope ...*

"No!" she yelled, startling the daylights out of Anne beside her. "No!"

She wouldn't let it take the ranch, this hungry monster who had already devoured so much. She saw again the Corley place going up in flames, and the looks on the faces of Rose and Owen Corley. New strength flowed through her exhausted limbs. She forgot her smoke-blurred, smarting eyes and parched mouth that felt like it was stuffed with cotton. She would defeat this enemy once and for all!

She was pounding furiously at the flames when Anne

cried out. Eve turned, but was caught from the other side and thrown violently to the ground. Her head struck something sharp. Just before the world went black, she saw stars dancing in front of her eyes, like flames from the fire ...

As she came back through a long, black tunnel, she heard a voice saying, "Thank God. She's coming to."

Another voice coaxed, "Eve, c'n you hear me?"

She meant to say, "Of course I can," but somehow her tongue refused to form the words. She opened her eyes wide as the anxious faces of Ben, Anne and Matt swam into view. *No, not just anxious.* Behind the cloak of smoke-stained grime, Matt's face was deathly white.

Why? Is someone hurt that badly? The hazy, floating feeling abandoned her with sickening abruptness, leaving her cold and shaking and all too aware of a sharp pain grinding in the back of her head. The rest of her body throbbed in one tremendous ache.

She tried to sit up, but Matt pushed her back. "Lay still. You've had quite a time."

Eve looked up at him bending over her, a solid tower of strength. "But I heard Ma cry out. Matt, what's happened?" Once more she struggled, and once more he gently pushed her back.

"Will you be still before I have to knock you out again?"

Not until Anne's fingers tightened on hers did Eve realize her mother was gripping her hand. "You gave us quite a scare, child." Anne's voice was light, but she couldn't conceal the worry in her eyes. Her face and clothes were streaked with soot, her hair loosed from its pins. Anne looked beautiful to Eve.

The Longing of the Day

Ben cleared his throat. "Hey, Little Bit," he said gruffly and gave her cheek an awkward pinch.

"Here," Matt put in as Jason handed him a cup, "drink this." He slipped his arm under her shoulders to raise her.

But as the cup touched her lips and the first sweet wetness trickled down her raw throat, she pushed the cup away. "That's water! You need it to fight the fire!"

She heard a low ripple of laughter around her. Matt chuckled as he once more held the cup to her lips. "The fire's out, Coppertop. We'll let you have all the water you want to drink."

She accepted the cup this time and drank gratefully. It was warm and flat and gritty. Never had anything tasted so good. When she had emptied the cup, she started to lie back wearily, but realized Matt still had his arm around her. She became aware she was lying on the hot ground and the cowhands, their faces smoke-darkened and solemn, stood in a circle around her.

"What happened?" she demanded once more.

Matt hesitated. "Your hair was on fire. It's all right," he said hastily as panic leaped into her eyes and her hands reached to feel her head. "Your hair's fine. Ma screamed at you, but you just kept swingin' your sack. I was close enough to knock you down and get the flames out. I guess you hit your head on a rock when you went down. I didn't mean to hurt you."

"I'm not hurt. Things are just kind of spinny."

"I can't understand why." But he couldn't carry through with his big-brother teasing as the words stuck in his throat.

"Is the fire really out?"

"Except f'r embers. We'll have to keep watch tonight, but the greatest danger is past."

"It didn't get to the ranch?"

"No, the ranch is safe. The flames didn't have a chance to get to it with you standin' in between."

The lighthearted banter was sweet to her ears as she leaned her head wearily against Matt's shoulder. Strange, how drained she felt. Ben and the crew, reassured she was safe, drifted away to begin cleanup operations.

Eve belatedly realized she was keeping Matt from his work. "Shouldn't you help clean up?" she asked fuzzily.

"I suppose I should be helpin', if you're sure you're not goin' to perform another fire dance."

"I won't. You go ahead."

"Only if you promise to stay here and rest, not go off an' top those ornery broncs we got down in the corral."

"I promise." He surrendered her to Anne's shoulder, and Eve watched him stride away to join the men loading the wagons. From her tiniest days he had been the adored older brother, always ready to spoil her or tease her or sympathize with her. How good he was to her. And what comfort she could draw just from his presence.

She was drowsing when she realized he had returned. "Is it the fire?" she asked foggily.

"I'm goin' to carry you to the wagon so we c'n leave."

"But I can walk."

"Quit kickin' or I'll dump you on your head again." She subsided and allowed him to carry her to the wagon.

In her semiconscious haze, Eve was only vaguely aware of the ride home. She knew Matt held her securely in his

The Longing of the Day

arms against the jostling of the wagon, and she rested her head against his chest with weary contentment.

She was dimly aware of being carried into the house, of being placed on her own bed and the sheet drawn over her. As Matt turned to leave, she caught his hand.

"What is it, Coppertop?"

"I like listening to it," she murmured.

"What?"

"Your heartbeat. It sounds so warm and safe. Comfortable." She yawned mightily on the last word.

"Go to sleep, my Eve," he said softly.

Her eyes closed, and she felt the lightest press of his work-roughened hand against her cheek as she slipped into dreamless slumber.

The ranch had been saved, but only through everyone's determined efforts. The range to the rear of the ranch, beyond the creek, was a charred-black wasteland, desolate and forsaken. Nightowl, the Arrow A's oldest cowhand, observed, "Like the back side of Hell'd look if the flames was stomped out."

In spite of all their efforts, it had been impossible to save the Corleys' Half-Moon ranch. Corley managed to push his herd across the creek ahead of the fire, but his outbuildings had gone up, and wind-fanned flames had leaped to the house, gutting it. Their lives, the clothes on their backs, the herd, and the charred ground beneath their feet — these, and their courage — were the only remnants at the end of that terrible afternoon. These, and one thing more — friendship.

Neighbors from many miles away began arriving, visiting where the Corleys were temporarily staying with their oldest son. And each family who came, knowing only too well it might have been themselves, left a little something. Bedding, foodstuffs and clothing were casually dropped by "to use if you can," given cheerfully from sometimes scanty stores to a family suddenly more in need than they. When the Corleys were ready to rebuild, if they decided to, these same friends would be there.

One spot of relief found in the whole sad business was the fire hadn't been deliberately set. The sun striking a spark of flame off a hot rock into tinder-dry grass. A careless drifter who left a campfire smoldering. Lightning was often the culprit. The cause would never be known. Apparently Ben had been right. Bold as they were up north, the Indians had not dared venture into their more heavily settled area.

Eve and Matt were discussing the fire an evening or so later as they sat on the back steps, hoping to catch a breath of cooling air. That day, like all the days before in this blistering month, had been terribly hot.

Except for a large lump on the side of her head, and a bald spot where her hair had been singed, Eve suffered no ill effects from her adventure with the fire. But now she shuddered. "When I think of what would have happened if it had come past the creek ..."

"But it didn't," Matt said quietly, "so just don't think 'bout it."

She sighed. "I know you're right. I should think of everything we have to be thankful for, instead of moaning about might-have-beens. Look at the Corleys, losing every-thing and not knowing how they'll ever get started again. It so easily might have been us — or Aaron, or Jason, or Luke." She hesitated.

"... Matt, can I tell you something?"

The misery in her tone startled him. After a quick glance at her shamed face, he said matter-of-factly, "Sure. You know you c'n."

"I haven't kept faith these last weeks," she whispered. "It's wrong, but I just can't seem to help myself."

"What are you talkin' 'bout?" he asked, puzzled. "I don't know anyone who has more faith than you."

"But I don't. That's just it. When we heard about the Lindermans, I just got so mad at God for letting it happen. And now the fire. He could have stopped both things, but He didn't. It just seems so unfair. I know I shouldn't feel this way, but I don't know what to do about it. I'm so ashamed."

"Why?" he demanded. "Because you're human? I don't think that's so terrible."

She was staring at him. "But I have so many doubts. I've never felt this way before."

How could he explain to her what he, himself, felt so deeply when he had never really put it into spoken words before? Seeing the dark pain in her eyes, he knew he had to try.

Struggling to find words that wouldn't fail her need, he spoke slowly. "At least you're honest enough to admit it. I think that's a whole lot better than someone who just accepts ever'thin' and never bothers to ask why. How c'n we know if we don't ask?"

"But what kind of acceptance is it to ask why things happen?"

"Askin' why don't necessarily mean not acceptin'. At least I don't think so. You think I haven't been askin' why all these weeks, same as you? Wonderin' what good could possibly come out of things so awful?"

"I didn't realize," she said slowly. "Do you think we'll ever find out why?"

"Only God knows, and so far He's not tellin'. If He wants us to find out, we will."

"You make it sound so simple," she said enviously.

"It's not, I know, but we have to do the best we c'n. Just remember, if God didn't want us to think, He wouldn't of given us the brains to do it with."

"Matt, you're impossible!" But she quickly sobered. "One thing I can't help thinking about is Ma. She feels awfully bad about the graveyard being burned up."

"I know. She hasn't said much, but you c'n tell how hurt she is inside. You know," he said after a moment, "it must of been kind of like losin' Elizabeth all over again to see the flames go over her grave."

Eve looked up at him, her eyes wide and serious. "You remember how we were talking once about what we would choose if we could have a secret wish?"

He smiled. "You wished f'r a locket. Have you changed your mind?"

Her voice trembled. "Now I'd wish for a white picket fence to go around Elizabeth's grave. Maybe then Ma could feel happier." She ducked her head, but not before he saw the shine of tears in her eyes.

The Longing of the Day

"Do you know," he reached over and gave the singed hair on her crown a teasing tug, "you are a special young woman?"

She shook her head. "But I'm not."

He smiled a little. "Not what? Special or a woman?"

She refused to smile back. "Either one. And wishing isn't going to make it so. I just want to see Ma happy again."

He saw the depth of her sadness. "I think you're pretty special. You care more f'r what happens to other people than 'bout yourself. That's a rare quality. And as f'r bein' a woman, well, it took someone who's all woman to do what you did out at the fire."

She brightened a little. "Do you really think so? Sometimes I feel like such a little girl. Some of my friends my age are already married, and I wonder how they can do it. I'd be scared to death!"

Matt didn't laugh. "You won't be scared. Not when it's the right man who loves and cares f'r you the same as you do him."

She sighed again. "You're so certain of yourself all the time. You never have any big worries beyond running the ranch. It must be nice to be so sure about everything. I bet you even know exactly the kind of girl — I mean, woman — you plan to marry." She sat up indignantly. "By the way, I saw you and Carolina Corley last night. You were behind the poplar, kissing. I was never so shocked in my life."

Lazily, he brushed at a mosquito. "That's what happens to people who snoop," he said unsympathetically. "They usually get more than they bargain f'r. But since you're so interested, she was just thankin' me f'r the goods we took her folks."

"Thanking you! If she'd thanked you any harder you both would have smothered. I was wondering if you were ever going to come up for air."

"You don't have to worry 'bout me or Carolina. We c'n manage just fine." He added slyly, "What 'bout you and Chase Aubrey? Seems to me he's been hangin' 'round quite a lot, and we don't need no freight hauled that I know of."

She tossed her head. "We're just friends, that's all."

"Uh-huh. Have you told him that? He looks more moon-faced every time he comes 'round."

"We're just friends," she repeated heatedly. "But we weren't discussing Chase and me. We were talking about you and Carolina. She doesn't seem your type at all."

"Why not?"

"She just ... just doesn't ... she flirts too much!" *There, it was out.* It had been bothering her ever since she had seen him with Carolina. "I just don't think you could ever really be happy with someone like that." She was no longer teasing, but deeply in earnest.

"No," he agreed, "but don't worry 'bout it. We're just friends." He said it mockingly, but lightly.

She looked relieved. "Well, if it's not to be Carolina, then who? You must have some idea by now." She wickedly taunted, " 'Let every man have his own wife.' "

His eyes slid over her. In the soft light from the kitchen, her hair was a shimmering flame. Her eyes were full of merriment and her lips parted a little as she leaned forward in interest. "As a matter of fact," he said slowly, "I don't know that I will ever marry."

"Not marry? Of course you'll get married. You have to!"

The Longing of the Day

After a startled moment, he grinned and drawled, "Not that I'm aware of, I don't."

"Matt, that's not funny. You know what I mean."

Her face was upturned to his, and his breath caught. He said lightly, "After all, after havin' been 'round two women like you and Ma f'r so long, it's not goin' to be easy to find someone who'll measure up to the standards I'm used to. I'm goin' to be awful choosy."

"Oh, Matt, I'm trying to be serious, and you just keep teasing! Really, you must have some idea what you want her to be like. Won't you tell me?"

He looked away from her, stretched his long frame out more comfortably against the stair post and said with studied casualness, "Oh, I guess she wouldn't be very tall. She'd prob'ly come to 'bout here on me since all the women I know are so much shorter'n me." He measured with his hand against his chest.

"Go on," she prompted, chin in hand and eyes rapt, "I bet she'll be beautiful."

He nodded. "As a matter of fact, she is beautiful, but the strange thing is, she don't even know it."

"She doesn't!" Eve sat bolt upright. "You mean there really *is* someone already?"

It was his turn to flush. "You know what I mean," he said hastily. "You wanted me to describe her as I see her, so naturally I have to talk 'bout her like a real person."

She studied him accusingly. "I thought for a minute there really was someone and you were being sneaky and not telling me. But go on. What about her hair? I know it's not this horrible red that mine is. I bet it's raven black! I read about that in my book, too. The lady with the locket had raven black tresses."

Matt's eyes went to Eve's hair, caught in its net at the nape of her neck, and he said slowly, "I don't think your hair is horrible at all."

She stared at him. "Matt, you're blushing! Just because you gave me a compliment. You don't have to be embarrassed with me, remember?"

He nodded, wordlessly accepting her explanation for his red face, knowing he couldn't possibly tell her the truth.

He was relieved when Ben appeared in the doorway behind them and announced, "Bedtime, Eve. It's gettin' late. You standin' watch tonight, Matt?"

Matt pushed rope-callused fingers through his already rumpled hair. "I'm on 10 to 2."

Eve jumped up and reached to hug her father. "Lucky you!" she flung over her shoulder. "All right, Pa. 'Night, brother. See you tomorrow." She waved cheerfully to him.

He watched them move away into the house, Eve chatting to her father about the Corleys. A great feeling of loneliness seized him, and in spite of the warmth of the night, he shivered.

Three evenings after the fire, Ben Clayton stomped into the kitchen where Eve was straining the evening milk and Anne was dishing up the supper. Anne took one look at his grim face, and her heart contracted. *Now, what's happened?* she thought. *There's been so much already ...*

"We'll be movin' the herd to Wildcat Creek tomorrow mornin'," he said abruptly.

"Ben, no." Anne's instinctive protest slipped out before she could bite it back. The trek of the herd from the home ranch to their summer feeding grounds was a yearly event; the mountains to the northwest sheltered a lush valley that remained green even in dry years. By timing the move carefully, and by shifting the herd so no single spot became badly overgrazed, Ben was able to bring his cattle through the summer. Skill, planning and an inborn knowledge and feeling for cattle and nature all played a part in his success, an ability evident in the good condition of his herd at summer's end. But never had he made the move so early. *If the graze gives out too soon ...*

Reading her thoughts, he said roughly, "I have no

The Longing of the Day

choice, Anne. If they stay down here any longer, we'll start losin' 'em. They had little enough grass before the fire. They can't possibly make it on what's left here."

Anne, knowing argument would be useless, pressed her lips tightly together. Once convinced of the rightness of a decision, Ben stood firm. What the cattle would do for grass and water later if they were moved to their summer pasturage so early, Anne did not know. The ultimate responsibility was on Ben's shoulders. He must do what he thought best and literally trust God that it would be right.

During this conversation, Eve's hands mechanically continued their task, but her heart caught when she heard Pa's decision. Unnoticed, she slipped outside into the violet twilight. Her footsteps carried her to the huge cottonwood shading the yard to the north. She leaned her head against the rough bark and watched the last rays of the dying sun.

She didn't have to be told Pa was gambling everything — the very future of the family — on this trip. He didn't even know for sure there would be sufficient grass and water once he got to the creek. But he would take the chance. He had to. Because with the grass destroyed here, there was no hope at all.

"Eve, they're lookin' f'r you at the house."

She jumped at Matt's voice behind her, blinked rapidly to clear the tear-mist, and drew a quick breath. As she turned to face him, she was grateful for the fast-falling darkness hiding her agitation. Strong and capable, he loomed before her, a steadfast figure in a world suddenly trembling beneath her feet.

He saw at once that she knew, and clenched his fists in

helpless rage at the circumstances tearing their lives apart. He would give his life to protect her, but how does a man fight an enemy he can't see?

They walked in silence to the house.

Ben sent Nightowl Jones into town to get supplies from the Clark's Valley Store. "Here's the list. Wake Clark if you have to, but get as much as you c'n." He thrust the paper at Jones as he climbed up in the wagon seat. "Nightowl." The gravity in Ben's tone startled the old cowman. Ben's mouth was a tight line. "I heard tell Clark's takin' cash on the barrelhead only. If there's any problem with puttin' it on my bill, tell him Miz Clayton'll settle up in the mornin' soon as the bank opens." Nightowl nodded and shook out the reins.

Matt, on his way to the barn, seeing Ben's grimness halted beside him. "I c'n go, Pa, if you think there'll be trouble."

Ben shook his head. "Nightowl c'n handle it. I need you here to start toppin' off them broncs." But his eyes followed the disappearing wagon a moment longer. "Never thought it'd come to this," he muttered, shaking his head. "Never thought it a'tall." He caught himself, tipped his head toward the corral. "Them jugheads ain't gonna work their kinks out themselves. We best get to it." He strode toward the corral as if the moment of uncertainty had never been.

With all cowhands pitching in, working by lantern light far into the night, they were able to complete the thousand and one details necessary for their departure in the morning. Horses were shod, equipment gathered, and wagons repaired and loaded. There was no lightheartedness and little talk. Grim necessity made it a task to be completed, and so it was. But the heavy silence of the men in the flickering lantern

The Longing of the Day

glow at that unreal hour, in contrast to their determined purposefulness, cast an eerie pall over the whole procedure.

Nightowl returned with the wagon piled high with supplies. He sought out Ben in the tack room and handed him the bill.

"Any problem?" Ben asked tightly.

Nightowl shook his head and grinned. "Clark says if he can't trust you ... what was his words? 'A man who wouldn't trust Ben Clayton's word wouldn't trust his own mother's.' You're to pay up as soon as convenient f'r you. He'd appreciate that."

Some of the grimness around Ben's mouth eased. With the world blazing to Hell around them, at least his word had been salvaged.

Anne tapped on Eve's door before first light. "I'm awake, Ma." At the muffled reply, Anne put her hand on the doorknob, then hesitated. She lifted her hand from the unturned knob, her fingers curling into her upturned palm. Another second of indecision and she slowly turned away. Rising, Eve dressed with shaking hands, her head aching and her eyes heavy from long hours of wakefully staring into the darkness.

Outside, silence hung over the world. The blackness pressed down, intense and threatening. Inside, in spite of the lamp-lit brightness of the kitchen, foreboding swamped the four seated with heads bent and hands joined in prayer at the table. Even with the hearty breakfast cooling in front of them, no one had much appetite. In other years there had been a definite stir of excitement at this move, an acknowledgment they were pitting their strength and ingenuity against the wiles of nature. This morning they knew only a deep, unnamed dread.

"... bless the work of our hands that it may prove pleasin' unto You. And Lord," in his earnestness, Ben's voice deepened yet more, "we ask that You be with all of us in these comin' weeks. We're goin' to be right busy, and it might seem like we're ignorin' You. Please don't ignore us back." Ben's prayers might not be strictly orthodox, but they sped straight to the point.

Eve's fingers, usually so warm and soft but now strangely cold and stiff, tightened around Matt's palm as she murmured "Amen" with the others. He turned to her, but she quickly withdrew her hand and busied herself arranging her napkin in her lap. Anne, similarly, was busy avoiding Ben's gaze.

Ben stared at his work-hardened hands clasped in front of him, as though the answer he sought would somehow be found there. Through the years, by the grace of God and hard work, his hands always managed to shape at least a measure of success out of potential failures. *Will they this time, too?* he thought. *God only knows.*

Rousing himself from his dismal thoughts, Ben glanced at the three glum faces and felt his stomach twisting. With effort, he grinned. "Well, now ain't we a sight! Anybody walkin' in here'd ask directions to the funeral plantin' f'r sure. Come on, Little Bit," he coaxed, "look on the bright side. No washin' of dirty, smelly long johns f'r the whole summer. I'd think you'd be dancin' on the roof at that!"

"Oh, Pa!" But Eve couldn't help a tiny smile forming. "You can't fool me. I know you're going to save them all and bring them back here in one big, fragrant lump."

The Longing of the Day

"You figure me out too easy," he complained. "Thought I was harder to trail than that."

Matt, with a clear glimpse of the visible effort they were making, chimed in, "Actually, Coppertop, he wasn't really plannin' on bringin' 'em home to you, you know." He held the questioning silence a tantalizing moment more. "He was figurin' on lettin' 'em walk back by themselves."

Anne's scandalized "Matthew!" was lost in the general uproar.

Ben managed to choke out, "Actually, I figured on givin' 'em a horse and lettin' 'em ride."

"That is totally disgusting, Ben Clayton! Such talk at the table!"

Having completed Anne's outrage, Ben said soothingly, "We are at the table, so I won't mention the subject of dirty, smelly socks."

Anne gave him her best glare. "I should hope not."

"I promise not to mention they're what I figured on lettin' walk back," he choked out between chuckles. "I guess they wouldn't be as well *suited* for it as the long johns, anyway."

Anne gave it up, buried her face in her napkin, and laughed until the tears came.

Before he mounted Latigo, Ben held Anne close for a moment, all the earlier lightness gone. He dreaded leaving her and Eve alone like this, without even the usual stove-up cowhand to offer token protection. And well she knew it. They both also knew there was absolutely no other choice. With all the years between them, they had no need for words. What could they say, anyway?

Matt and Eve also stood together for a few moments.

The anxiety, lifted for a few moments at their teasing, again darkened her eyes, but she forced a smile. "Take care, brother."

"I will. You and Ma be careful, too, hear?"

"We'll be all right." She hesitated. "We'll miss you."

That was all, but Matt understood. It was not the way of the Clayton women to send their men off with tears and lamentations. Eve would not speak of her fears and anxieties, of the coming loneliness that would be hers. The men were burdened enough. Of no use to add more. So she did her best to smile, and Matt gave her a quick hug. "Bye, Coppertop." He hurriedly mounted Tumbleweed.

Anne and Eve waved as darkness swallowed the departing figures. Only after the hoof beats died away did the women trudge bleakly back to the suddenly too-large house.

"Thy will be done." Words so easy to say, so difficult to truly accept. This was hard faith, as it had never been before, at least for Eve. Anne, on the other hand, was much more familiar with it. But accept and live by those words they must. To reject would mean reducing both of them to a state of frozen fear. Anne understood her daughter's torment but was helpless before it. For all her assurances, she could not give the younger woman what the hard passage of years had taught her, knowledge that, one way or the other, whatever happened would ultimately fit God's plan for them. Anne told Eve, but only time and Eve's own heart could make her truly understand the total giving over of one's cares to Him was not weakness, but strength.

The Longing of the Day

With the men gone, the household tasks were lightened, but other outside chores, such as cleaning the barn, caring for the new litter of pigs and all the horses fell on their shoulders. They came to be grateful the present work was so pressing because, in keeping their hands busy, their time for worrying about the future was lessened.

Clothes must be washed and ironed, an arduous enough task at any time, but more difficult now with the drought. Years ago, Ben rigged a system whereby water could be pumped directly into the kitchen from an underground spring behind the house. Before, even in dry years, the spring always yielded an abundance of water. But never had there been such a year as this.

The flow was still coming through, a slower, decreased amount, and it was murky with an unpleasant muddy taste. Ever since Willow Creek had become a mud-caked bed with only a few stagnant pools behind the house, a deep fear haunted Anne that the underground supply would disappear, too. She had become adamant they not waste a drop, so they cut back sharply on the amounts they normally allotted for household tasks, sorely trying Anne's housekeeping heart.

And they still had to eat, even if cooking for themselves held none of the satisfaction they felt when they could prepare a hearty meal for Ben and Matt. By unspoken agreement, they cut their meals short and did no extra baking. Neither one had much appetite, anyway.

With Ben and Matt gone, the chore of milking was added to the other household duties. This task, too, had developed its painful side, for without adequate grass and water, Buttermilk was becoming thinner by the day. Her hip sockets protruded, and her ribs stuck out. All day she bawled and sometimes far into the night. Each day she gave less milk, and what she did yield was thin and bitter. Nevertheless, they shared this twice-daily responsibility until the morning Anne, her face white and set, came in with the bucket. The small amount it contained was pitiful to see. Eve took the pail, and from that time on, quietly assumed the chore herself.

They had no idea how long the men would be gone. They knew the main body of cowhands would remain with the herd, but Ben had promised either he or Matt would return to the ranch to make sure they were getting along all right. One bright spot in their otherwise work- and worry-filled days was the anticipation of this return. They made a little game of speculating which one would come and when it would be. They had to laugh at themselves for doing so, but it was good to know that in spite of the loss of so much else this summer, humor, their friend, remained loyal.

Within a day or two of Ben moving his herd out, Jason and Luke departed with their cattle for their own summer grazing grounds, leaving Becky and Hannah, the daughters-in-law, to carry on even as Anne and Eve were doing.

On a warm evening a few weeks after these latest departures, Anne was sitting on the back steps where it was cooler than in the house. Eve was in the corral, currying her mare, Thistle. She didn't really have much heart for it, but at least it kept her hands busy. She and Anne had become good at inventing little tasks like this.

Eve paused to push her damp hair back from her flushed forehead. As she straightened, she caught a glimpse of a cloud of dust to the south. "Ma, someone's coming."

The Longing of the Day

Anne put aside the stocking she had been listlessly mending and stood up. Her hands automatically smoothed her hair and apron. Currycomb in hand, Eve came out of the corral to watch the wagon draw near. "It's Becky and Hannah!"

The team pulled into the yard amid shouts of glee from the youngsters piled in the back. With suddenly lightened hearts, Anne and Eve began lifting the little ones from the bed. After hugs of greeting, the six older children, seemingly oblivious of the heat, scattered to play.

Talking and laughing, the women settled on the porch steps, Eve holding Hannah's youngest, Micah, on her lap, and Anne cuddling Becky's 2-year-old Patience. "Talk about a happy surprise! We're so glad you came."

Hannah, tall and black-haired, looked uncertain. Once she had been bright-eyed and merry, always ready for a bit of frolic. But five years of marriage to Luke had dulled the snap of her green eyes and made her retreat into herself when she was with him. She was only 23, but hard work, a scarcity of the affection doled out by her husband, a collapse of romantic dreams into the harsh reality of the drudging life that was now hers, and too many children too quickly, had all aged her. She looked more than her years now. By the time she was 30, she would be an old woman. Now she said apologetically, "We hoped you might like some company. We've just been too busy to get over before."

Becky nodded agreement. She was short and rounded, with soft brown hair, mild blue eyes and rosy cheeks. Kindhearted and merry, she was also intensely energetic as her neatly kept home and well-tended children proved. She was chatting now in her breezy way. "Hannah's right. With Jason away, I haven't been able to catch up on anything. I tried to clean house today and had everything dusted shiny as a new penny. Would you believe not two hours later, it looked like I hadn't done a thing? It was all grimy and gray, just as bad as when I started."

"We tried to do laundry today," Eve chimed in, "but it came out so gray and dingy." Anne shifted protestingly, but Eve was determined to have her say, now that she had an audience. "It did, Ma. We might as well admit it and not be embarrassed about it. How is anything supposed to stay white, or clean, with all the grit and ashes in the air and not enough water in the creek to slake a snake, let alone do a proper washing?"

"I agree with you," Becky said emphatically. "Even sun-bleaching doesn't seem to help much. You'd think all this sunshine and heat'd be good for something. But if there is anything, I haven't found it yet. My chickens are even starting to fall off on their laying, on top of everything else. We've been eating a lot of eggs 'cause they're so easy to fix. But enough grumping," she laughed. "My goodness, I'm starting to sound like Pearl Gilby."

Anne smiled. "You have a ways to go, I assure you." The town's inveterate gossip would, undoubtedly, have been highly indignant.

Amid moist explosions of laughter, Becky pushed on with her explanation. "So, heat and work or no heat and work, tonight I decided to come anyway. We got to Hannah's just as she was leaving for here, too. We hope you don't mind an invasion of all of us."

The Longing of the Day

Anne suspected Becky's encouragement had persuaded Hannah she really wouldn't be in the way if she came. She silently blessed her older daughter-in-law, her eyes bright as she expressed her pleasure aloud. More soberly, Anne asked how they were getting along with Jason and Luke gone.

Both women assured her they were managing. "If only this heat would let up a little," Becky moaned.

Hannah laughed. Once assured of her welcome, she could still be as much fun as anyone when away from Luke. "Strange, isn't it? In July we wouldn't mind shoveling snow, and in January all we can think about is how nice it would be if it was hot like summer!"

Patience stirred in Anne's arms. "Pa all gone," she contributed, her brown eyes wide and mournful.

Anne pressed her cheek against the little girl's soft hair. "I know, child," she said gently. "I know."

The little group fell silent, their thoughts slipping away over the miles to where the men were encamped. They would be settling the herds for the night by circling them slowly, gradually drawing them in, while the first star pricked the vast curtain of evening sky. Eve softly voiced their common thought. "I wonder how the ... cattle are making out?"

Each listener heard the tiny pause and privately added a particular name as she considered the question. Aloud, they speculated on how things were going, assuring themselves and each other everything would be fine.

Ten-year-old Jared came racing up, followed in a straggling line by the younger children. "Jared, slow down," Becky admonished before he could speak. "It's too hot to be running like that."

"But Ma," he panted, "someone's comin'. It looks like Aunt Cat."

The group on the steps rose and turned as one as the wagon rattled into the yard. Catty, her bonnet hanging by its strings down her back, jerked the horse to a halt and wrapped the reins around the whip socket. Anne plopped a startled Patience down onto the porch step, hurried over and helped Cat down over the high wheel. Her usually neat blond hair was windblown from her rapid ride, her blue eyes wide with fright.

"Cat, what's happened?"

"Oh, Ma, I just had to come."

Anne glanced at the children standing wide-eyed nearby, but Becky was already speaking. "Go play, all of you." They looked uncertainly at her, at Catty. "Now!"

Eve spoke up. "Come down to the barn with me. You can see Lass' puppies."

Their attention diverted, they crowded around her, chattering excitedly. She handed little Micah to Hannah, took Patience and 3-year-old Isaac by the hands, meanwhile assuring the others they could each hold a puppy. Promising to be careful and to take turns, they crowded close as they scampered toward the barn.

"Now, Catty, come sit down." Anne led the trembling young woman to the steps. "Would you like a drink of water?"

"We'll get her one, Ma," Becky said quickly and pulled a surprised Hannah with her into the kitchen.

"Aaron's gone."

Anne let out her breath. "When?"

"This evening. He doesn't know when he'll be able to

The Longing of the Day

come back." The words stopped on a sob.

Anne hesitated. "You knew he'd have to," she murmured.

"I've been telling myself that for days. I thought I was ready for it. But when it actually came time ..."

"I know." Anne was deeply sympathetic. "I'm not used to it even after all these years."

"It's not just that, Ma." Catty colored.

Anne waited. Catty looked up, then dropped her glance to her hands twisting a fold of her skirt. She looked up again, and Anne saw Catty's eyes were bright, a smile tugging at the corners of her mouth. "Is there by any chance something you haven't told me?"

Catty, suddenly radiant, nodded. "There's going to be a baby. Aaron's and mine." Her voice was soft with wonder.

Anne gathered her in a big hug. "That's wonderful! You've been hoping so long."

"Ma," Catty's eyes clouded again, "Aaron doesn't know. I wanted to tell him before he left, but I just couldn't. He had to leave. He couldn't keep the cattle here. And I didn't want him to worry about me when he had no choice except to go."

"Oh, child, what a shame." Anne's heart ached for her. "When will it be?"

Catty's eyes lit up again. "December. Just about Christmas."

"What a perfect time! I'm so happy for you."

"I just wish Aaron could know." Her voice trembled.

"I understand, truly." Anne touched Cat's tumbled hair. "But what about Becky and Hannah? I'm sure they'll be delighted to hear about it."

Catty's hand covered her mouth. "I forgot all about them."

When Anne called, they came a little hesitantly, but their genuine pleasure at the news soon had Catty beaming.

That night, Anne confided Catty's secret to Eve, who smiled with uninhibited delight. "A bun in the oven, at last!" Seeing Anne's "The Mother Look," she said hastily, "Cat and Aaron are expecting a little visitor from above. How wonderful!" She clasped her hands and raised her eyes heavenward.

Her mimicry of Carolina Corley was perfection itself and earned her another look that faded the first one into insignificance. "Sorry, Ma, it just slipped out."

She hung her head, so she failed to see how hard Anne bit her lip to keep from laughing. Eve *was* getting better. Only occasionally anymore did she slip. Anne had worked so hard to "civilize" her. So why did she feel this sense of loss tugging at her heart?

Long after Anne had settled into the bed, too wide and empty without Ben's back to curl against, her thoughts lingered on her daughter. She knew that in spite of Eve's surface cheerfulness, she was deeply troubled by all the ill luck that had befallen them this spring. But how could she help her? Was any help possible when the answers Eve sought must come, in the end, from her own heart and soul? Was this time of walking through fire necessary to each human being that only then she might know herself with all evasions stripped away?

Anne remembered so well the time of her own soul's deepest torment. Looking back 21 years to the innocent, accepting girl she had been made her cringe even now. So smug, yes, smug, in her belief she had full understanding and acceptance of the way of life.

The Longing of the Day

But she had learned, in full measure, the error of her attitude in the weeks following Elizabeth's death. Those black hours were seared into her soul, those days when nothing — not Ben, nor the boys, nor their wants or needs — had the power to penetrate the rock her heart and soul had become.

How long it might have gone on, she had no way of knowing. But it ended on another black night in July, five months after Elizabeth's death. Now, she could only pray Eve never need such a harsh lesson to awaken her.

How many dreams, how many hopes Anne had for her! Uneasily, she wondered how Eve really felt about Chase Aubrey, the blond giant who delivered freight to all the surrounding communities. He came with punctual regularity to visit Eve ever since the Brices' Christmas party. Eve didn't seem to mind. But Anne wondered if her daughter realized the truth of his feeling for her. For all his size and awkwardness, he was a gentle young man, and Anne could find no honest reason to fault him. And yet ...

Her motherhood wondered now, as so many times before, whether she should say anything, knowing the heart will follow its own path in spite of a thousand loving words. In the meantime, Eve seemed content enough being home, working at the tasks around the house, unconsciously adding her own bit of sunshine to the mundaneness of life.

Indeed, Anne found it difficult to think of Eve, her own baby, being married and with a home and babies of her own. How empty the home would be without her! Yet Anne had to smile at her own reluctance. She knew well enough the time would come for Eve to go, and Anne must be happy for her even as she had been for all the others.

Her thoughts turned to Catty and her heart recognized the selflessness and love it had taken not to tell Aaron about the coming child. Anne had suggested Cat stay with Eve and her, but she had refused. Aaron was counting on her to run the place, and she couldn't let him down.

"You understand, Ma."

Of course, Anne had understood.

What she couldn't comprehend was Luke's behavior. What made him act the way he did? Were she and Ben to blame? Even when he was a small boy, he had shut himself away from all their attempts to talk to him, to give him affection. Ever holding himself aloof, he scorned all their efforts to show him they cared.

The unceasing ache in Anne's heart was a constant reminder of failure, even as the careworn expression on Hannah's face was another reminder. She was a good daughter-in-law, and she was paying a terrible price for marrying Luke.

Anne's mind twisted sharply away from the disloyal thought, knowing, deep down, that it was true.

How quickly the years had gone that she was to be a grandmother for the ninth time. She wished she could share the news with Ben.

So her thoughts ran and drifted until she slept, and the stars moved slowly overhead to another day with its round of work, its uncertainties, and its small joys.

On a sultry morning, Eve emerged from the barn with her scant ration of milk. The eastern sky was stained crimson, and she paused a moment, drinking in the splendor. The warm breeze brushing her cheek promised another burning day.

Her shoulders slumped as dejection overwhelmed her. She had tried so hard to fight a good fight. But she was so weary. The unending heat, the constant worry and fear for the future, the unceasing effort to be hopeful and cheerful in Anne's presence, the aching loneliness she had felt since Matt had gone — all these beat upon her until at times she felt she must sink to her knees and hide her face against the uncaring ground.

Such a moment was this.

If only she could give way to the hot pain inside her! If only ... but Ma was calling from the back door, breakfast was ready, and the new day was waiting to be got through, somehow. She slowly straightened her shoulders and turned with the bucket toward the house.

Anne had come down the steps. "You finished milking?"

"Sure did, Ma. Isn't the sunrise beautiful?"

71

The Longing of the Day

Neither spoke as they stood a moment, watching the eastern skyline. The sun, shining through a pall of smoke, glowed blood-red. Finger-clouds, trailing away from the sun, were tipped with the same brilliant flush. Yesterday the smoke-haze was barely perceptible; much heavier this morning, it tinted the sky with breathtaking color. The two women felt deep foreboding as they viewed the spectacular display, for they knew it meant somewhere there were new fires. Anne finally broke the silence. "Breakfast is ready."

While they were eating, both heard the far off sound. They glanced at each other as the thud of hooves grew louder. Thistle, down in the corral, whinnied a greeting. Hand pressed to her breast, Anne pushed back her chair and took a step toward the door. Eve, gripping her fork, waited with held breath. There had been a great many out-of-work cowhands passing through the area this summer. Most were courteous. Some were seedy beyond a traveler's normal unkempt state. All were hungry. "Mind, now, Eve, you stay out of sight." Anne reached for the shotgun kept ready by the door. One could never tell.

"Hello the house!"

As the resonant voice filled the spaces of the kitchen, the tension whispered away. Anne's face became a glad smile as she cried, "Ben!" Shotgun still in hand, she ran to open the door.

By the time Eve reached the porch steps, Ben had dismounted, and Anne, shotgun and all, was flying into his outstretched arms. Eve gripped the railing, her eyes searching eagerly, futilely, beyond her parents for Matt.

His arm circling Ma's waist, Pa was coming toward her.

"Hey, Little Bit! This is quite a reception, ain't it! Think we can persuade your Ma I ain't dangerous?" He gestured toward the 12-gauge shotgun still clutched in Anne's hand.

"Oh, my word!" Staring at the shotgun as if questioning how it came to be in her grip, she thrust it at Ben.

"Careful there, my Anne! I'm right glad to see you, and I'd sure like to be able to prove it. You wavin' that thing around like that just might blow my chances away."

"Ben!" Anne turned strawberry red.

Her thoughts tumbling, her heart pierced by sharp disappointment at the realization Matt hadn't come, Eve for the moment could find no words of greeting. Numbly, she stared from Ben's wide grin to Anne's blushing radiance. Would she, could she, honestly have denied them this moment? Taking a deep breath, she abruptly let go of the rail and raced to meet her father.

While Ben shed Remington and holster and began to wash up, Anne bustled happily about the kitchen, preparing special dishes to add to the simple breakfast she and Eve had already begun. "You don't need to go to extra trouble, my Anne," he protested good-humoredly. "Any kind of home-cooked food is goin' to taste great to me." But he was home, and her joy needed to take tangible form.

Between mouthfuls of the fresh, hot eggs, bacon and biscuits, Ben recounted moving the herd. "It took us three full days to get there. We planned to travel mainly at night so it'd be cooler, but there just wasn't no water or grass. What wasn't burned up was dried up. So we pushed on, figurin' it'd be better to get 'em there first and let 'em rest afterward. I can't even begin to describe to you trailin' them critters across that dry stretch." For Ben to be wordless on any subject, let alone that of beef animals, painted its own frighteningly vivid picture of the hot, dry trek across the blazing plains with cattle that were all but dead of thirst.

"We reached Wildcat Creek 'bout sundown the third day. After what we seen on the way, and not knowin' what we'd find when we got there, we figured we'd hit a bit of paradise. Water and green grass. 'Course the critters smelled the water while we was still a good ways off and there was no holdin' 'em, so we let 'em go."

"It must have been beautiful," Eve said wistfully.

"Will there be enough grass and water to hold them through the summer?" This question had been plaguing Anne ever since Ben had announced the move would take place. She could wait no longer to find out.

He looked bleak. "I don't know. All I c'n say is they're better off up there than they would be here. F'r now, anyway."

Anne, the familiar heaviness settling in her chest, asked no more questions. Never the most subtle of subject changers, Ben turned abruptly to Eve. "How've things been goin' here, Little Bit?"

"We've found homes for all of Lass' puppies." Eve's enthusiastic checklist blithely neglected to include such details as the shortage of food and the poor condition of the animals. "Chase Aubrey is going to take the last one. He says she'll be great company on his freighting trips, runt of the litter or no."

"How're the supplies holdin' out?"

Eve could not dissemble at this blunt question and looked up uncertainly at Anne. Ben read her hesitation correctly, and the lines in his forehead deepened.

"Ben, we have plenty to eat. Don't fret about it!" Anne chided him, but he continued to look grave. It was her turn, then, to change the subject. "You should have seen us when Suzie tried to escape from her pen! Three times we had to reinforce the siding to keep that sow in."

"I'll take a look at it for you, my Anne."

"You don't have to do that, Pa. It's as secure as can be. Ma's turned into a regular carpenter," Eve boasted.

Anne chuckled. "I had to. It was either that or chase down that sow and 11 shoats. What a spectacle that would have been!"

Eve made a sound between a squeak and a giggle. "The skunk was spectacle enough!" At Anne's warning glare, Eve clapped her hand over her mouth.

"What about a skunk?" Ben glanced from his daughter's guilty face to his wife's red one.

"Nothing," Anne said hastily.

"What happened?"

"Nothing, really," she said with dignity. "We just caught a skunk in the hen house one night."

"Well, that's good. What's so secret 'bout that? Unless ..." The light of suspicion dawned in his eyes. "Did you get squirted?" he demanded incredulously.

Anne sighed and gave in. "Just a little."

Ben turned to Eve, who was choking with laughter. "Come clean," he said sternly.

Eve whooped. "It took her a long time to do that!"

"Eve!" Anne was aghast.

Ben finally pried the story out of his daughter, while

The Longing of the Day

Anne sat glowering.

"We heard a racket in the chicken house one night, and Ma dashed out in her bare feet and her nightgown, catching a huge skunk in the act of snatching her best laying hen," Eve said. "By the time I arrived, Ma had hold of the skunk by the tail. He'd hooked his front and hind feet together and was spraying for all he was worth. She was screaming for me to bring the butcher knife ..."

Eve's words were lost in a new fit of giggles, but by this time Ben had gotten the picture and he, too, was roaring with laughter. Even the dangerous look on Anne's face failed to sober him.

"The butcher knife? We'll have to keep your skills in mind at the next calf roundup," he choked.

"When you are quite done," Anne said icily, "you may be interested to know there is one skunk that will never spray or do anything else again. When Eve finally brought the ax, I took care of him in short order."

Ben did his best to sober up, a difficult thing to do with Eve sitting across from him still giggling. "I'm sure you did, but why didn't you just drop him? I'd think he'd of had enough of hen houses and hens by that time."

"Because," Anne said with dignity, "I didn't want him to come back the next night."

"I bet you didn't!" He gave up his attempt to be serious and collapsed into laughter once more, holding his nose delicately.

Eve sat up and took a deep breath. "I'm sorry, Ma. But if you could have just seen and heard yourself! I didn't know you knew all those words," she said admiringly.

Anne studied her daughter thoughtfully. "You're right.

After all, it might have been you. I can see how funny that would have been."

Eve shut up.

"As for you," Anne said coolly to her husband, "you're so busy holding your nose, I guess you wouldn't be interested in the news about Catty."

Ben stopped clowning. "News?"

"Well, I'm glad to see your mind has more than one track. But maybe I just won't tell you."

"Aw, come on, Anne. We're sorry, ain't we, Eve?"

"We sure are, Ma. Go ahead and tell. You've been waiting and waiting to."

Anne relented slowly. "Only if you promise to drop the other subject." Her anger gone, her face lighted with the joy of telling that there would be another grandchild for them by Christmas.

Ben blinked and grinned. "That's great! I bet Aaron's the proud one." At her expression he stopped, bewildered. "He is happy 'bout it, ain't he?"

"He doesn't know. Cat was really torn between telling him before he left and saving him the worry of being so far away from her. Right now, she's still figuring if he doesn't know, it's better because he has enough on his mind. But I don't know how much longer she can hold out."

Ben shook his head. "She's prob'ly right at that, it bein' the first one and all." His eyes went to Eve. "Seems like a few days ago you and me was havin' 'em, my Anne. Now those babies are presentin' us with grandbabies!"

"I know. Where did the time go?" she asked wistfully.

He felt her painful memory of baby Elizabeth. Helpless,

The Longing of the Day

he turned abruptly to Eve. "Got a message f'r you from Matt." He drew a folded paper out of his pocket.

Her heart suddenly beat faster as she read her name, penned across the outside.

Anne looked up with quick interest.

"I been wonderin' what he had to say that he couldn't tell me to tell you," Ben remarked. "Go ahead and read it to us."

"But Pa, it's my letter!"

Anne put in, "Now, Ben, don't tease. You know how Matt's always doing little things for her. He thought this would please her." She glanced at her daughter's suddenly bright face. "I think he was right." She began to stack the sticky plates. "You go and read it. I'll start the dishes."

Eve flashed her a grateful smile. "Thanks, Ma. I won't be long."

As she started outside, she heard Ben grumble, "I still don't see what all the fuss is 'bout."

Outside, she chose to climb the ladder to the loft of the carriage house, a building attached by a breezeway to the kitchen. The carriage house was a kind of all-purpose room. They had never kept a carriage there, because they didn't own one. But as Ben pointed out, they surely would some-day, and it was best to be prepared. In the meantime, the building was used for storage and as a sickroom for such animals as Ben wanted to keep a closer eye on. For this lat-ter purpose, the loft was always kept filled with fragrant hay. Anne had protested furiously about mice invading her kitchen, but Ben had assured her the cats and he would hold vigilante-style necktie parties with the mice as honored guests. Unwillingly, she had given in, but over the years whenever any whiskers put in an appearance, she told Ben so. Immediately, loudly and clearly. Over all her protests and dark threats, the carriage house loft continued to hold its abundance of hay, cut by Ben and the boys from the wild grasses of the plains.

Eve was glad that, in spite of her mother's objections, the hay had remained in the loft. All through her growing-up years this room had been her own special haven in times of sadness or joy.

Now the supply of hay was reduced because they had been doling it out to Buttermilk and the horses to supplement the bare amount they were able to scrounge from the plains. But enough remained to make a comfortable seat. After she climbed the ladder, she settled herself in the pile and slipped Matt's letter from her pocket.

In delighted anticipation, she studied the letters of her name written on the outside. The first letter she had received from Matt was when she was 8 and he 14, when he was on his first cattle drive. In his pride and new-found manliness, he had written her when the herd reached its destination. No matter to her that the letter was delivered long after he had arrived back home. It was the first letter she had ever received from anyone, and she proudly carried it around with her until it had crumpled into nothing from so much handling.

Only years later did she learn of the cruel teasing Luke had inflicted on Matt because of that letter. For it had been out of Eve's and his parents' hearing that he had taunted Matt about sending a letter that took longer to reach home than he did. She had seen Luke's bloody nose, but then he

The Longing of the Day

was always fighting with someone. Matt continued to send her letters when he was away from home, if opportunity permitted. Luke teased her, but she just threatened him with a knuckle sandwich for lunch. He had laughed long and hard over that, but he had never blatantly twitted her about it again. She suspected he knew she'd do exactly what she'd said. *Behind the back has always been so much more Luke's style, anyway*, she thought wryly.

With a shrug, she dismissed Luke from her thoughts and eagerly studied the folded paper in her hands. Her name was written in firm, square strokes. Turning it over, she saw he had fastened the edge with a dab of flour-and-water paste. She smiled to think of him snitching a bit of flour from the chuck wagon.

At last, having drawn out the moment of anticipation, she carefully broke the seal and unfolded the paper.

"*Hello, Coppertop,*"

She grinned. No formal "I take my pen in hand ..." but rather a greeting so familiar she could hear his teasing voice.

Pa will be leaving soon to head back to the ranch, so I'll just write a quick note to have him give you. I hope all is going well for you and Ma. The cattle are faring pretty well here, but Pa will tell you all about that. Earlier tonight on watch, after Pa said he'd be going back home, I got to thinking.

Sometimes when it's moonlight and the cattle are quiet and there isn't much to do but think, I play our game. Remember? What we'd wish for if we could have anything we wanted.

Louise Lenahan Wallace

When Pa talked about home and Ma like that tonight, I got to puzzling it out.

It came down to two choices, and I still can't make up my mind. Maybe because it's so hot even now after midnight, but I got to thinking of some of the winter nights we've spent with snow and wind screeching outside and all of us inside by the fireplace, safe and warm. You and Ma sitting in your rocking chairs, sewing, and Pa reading from the Bible. Remember how he always mumbles at first because he's so embarrassed? Then his voice gets real deep and full when he gets going.

That's my wish — to have it be like that again. No drought, no worry, just a family. Together. Pa's getting ready to go now, so I must close. My other wish? To be eating one of your pumpkin pies!

> *Take care,*
> *Matt*

Eve smoothed her fingers over the paper. Her ears were so used to his cowman's drawl, it always surprised her a little to read his precise writing. Curious how Anne's determined efforts at home teaching asserted themselves.

"Eve! Eve, come quickly!"

She scrambled down the ladder. "Coming, Ma!"

When she reached the kitchen, Anne swung around from the sink, suds dripping unheeded down her elbows. "We'll have to hurry and get our work done early. Pa wants to go see Catty this afternoon. He's planning to stop by to see

The Longing of the Day

Becky and Hannah tomorrow to make sure everything's all right with them. He wants to leave tomorrow evening to get back, so there isn't much time." As she mopped her arms with a towel, Anne's pale face betrayed to Eve what her calm voice would not.

Eve's heart sank. "So soon?"

"I know, but he feels he has to get back. Let's just appreciate the time he's here and not waste it fretting." Anne reached for a basket. "We'll be getting to Cat's just about dinnertime. Let's take a few things with us." Even as she was speaking, she was piling eggs, a jar of blackberry jam and some potatoes into the hamper.

All through the morning's work, the letter lay in Eve's pocket, mutely, yet tangibly, signaling Matt's nearness.

When they reached the little house Aaron had built for Catty, they found her blooming in spite of the heat and the discomforts of pregnancy. Becky had "loaned" 10-year-old Jared to her, and he had been manfully doing the heaviest of the necessary chores to spare her.

She greeted them happily and while Ben and Jared set off on a tour of the grounds and buildings, the three women laid out the simple dinner.

Gathered about the table, heads bowed and hands joined, Ben gave thanks. "And bless all our loved ones, both here present and those who are here in spirit and thought. Guide the work of our hands that it may prove pleasin' unto You ..."

As Eve heard the words, familiar to her from earliest memory, something stirred deep within her. Another feeling, as old as herself and therefore never questioned, began to spread its warmth through her veins. The security of knowing she was deeply loved. Safety taken for granted until it was threatened. Could this be the answer to her desperate search?

The half-formed thought snapped off as Ben finished his prayer and reached for the potatoes with one hand and pointed the serving spoon at Jared with the other. "He may be between hay and grass, size-wise, but he's sure doin' a man's work."

"He's been a big help to me," Catty put in with a grateful smile.

Jared squirmed with embarrassment and pleasure, then abruptly sat up straight. "While Uncle Aaron's gone, I'm supposed to be the man of the house. I promised Ma."

"You're doing a fine job," Catty assured him. He grinned again, and in the gesture was the foreshadowing of carefree boy becoming a responsible man.

As they ate, the talk turned to the subject so important to them all — the cattle. Ben, guarded in his comments, refused to deceive them by holding out false hopes. Catty was cheerfully optimistic. Anne was cautious in her hopefulness. Eve, her hand resting lightly on the pocket that held the precious letter, was neither optimistic nor cautious. She said little aloud, but silently breathed over and over, *Please, God, it will be all right.*

"By jimminy!" Ben slapped his hand down on the table, causing the salt to spill and everyone to jump a foot. "I got so busy yammerin', I clean f'rgot to tell you the bad news."

"What's happened?"

"What's wrong?"

"Ben, what's happened now?"

Ben raised his hands to quiet the chorus of feminine anxiety.

The Longing of the Day

"Don't know how I could of f'rgot. Gettin' old, I guess."

"Ben, if you don't tell us right now ..." Anne said, exasperated.

"All right, all right. Just let me get it straight as I heard it. You know how the Brices work the summer grounds south of us. Will Braden works f'r them ... still can't persuade him to come work f'r us, even after he practically grew up here. I keep tellin' him there'd be no favorin', but he says ..."

"Ben!" Exasperation had become warning.

"Oh, all right. Will busted his ankle last week."

"What?"

"How?"

"Is he all right?"

"Was there any blood?"

Ben grinned and turned to his grandson. "No blood," he said apologetically. Jared subsided, disappointed as only a 10-year-old boy could be.

"Ben!" Warning had become full-fledged threat, and wisely, he finally relented.

"Way I heard it, Will was coaxin' a cow back to the herd, and a jackrabbit popped up smack under his mount's nose. His horse stopped, but Will didn't. Ol' Will just went a sailin' so fine over that horse's head, ass — heels," he amended hastily, "over teakettle. When he landed, his foot come down in that jack's burrow hole and snapped his ankle clean as spit. They splinted him up, but f'r some reason it ain't mendin' right. So when Brice found I was comin' this way, he insisted on Will goin' to Doc Fergus.

"I dropped him off there, and Doc was still fussin' over

84

him when I left. He's makin' Will stay in town today and tonight. I c'n pick him up on my way out tomorrow and take him to Brice's ranch. Doc don't want him goin' back to the herd till he heals. Will was madder'n a wet hen, I'll tell you. 'Specially when Doc told him it'd take six weeks to heal if he did what he was told. Will was gettin' right vocal 'bout it."

"And if he doesn't do what he's told?"

"If he don't, he'll be limpin' permanent."

"Is he going to follow instructions?" Eve asked anxiously.

"He was still flappin' and squawkin' when I left, but I reckon he'll follow 'em. Doc's a real good persuader that way. A gimped-up leg never could do the job an ungimped one c'n, and Will knows it."

"He will be all right, though?" Anne's motherly concern made Ben smile.

"Sure. His pride's hurtin' more'n his ankle, I reckon, at havin' to spend six weeks at the Bumblin' B instead of out on the range where he belongs."

Anne's wholehearted sigh of relief was echoed by Cat and Eve.

Jared, who had been leaning forward and listening open-mouthed, piped up. "Went ass over teakettle, did he, Grandpa?"

Ben grinned around Anne's horrified exclamation. "That he did, son."

Jared, eyes shining, relaxed in his chair. "Wow!" His wholehearted sigh was one of admiration.

Back in her own room that night, Eve sank into her rocking chair, buried her face in her hands, and tried to put into words the realization that had come to her. All her life her parents had disciplined her, not for the sake of punishment

The Longing of the Day

but because they loved her and wanted her to be the very
best of which she was capable. Could this not be God's plan
with her, too? Was He trying to teach her self-control now
so she might not bring greater harm to herself later for the
lack of it? *But why did that sound so familiar?* She reached
for her Bible and hastily turned the pages.

> *... this is my prayer: that your love may more and
> more abound both in understanding and wealth of
> experience, so that with a clear conscience and blame-
> less conduct you may learn to value the things that are
> really important ...*

Such a simple answer after all her frantic questioning!
How many times in her life had she read those very words?
Strange that only now was she glimpsing their full meaning.

When she finally rose from her chair, sleep was impossible,
so she wrote a cheerfully newsy note to Matt, with no hint of
the disappointment she had known when he hadn't been able to
come home. She was relieved he'd never find out how she'd
reacted. He'd tease the daylights out of her for such nonsense!
She told him a little of her discovery. But, new as it was to her,
it was hard to find the words to put on paper. If only she could
see him. Somehow, in their discussions, banter though he
might, he usually managed to make even her most jumbled
thoughts seem sensible.

The next evening as Ben was strapping on his Remington
and preparing to leave, she dashed to her room, took the note
from Matt's book where she had placed it for safekeeping,
and hurried to hand it to Ben.

"I feel like the Pony Express," he teased. "Sure, I'll deliver it. But now I got to spend the whole ride back wonderin' what you have to say that you couldn't tell me to tell him. Somethin' tells me I been down this trail before." He sighed and grinned. Putting the letter in his pocket, he gave her a quick hug. "You mind your Ma," he said as if she were once again 10 years old.

"I will, Pa." She stepped away so he could say goodbye to Ma, then, with a wave of his hand and a drum of hooves, he was gone.

Anne and Eve looked at each other, then away.

The loneliness had returned.

ANGELA MOERLIEN

5

The bean, squash and cabbage leaves drooped in the heat. Entering the garden enclosure, Eve moved among the limp pea vines, picking a small panful of pods for dinner. The garden was a major worry these last weeks. They poured every drop of water they could spare on it, but the plants were woefully stunted and their yield poor compared to past years. There was barely enough for the two of them right now. *What will happen this winter?* Tiny fingers of fear tickled down Eve's back. They had always depended on summer canning to feed them through the winter.

Behold the fowls of the air ... Consider the lilies of the field. ... In Eve's opinion, the birds were doing just fine, taking as they were the choicest pickings from the Clayton garden. As for the fate of the lilies, as far as she knew, none grew around here. *But the flowers she had seen this summer didn't seem to be in great shape if the truth were told.*

"Just teasing, God," she amended hastily, lest He think her attitude unseemly.

A bee bumbled its way under the deep brim of her sunbonnet. She stood stock-still as it fumbled angrily, seeking

The Longing of the Day

escape. Mumbling and muttering, it finally found the edge and freedom. Releasing her breath in a gust of relief, she yanked off her bonnet. Trying to cool her scalp, she pushed her fingers through the hair coiled heavily at the nape of her neck.

Retying her bonnet strings, trying to ignore the tunnel of heat thus created, she stooped to pick up the pan and heard the clop of hooves. She turned and saw her best friend, Polly Brice, riding up. Polly caught sight of her and began to wave frantically. "Eve, guess what?"

Eve's suddenly cold hands gripped the sun-hot pan. *What had happened to get Polly so excited in this heat? Surely it couldn't be bad news.*

Polly tied her mare in the shade of the cottonwood and rushed over to Eve.

"Polly, whatever ..."

"Phil and I are going to be married!" She grabbed Eve by the arms and — pan and all — began to dance joyfully, the pods bobbing up and down in rhythmic accompaniment.

"Married! I'm so happy for you! When?" Eve's last words were a bit breathless because of Polly's excited turning.

"Saturday. I want you to be my attendant. Phil's asking Will Braden to stand up with him. You will do it, won't you?" she pleaded, now breathless herself.

"Saturday? So soon? But ..." Eve could scarcely take it all in.

"We know it's awfully fast, but Phil has to go to Chicago on a buying trip for the store, and he wants me to go with him. I'm so excited. I can't really believe it yet! You will attend me, won't you?" she asked anxiously.

"Of course. You know I'd be delighted."

Polly's pleading expression became sunshine again. "I'm so glad! Will's ankle is healed enough, so he doesn't even need his crutches anymore. In another week or so he'll be going out to the herd, too, so we're doing this just in time."

Eve broke through the excited rush. "What will you wear?"

"We're going to fix Ma's wedding dress. She's always planned I should wear it. And I want you to wear the green dress you wore to the Christmas party. It was beautiful on you. Say you will!"

Eve resisted the impulse to laugh as Polly's mood changed yet again from eager to dreadfully serious. She reached out to hug her friend. "If that's what you want me to wear, then of course I will."

"Can you and your Ma come this afternoon and help us get ready? We've a million things to do, and Ma says she needs your Ma's help, please."

This time Eve did laugh. "Yes, we'll be happy to come."

"Thank you! I have to go. See you in a little while." With a last quick embrace, Polly hurried to her mare and waved as she disappeared around the corner of the barn.

With a funny feeling tugging at her heart, Eve watched her go, then turned quickly toward the house.

"Ma!"

Saturday's unusual events made a trip to town a necessity. Except for church, they had not been for several weeks and so had accumulated a list of errands to run.

The Longing of the Day

Eve and Anne set out early the next morning, hoping to get back before it became unbearably hot. The 45-minute ride was spent in anxious discussion of what to buy. They could agree only that it had to be very special.

They pulled up in front of the Clark's Valley Store and easily found a space to leave the buggy among the few wagons and horses already hitched there. As they stepped to the boardwalk, Eve glanced up the street. A strange feeling of desolation shook her. The street was quiet, even for this hour of the morning. Usually a fair-sized group of citizens could be seen coming and going about their business. Today the sidewalks and the town itself seemed all but deserted, so many men had taken their herds to summer grazing grounds.

From under her bonnet brim, Eve glanced at her mother and saw she noticed, too. Anne, tight-lipped, led the way into the store. The interior seemed cool and dark after the hot glare of outdoors, and Eve felt Anne relax a little with the relief of it.

They went immediately to a side counter containing glassware of almost every description, from cheap and gaudy to exquisite and expensive. After much earnest discussion over the merits of various pieces, Eve finally narrowed her choice down to a delicate cut-glass vase just large enough to hold a single rose, and a porcelain candy dish edged with tiny sprays of hand-painted violets.

She wavered so long, Anne finally gave up on her and moved on to complete their other purchases. Just as Eve almost definitely decided on the candy dish, she heard a deep voice at her elbow speak her name. She turned to find Chase Aubrey standing bashfully behind her.

"Why, Chase, how are you?"

"I'm fine, thank you." Searching desperately but determinedly for something more to say, he gestured to the spool he was holding. "I came in so I could get some thread. I have a little sewin' to do." His face immediately turned as red as the thread he was holding, giving Eve a strong suspicion it was his long-handled underwear that needed mending.

He was so painfully embarrassed she had a sudden vivid mental picture of him sweating as he bent over his long johns, working a needle and thread that were all but lost in his big fingers. She wouldn't have hurt his feelings for the world, but she felt an unholy chuckle rising. She gulped, choked, and felt her own face redden.

He peered at her anxiously. "Eve?"

"I just swallowed wrong," she managed to gasp.

"You be careful. That could be dangerous," he said solemnly, and she choked again.

Fortunately for her breathing abilities, Anne appeared beside them.

" 'Mornin', Miz Clayton. Eve and me was just talkin'." Unconsciously he gestured with the spool, and Eve bit her lip fiercely. *I will not laugh. I will not!*

To her vast relief, Chase said reluctantly, "I guess I got to be goin'. Will I see you Saturday, Eve? At the weddin'?"

"Definitely! Polly asked me to be her attendant. Ma and I are going over early so we can help out," she managed to tell him demurely.

He looked disappointed at her last words. "I'll see you there, then." For a reason she couldn't begin to figure out, he turned red again and hurried off.

The Longing of the Day

She turned back to the shelf of glassware and snatched up the vase. "I decided on this after all," she said brightly.

All too aware of Anne's intent gaze, she concentrated her attention innocently on the vase. She was relieved when Anne said nothing, obviously deciding not to press the issue. But why was she so relieved? Chase was a nice enough fellow, and he clearly liked her a lot, even if he was bashful about it. He had dignity, too, in spite of his shyness. The woman he married would always be treated kindly, she was sure.

The remaining hours until Saturday fairly flew in the flurry of preparations necessary for the wedding. Anne and Eve helped Polly and her mother with all the tasks of cooking, cleaning, sewing and baking. Somehow it was all done in time, and suddenly Eve found herself standing beside Polly as her childhood friend became a married woman.

How would it feel, Eve wondered, watching Polly and Phil smile nervously at each other as they exchanged rings, *to belong entirely to another and he to you, to be one in mind, one in heart, and one in affection?*

Will Braden, on Phil's other side, smiled warmly and reassuringly at her as if sensing her sudden feeling of confused loss. He and Matt were chums from boyhood, and she had known him literally all her life. Somehow, she couldn't really mind if he knew how she felt.

After the ceremony, Will claimed Eve for their first dance, as was his privilege since he was Phil's groomsman and she Polly's attendant. "Are you sure your ankle is up to it?" she asked anxiously.

"It's up to it. But I don't know whether your feet will be, time we're done." He grinned ruefully and ran his fingers through his unruly mop of dark hair. "With my big boots steppin' on your small shoes, you just might need splintin' yourself!"

"I'm not worried," she assured him loftily as he took her in his arms and they began circling. "My feet may be little, but they're tough."

He grinned and guided her past Grandma and Grandpa Ruston. In spite of his 86 years, Grandpa was swinging to the music with cheerful abandon and obviously having a grand time. Grandma and her 82 years were doing their best to keep up with him. "I suspect he's been nippin' at the hard cider," Will whispered. "And Grandma looks like she could use a swallow or two!" Eve, following his glance, had to chuckle in agreement.

When she looked back at Will, she found his black eyes intently studying her face. "You look mighty pretty in that green dress," he said gallantly.

Startled, she met his gaze directly for a long moment, feeling a strange stirring within her. "Why, thank you, Will. You look mighty handsome yourself."

He tipped his head toward Phil and Polly waltzing nearby. "Sure seems strange to think of them married, don't it? Seems only a day or so ago, we fellas were chasin' you girls with frogs. Now those two are married, and you're all grown up, too. When the cowhands get back from summer herd, you better watch out. Just don't forget," he said gruffly, "I saw you first!"

The Longing of the Day

She laughed, her heavy heart suddenly lightening, the curious stirring stronger. "As long as you promise no more frogs," she teased.

He looked down, all his laughter gone, and his arm tightened around her. "I promise," he said softly. "No more frogs."

She smiled happily up at him, completely unaware of Chase Aubrey glowering nearby.

Anne watched the little scene unfold, but she wasn't the only one. Tegan Brice, Polly's mother, paused beside her and said sagely, "Mark my words, Anne, that daughter of yours will be getting married next."

Anne's attempted smile was not very successful.

On an oven-hot morning weeks later, Eve fled from the house. She didn't care where she was going. She just had to get away, and outdoors was no hotter than all the burning inside her.

Ever since she made her joy-filled discovery the night of Pa's visit, she had tried so hard to be worthy of God's trust in her, to show Him that she, in her turn, had total trust in Him. But there were still times, such as now, when, in spite of all her efforts, she felt like Nineveh of old, so "empty, and void, and waste."

She and Ma were both frazzled with the unending heat and work and worry and waiting. Humor, heretofore their staunch ally in their long battle, had deserted the ranks and refused to return.

The sun beat down mercilessly on her bare head. The

ground was so hot it burned her feet through her shoes. The brassy blue sky and the blackened, baked, crack-pitted plains stretched as far as the eye could see. *Was there any place in all the world for her to turn?*

Instinctively, her footsteps took her to the carriage house. The loft would be stifling in this hour of midday heat, but no more oppressive than the pain within her. She reached the haven of the upper floor, threw herself face down in the prickly hay and buried her head in her arms.

She lay thus for a long time, rebellion seething within her. *It is not fair! It just wasn't fair. Just because Ma was hot and tired was no reason to take it out on her. Wasn't she tired, too? Wasn't she just as worn out as Ma? Yet, apparently Ma could yell at her, but she couldn't yell back.*

Would this heat never end? She'd give anything for a cool breath of air. *Anything!* Even as she clutched furiously at handfuls of straw, something tickled the back of her head. Her tired mind failed to register the sensation at first. It came again, a lifting of the hairs at the nape of her neck. She raised her tear-stained face and unbelievingly held her breath. At the third puff of cool air, she scrambled to her feet, stumbled to the west window and leaned out.

The breeze struck her flushed face full on. She gasped, drinking in deep draughts of coolness. She wheeled and raced down the ladder, almost falling off in her haste. "Ma! Ma! Come quick!"

Anne yanked the back door open. "Eve, what in heaven's name ..." Her impatient words broke off as the breeze touched her face. Incredulity replaced her angry expression. Still clutching her dishtowel, she ran down the steps.

The Longing of the Day

Joy, wild and sweet, broke over her. Wordlessly, simultaneously, she and Eve turned and raced for the north corner of the house. Far away on the horizon, but undeniably drawing closer, a great, black cloud shadowed the heat-stricken earth.

They watched it in breathless silence, their exhausted beings drinking in the sweet coolness flowing in increasing strength around them. Anne hurried to the house and began throwing open all the doors and windows. The freshness rushed in, dispelling the stifling, stale air that had been a part of their lives for so long.

Back outside, they could see the black curtain of rain falling from the cloud. Neither dared speak for fear it would disappear, or worse yet pass by and miss them completely. They smelled the musty earth now as the drops pounded the parched ground. Lightning zigzagged blindingly. The roll of thunder was deafening.

Still they stood and watched it come closer and closer until it poured on them, filling their weary bodies with new life, sinking deep into their very souls.

When a little sanity finally returned, they retreated indoors. The rain drummed on the roof, gushing over the eaves, soaking into the wood of the house and sliding down to the parched ground where the thirsty earth greedily drank it.

Hours later the pounding lessened, became intermittent, then ceased. The storm had passed, leaving a clean, sparkling world behind. It had taken with it all the harsh tension, leaving only a blessed weariness.

Anne and Eve had set out all the rain barrels, and now their first priority was to shampoo their hair, luxuriating in the feel of having it really clean again. Their next move was for each to immerse herself in a long, hot, soaking bath. After all the weeks of basin-bathing, they felt almost wicked to be using so much water. Almost. But not wicked enough to keep from fully enjoying it.

In spite of the muddy roads, in the cool of the evening, they set out in the buggy to visit Becky. They met Hannah and Becky, with the children piled in the back of the wagon, on the road coming to the home ranch. Together, they turned toward Catty's and found her with Jared outside, drinking in the beauty of the spectacular sunset. They all sat on the steps enjoying the freshness, no one saying much until Catty softly voiced their joyous knowledge. "Soon, now, they'll be coming home."

Now the days, long filled with anxiety and tension, held out the sweet anticipation of hope to be fulfilled. Each morning Anne and Eve asked themselves and each other, "Today?" and each evening, "Tomorrow?" They tried not to be impatient but were disgracefully unsuccessful.

In the meantime, the sun continued to shine brightly over the plains, and on her way to the barn a few mornings after the rain, Eve saw a mist of green over the red-brown earth. *The grass was up!* Milking forgotten, bucket still in hand, she raced back to the kitchen where Anne was setting the table. "Ma, come look!" Anne did so, wondering at her daughter's broad grin, but when she saw, her smile became as bright as Eve's. They staked the animals out to graze, and in just a few days' time had the satisfaction of seeing them take on new flesh.

They were outside removing clean clothes from the line when they heard the rapid beat of hooves coming from the

The Longing of the Day

north. They turned, the light of hope bright upon them. The hooves pounded louder as Ben and Matt rounded the far corner of the house, their yells of triumph splitting the air.

Anne was already racing toward them. Ben dismounted and swept her into his arms. Lass, usually so dignified, was leaping and cavorting in an ecstasy of excitement, plumed tail waving so fast it was only a blur. Eve held back, drawing to her heart all the joy of this long-awaited moment.

Now Matt was striding toward her, taller and broader of shoulder than she remembered, his skin deeply bronzed by weeks outdoors. She had no way of knowing the whirl of thoughts engulfing him in those seconds as he took in the sight of her. She had thinned down, and the Lord knew there had been little enough of her to begin with. Her face was drawn as though she had endured great weariness, but her eyes were alight with glad welcome.

He stopped in front of her. But no words came. He had awaited this meeting so long; how could mere speech possibly convey all it meant? His first impulse was to reach for her hands, but, reversing movement, he swiftly removed his hat, revealing the pale stripe on his forehead in sharp contrast to the rest of his dark-tanned face. The strip of hat-protected skin amused her at first glance.

He grinned. "Hello, Coppertop."

Her lips moved, but no sound came. Finally, "Matt." All the joy of the world was held in that moment of knowing he was safe, knowing he was home.

Anne and Ben came up, and he turned away to give Anne a bear hug. She and Ben, talking and laughing, didn't notice the silence of the two young people.

While Ben and Matt tended their horses and washed up, Anne and Eve prepared a hasty meal. It flashed through Eve's mind that this homecoming was very much like the one earlier in the year, after they had been away on spring roundup. So much alike, and yet something was different. That earlier time they had been carefree and full of hopeful plans for the future. The long, dreadful summer had taught them many things. Looking back to the young girl she had been, she wondered at herself. *Was it really only the span of a summer? It seemed to have been years.*

Matt and Ben's stomping arrival from the corral interrupted her thoughts. How good a sound it was in a house far too quiet all summer. And how good to hear their voices fill the rooms that heard only women's voices for so long. Before he even washed up, Ben began telling Anne all their adventures. Matt let him do most of the talking, even as Eve let Anne ask most of the questions.

Ben related how the graze and water had all but given out on the creek. "The cattle had it picked so clean you coulda found a pin if you'd dropped it." Now it was over, he could tell of the worry that had lived with them night and day. Tell of it and even joke, though it had been a life-and-death matter at the time.

"When the rain come, it was like the Lord'd opened all the floodgates. You should of seen it, though I guess it must of poured here, too."

Without waiting for an answer, he plunged on. "We thought the herd would run out on us when it first started comin' down, with the thunder and lightnin' and all. You know how they'll spook at their own shadows. We was all

The Longing of the Day

set f'r 'em to go. Would you believe they didn't? They milled around and bawled, but that was it. They actually stood there and let all that water pour down on 'em.

"I never seen anythin' like it in all my days. It was as if they was just standin' and soakin' it up." He paused for breath. "I guess you might say we was as dumb as the critters, 'cause we just set on our horses and soaked it up, too."

Anne put in, "I never heard of them standing still in a thunderstorm before."

"I hadn't neither. Maybe they figured if they moved, they'd miss the water." Ben roared at his own joke.

"Did they really come through all right then?" Anne couldn't keep the anxiety out of her voice.

He sobered. "We did lose some. I'll have to go over the books. Before it rained it was almighty bad up there. A few more days and we'd have lost a whole lot more. As it was, I think they didn't spook 'cause they just didn't have the strength."

He fell silent, remembering, having unwittingly revealed the extent of the wretched situation to the women who had waited unknowing at home.

As Eve was helping Anne finish up the dishes, she suddenly realized they hadn't brought in the wash from the line. She slipped outside and stood a moment, face uplifted to the starry sky. As she reached for the last dress, Matt's voice behind her made her jump.

"Here you are," Matt said. "I was wonderin' where you'd made off to."

"I just thought I better finish bringing in the wash before the night damp gets to it."

He reached to take the basket from her, and they walked a few steps in silence. He glanced down at her. "You've been awful quiet this afternoon. Pa was so busy tellin' our adventures that we didn't get much chance to hear how you got on other than Polly and Phil's weddin'."

"That was definitely our biggest excitement. You know how it goes around here."

"They sure did it up quick, didn't they? I wish I could of been here. Leave it to Will to break his ankle so he'd be around f'r the big doin's. Some fellas have all the luck!"

When she didn't respond with a swift retort or even a chuckle, his look changed to one of questioning. "Eve? Is somethin' botherin' you?"

She was remembering the warmth in Will's black eyes and his sympathetic understanding the day of the wedding. But how could she put into words, even to Matt, this new awareness within her that was fragile as a bubble? An awareness that even all Chase Aubrey's awkward shyness had not stirred.

They stopped by the porch steps as Lass came bounding up. Belatedly, Eve smiled up at Matt. "Ma and I kind of got cabin fever from there being just the two of us here so long, but that's all over now."

"I take it the unfair way things turn out doesn't seem quite so unjust now?"

So he hadn't forgotten. But she should have known he wouldn't. She bit her lip. "It's been easier since it rained," she admitted, "but I know it goes deeper than that. I'm still trying to sort it all out, and I think I'm truly beginning to understand, at least a little. What we want, and what He

The Longing of the Day

wants for us, aren't always the same. But He does have His reasons. I ... I can't really put it into words yet."

He smiled in understanding, remembering well enough his own difficulty in speaking his deepest emotions aloud. "I'm glad you've made a start. That has to be the hardest part ... beginnin'. If you do want to talk, just remember I'm here. And now," he asked briskly, "any other scandal I've missed? I know you women just can't resist gossip!"

"Look who's talking," she retorted. "You men are worse than we women ever thought of being."

He grinned so sheepishly she had to laugh. Relenting, she said, "No, nothing I can think of. Except Catty's baby!"

"It's a mighty fine thing," he agreed. "Catty always has been a good hand with the little ones."

"But this one will be her very own," she said enviously.

"I don't know. I think maybe Aaron had just a little to do with it."

She blushed but returned with quick scorn, "Men! You think you know all about it."

"You'll have to admit we must know somethin'. Look at all the results we get with our efforts."

She blushed furiously this time and turned her head so he might not see. But she wasn't fast enough.

He glimpsed her red face and felt swift shame for embarrassing her, even in fun. Although he suspected they sometimes went further in their joking and foolishness than Anne would have strictly approved, it was only in fun, and Eve didn't seem to mind. Indeed, more often than not, she got in the last word. Only occasionally, as now, would she have no answer for him, and he would know he had gone too far.

He set the basket on the ground, and dropping to the step, motioned for her to sit beside him. Cheeks still pink, she did so, clasping her hands in her lap.

Lass had stretched out on the porch. Now she thumped her tail against the boards and thrust her cold, moist nose under Matt's hand to be petted. He scratched gently behind her ears, and her eyes half-closed in bliss. He glanced sideways at Eve. "Pa gave me your message."

She made a wry face. "It was pretty dull, I suppose, but what can you write about when the most exciting thing that happens is you find three new freckles on your nose when you thought you were finally getting rid of the pesky things?"

She looked so disgusted he knew better than to make light of it. So he said with maddening masculine practicality, "Better three than four. Besides, your letter wasn't dull. It was ... interestin'."

She eyed him warily. "Interesting?"

" 'Specially the part 'bout Ma and the skunk."

"Don't tell her I told you! She was mad enough I let it slip to Pa. If she knew I told you, too, she'd never forgive me. But I just couldn't resist!" Even yet, unrepentant laughter bubbled up within her.

Eyes twinkling, he raised his right hand. "I won't breathe a word of it." Then, laying his lightness aside, he said, "And I was just teasin' you before. Your letter really was interestin', and I appreciated gettin' it."

Words. Common, everyday expressions. How could she know he treasured that scrap of paper, carried it with him by day, and at night in the vast, lonely dark, taking it out — not to read, for he had long since memorized it — but because

The Longing of the Day

the tangible feel of it in his hands brought her near and made the ache of the night a little more bearable?

He could tell her nothing of all this. He could only sit beside her as he longed to do all those empty days and nights and feel a great peace and quiet within him. He could not, would not, let his mind dwell on the future. Here and now had to be enough.

And, for the moment, it was.

During the week after Ben and Matt returned, Jason, Luke, and Aaron brought their cattle home. Weathered, weary and grim, they set about tallying the toll the difficult summer had exacted on their herds.

Luke was hardest hit — he had lost nearly a third of his cattle before the rains finally came. But then he always seemed to come off second best to the other boys, a fact he was well aware of and tried to cover with bluff and bluster. His ranch always had the look of needing repairs, of sagging a little. His cattle always seemed slightly more gaunt than anyone else's. He, himself, perpetually wore a faintly haggard expression from trying to provide more than just a bare existence for his family, his soul sagging a little, as it were, under the burden of life.

Anne and Ben spent many dark hours wondering, worrying they had failed Luke somehow. But how? They did their best to treat all the children equally. What made the difference? Given the same circumstances, what made one man succeed where another failed? Was it luck? Fate? Or just a bit more knowledge and skill that no amount of years or

The Longing of the Day

learnin' could give a man if he wasn't already born with it?

So Ben's thoughts ran this mellow September Sunday as he sat at the head of the dinner table and gazed at the family ranged on both sides of the board. It was the first time they had all been together since early spring. Thinking of Anne, he glanced at her and smiled as he read the pleasure in her eyes. His smile deepened to a grin. *A woman to ride the river with! She keeps me on my toes, f'r sure.*

Catty and Aaron, sitting next to Anne, were wrapped in a world of their own. Aaron had raised holy Hannah when he got home and found Cat like she was. But he was also tremendously proud. His blue eyes spoke more than words could as he bent his head down beside her fair one to whisper in her ear.

Eve sat next to Catty, and Ben's glance was a little perplexed as it settled on his youngest child. *She's growin' up so fast.* She had been such a little bit of a thing when she was born, following as she did after such strapping brothers, and as such whimsy will, the nickname had stuck. He saw now she had blossomed in spite of the hardships of the summer. On the heels of this thought came the startling realization of how very much like Anne she was becoming.

Ben watched as Eve passed the basket of rolls on to Matt. Uneasiness nudged Ben. *Somethin's botherin' the boy and has been f'r quite a while.* He'd noticed it during their stay at the Creek and off and on since they'd been home. But the time for discussing it was never right, partly because Matt had become more reserved and sober these past months. *Not that he don't have reason to, the way things have gone with the ranch this summer.* Still, Ben sensed it was more than that. He would have to talk with Matt soon. *And yet, would such a talk be pryin'?* Matt was a man now, undeniably, with the right to handle his own affairs.

"Pa?"

Ben brought his attention back to the conversation to discover Jason regarding him questioningly. "I just asked if you've reached your final tally yet. We know pretty well where we stand, but you haven't said much, Pa."

Ben took a slow swallow of coffee. "My count ain't as high as I'd hoped."

"Will you be sendin' any to market?" Only Luke could make such a simple question sound like accusation and judgment rolled into one.

Ben tried to keep the bitterness out of his voice. "None of my cows are in any shape to sell. I'm goin' to have to hold 'em over 'til spring."

Aaron, eyes on the knife he was twiddling between his fingers, shifted in his seat. "They're sayin' this winter is goin' to be a rough one."

Jason's brown eyes were sober. "I've heard that talk, too. Grandpa Ruston was by the other day, and he was sayin' that in all his years of fur trappin' up the Yellowstone he never saw nothin' like what's goin' on now. Says that on Catfish Pond the muskrats are buildin' their houses twice as high as usual, and they're makin' the walls much thicker."

Silence descended over the table at his words. Luke, not to be outdone, put in, "I know my horses are growin' mighty long coats already."

Ben's fist closed around his empty coffee cup. "All the signs are sure enough pointin' to a hard winter. I hate to hold

109

The Longing of the Day

the critters over 'til spring, but even if they was in any shape to sell, with the market gone bust, there's just nothin' else to do."

Lately, the Laramie paper Ben received was full of news of the failing cattle market. Eve, seeing her father's grim expression as he laid his paper aside, took to reading it quietly. One day she came in to find Anne poring over it. After that they discussed it together and so came to understand better the longwinded discussions Ben was so fond of.

From reading and listening, they knew that, in a vicious circle, the drought had spread to the Midwest corn belt and created a shortage of feed. The rush to sell surplus cows caused Chicago beef prices to fall steadily. With no demand for cattle, the bottom fell out of the market. Thus Ben couldn't sell his cows even if they had been in any shape to. Eve thought that, with the coming of the rains, their troubles would be at an end. She was discovering they weren't to be let off that easily.

The earnest discussion continued as the afternoon wore on. At times the talk reached debate proportions as they aired their ideas on cause and effect.

Luke put it all down to the bad weather. "How c'n a man fight it? He sure enough can't change it!"

"The range is just plain overstocked — too many cattle and not enough acreage to feed 'em," Aaron argued. "All the absentee ownership's a lot to blame f'r that. How c'n a man know what's goin' on with his herd when he's a thousand miles away? This situation's been buildin' up f'r years, but everyone's ignored it."

Ben pounced on that one. "How would you go 'bout

changin' it? Some men 'round here have been raisin' cattle since before you was born. I suppose you could handle things better?"

Aaron ignored the sarcasm. "Less cattle per acreage, maybe let the grass lay idle a while to rebuild itself."

Ben snorted. "How long? A year? Two? All the grass is taken up 'round here. There's no room f'r expansion. So what you want to do is tell a cowman on the way up to cut down on the size of his herd. I'd like to see you try that one!"

Aaron subsided, having heard his father-in-law's views on that subject before. But was Ben really wrong? A man worked to increase his herd, not cut it back.

Jason put in, "But Pa, isn't a little setback now worth it rather than face complete disaster later on? It's comin'. You know that as well as the rest of us."

Ben jumped to his feet and began to pace. "Not necessarily. We've had bad winters before."

"Maybe not this year, true. But it is comin'. God help the man who ain't prepared."

"Risks are part of a cowman's life. If he's afraid of the odds, he should throw in his hand, get out of the game."

"It's just common sense to look ahead."

Jason well knew argument with Ben was useless. But there was a scrap of comfort in knowing Aaron and Matt agreed with him rather than Pa. He knew they did. It was plain on their faces.

Ben saw it, too, for he shifted his attack to them.

"Come on, you two, speak up. Is Jason the only one with a tongue or guts to use it?" Thus he baited them, urged them to argue with him, for a rousing debate was to him as salt to meat.

The Longing of the Day

Anne invited the whole group to stay for supper, but one by one, they declined. Chores were waitin', and they didn't want to be too late gettin' home to do them.

After the wagons rattled away, Anne and Eve returned to the house to start fixing supper, and Ben and Matt headed for the barn. After they completed the evening chores, Matt wandered off toward the corral. Ben watched him go and remembered he wanted to talk to him. He followed and leaned his arms against the gate post. Matt, staring moodily at the milling horses, didn't speak.

Uneasiness nudged Ben again. *What's troublin' him?* He tried. "You know, Matt, I'm sure glad you're here on the ranch. Luke, Jason and Aaron have their own families and responsibilities. With you though, well, it's a comfort to me, son, knowin' you're right here to face things with me." This approach wasn't easy for Ben. *How does a man tell a son how he feels?*

He kept his eyes on the horses while he spoke, but when Matt didn't answer, he glanced sideways. Swift shock punched through him.

Matt was gray as death come a-callin'. His hands clenched the fence rail, and his eyes were full of despair as he stared straight ahead.

"Matt, what's the matter?"

He drew a shaky breath. "Nothin', Pa."

"No," Ben said sharply. "You can't look that way then tell me nothin's wrong. Somethin's been eatin' at you f'r quite a while. I don't want to pry, but if you want to talk, I'll listen."

"I just don't want to be a disappointment to you and Ma.

You're countin' on me. I know that, and I sure don't want to fail you."

"I don't understand. You mean you boys with your new-fangled ideas f'r runnin' the ranch and me claimin' the old ways are best?"

That was not what Matt meant at all, but it was far easier to agree than try to explain what was really wrong. How could he tell Ben the whole truth when he dared not admit it even to himself?

"Matt," Ben shook his head, and his face held a strange sadness, "times change. A man has to change with them. If he's not willin' to accept new ideas and ways of doin' things, he might as well be six feet under, pushin' up daisies." Matt started to speak, but he went on quickly, "When we settled here we had a dream that one day we'd have the finest cattle ranch in Wyomin'. We've worked toward that goal all these years the best way we knew, with the best knowledge and equipment available to us, always keepin' in mind we was buildin' f'r the future.

"Our span of time will be up eventually, then the ranch and the dream will pass on to you young ones. It'll be your turn to carry on your dream the best way you c'n. We ask only two things of you." Matt had never seen Ben look so solemn.

"One is you all do your best. The second is f'r you, personally. If Eve hasn't married when the time comes, I want you to promise to take care of her. Since you're the brother she's always been closest to, we'll give her into your keepin', knowin' you'll do right by her. The same with Ma. If somethin' happens to me, I know you'll take care of Ma."

The Longing of the Day

Matt's throat was tight. "I'll take care of them."

Ben grinned and looked a little embarrassed. "And to close this fine speech, I just want to say you could never be a disappointment. You've been a fine son all these years."

Overhead a flock of geese winged their way southward toward freedom from cold and hunger — did it because instinct told them to. Matt watched them fly out of sight before his gaze returned to the horses.

"But what if it don't work out the way you've dreamed all these years?"

"That's always a possibility." Ben spoke matter-of-factly. "But I don't see any real problem. The others got their share of the ranch when they married. We figured we might as well give it to 'em now as later. I've got it all mapped out equal as we could make it. When Eve marries, she'll get her share. It's over to the northeast. The home acreage'll go to you. We figure that's fair, all the time and work you've put into it with me. If you marry while Ma and me're still here, it's still yours. We'd have a little place to ourselves out of your way so you'd be free to come and go. The only requirement in all this is, if anyone sells his share, he sells it back to the family."

Matt knew most of this — they had talked about it before. But he hadn't known he was to get the home acres. A year ago he wouldn't have believed his good fortune; now he felt cold desolation. Something of his thoughts must have showed in his expression for Ben said sharply, "Don't you like the idea? We thought it'd give you pleasure."

"Pa, it's generous of you. I sure never expected it." It was a relief to be able to speak the full truth about something.

"Generous has nothin' to do with it. It just seemed the right way, knowin' you feel the same as we do 'bout the place. It's not like we'd be tyin' you down here when you was up and itchin' to be off."

Again he could speak the full truth. "No, I don't want to leave here."

"That's quite a relief! The way you was draggin' 'round, I was afraid you was maybe frettin' to take off." Ben chuckled at his own foolishness in worrying so needlessly. "Then we agree, whatever comes we'll face it together." As Matt nodded wordlessly Ben added, "There's nothin' the two of us can't lick, even as bad a winter as they're all claimin' we're in f'r. Together, son, that's the way we'll meet it — head on! Hell's fire, I thought maybe you was havin' woman troubles." Ben's relief made him jovial, so he failed to see the sudden darkening in Matt's eyes.

"Now that would be serious," Ben continued. " 'Course I don't know how much advice I could give you there. You young ones are a lot smarter than my generation was at your age." He sighed with mock heaviness. "I don't know whether that's good or bad. Learnin' c'n be mighty interestin'!" He laughed heartily and clapped Matt on the shoulder. "Let's go in, son. I suspect supper's almost ready."

Matt's heart and mind were still in chaos as he and Ben turned toward the house. He was fully aware the burden of his problem was his own. No one else could solve it for him. Ben thought he had helped. He had tried, anyway, and if he didn't yet suspect there was more to it, Matt wasn't about to give him the chance.

So he asked with great casualness, "How 'bout you and

The Longing of the Day

Ma? Was she the first girl you ever loved?"

Ben looked surprised but smiled. "Men do a lot of talkin' 'bout all their conquests, but that's what most of it is — talk. If you ain't already found that out." He put his hand on Matt's shoulder and faced him squarely. "Son, she was — and is — the only woman I've ever wanted — needed — to marry. There's a big difference, you see, between wantin' a woman and wantin' to marry her. When the right one comes along f'r you, you'll understand. And now," he said briskly, "let's get that supper. I'm hungrier than a beaver with a toothache."

His arm still around Matt's shoulders, they went up the steps and into the brightly lit kitchen where Anne and Eve waited for them.

Long after Anne lay sleeping beside him that night, Ben remained awake, staring into the darkness. His thoughts kept chasing themselves through his mind, making sleep impossible. So many nights had been like this lately, when he would go back over the events of the summer and wonder what he could have done differently. What could he change if he had a chance to do it all over again? The answer was always the same. *Nothin'.*

Dealt the same hand again, he would play it the same way. Circumstances themselves had made any other course impossible. But to be brought from the high tide of their springtime hopes to this grim knowledge that by next spring they might be bankrupt was bitter medicine, indeed.

Louise Lenahan Wallace

He must be gettin' old to be so pessimistic, he reflected wryly. There had been other years when the bright dream was shattered by the heavy hand of circumstance, but he had been young then, with years left in which to try again. At 58 there weren't that many chances left.

Finally, unable to lie still any longer, he sat up and glanced over at Anne. She was sleeping quietly, curled on her side facing him. He rose, careful to make no noise, and stepped to the window.

He gazed unseeing out into the moonlight, his mind loping the back trail of years to the time when he had brought Anne out here. How young they had been, and how hopeful, how confident they would succeed.

He first came to Wyoming — then Nebraska Territory — with the Eleventh Ohio Volunteer Cavalry during the Civil War. Their assignment was to build a fort on the Overland Stage Road after increasing Indian harassment had caused the route to be moved southward from the Oregon Trail.

During the time he served at Fort Halleck, he had ample opportunity to study the countryside. Most people immigrating to California and Oregon regarded these plains as a wasteland — a stretch of territory on their journey to be hurried through as fast as possible.

But he knew he wanted to work with cattle. He had been on his own since he was 11, and he worked at any job that would enable him to buy food for his adolescent ravenous belly. Blacksmith's flunky, dishwasher, stable work — he had done 'em all. While he worked at a livery in Marietta, trail boss Hiram Sparks had spied him, sized up his muscles and thoroughness in completing a task once started. Sparks

The Longing of the Day

signed him on to help push a herd through to Missouri to supply the California immigrant trains.

That was the beginning.

From there he eventually found himself in Texas working cattle. The business in those days was a far cry from present-day methods and standards, but it was on those lonely windswept plains that, at 15, he glimpsed his dream for the first time.

During the years that followed, when he returned to Marietta and married Anne, the responsibilities of a growing family had forced him to lay aside any plans for such a wishful future. But, sent to Wyoming by the Army in 1862, he had looked on the expanse of sage and grassland and saw what almost no one else could — that it was prime cattle country for a man with a dream and determination.

His three-year enlistment over, he brought Anne, Jason and Luke from Ohio. *How right it felt, risking everything!* They began raising cattle for the Army — first for Fort Halleck, then after it closed down in '66, Fort Sanders. After the transcontinental railroad was completed in 1869, thus making the entire country a potential market, they had settled down in earnest to build their ranch — their dream.

They started with just the one room that was now the sitting room. He remembered Anne's happiness that first fall, when he had put down a wood floor over the bare dirt that had served them during the summer. That floor was their first big triumph and signal of success. Many families lived on dirt floors for years. But he and Anne were different. They would succeed where so many others failed! And they had laughed together in their young happiness.

Louise Lenahan Wallace

He had trailed in 40 head of prime beef for their start —
no more scrub cattle for them. Over the years, the house, the
herd and the family had grown. It was a slow, sometimes bitter, often painful growth, but they held on, refused to quit
when so many others had given up, beaten by the harsh
demands the land exacted from those who dared challenge
it. Their closest neighbors, the Jamisons, did not give up, but
they paid the highest price of all.

His thoughts turned to the tiny cross on the hill behind
the house. Baby Elizabeth's death was the bitterest blow of
all. She was born in late February on a dreary day made suddenly beautiful by her arrival. Their happiness at her birth
and their joy of having a daughter were short-lived, for at
sunset she died. They had never known exactly why.

Maybe it would have been easier to bear if they had
known. Heart-tearing uncertainty and grief lived in the
house with them long after the spring rains greened the grass
over their baby's grave. And always their hearts would carry
the knowledge that which has been given, can be taken
abruptly away.

How many times over the years that truth had reared its
ugly head. Droughts, blizzards, disease. Each time success
seemed just over the next rise, calamity snatched it from
them. They got along, but it was always "next year" the tide
of wealth would surely roll over them.

He thought of Anne, with her deep faith, her fine education and her love of books, coming here with him all those
years ago. He saw himself as he had been, with little working knowledge of God, social ways or books. All his time
and learning was in cattle. She never spoke against him for

119

The Longing of the Day

this but had quietly, determinedly, passed her knowledge on to each of the children in turn as best she could.

She asked only two things of him before they pulled up stakes and came out here to the end of the world. She had wanted the children to be educated, even if it meant taking time away from the ranch work. He stiffened his neck at this and insisted the boys would get all the learnin' they needed polishin' their pants in a saddle. Look at him, he had said, only a year or two of real schoolin' and he was gettin' along fine in the world. Wasn't he? And his boys would, too!

But she had stomped her foot down firmly. It was the first time she'd ever balked at him. And in the end he gave in, never admittin' to her that his real reason was fear that with learnin' the boys would look down on him, think less of him for his lack of knowledge.

It hadn't worked that way, of course. *Seems the things a man most fretted 'bout never happens.* Anne held her school in the evenings or at such odd times as they were all together. He found, by listening secretly, that he was picking up quite a bit of information himself.

Surprisin' what a man could learn by keepin' his mouth shut and his ears open. For the first time it occurred to him to wonder if Anne worked it that way on purpose. Wouldn't surprise him — she was usually a jump and a half ahead of him anyway.

Her second condition, religion, was a different matter. Living outdoors in the saddle, he came to know a God different from the One in a meeting house who dispensed justice or wrath or kindness at His whim. His was a God of nature — of storm and wind and cloudless summer sky.

Sitting on his horse and looking up at a winter night sky of a million stars, he was in a church that held no question of either God's goodness or His presence. But how could he explain it to Anne? He understood well enough how she felt. She was determined that, living in an uncivilized place, her family must not lose their own civilized ways in the process. As it would have been so easy to do. Again she refused to budge, had in fact balked like the orneriest mule he'd ever seen, until he agreed.

She was right, of course. He freely admitted it now, but for sure not then. The lack of a proper church necessitated their making their own services. Saturday nights when they had enough water, they all bathed. And Sunday mornings, dressed in their best, hair combed and faces scrubbed, they gathered solemnly for prayers and Bible reading. Week after week, year after year, they did it as regularly as though a church bell called.

Funny to think, when a church had finally been organized in town and they had started goin', he had really missed the home meetings, felt like somethin', well, vital had gone out of their lives that even services with a real minister couldn't replace. Quite a change for a man whose former personal acquaintance with the Almighty was a mumbled Lord's Prayer.

That agreement, and the one about education, at least, he had kept. But as he recalled all the other fine promises he had made Anne in those long-ago days, he smiled sourly. *What a job I've done of keepin' them!*

He sighed, his bitterness washing away in a great tide of weariness. Matt was right. He was countin' on the boy more

The Longing of the Day

than he realized. Matt saw the truth even before he could admit to himself he was ready to hand over the reins of his horse, that he was ready for younger shoulders to heft the weight of the ranch.

The pain burned in his chest like a ball of fire suddenly thrust inside him. As it traveled down his left arm, he dug his nails into the sill, breathed slowly, and waited with forced patience for it to pass. It had been ailin' him, comin' and goin', for almost two weeks this time.

Anne's voice came out of the darkness. "Ben, are you all right?"

He didn't turn as the pain finally, slowly ebbed. It didn't go away completely, and he knew only too well that it wouldn't. It would crouch, waiting and grinning wolfishly, ready to spring when he least expected it. "Of course. Go back to sleep, Anne."

The springs creaked as she left the bed. She put her hand on his arm. "You mustn't tear yourself apart. There's nothing else you could have done that would have made things any better. You did your best. That's all anyone could ask."

He looked down into her eyes and, in the moonlight, saw the love and trust reflected there. He cupped her face with his work-callused hand and shook his head. "I think you know me better than I know myself."

She smiled. "After 35 years I should know you pretty well."

He thought again of his conversation with Matt. "F'r better or f'r worse. When you said that all those years ago, I bet you didn't realize how much 'worse' there would be."

"I guess," she said thoughtfully, "you might say I didn't

know how wonderful the 'better' would be."

"Do you truly mean that, my Anne?" Suddenly he had to know. He had to hear her say it.

She dropped all pretense of teasing and laid her hand gently against his cheek. "My dearest, no woman has ever been more blessed than I. We've had hard times, yes. But being there for each other, no matter what, it's brought us through so much. I can't imagine life without it — or without you."

He gazed at her for a long, searching moment. "I know I don't say it often, but I do love you very much."

He bent his head to kiss her, and all the years, all the troubles, and all the difficult times slipped away.

"The only woman," he whispered, holding her close. "The *only* woman."

Dusk coming softly to the surrounding countryside brought warning of winter's approach. The night breeze, as it stirred the leaves of the cottonwoods and moved on to brush away the smoke curling lazily from the chimney, spoke strongly of the coming coolness. It was in the crispness of the air and in the brightness of the stars.

Inside the house, the family of four, each busy with his or her own task, gathered near the fireplace. The light from the fire threw flickering shadows on the walls and seemed to swallow up the glow from the single lamp burning on the table. The area in front of the hearth was sufficiently well lighted for them to work, but the rest of the room was dusky.

At the time when Anne and Ben built this room, when it was the entire house, stoves had been considered much better for heating purposes than fireplaces. But having more rocks in the creek than dollars in his pocket, Ben decided to go with the fireplace.

Later, when they added the bedrooms, they put Ben and Anne's room at the northwest corner, facing the front of the house, with the fireplace and Catty's and Eve's room sharing

The Longing of the Day

the remainder of the north wall. Both bedrooms were built with a separate hearth that connected to the main chimney, a luxurious comfort on bitter winter nights. The boys' room was in the corner formed by the ends of the kitchen and the girls' room. This had become Ben's office after Matt chose to move out to the bunkhouse.

Comfortable was the word Matt finally decided fit the sitting room. From the bright, braided rugs on the scrubbed wood floor, to the crocheted throw on the couch and the whatnot shelf in the corner, it reflected Anne's personality. Always neat and clean, with few frills, it nevertheless wore its furnishings with grace. For anyone who was tired or anxious, just the act of walking in and sitting down in this room was soothing.

Matt had no idea how Anne managed to give so much of her own self to the room; he hadn't even recognized it as such for a long time. But it was true: As the room was, so was Anne herself. Fastidious in her personal appearance, efficient in working at the tasks around the house, she always had time for anyone who was hurt, troubled or just in need of that special warmth and caring that were so much a part of her. Just to be near her was healing.

Tonight, however, there was no peace in Matt's troubled soul. From his position on the floor beside the fireplace, he could watch the others quietly and be unnoticed himself as he whittled a piece of wood.

Anne sat in her rocking chair beside the round table that held the lamp. She was sewing, her head bent over Ben's shirt in her lap. The pool of lamplight picked out the silver in her once glorious red hair, and her hands, busy with the material, showed the effects of much hard work over the years. Her face, however, held as much kindness and caring as when, long ago, she cradled and reassured a certain bewildered little boy who used to wake with huge tears running down his cheeks.

Matt remembered that little boy.

Anne raised her head from the collar she was turning and commented to Ben how good the fire felt. Ben nodded his head and replied that after the summer he'd never figured to really enjoy heat again. Anne laughed, but Matt saw Ben did not smile.

He saw something else. *When had Ben aged so noticeably?* He felt a sharp pang as he realized the other man's hair was completely gray and lines were deeply etched into his face. But, Matt wryly acknowledged, there was no doubt Ben could match him for a full day's work. *Strange,* he reflected, *the people around us become older, and we don't even notice, until something happens.*

These two people were more than just parents to him, as they had loved him and brought him up. He owed them more than he could ever repay. He knew they expected no return from him, any more than any loving son would give. Here his thoughts faltered, for he knew one way he could do right by them.

His heart beating faster, he raised his head to look at Eve, and for the first time that evening, his eyes brightened. But only for a moment. He dared not gaze at her longer for fear someone would see and read in his eyes that which he kept concealed in his heart. Even as his glance sought her face and turned quickly away, he knew she had never been more desir-

The Longing of the Day

able — or more impossibly distant from him.

She was knitting, her head bent a little as she counted stitches. The firelight caught and reflected the rich copper of her hair, turning it to living flame. Her nose was wrinkled, a sure sign of her concentration and one that always made him want to chuckle. However, he learned long ago, ruefully, it was wise to restrain the impulse.

He was *brother*; she was *sister*. Thus had they always accepted it, even as everyone around them had accepted it. He was 6 the autumn she was born, and from the very first moment there was a special closeness between them.

From the beginning it was to Matt that Eve turned whenever she was troubled or unhappy. She tagged after him, even when her toddling steps couldn't hope to keep pace with his surer stride. It was he who helped her discover the fascinating world of the ranch and explored it with her, from bird nests in the very tops of the trees, to the creek running behind the house, to their own special hiding place on the roof of the carriage house.

The roof was gained by going through the loft window and then by perilously climbing up, using the finger and toe holds he had taught her. Once on the roof, they would lie flat on their stomachs, heads buried in their arms. Shaking with childish giggles at their daring, hearing the other children calling, they knew full well that if their parents caught them, they would have their backsides paddled but good. But they were never found out. More miraculously, Matt now knew, they had never broken their necks.

When did childhood's rollicking comradeship become the man's abiding love? The two essences were so deeply

128

intertwined within him that he did not know.

He was startled out of his thoughts by Eve, laughing and calling to him. "Brother, did you hear me? Do you like it?" She held out her knitting, and he saw she had completed a scarf. "I made it just for you, since you seem to have misplaced the one you had last year ..." her voice was severe even as her blue eyes lit in fun, "... and the year before."

He stood and carefully shook the wood chips from his lap into the fire. He held up the scarf. "Snowflakes. That's quite a fancy pattern. I promise not to lose this one. After all the hours of work you've put into it, I wouldn't dare." He grinned. "At least not 'til winter's half over!"

"You! I've never heard of anyone losing scarves like you do. It's a wonder your neck doesn't freeze right off."

He was suddenly solemn again. "I promise I'll keep this one. I'll make sure nothin' happens to it." He turned, picked up the piece of wood he had been whittling and held it out to her. "I've got somethin' f'r you, too."

She turned it over in her hands wonderingly. "Matt, it's beautiful."

It was the tiny, carved likeness of a deer in full flight. Every fleeting, graceful line was captured, giving the sensation of fluid movement and life to the little figure.

Anne and Ben held it and marveled. Matt had always had this talent, but it never ceased to amaze them.

Eve took it back carefully. "Thank you. I'll treasure it always." Impulsively she stretched on tiptoe to press her cheek to his. "You're the best brother anyone ever had."

Her touch sent sweet joy surging through him; the reality of her words was a bitter wind blowing over him. Unable to hide his feelings, he turned brusquely away and brushed stray wood shavings into the fire. He sensed her puzzlement but didn't know what else to do.

He was saved by Ben. "It's late. We'd best be readin' our chapter." But Matt's relief was short-lived. As it turned out, the passage that night was from the *Song of Solomon*, a choice not exactly beneficial to Matt's present frame of mood. *By night on my bed I sought him ... Thy two breasts are like two young roes. ...* With a strangely dull feeling of finality, Matt listened to Ben's embarrassed but determined-to-get-through-it reading. *How fair is thy love, my sister ... How much better is thy love than wine. ...*

Ben, with an audible sigh of relief, finished, and Matt knew he couldn't put it off any longer. He faced them and said quietly, "Ma, Pa, I'm goin' away. I'll be leavin' before first light, so I'll say goodbye now."

Anne and Ben stared at him, unbelieving. He saw Anne's hands, white-knuckled, grip her sewing. Ben suddenly looked very old and tired. And Eve ... the pain in her eyes cut him to the raw. It was she who finally broke the shocked silence. "But why? Why must you go?" It came out a choked cry.

From what source he was able to draw strength, he never knew, but somehow he managed to face them all and say cheerfully, "After all, I'm almost 25. It's time f'r me to go. I won't be leavin' you short-handed, Pa. You know how you're always wishin' Will Braden'd quit bein' so stubborn and sign on here? Well, I got 'im to change his mind. He'll be right tickled to come here in my place. 'Course it's comin' on to winter, so he won't expect any pay, just meals and a place to sleep. He won't cost you any more than I would. And you know yourself he's a good, steady cowhand and reliable." He stopped, unable to continue with their eyes on him like that, feeling they were reading the depths of his soul.

Anne finally stirred. She had been watching him searchingly all the time he was speaking. "Matt, are you sure it's what you want to do?"

No! he wanted to cry out. *It's not what I want. I want to stay here. With Eve. I want to love her and honorably claim her as my wife before all of you. As I have a right to do!* His thoughts mired painfully. As he could have done had Fate not stepped in a long time ago ...

"Matt," Ben's voice brought him back, "your Ma asked you a question."

He saw Ben was waiting for an answer, that they were all waiting. Silently he drew a deep breath. " 'Course it's what I want. I wouldn't be goin' otherwise, would I?" He even managed a careless laugh.

Ben's eyes bored into him. "I was countin' on your help this winter. I had no idea you was plannin' on cuttin' out. From all the signs, it's goin' to be one hell of a winter. You've seen f'r yourself. And comin' on top of this summer ..."

He gazed at Matt for a long, hard moment. When he spoke again, his tone held a cold fury Matt had never heard directed at himself before. "I thought we agreed we would stick together this winter. I thought we agreed it's the only way we'll make it to next spring. And now you want to trot off carefree and happy.

"Matt, you gave your word. In my day when a man did that, it meant somethin'. He might not have another possession to his name, but if he made a deal on his word alone, it

The Longing of the Day

was as good as if it was signed in gold. If a man didn't have another thing, he had that."

Matt felt as if he had been flicked raw with a whip. He knew Ben was right. He had spent long hours arguing this very point with himself. But what other choice did he have? He just couldn't stay here any longer. "I'm sorry, Pa," he said quietly. "It's just somethin' I have to do."

Ben's voice shook with disbelief. "I was dependin' on you. And now you're goin' to walk out, and all you c'n say is you're sorry? I'm sorry f'r you, Matt. You may be gamblin' more than you realize right now. Some day you might want to give your word again, and you might find it won't be so easily accepted."

Ben's eyes held deep hurt. "You've been like our own flesh and blood to us all these years. We've tried to show that's how we felt 'bout you in every way. In some ways, maybe, you've been like more than our actual own. At least I thought so. Until now. But no son of mine would ever walk out like you're doin'." Shoulders bowed, he turned slowly away to his bedroom. The door clicked shut.

Pain seared Matt. *It's not that I want to go,* he wanted to bellow to the closed door. *I just have no other choice. Except to stay here, and that could only hurt you even more.*

Anne stepped forward and took his clenched hands in hers. "You know I don't want to stand between you or take sides. That wouldn't be fair to either of you. But you and Catty have been as dear to us as any of the others. Nothing can ever change the way we feel about you." She hesitated. Her gaze went to the closed bedroom door and lingered there a long moment. "He didn't mean it," she whispered. "He couldn't.

It's just such a terrible blow. He *was* counting on you."

The stark statement cut him even more deeply than all of Ben's rough words. Her voice strengthened as she faced him directly once more. "When you were 5 years old, we had a God-given responsibility to correct you when you made a wrong decision. Now you're almost 25, and we have a God-given duty to let you make your own choices and to let you take the consequences."

He saw the shine of tears in her eyes and could scarcely speak for the ache that was in him. "I'll take the consequences, Ma."

Only then did he turn to face the first consequence, standing white and dazed beside him, her hands clasping each other tightly. He had intended to take her hand and tell her "Goodbye, sister," with casual cheerfulness. Now, looking into the depths of her blue eyes, bright with unshed tears as they were, he knew he couldn't. To touch her at all was to betray himself. So he only said quietly, "Goodbye, Eve."

He turned, had his hand on the doorknob when she spoke suddenly. "Wait, Matt, I'll walk out with you." She grabbed her shawl and drew it over her shoulders before he could protest, even had he wanted to.

The night was very clear and cold. The walk to the bunkhouse was too short.

He stood at the door, gazing at her for one last, precious moment. In the moonlight he could see her expression was deeply troubled. "Must you really go, brother? If only ..."

He broke in, unable to endure more. "Yes, I must! Why can't you let it go at that?" His voice broke, and she stared at him, bewildered.

The Longing of the Day

"But Ma and Pa need ..."

"It's just somethin' I have to do." His voice was chillingly quiet, made more so by his very desperation that she not seek further. They had had differences, of course, when they were growing up, for she had Ben's stubborn temperament that could quickly become full-fledged fury when she felt she was being unjustly crossed. Not often, but once in awhile since she had ceased to be all knees and elbows, freckles and wild, fly-away mane of red hair, her anger been directed at him. It was now.

"All right, go." Her voice was as cold as his had been. "But I just don't understand why!" She turned and ran away from him, back to the house.

He winced. The last thing he desired was to leave her with bitterness between them. He started to call after her, to tell her to wait, but stopped. *What good would it do, anyway?*

The cowhands who would stay the winter were already snoring loudly. After he packed his war bag, he stretched out on his bunk, hands locked behind his head.

He stared up at the ceiling, waiting out the hours to morning.

He rose before first light, gathered his belongings and quietly left the bunkhouse. He stood a few moments, the chilly air closing around him. It was dark and quiet in this time before dawn. The moon had set, leaving only the stars to light the world.

He intended to go away without seeing anyone, but when

he led Tumbleweed out after saddling him, he saw the light gleaming in the kitchen. Desolation swept him. He didn't want to see anyone. He just wanted to get away. Must he go through having to say goodbye all over again?

Even so, he hesitated. If Anne were going to all the trouble of fixing breakfast for him, he couldn't very well just ride away without acknowledging her effort. He wasn't hungry. His stomach felt like a cold branding iron had lodged at the bottom, but he couldn't deliberately cause more hurt than he already had.

Reluctantly, he led the bay over to the back door and tied him to the railing. He stepped into the light and warmth of the kitchen, saying, "Ma, I ..." and stopped, stricken.

It wasn't Anne who turned, cooking fork in hand. It was Eve. He stared at her, dismay and joy battling within him. He felt the blood beating up into his face and, clumsily, dropped his hat. He bent to retrieve it, a good excuse for his redness, he hoped, as he straightened up again. "Eve, I didn't expect you to be up. I thought Ma was fixin' breakfast."

Her eyes were shadowed as though she hadn't slept much, but she answered saucily enough, "What's the matter? Don't you like my cooking?" She gestured with the fork to the bacon sizzling in the pan.

"Sure. I just didn't expect to see you up this early."

She wrinkled her nose at him. "Just you never mind about that. I may like to sleep, but I have been known to get up before daylight once or twice in my life. You just sit down and let me tend this bacon before it burns."

She turned back to the stove and busied herself with the fork and the coffeepot. Shedding his coat and hat, Matt

135

The Longing of the Day

watched her, telling his thudding heart to shut up before she heard it clear across the room. She was wearing a blue robe and the deerskin slippers he had made and given her last Christmas. The robe was belted around her slender waist. A bit of white ruffle showed at the hem as she reached for a plate. Her burnished hair was tied back from her face with a blue ribbon and fell loosely over her shoulders in a shimmering mass.

Too heart-weary to struggle longer, he gave it up and let the pounding of his blood admit what he had tried so long to deny.

She set a cup of coffee and a plate of bacon and eggs in front of him. The soft fragrance of her hair as she bent near almost undid him. Murmuring his thanks, he reached for his coffee cup with a decidedly unsteady hand. He felt as shaky and awkward as any new-dropped, wet-behind-the-ears calf trying to stand on its legs for the first time. He just hoped to God he didn't look that foolish. He sternly told himself this was Eve, and he had known her all her life.

Because he had to say something, he asked, "Aren't you goin' to eat?" When she shook her head, he said gruffly, "You better. You're so little, if you don't eat somethin' to weight you down, you'll blow away."

"Are you trying to tell me my cooking's that heavy? Thanks a lot!" But she went to the stove and returned with a plate and cup. She put them in the place across from him and sat down. When she made no move to eat, he looked over at her and saw the shadow that had lifted at their teasing had come back.

He quit trying to fool himself with dumb remarks. This

136

was, indeed, Eve. Clear thought, having for a few moments taken a wild gallop, returned with the old familiar ache as its rider. "Are you all right?"

She nodded, then shook her head. "Matt, I ... I just wanted to say I'm sorry about last night." He moved his hand in a dismissing gesture, but she went on quickly, "No, I mean it. I shouldn't have lost my temper that way. You have your reasons for going, and whatever they are, they're good ones or else you wouldn't be doing it." She was looking at her hands clasped tightly in her lap. "I thought about it for a long time after I went to bed. I finally figured out what the matter is."

Quick alarm raced through him. *If she knew ...*

Head down, she didn't see and went on resolutely. "I finally realized I was scared." She looked at him then and tried to smile. "I was scared because you've never gone away before, except for cattle drives and such. And I always knew you'd be back. But this time isn't the same. You won't be coming back. I guess I've just gotten so used to you being here to talk to and everything, it frightened me to think of you being gone."

Her eyes, meeting his, were pleading. "Isn't that silly?"

His first reaction was overwhelming relief that she didn't know, and then the full import once her words struck him.

No, it could never be the same. Not ever again would she be only *sister* to him. She knew she wasn't, of course. There had never been any secret made of it, although Ben and Anne were reluctant to speak of it beyond the basic facts. After she was old enough to understand, she was told, even as his true sister Catty had been, that the Claytons were parents to the Jamison children in love only.

The Longing of the Day

They were raised together to feel they were all brothers and sisters, and Matt knew, was as certain as he had ever been about anything, this was how she felt about him. He knew her too well, loved her too long, to doubt it. She would be shocked, perhaps even revolted — he used that harsh word flatly, knowing it for a very real possibility — to learn his feelings. That would be more unbearable than the present situation. So he held himself tightly in check, taking infinite care that she not know.

Of course, in the darkest hours of the night, he had asked himself whether she felt the same way. But he had only to look into her clear eyes to know the truth for what it was.

All this ticked through his mind even as he wondered how he could answer her. Using every ounce of strength he possessed to keep his voice calm, he said, "Eve, you mustn't feel that way. I'll be back. You can't be thinkin' I'm leavin' forever. I'm not, honest. This is just somethin' I have to do." He chose his words very carefully as he looked directly into her eyes. "And," with the barest pause, "I would hope, as close as we've been, you'll think of me once in a while even if I'm not here. Just as I'll ..." He stopped and swallowed, "Just as I'll be thinkin' of you."

Some of the sadness left her at his words. She even managed a trembling smile. "You always know how to make me feel better when I'm blue. And you never tell me I'm acting silly even when I am, and I know it. No one else would put up with my foolishness, so I guess I better get it out of my system before you go!"

Her words brought him back to the reality of the situation. "What we better do is eat this great breakfast before it gets well-water cold." He reached for a piece of toast.

She laughed and brushed at her lashes with her hands. "There's plenty more on the stove, keeping hot. Just let me know when you're ready for a refill."

They ate in silence for the most part, and he wondered what she was thinking. He had spoken brave words, but when she refilled his cup it took all his willpower not to reach out and take her in his arms.

He lingered over his coffee, prolonging this brief time with her as much as he dared. How good it seemed, how right that they, just the two of them, should be sharing breakfast in the warm, lamplit kitchen with the rest of the world shut out.

Finally, there was nothing to do but go. He stood and buckled on his gunbelt. As he reached for his coat and hat, she turned to the stove and brought back a flour sack tied with twine. She laid it on the table. "I fixed you some food to take along. Figured you could use some coffee and bread and such."

"Now that was right thoughtful," he said with all the cheerfulness he could muster, deeply touched by this last little gesture.

Her eyes were deep and dark, and the sadness returned as she gazed at him. Her head came only to his chest, and she looked so small and fragile.

He meant only to take her hand, to tell her goodbye. But looking into the depths of those blue eyes, knowing this was goodbye, all his love and longing suddenly overwhelmed him.

"Eve," he said huskily and reached out to draw her to him. Her eyes widened, but whether because of shock or

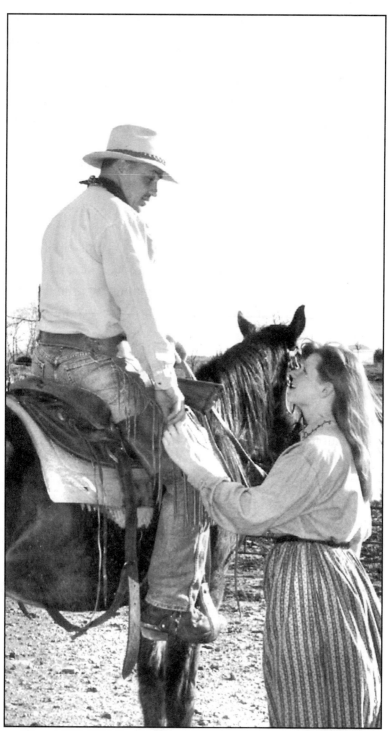

---

because she didn't fully realize his intentions were less than brotherly, she made no struggle. As his arms circled her, pulled her to him, his hands caught in the flaming mass of her hair, and he thought the fire of it would consume him. But he was beyond hesitation. He simply, hungrily, drew her hard against him.

With the soul-singing reality of holding her in his arms — a reality so long desired, so long despaired — the last vestige of restraint, that he had clung to so doggedly, melted without a murmur.

Without volition he bent his head down. His mouth found her lips, and for one brief, timeless moment of eternity, joy surged through him.

Until he felt her shudder, her body stiffening against his.

When shocked realization of what he was doing lanced him like a knife.

He released her hurriedly, not daring to look at her, yet horribly aware she was standing frozen, back of hand pressed to mouth. *Her eyes* ... Powerless to bring himself to look into those eyes, to read what he knew was written there, he grabbed the flour sack and rushed out the door.

Wheeling Tumbleweed away from the house, he urged him to a pounding run. Over the sound of the hooves, he thought he heard her call.

But he knew there was no way he could face her after what he had done.

8

Matt rode north many miles in his search for work. He had made up his mind at the outset he would not take a job in the immediate vicinity of the home ranch. If he did, it would only defeat his purpose in leaving. He must be far enough away that he could visit home only infrequently.

So he rode north and west across the plains. He had heard much talk of this part of the Territory. It was definitely rougher and more unsettled than the southeastern area. After only a handful of years since this part of Wyoming opened to settlement, the Indians still weren't happy about it. Raids on ranchers and settlers alike attested to their anger.

Indians weren't the only problem up here, however. Near the headwaters of the Powder River was a region 35 miles long called Red Canyon. Outlaw gangs, using this canyon as a headquarters, regularly rode forth to raid, rustle and generally terrorize the countryside. Afterward they would slip back to their hideout, secure in the knowledge no one could track them by earth. There was only one entrance on the canyon's eastern side easily defended by a few armed men. Thus they could strike any time, any place, with little

The Longing of the Day

fear of retribution.

Yet Matt rode forward with no hesitation. If a rougher way of life and danger lurked here, there also loomed the vastness of the wide-flung land where a man could breathe deep and forget the only young woman who gave meaning to life.

He inquired at several ranches, but the answer was always the same — no one was hiring. They were cutting back this time of year, same as always. However, as he soon discovered, there was a new twist to laying off the cowhands this season.

In past years a cowman who was let go had several choices. He could leave the ranch and head into town where he might find a job tending bar, cleaning stables or washing dishes. Or he might remain on the ranch and work without pay, receiving only room and board in return. A third option was to ride the grub line. If he had a good horse and saddle and the necessary desire to see the country, he could travel from ranch to ranch throughout the winter, timing his arrival at each new place to coincide with supper time. The code of the times decreed that no one, friend or stranger, be allowed to leave without a good meal under his belt.

Now this open-hand hospitality was undergoing drastic change. At ranch after ranch, Matt was told sure he could join 'em for dinner, but it'd cost him four bits. At first he couldn't believe it. No rancher he knew would dream of charging 50 cents for a meal. A man shared what he had in the way of food with no thought of exacting payment for it.

But after being confronted with this same response a few times, he realized it was indeed a true fact — and a spreading one. Wyoming ranchers, hard hit by the bad summer and trying to cut down on the extra expense of stray men at the table, were demanding they pay for the food they ate.

He began to understand how truly devastating the summer had been, and it was then that he fully appreciated the packet of food Eve prepared for him. Not being the proud possessor of any extra 50-cent pieces, with Eve's supplies he was able to forego stopping at a ranch when night came. Each evening he fixed himself a small campfire, and after eating, rolled up in his blankets, face to the stars.

He would lie, hearing Tumbleweed crunching grass close by, the small sound of it loud in the listening stillness. The stars, shimmering overhead, were touchably near. The man, the horse and the stars were alone on the vast, empty plains.

Strangely enough, Matt felt far from alone. It was as though, in going away, he chose the one trail by which he could always remain near to those he had left.

Deep weariness sapped him as he realized his staying would have shattered their closeness as a family. That, weighed against the burden of his leaving, was surely far more important. Caught between two paths of causing them pain, he chose the fork that would give them less hurt later on.

So he lay and gazed at the glimmering stars, listened to his horse graze and felt the stillness of the night around him.

And told himself grimly that it was true.

Thus, he eventually rode into Crooked Fork Valley. Here, as everywhere else in Wyoming, the grass lay sparse

The Longing of the Day

and brittle so that it crackled when Tumbleweed trotted through it. He glimpsed a cluster of ranch buildings just before noon and cantered Tumbleweed toward them, neither hopeful nor apprehensive. If there was no work here, as there had been none at the other places, he would go on. It was that simple.

The main ranch building was of logs, set in an open space upon which the sun, in summer, would blaze mercilessly. But in a country where Indian harassment was not yet a thing of the past, shade trees providing concealment were foolhardy. The outbuildings were a combination of log and sod — not fancy, but durable. The place had a look of well-run efficiency, and Matt felt a stir of pleasure for the first time in days.

As he neared the corrals a tall, powerfully built man in his mid-50s was preparing to dismount from a buckskin. The rider's hair was iron gray and he wore a drooping mustache the same color. Dressed in well-worn range clothes, he had a definite air of authority.

Matt knew after one look this was the man he wanted to talk to.

He walked his bay over to the buckskin. The other man had dismounted and watched his approach through narrowed eyes. When he spoke, his voice was rusty, as though he were more used to speaking to cattle than to men. "Light down, stranger. What c'n I do f'r you?"

Matt pulled Tumbleweed in and stepped to the ground. "I'm lookin' f'r the owner of this spread."

"You found him. I'm Lafe Bardlow, owner of the LB. Covers all you c'n see from here and then some. What's on

146

your mind?"

"Name's Jamison. I'm lookin' f'r work."

Bardlow's eyes pierced him. "Work, huh? You any kind of cowman a'tall, you know ranches are layin' off, not hirin' this time of year." At Matt's acknowledgment, he frowned. "You know, yet you're askin' me f'r a job. Why?"

"I need work. I like the looks of your place."

Bardlow studied him for several seconds. "Where'd you work last?"

"The Arrow A, north of Laramie."

"That'd be Ben Clayton's spread. I've met him. A good man, knows his business. Did you say your name's Jamison?" he asked suddenly.

Matt stiffened as he saw realization strike the other man.

"Jamison. Heard of you, too. Ben was mentionin' it. You been raised in his ways, then you know cattle. It ain't my place to ask why you left there. In this country a man's business is his own, long as he's not tangled up in somethin' dishonest." Bardlow's eyes, the color of steel, bored into Matt. "One fact I have learned — a man's character usually shows up in his work, be it good or bad." He spoke with sudden decision.

"All right, Jamison, if you're Ben Clayton's kin, that's good enough f'r me. The truth is, I c'n use another good man right now."

Matt drew a deep breath. "Thanks, but I can't take the job."

Bardlow's mouth fell open. "What the hell do you mean you can't take the job?" he demanded angrily. "You come lookin' f'r work, I hired you. Now you want it or not?"

Matt spoke quietly. "Yes, sir, I do want it. But not under those terms. Not just because Ben Clayton raised me. I want to

The Longing of the Day

be hired on my worth, not his. Thanks, anyway." He started to mount Tumbleweed.

"Wait a minute." Bardlow's eyes probed Matt deeply for a moment, then he chuckled. "You'll do, son. You'll do. The fact is, I don't like to hire men who can't stand on their own worth. You'd be no good to me if you was willin' to trade on Ben Clayton's reputation. I don't need that kind of man." He stuck out his hand.

Matt let out his breath and they shook. "Put your gear in the bunkhouse," Bardlow said, "I'll take you out to the herd after I check somethin' in the house." He strode off, but momentarily turned back. "Pay is bed and board. That's all I c'n afford this winter. Come spring, you'll be hired on regular."

Matt untied his bedroll from the saddle. "Fair enough."

In the bunkhouse he shoved his war bag under an empty cot and returned to his horse. Bardlow soon joined him, and they rode off to find the men holding the herd. "I been here goin' on six years now," Bardlow informed Matt. "It started small, but it's growin'. Right now I got six men besides the cook workin' under me. You'll meet 'em all, of course." He lapsed into silence.

The herd grazed in a valley to the west. The calls of the cowhands keeping the strays in check drifted toward the two who had halted their horses on a rise to watch. Bardlow explained. "I'm goin' to try to keep 'em fairly accounted f'r this winter. Seems to me we're in f'r a right rough one. I don't have so many cows I c'n afford to let 'em wander off 'til spring and still hope to find 'em. That's what I meant about needin' another good man. We're goin' to ride herd on these critters day and night, hell or high water — or snow."

148

He turned that intense look on Matt.

"Does that fash you? 'Cause if it does, the gate's still open. You c'n ride out now and never set foot on this spread again."

Matt set his jaw. "That kind of work suits me just fine."

"Good. There's Rand. Let's go," and he started his horse down the slope.

Matt watched as a short, spare man rode up on a roan and reined in beside Bardlow. In a surprisingly deep voice, he said, "Ever'thin's under control, boss." His gaze flicked over Matt.

"Good. This is a new man, name of Jamison. He's on f'r the winter. Jamison, this is my right-hand man, Delt Rand. You'll be takin' orders from him same as if they come from me."

Rand was around 35, his spare figure wiry. With brown hair and eyes, he looked completely undistinguished, but Matt sensed the same air of authority about him as about Lafe Bardlow. Here was a man who could do his job and do it well, with no nonsense tolerated from anyone else.

His eyes measured Matt, his face neither approving nor disapproving, merely waiting. "Howdy, Jamison. Welcome to the LB."

Bardlow put in, "You show him the ropes, Rand. Have him meet the other men. I'm goin' to check on the north side."

He rode off and Rand spoke up. "Might as well meet the men first." As he started to walk his horse, Matt and Tumbleweed fell in beside him. "Mr. Bardlow didn't say. You worked 'round here before?"

Matt kept his gaze ahead on the herd. "I come from the Arrow A, north of Laramie."

"That's a fair piece from here." He spoke only as stating

149

The Longing of the Day

a fact. When Matt didn't answer, he went on, "We're not as citified up here. This country c'n be rough on men and cows. One of the cowhands got hisself turned into a pincushion just last week. Was out by himself and tried to stop some bucks from borrowin' a stray cow. Not much danger from Injuns if you don't go wanderin' off, but they do like to bedevil." He shot a sideways look at Matt's Colt.

Matt acknowledged the warning. "Sounds like he forgot to use common sense."

"Sully knew, he just didn't heed. 'Round here, one mistake c'n be too many."

"Not much different from any place else then. I like it up here. A man c'n feel free."

"That he c'n. There's still plenty of wide-open spaces. I like it, myself." Rand caught sight of a rider approaching and called, "Hey, Gaines, over here."

The man loped his horse up to them and reined in.

"This is a new man, name of Jamison, from down Laramie way. Jamison, Jack Gaines."

Each man acknowledged the introduction, Matt reserved and Gaines casually cheerful.

As Gaines rode off to bring in another stray, Rand said easily, "We all get along right well here. Each man knows his work and does it." He said it casually enough, but again Matt got that impression of no-nonsense authority.

It suited him just fine.

The men broke for the midday meal, and Matt met the others: KC, with the gambler's eye; Canto, whose deep, rich singing voice had given him the only name anyone knew or would ever know; Red, a shirt-tail cousin of Gaines who could count on the toes of one ample foot the months he had been shaving, but did his best to give the impression he was a man of the world; and Dan Mackley. Once Dan had stood straight, tall and strong in the fullness of youth. Now his seamed, leathery face and stooped, rounded shoulders spoke eloquently of time, the great ravager. He stuck out a callused paw. "Glad to make your acquaintance," he told Matt with quiet reserve.

During the afternoon, Matt found himself put to the test several times to show his ability. That was all right with him. He didn't do anything he hadn't done a thousand times before. As he nudged a reluctant steer back to the herd, he saw Bardlow watching him but couldn't read his expression.

Riding back to the ranch that evening, Rand pulled his horse up beside Matt's. "I just spoke to Mr. Bardlow."

Matt waited.

"He's right pleased with hisself f'r hirin' you. Just thought you might be interested to know." He gave Matt a friendly grin and rode off.

Matt's eyes followed him and a sudden sense of well-being warmed him.

Dan Mackley rode up beside him. "I heard Rand just now. Them's high words of praise comin' from Mr. Bardlow. He don't say much. Just expects a man to know his job and do it. Good words are pretty rare with him."

Matt's feeling of pleasure deepened. He didn't say anything, and Dan chuckled. "Go ahead and feel good. I'd say you'd earned it!"

151

The Longing of the Day

That night in the bunkhouse, KC, deck in hand, approached Matt. "How about a little game, friend?"

Matt shook his head. "I'm right low on cash at the moment."

The gambler grinned. "Be glad to stake you." When Matt still refused, he shrugged. "Have it your way. Maybe some other time." He stalked off and started wrangling Gaines to play a friendly hand.

Matt stretched out on his bunk and closed his eyes. He had drawn the 10-to-2 watch along with Dan Mackley, so he needed to get some sleep while he could, if he could. KC had talked Gaines into playing cards and was now winning, to judge by Gaines' blustering.

It was typical bunkhouse fare, probably going on right now in a hundred other rooms just like this one. The stove glowed warmly enough, but outside its immediate vicinity as Matt was, the room was chilly. The walls were a patchwork of old newspaper stories and patent medicine ads. Some previous owner of Matt's bunk, in a burst of genius, had even pasted pictures of ladies' corsets to the underside of the bunk above. Wrinkled as they were from the pasting and brown around the edges, Matt wondered drowsily whether they served the purpose for whoever went to all the effort of putting them up there.

Clothes were hung up "on the floor," and a pungent smell lingered, compounded of skunk tallow, unwashed bodies, smoke and grease. Even with his eyes closed, Matt knew just by breathing that he was in a bunkhouse.

He woke shortly before 10. He had a knack of setting a mental clock before he went to sleep and waking precisely when he wanted. He had been able to do it as far back as he could recall, and at no time did it come in so handy as when he had to stand night watch. He was tugging on his boots when Rand walked in and glanced around at the snoring men. When he saw Matt was already up, he nodded to him, walked over and called Dan.

Matt watched the older man come up silently, immediately wide-awake, and guessed Dan had seen days and nights among Indians. He spoke quietly to Matt, and they pulled on their heavy coats before stepping outside.

A brisk wind blew from the north. "Either I'm gettin' old or we're in f'r one hell of a winter," Dan grumbled.

Matt grinned. "I thought we had one hell of a summer. I, f'r one, sure don't want the winter to be that warm."

Dan muttered under his breath something that would have shocked his Granny and shot him a look of utter disgust. Matt's grin widened.

At the corrals they saddled their night horses. Dan eyed Matt's mount, a nondescript gelding. "I see you got ol' Buttercup. He don't look like much, but he sure c'n see a chunk of coal in a cave at midnight."

"I hope I got a good string. They ain't much f'r looks, but then looks never stopped a stampede."

He had picked out his string, the horses that would be his alone to use as long as he worked for the LB, and turned his own bay into the corrals earlier that evening. Now, only time and trial would tell whether he had chosen well.

"Buttercup, here, tried to bite me," he said gloomily, "so

The Longing of the Day

naturally I had to pick him so I could show him who's boss."

"That's Buttercup, head of the welcomin' committee!"

They mounted and rode out to the herd. Everything was quiet and remained so during their four-hour stint. At the end, after Canto and Gaines, the latter still grousing about the month's wages he had lost, put in an appearance, Dan and Matt returned to the bunkhouse.

"We had an easy time tonight," Dan commented. "Too bad we can't always be so lucky."

They parted, to catch a couple hours of sleep before morning.

And the days and nights, each with its pattern of work and sleep and work again, dropped like missed stitches until October and part of November quietly raveled away.

9

Wednesday, Nov. 17, was a day that never showed dawn. With the gray half-light of the morning came a curious sense of foreboding. It was quiet, too quiet, as men and cattle waited.

The cowhands carefully circled the jittery herd, singing softly to try soothing them. Rand and Bardlow moved among the men, cautioning them to go easy. "It won't take nothin' to spook 'em. They're just itchin' to go."

The snow caused it, finally. Powdery, fine and dry, it came from the north with a snarling blast. One instant the herd was there, the next it was gone. In that same fraction of time, visibility became nil.

All-enveloping whiteness rushed at Matt, scratching viciously at his eyes, tearing his breath away. The wind wailing in his ears drowned out all other sound. The temperature plummeted in those few seconds, but it was no colder than the sudden icy knot in his belly.

He knew Rand and Bardlow were someplace ahead and the herd had been to the east. Trusting Shadow's instincts and sure-footedness, Matt gave him his head, and they started forward into the swirling madness.

155

The Longing of the Day

Thus began one of the eeriest rides Matt had ever experienced. He knew they were moving forward, yet they seemed not to be. Somehow he felt as though they were standing still while the storm tore past them at breakneck speed. He knew it couldn't be so. Yet the impression persisted as gullies and rises flattened beneath Shadow's flying hooves. Rocks and bushes loomed up weirdly in the blankness and fell away as the horse cut and dodged. Traveling along the perimeter, keeping pace with the panicked creatures, Matt finally felt them begin to turn and slow. Then stop.

In spite of the biting cold, he was drenched with sweat as he pulled in his mount.

Now the harm was done, the wind began to ease a little. With the snow no longer being blown so fiercely, shapes and figures began to emerge from the powdery haze. By some miracle, no one was lost or trampled, but the herd was scattered far and wide. Bardlow's face was grim as he issued orders to start roundin' 'em up.

Rand was the one to turn the herd. Matt understood more than ever why Bardlow depended on his foreman so much. Even when a man could hear and see, turning a stampede required the highest kind of skill. Literally deaf and blind in the storm, Rand took a terrible chance. One misstep of his horse, one miscalculation of the movement of the herd, and he would be ground to nothing beneath a thousand angry hooves. But his horse hadn't stumbled, and he hadn't guessed wrong.

They set to work rounding up the scattered cattle, unaware the storm marked the beginning of a winter that would be branded in their memories forever. Isolated as they were, they had no way of knowing until much later that all the cattle country from Texas to Canada had been hard hit, that trains carrying passengers, mail and supplies were stranded on the open plains for days before they could be dug out. Telegraph lines were knocked out, completely isolating some communities, and travelers, caught on the open road between their homes and town, froze to death before they could reach shelter.

On the LB, their own trouble was too immediate, too real for them to give much thought to the outside world. They worked night and day to reunite the herd and keep it together after that first all-out stampede. When Bardlow made his final tally, 16 head were missing. The cowhands searched with painstaking care long after the blizzard had blown itself out, but they were gone, apparently having drifted on with the storm. Whether they would find them again in the spring, no one knew.

It was bitter cold and made worse because the powdery snow was so fine it drove through every crack in a building. The wind blew so hard the briefest opening of a door sent snow blasting to the farthest corner of a room. The north wind, blowing down from the Arctic, caused temperatures to plunge far below zero. The cattle, then, must be kept moving, for to lie down in the snow was to die. Since they were reluctant to move under their own steam, the men had to continually prod them to be up and moving.

The cowhands also had to shovel away the snow blanketing the grass, so the cattle could feed. This exhausting task was necessary because a cow, not having the wits to paw the snow away, would starve to death even though grass lay just beneath its hooves.

The Longing of the Day

The remainder of November passed in a nightmare haze of wind and ice and balky, hungry cattle. Thanksgiving came and left without the men being aware of the day. They were in the saddle where they had been for many days and nights before, where they would remain for many more to come.

At last, the first week in December, the weather moderated. After the cold eased up for a day or two, Red voiced the hope that perhaps the worst was over. No one in the bunkhouse even bothered to reply. The others had been cowmen too long to entertain any such wishful thought.

During this calm, Bardlow decided it would be safe enough for them to return to their four-hour-watch routine. Everyone had lost sleep during these last, hectic weeks; there was every possibility they would lose more in the time to come. They might as well catch up while they could.

One evening during this lull, Bardlow strode into the bunkhouse. He surveyed the lounging men and said bluntly, "I need two men to go to town f'r supplies and mail. I'd go myself, but I can't leave here. Any man willin' to take on the job, let me know."

The men silently surveyed one another. It was 25 long miles to town; the weather might break at any time. If it did and a man was caught out in the middle of nowhere ...

"I'll go," Matt said abruptly, swinging his feet to the floor.

The men's eyes focused on him, but they kept their opinions to themselves.

"I'll go, too," Dan Mackley said quietly.

Bardlow's gaze shifted from Matt to Dan and he slowly nodded. "Come to the house. I'll go over the list of supplies with you."

He walked out, leaving a vast silence behind.

"Well," said Dan, "standin' here won't get the wood chopped." He reached for his coat.

Matt pulled his collar up as they stepped out into the yard. The snow crunched underfoot.

Neither one spoke as they headed for the house.

Matt had been in the main building only for meals. Now they entered the kitchen and waited. The cook, short, balding, and to judge from the non-existence of his waistline, immensely fond of his own cooking, was kneading bread dough and looked up as they entered. "Supplies gettin' mighty low," he grumbled. "Glad somebody's finally goin' or this outfit be eatin' saddle leather 'fore long." He punched the dough vindictively.

Bardlow's arrival spared them the necessity of a reply. "Sit. Coffee's on the stove." He poured himself a cup and turned to face the two waiting by the table. He surveyed them a few seconds as if measuring them. They were an unlikely combination. Dan was round-shouldered, grizzled, and faded. Matt stood tall, straight and clear-eyed.

Bardlow trusted his instincts and was seldom wrong about a man. He was not surprised these two volunteered, but he was glad. "Here's the list, with the very minimum of what we c'n get by with. Get more if you c'n. Supplies might be short in town, too. Just do the best you c'n." He shoved the paper toward them. "Read it over. You got any questions, ask."

The two men bent over the paper, studying it. Dan's lips moved soundlessly as he read. Matt straightened and waited. At last Dan raised his head. "Seems clear enough to me." He

The Longing of the Day

looked at Matt, who nodded.

Bardlow stood. "You'd best start before first light tomorrow. It'll take you most of the day to get there. You should have time to get the supplies and load 'em before the store closes. Zack Davis will let you keep the sled in his livery stable overnight." Again that piercing look.

"I expect you two to stay with the sled all night. Those supplies get stole, there's goin' to be bellies and backbones rubbin' acquaintance before we c'n get more, and that's plain fact. You'll be able to start back first thing Friday mornin', day after tomorrow. That'll get you back here Friday night if ever'thin' goes right."

"Which team should we take?"

"Star and Sugar. They're in the barn tonight, along with the sled. I'll give you the money in the mornin'. Any other questions?"

Both were silent.

"Then I'll see you at four o'clock." As they reached the door, his voice stopped them. "I appreciate this."

They went out silently. In the sharp cold once more, Dan spoke. "It appears we'll be doin' a little travelin' tomorrow."

"Uh-huh. Got your society duds all ready to wear?"

"Society duds!" Dan spat. "It seems the only society we're goin' to see is at the mercantile and the livery stable." He quirked an eyebrow. " 'Course, there is Les Hooper's daughter. She helps him in the store. She's 35 if she's a day, and she's on the lookout f'r a man. I'll be sure to introduce you," he finished brightly.

"Thanks. She sounds like a real treasure, but more your age than mine. I just couldn't take her from you and all your sophisticated charms."

Dan groaned. "She looks at me with those big, sad eyes whenever I go in the store. It's like she knows I'm guilty of somethin', but she forgives me anyway. What it's supposed to be, I've never figured out."

"Why don't you ask her? She'll prob'ly be glad to refresh your memory."

"I may be guilty of a thing or two, but it sure ain't been with her!" Dan said indignantly.

"You goin' to be honorable and marry her?" Matt was all concerned seriousness. "I'll be glad to stand up with you."

"Marry her!" Dan snorted. "I been wearin' single harness too long to start pullin' double now. 'Specially with her!"

Matt slapped his thigh. "That's why you volunteered f'r this job! You just couldn't wait to see her again."

"I couldn't? That's f'r you, my fine friend!" Dan bent down as he spoke, picked up a handful of snow and flung it at Matt. It caught him full in the face, and it was Dan's turn to snicker at the other's outraged expression.

Matt promptly stooped as though to scoop up a handful of snow. When Dan also bent over, he lunged, tackled him and shoved his head into a drift for a royal washing. Dan sputtered and struggled, but Matt held on. "Say 'Uncle.' " Dan sputtered again. "Say it!"

Dan managed to pry his face out of the drift. A scarlet blaze branded his cheek, and his nose glowed cherry. With his eyebrows crusted white, and snow clinging to his cheeks and jaw, he resembled nothing so much as an outraged Saint Nick. "How in thunder c'n I say it when you got my mouth shoved full of snow clear to my tonsils?"

The Longing of the Day

As Matt pushed down once more, "All right, all right. Uncle!" Dan roared.

Matt snickered, let go, and immediately received another face full of the icy stuff as Dan grabbed a handful and flung it, all in one swift motion. Matt gasped, choked and collapsed into laughter. Dan grabbed Matt's head to push it down in the snow, and Matt raised his hands, a strategic error Dan promptly took advantage of by pushing harder. The drift loomed hugely before Matt's eyes and nose. "We're even," he managed. "Uncle!"

Dan let go. They glared at each other and burst out laughing. Steadying each other, still chuckling, they turned toward the barn to check the horses and sled.

Later, lying on his bunk, Matt realized it had been the first time he had laughed like that in a long while. He thought of Eve, and turned over with a thump. He wouldn't think of her tonight. He couldn't.

He forced his thoughts back to the tussle in the snow. "So ol' Dan has a gal chasin' after him. From what he says, she must be somethin' else. This trip just might turn out to be very interestin' after all."

Matt had set his mental clock before falling asleep and woke shortly before four. He lay a minute, listening to the chorus of snores around him and thinking of the long, cold day ahead. Reluctantly he pushed his warm blankets aside and swung his feet to the icy floor.

He tugged on his stiff, cold boots and bent over Dan's

bunk. A man never touched another to wake him. To do so was for the waker to run the risk of having his face rearranged. So he called, "Hey, Dan, up and at 'em!" To be quiet was not necessary. With all the snoring, a train could have roared unheeded through the room.

Dan sat up silently as always. Instantly awake and alert, he reached for his boots. As he tugged them on, he had a few choice words to say about their lack of warmth. Matt grinned. Dan might wake up fast, but it sure didn't do much for his personality.

He didn't expect the icy water in the washbasin to help much either, but after a vigorous splashing and grumbling, Dan turned. "Now I've said my prayers, let's go eat!"

As they crossed the silent yard to the house, the sky hung wide with stars. They could only hope there would be no storm while they were gone. Their breath held white before them and the snow squeaked underfoot — the only sound in all the stillness.

The light in the kitchen glowed brightly in the night as they stepped onto the porch. Through Matt's mind flashed the memory of another morning and another breakfast, but he thrust it fiercely aside.

Crusty was pouring buckwheat batter onto the smoking griddle. "Help yourselves to coffee. You c'n eat in a minute." He went on with his work without so much as glancing at them.

Bardlow strode in. " 'Mornin', boys."

Crusty filled their plates, and they pulled out chairs and sat down. They ate heartily, for both were aware it would be a long, cold trail until suppertime.

The Longing of the Day

When they pushed back their plates, Bardlow disappeared into the other room. He came back in a few moments with a money belt in his hands. He placed it on the table. "You c'n decide between you which one'll wear it. There's adequate to cover any expenses you'll have. If you c'n bring some back, so much the better, but the important thing is to get all the supplies you c'n."

Matt's eyes met Dan's and he pushed the belt toward the older man. "You wear it."

Dan started to speak, hesitated. He picked up the belt, buckled it on under his shirt and buttoned his coat over it. Bardlow, who watched intently, nodded in satisfaction.

They picked up their hats and turned to the door. "Wait, boys." Bardlow dug into his pocket and held out two 5-dollar gold pieces. "Just a little somethin' to show my appreciation. Might as well give it to you now as later."

Dan and Matt looked at each other. It was Matt who said, "You don't have to pay us extra."

Bardlow's voice was gruff. "If I thought I had to, I wouldn't. You don't need to mention it to the others, however." The last statement was an order. "And you'd better be gettin' along. You're burnin' daylight."

Outside, Dan raised a grizzled eyebrow and Matt shrugged. They went on to the barn.

The trip into town was, in itself, uneventful. They saw no one and nothing except miles and miles of ice-covered plains. The sun came up in a burst of color that was reflected on the white carpet of snow. As they drove along, somehow words weren't really necessary between them. Each was comfortable in the other's silence.

164

Suddenly, Dan began to sing vigorously, if off-key. *Old Bill Jones had two daughters and a song. One went to Denver and the other went wrong. His wife she died in a poolroom fight, but still he keeps singin' from mornin' till night.*

Caught up in the plaintive lyrics, Matt joined in and they let loose their voices for all they were worth. *Ride around little dogies, ride around them slow, for the fiery and snuffy are a-rarin' to go.*

They finished on a note that would have done credit to a dying bull. Roaring with laughter, they stopped to rest the horses and went on to sing, *Come all you young men who handle a gun. Be warned of shootin' after the down sun ...*

They kept going as one tune sparked memory of another. Some were ribald, some sad, some hilarious. A cowman with a song was never alone.

Almost before either realized it, they swung into town. They had made good speed and had ample time to fill their list.

Matt had forgotten about Les Hooper's daughter until they reached the front of the store. His curiosity newly sparked, he said with great casualness, "By the way, what's the name of the storekeeper's daughter? I think you forgot to mention it."

Dan eyed him with surprise, then suspicion. "Why?"

"Just curious."

Dan scowled. "Florabelle. And don't you go shootin' your mouth off."

"Why, I wouldn't dream of it, partner. You know me better than that." He was all injured innocence.

"Yeah, I know you. That's what I mean."

Matt followed him to the door. "Go on in," he prodded.

The Longing of the Day

"She's waitin' just f'r you!" He barely managed to duck Dan's swing at his head. He snickered as Dan opened the door. At the older man's glare, he gazed back with wide-eyed innocence, then grinned again behind Dan's back.

After being out in the brightness of the snow for so long, the interior of the store seemed very dark to them. Even after their eyes adjusted to the change, the room was still dusky.

The mercantile had every object necessary to sustain life on the plains. Hardware — from buckets, stoves and coffee grinders to ready-made saddles — lined the wall to their left. Along the opposite wall hung an incredible array of stacked hats, coats, shirts, long handled underwear, dresses and dress goods. The wall broken by the door behind them supported a floor-to-ceiling case full of patent medicines guaranteed to cure everything from lice — "mechanized dandruff" — to hoof-and-mouth disease. Even the floor was jammed with sacks, barrels and boxes containing cheeses, crackers, coffee beans, tea leaves, dried beans and apples; tins of tomatoes, peaches and milk; flour, sugar and cornmeal.

The area behind the counter, which held the cash register, was given over to pigeon-hole mailboxes, and on the counter itself reposed a basket of onions and turnips, doubtless given instead of money for goods received. It was an overwhelming, chaotic assortment. Over the whole room hung a heady odor of whiskey, liniment, axle-grease, tobacco, spices, leather, fresh-ground coffee, and the slightly stale smell of a room that has been kept closed for many days and has picked up dampness in the process.

The storekeeper drifted toward them, stopping twice to sneeze. Heavyset, probably pushing 60, he had a fringe of

166

white hair around his ears and a bald dome above. The eyes behind his steel-rimmed spectacles were beady and darting. *Like a snake's*, Matt thought, half expecting to see his tongue flick in and out. Letting go with a sneeze that shook dust from the rafters, Hooper drew out a handkerchief and vigorously blew his nose. Replacing the cloth, he extended his hand to Dan.

"Just can't seem to shake this cold," he explained in a curiously high-pitched voice and sneezed again. "It's been quite a while since any of your crew's been in. You haven't been sneakin' off to Ziv Vladimir's and gettin' your supplies there?" He asked as a big joke, but his voice held a definite edge.

"Who's Ziv Vladimir?" Dan asked interestedly.

"Why, he came to town a couple of months ago and set up shop down the stre—" Hooper snapped his mouth shut. "Who's this fella?" he asked hurriedly. "He ain't been here before." While he made this astute observation, his snake-like eyes flicked over Matt.

There was a dangerous glint in Dan's eyes. "This is Matt Jamison. Matt — Les Hooper. He owns the store. So far it's been the only one within 50 miles of anywhere. This Ziv Vladimir, he sell general merchandise same as you?"

Hooper ignored Dan's blunt question and hastily stuck out his hand to Matt, who took it and dropped it quickly. It was soft and white and slightly damp. Hooper didn't notice, or chose to disregard, Matt's reluctance. "Pleased to make your acquaintance, Matt Jamison. Right pleased, indeed." Giving Dan no chance to inquire further about his new competition, Hooper suddenly bellowed over his shoulder, "Flora, we got customers!"

The Longing of the Day

"Coming, Pa," sounded from behind a curtain beside the mailboxes, and in just a moment, a woman appeared. She had her hand to her hair as if making a last-minute adjustment, but when she saw Dan, she hurried forward, hands outstretched. "Why, Mr. Mackley, we haven't seen you for ages. How nice that you've come again."

The inference that he had come to see her, and not just on business, was too plain to be missed. Dan stammered, gulped, and rescued his hand. Matt poked him, but when Dan glared at him, he just looked back, wide-eyed.

Dan said too rapidly, "We've come f'r supplies. F'r the ranch," he added unnecessarily. "This is Matt Jamison," he finished in quick triumph.

She turned her eyes, so big and black and solemn, like a mournful chipmunk's, to Matt. She rejected him as a suitor in one quick glance, but he was, after all, a man even if a young one. "How do you do, Mr. Jamison?" Her voice was like new honey. "It's so nice to meet you!" She held out her hand.

He took it, and dropped it as quickly as was decently possible.

Whoever named her "Beautiful Flower" had, unfortunately, failed to see the prophecy come true. She was slender, and she didn't wear spectacles, but with the same exaggerated politeness, high-pitched voice and warm, moist hands, she was certainly Les Hooper's daughter. Surprisingly enough in view of her father's crowning lack, her hair was beautiful. Abundant, black and gleaming, it was piled carefully on her head. As her one redeeming feature, she made the most of it.

She fluttered her lashes at Matt and turned her attention back to Dan. "How have you been faring at the ranch?"

He swallowed and said too hastily, "Just fine. We do need supplies, though." He shoved the list at her.

She took it carefully. "Of course," she murmured. "Let's see what you have here." Behind her back Dan cast an appealing look at Matt, who just smiled wickedly.

It took some time to fill the list, but eventually they had everything gathered into a large pile. They knew Bardlow would be pleased they were able to get everything and in such ample amounts.

The last item on the list was mail. Flora turned with a swish of skirts to the pigeon holes. "Let me see. Yes. There's quite a bundle here."

She handed the stack to Dan who took it hurriedly and retreated. Flipping through the pile, he said apologetically to Matt, "I don't know why I bother to look. I never get anything."

Matt heard a strange note of lonesomeness in his voice and wondered whether Dan had anyone to write him. He promptly forgot the fleeting thought as Dan said, surprised, "Here's one f'r you."

Matt eagerly reached out, but now it was Dan's turn and he was going to repay him in spades for all the taunting Matt handed out about Flora. So he backed away, waving the letter tantalizingly. "Such purty handwritin', so nice and neat," he said admiringly. He held it up to his nose and took a long whiff. "Does it ever smell good!" He rolled his eyes up and pretended to swoon.

Matt was not noticeably amused. He knew Dan was determined to have his fun, to rub it in for his own lack of sympathy earlier. But he wanted that letter, and the only way to get it was to play along with Dan's little game. So, with an offhanded casualness he was far from feeling, he asked, "Is it from Laramie or Cheyenne?"

Dan studied the postmark intently. "Laramie," he finally offered triumphantly.

Matt heaved a sigh of disappointment. "If it was from Cheyenne, I'd be fightin' you f'r it 'cause there's a gal there I've been waitin' f'r a letter from. But this one ..." He shrugged and turned away.

Dan stared at him suspiciously, but he was so obviously uncaring whether he got to read it or not that there was no fun left in teasing him. So he handed it over with no more fuss.

Matt grabbed it and grinned. Dan let out a howl as he realized Matt tricked him and tried to snatch the letter back. But Matt had it now, and he held on to it, backing away from Dan's grasping hands. Then he forgot Dan as he turned the envelope over and saw the familiar handwriting.

Matt felt quick hope as he took the envelope, then swift disappointment as he recognized Anne's script. Even as he opened it, his spirits rose once more. After all, a letter was a letter, even if it wasn't directly from Eve.

He lifted out the paper, seeing Anne's face as she told him goodbye that last night. And Ben's face, too.

Dear Son,

We received your letter telling of your safe arrival at the LB. We were very glad to get it and are happy you are doing so well.

It gets colder here each day, although there is no snow yet. Ben has been preparing as best he can for the winter. Will is a great help to him and seems to have settled into working here very well.

We all have our health and hope you have kept yours as well. Somehow the place seems much larger since you left, and much emptier. But as I said before, you're a grown man, and we must accept your decision. Just know if you should decide to come back, we will,

The Longing of the Day

all of us, welcome you. Ben was very unhappy at first as you well know, but since has resigned himself. I won't pretend he isn't still hurt — he had so many plans. He assumed that what he wanted, you wanted, too. He realizes now how unfair that was to you.

We will have Christmas here as usual. If you can find it at all possible to come, please do so, son. The day won't be lavish, I'm afraid, but at least we'll all be together. Eve and I are already figuring what we'll have for dinner, and I'm glad to see her take an interest in things again. She's been so quiet lately.

I must close for now, son. Ben is waiting to take this letter.

We hope with all our hearts to see you at Christmas.

Your loving Mother

Matt finished reading and drew a long breath as hope and despair mingled within him. He wanted to go, but how could he?

Dan, all teasing forgotten, stood to one side, quietly watching. As he caught Matt's eye he said carefully, "Not bad news, I hope." It was question and statement at once. Dan would help, but he would not pry.

"No, not bad news. It's from my — my Ma." If Dan noticed the hesitation, he gave no sign. "She wants me to come home f'r Christmas."

"I thought it was bad news, you looked so douncy. Christmas, huh? You better take her up on that. Christmas in a bunkhouse ain't much to speak of." He looked at the list one final time. "That seems to be it."

Matt stuffed the letter in his pocket. "You goin' to pay now?" Flora, who had been watching with avid curiosity, bent to add the charges up.

While he waited for them to finish, Matt glanced carelessly around the store and noticed Hooper had lighted lamps against the encroaching gloom. Matt hadn't realized it was so late.

He casually surveyed the glass case of the counter in front of him. The case contained an array of rings, brooches and bracelets. But he scarcely saw these, for his eyes lighted on a gold locket.

Eve's voice came to him from across the months. *I would so like to have a locket in the shape of a heart.*

He closed his eyes as, for an instant, she was so near, so real.

"Matt?"

He turned his head. Dan was eyeing him anxiously. "You all right?"

"Sure, I'm fine," he managed.

Dan frowned, but Flora spoke quickly, saying she reached her total. Dan turned back to her, and Matt looked into the case again.

He didn't know much about lockets, but this one was gold colored with a design of leaves etched on it in fine lines. And it was heart-shaped.

His own heart beating faster, he gestured to Hooper, who hurried forward. Matt indicated the locket. "C'n you take it out of the case?"

Hooper extracted the locket and held it up by the chain. "Right nice, ain't it?"

173

The Longing of the Day

Matt examined it carefully. Even with his ignorance of such things, he thought it was pretty. He could picture it hanging at Eve's throat and knew she would like it. "I'll take it. How much?"

"Two dollars and 50 cents." When Matt looked shocked, Hooper said defensively, "It's genuine gold plate on the heart and chain both. Guaranteed not to turn the young lady's neck green."

He didn't really care how much it cost. It would be worth every cent to give Eve pleasure. He handed the necessary amount to Hooper, who beamed. "I believe I have a box just the right size for this to go in. Shall I get it?"

Dan had his back turned, apparently unaware of the purchase. Hooper brought out a small box and laid the locket in it. "Some young gal will be mighty pleased when she opens that lid." He quirked an inquisitive eyebrow, but Matt said nothing. Hooper handed him the box, watching him with frank curiosity.

Matt joined Dan, who put the last of the money on the counter. "It'll just 'bout take it all," he said grimly.

Matt eyed the supplies piled on the floor. "I think Bardlow'd rather eat food than money any day," he said firmly. "Besides, he told us to do our best. I'd say that's just what we did."

"I sure hope he sees it that way."

"He will. Come on, let's start loadin' these supplies. I'm hungry as a winter-starved bear."

Bringing the sled from the livery, they set to work, loading as quickly as they could against the cold of the fast approaching night. At the stable, Davis, the owner, showed them where to put the sled, lending a hand with the business of unharnessing the team. While they were thus occupied, Dan asked casually, "Say, Davis, do you know this Ziv Vladimir that Hooper was mentionin'?"

"Sure do. He's been in town two or three months now. Come from some place 'cross the water called St. Petersburg. I never heard of it, but he says it gets right cold there. I told 'im wait 'til he sits out one of our winters — then we'll talk cold! Know what he did? He laughed. Like I'd told some side-splittin' joke." Davis scratched his jaw bemusedly. "Anyway, he just showed up one day with a wagon full of supplies. Started sellin' stuff right and left. Good merchandise. Good prices. After he sold all his supplies, he sold the team and wagon."

Davis began measuring out grain as he continued, "He rented out the saddle shop that's been standin' empty since old man Cullin died last winter. Folks was suspicious at first — him bein' so foreign lookin' and all and comin' to town with a lot better deals than what we've been used to gettin'. But times change; folks has to change with 'em."

Matt started. Where had he heard that before? A flock of geese honking overhead ... Ben's voice, with its strange note of sadness. *Times change* ... Matt suddenly shivered, as if one of those geese had stepped on his grave.

"... easier f'r some people to gripe than change."

"You take your business to him?" Dan asked bluntly. "You trust him to run a fair deal?"

Davis picked up a currycomb. "That team and wagon I was mentionin' he sold? I bought it, and I ain't regretted it. So I reckon I do. It's kind of refreshin', after Hooper's had

The Longing of the Day

his thumb on this town f'r so long. Hooper still has the post office, though. So I guess we'll have to put up with him f'r a while longer." The horses tended, Davis disappeared into his office at the rear of the stable.

Dan stared thoughtfully after him. "I think Bardlow'll be right interested to hear all this," he said, half to Matt and half to himself, so he didn't notice Matt's silence. He shrugged and stretched his muscles hugely. "Let's go eat!"

"Good idea." Matt's casual tone of voice surprised himself. "You go first. I'll stay with the wagon."

Dan started to protest, but Matt cut him off. Dan gave in reluctantly, saying he'd be back as quick as he could.

Matt, glancing over his shoulder to the office, saw no sign of Davis. He eased himself down into a pile of hay until he was stretched full length against it. Drawing the little box out of his pocket, he lifted the lid and carefully took out the locket. The gleaming bit of gold seemed somehow lost in his big palm.

He closed his eyes and let the sweet, warm rush of memory cover him like a quilt.

"Matt, where are you?"

He hurriedly returned the necklace to his coat pocket and scrambled to his feet. "Here. That sure was fast," he added as Dan came up holding a tray covered with a napkin.

"Brought us back some eats. Figured it wasn't quite fair, me fillin' my belly while you was sittin' here hungry."

"And they let you bring a tray and dishes. How'd they know you'll take 'em back?"

"They're very trustin'. When I take the dishes back, I get back the 6 bits I had to fork over as security."

176

"Six bits? These dishes must be genuine silver!"

"You'd think so. Anyway, let's eat. I'm plumb famished and I been smellin' this all the way over here."

Matt drew a barrel forward, and Dan carefully set the tray on it. Dan pulled off the napkin and they both deeply inhaled the fragrance of steak, hot apple pie and fresh coffee. Sitting cross-legged in the straw, they ravenously ate to the last crust.

With a sigh of deep contentment, Dan settled into the pile of hay and pulled out his pipe. Ruefully eyeing the straw heaped around him, he put it away reluctantly. Matt collected the dishes and replaced them on the tray. "I'll take these back. Where'd you get 'em?"

Dan yawned. "Straight across the street. And don't forget my 75 cents!" he called as Matt headed out the door.

He returned the dishes and collected Dan's money. Back outside, he paused. It was full dark now and the town was quiet. The entire business section seemed to be spread along this one avenue. The homes of the townsfolk, he assumed, made up the rest of the streets.

He jammed his hands into his pockets and glanced in the direction of the general store. A light burned there; obviously they were still open for business. He knew what he had to do, no use putting it off. He crossed the muddy street that, with nightfall, was beginning to freeze up again. His boots cracked against the newly formed film of ice covering the slush. During the day there was too much traffic for the mud to remain frozen. Teams and sleds and human feet kept it churned to a sticky mire.

He reached the boardwalk and swung with purposeful

The Longing of the Day

stride past the jail, the doctor's office and the hotel. Perhaps 18 buildings in all made up the business section; at least four were saloons. A church sat at the end of the street and beyond that stretched the empty plains.

He paused at the door of the mercantile and squared his shoulders. Flora wasn't in sight, but Hooper, behind the counter, looked up with a large smile. "Did you forget somethin'?" He was openly curious.

"I need to buy a sheet of writin' paper and an envelope," Matt said shortly. "I'll need a pen and ink, too."

"Oh, you goin' to write the young lady a letter, too?" Hooper smirked. Matt fought the desire to plant his fist against his laughing mouth. He said nothing as the storekeeper laid a sheet of paper, an envelope, a pen and ink on the counter. "That'll be two bits, and two cents for postage."

Matt put the coins down, folded the sheet carefully, and stuck it in the envelope.

Hooper couldn't stand it. "She is a very lucky young gal to receive a locket *and* a letter all at the same time," he hinted.

Matt strode to the door, determined not to answer. But suddenly, unexpectedly, humor and its array of possibilities poked at him, so he couldn't resist, after all. "The letter is f'r my mother, and the locket is f'r my sister. 'Night." He breezed out, wishing he could be a fly on the wall to see the other man staring after him with his mouth open and wondering who they were really for.

Matt hurried back to the livery, hastily shutting the door on the sharp cold.

"There you are," Dan said. "I was beginnin' to wonder if you'd got yourself lost. Did you get my money back?"

Matt handed it to him. "I went back to the store to get some paper. Might as well answer my letter while I'm here in town and c'n mail it." Pulling Anne's envelope and the sheet of writing paper out of his pocket, he flopped down in the hay and began to read the letter again.

Dan watched him but said nothing until Matt lowered the paper and sat staring ahead. Picking up a handful of straw, Dan meticulously began to even the ends. "Sometimes if a man has a problem, it helps if he c'n talk it over," he offered quietly.

Matt's jaw tightened, but he said nothing.

"I don't mean to pry. A man's business is his own."

Matt sighed. "You're not pryin', and there's not really any problem. They want me to come f'r Christmas, and I don't see how I c'n."

"Why not?"

"After all, I've only been on this job a couple of months. Bardlow wouldn't exactly appreciate me runnin' off just because it's Christmas. The way the weather's been, we're more'n likely to get more bad storms any time. I can't just go traipsin' off and leave my job."

Dan was silent while he pondered. Finally he said, "You're right. You should be here in case somethin' comes up, but Christmas ain't just any day, especially if you're lucky enough to have a family to share it with. Good Lord, Matt, Bardlow ain't a slave driver. The least you c'n do is ask him."

Matt realized the truth in Dan's words. And yet, he just couldn't go home, could he?

He stared at the blank paper. Dan, head bent, carefully

The Longing of the Day

arranged his straws.

"I just don't know." Matt tossed the paper aside. Jerking to his feet, he paced to the wagon and back, Ben's voice ringing in his ears. He'd given his word on this job; he couldn't just take off when the fancy suited him.

He jammed his thumbs into his pockets.

No, he couldn't do it. He'd just have to write and tell them so. His duty was to stay with his job, and that's what he'd do.

He sat, dug the pen and ink from his warbag, and resolutely picked up the paper. He was aware of Dan watching him, but he wrote firmly:

Dear Ma and Pa,

His hand trembled slightly, but he ignored it.

> *Your letter reached me, Ma. I'm in town buying supplies, and it was waiting here. I'm glad you all have your health. It's been cold with much snow here. We had a pretty bad storm the middle of November. Did it hit you, too? So far the cattle are doing all right. Mr. Bardlow has us watching them closely.*
>
> *I'm sorry, Ma. I just won't be able to make it home for Christmas. The weather is too uncertain to risk it. I know you'll understand.*
>
> *Give my love to Catty and Eve ...*

He looked up, involuntarily, at Dan. The older man was sitting, gazing ahead at nothing, obviously deep in his own thoughts. As if aware of Matt's eyes on him, Dan sighed and looked over at him.

"You look like you was a million miles away, Dan."

"A lot of miles and a lot of years." He stood. "You finish your letter?"

"Almost."

Dan studied him. "You're not goin', are you?" At Matt's shake of the head, Dan said softly, "You're a fool, Matt Jamison." Flinging his handful of straws aside, he strode down the corridor to the office.

Matt heard Zack Davis greet Dan cheerfully. He let out his breath slowly, closed his eyes and leaned back into the pile of hay. What in God's name was he going to do?

Emotions he had tried so desperately to subdue these past weeks surged over him. He tried so hard to do right by Eve. He thought being away from her would help him get over his deep longing for her. He hoped by not seeing her every day, by not hearing her singing and her laughter, he would be able to forget her.

He had found, though, that it wasn't true.

Even though living near her, coming into contact with her a dozen times a day, always aware of the part he played, had been difficult, at least there was bittersweet comfort in her presence. Away from her there was nothing but loneliness and heartache, try as he might to banish such feelings. Until the night, when she would come into his dreams.

For a little while then, all would be joyous and right and good. Until he woke. To emptiness. He would lie, wishing futilely for sleep, for the sweetness of her presence, for the wondrous feel of her lips on his. He would know, with

The Longing of the Day

agonizing clarity, how it could have been except for the events of one bitter night long ago.

He had been just 3 years old and he had only snatched memories of that night — a vague, confused remembrance of water, bushes and Catty wailing in his arms. The rest was blotted out, blended only into one terrifying sensation of calls and cries and high-leaping flames.

His thoughts turned to the man and woman who died that night. His parents. They had given him birth, were everything to him for the first three years of his life. And he had no memory, none at all, of either of them.

"Finish your letter yet?"

Matt hadn't heard Dan come back from the office. He held up his paper. "Not quite. I'll be done in a minute."

Dan was silent. It was certainly not his business whether Matt went home or not. He knew that in later years, when the chance to go home and be with loved ones was gone forever, Matt would look back and deeply regret this decision. How well Dan knew the feeling.

But he could not tell Matt. No one could tell him. Dan suddenly felt incredibly old and tired. He shouldn't have allowed himself those moments of looking into his own past, remembering Bethany and how it had been in the days when he had been young.

"Which one of us is goin' to take first watch?" he asked brusquely.

Matt, surprised at his tone, said, "I will. I want to finish my letter, anyway."

"So be it. Wake me when it's my turn." Dan settled back in the hay and pulled his hat down over his eyes as if, by so doing, he could shut out the haunting realization of how very much like him when he was young, Matt was right now.

Matt, puzzled by Dan's abrupt behavior, looked down at his letter. He'd best finish it. So he wrote quickly, *and my best to Becky, Hannah and the boys. Love, Matt.*

He drew Anne's letter out of his pocket once more. So Ben was still hurt, still felt betrayed by his leaving. How much more hurt and angry he would be if he knew the full truth! And that part about Eve. If she was sick ... But there was no use fretting, seeing trouble where there was none. She was well, surely. Ma said they were all well.

He folded the letter carefully and placed it in the envelope. He glanced at Dan and saw he slept.

He drew the box out of his pocket, held the locket in his hand. The light from the lantern touched the gold and made it gleam softly.

In the chill, gray light of dawn, they started back to the ranch. Dan had apparently recovered from his bad mood of the night before, for he was cheerful enough as they started out. Both felt apprehension, for the sky was gray and heavy, and a peculiar hush was over all the plains, sure signs the mild spell was over and more snow on the way.

Carefully studying the sky, they decided, with luck, they could reach the ranch ahead of the storm. They pushed on the lines, however. To be caught on the open plains when a blizzard struck was to invite death.

There was no singing and joking on this return trip. There

The Longing of the Day

was little conversation of any kind. They didn't need to put into words what their quick glances at the leaden sky told them. They both knew it; talking wouldn't change anything. As the white, empty miles slipped by, about the only words spoken were to the horses, urging them to go a little faster.

They made it back to the ranch only minutes before the first wind gusts of the storm were upon them. The men came piling out and a cheer rose as Dan drove up with the sled piled high with goods.

Willing hands made short work of unloading the supplies, and Bardlow indicated his satisfaction with their efforts. When they admitted they spent all the money, he dismissed their uneasiness with a wave of his hand. "From the looks of things, at least we'll be eatin' regular f'r quite a while."

Dan told him briefly about Ziv Vladimir. "That's right interestin' news," Bardlow mused. "We'll keep it in mind f'r next time, especially if Zack Davis speaks high of him. Zack's one to ride the river with, f'r sure."

Duty done, Matt and Dan retired to the bunkhouse where they had an eager audience waiting to hear their adventures. Going to town was a big event, even when it was just for supplies, and Matt and Dan were regarded as akin to world travelers and must relate their tales as such.

Dan was describing, with appropriate gestures, Hooper's nauseating politeness and his unmistakable eagerness to get his hands on their money. His listeners were nodding wry agreement — they, too, had done business at the mercantile — when the door slammed open and Rand stuck his head in.

"Ever'body out! The storm's pickin' up!"

As Matt swung up on his night horse, Dan pulled his own

184

mount up and leaned over to chuckle, "Fame sure is fleetin', ain't it? Heroes one minute and plain ol' cow nurses the next." He started his horse moving, and Matt fell in beside him.

"You said it! But I don't think I'd trade cow nursin' f'r all the fame in the world."

"All the cussin' may blister the paint off the barn, but I don't think you'll find many cowhands who'll give you an argument." Dan cocked an eyebrow. "It's right nice to know I'm not the only idiot in the world. Goin' out on a night like this instead of havin' a job where I can sit cozy by the fire. I must be cracked in the head!" He rode off to his post, and Matt's gaze followed him through the gloom of the storm.

He shook his head and spoke quietly to the departing figure. "If you're an idiot, then I hope I'm as big a one in 25 or 30 years."

He pulled his horse's head around. "Come on, Buttercup, let's make tracks!"

The light, shining from the windows of the bunkhouse, made squared yellow patches in the snow that had already fallen that day. It could do little more, however, than pierce a few feet through the curtain of snow still coming down.

Inside, KC attempted to get up one of his interminable poker games. He approached Matt, who lay on his bunk reading a dog-eared magazine about Sam Slade in the Wild West.

"How 'bout you, Silent? Wanta play?"

"Not me. Maybe some other time."

"That's what you always say," KC complained. "One of

The Longing of the Day

these times, I'm goin' to hold you to it."

Dan Mackley came to stand beside Matt's bunk. They watched KC approach Red.

"I always thought it worked out so a man'd win some and lose some. But it seems like he never heard of that rule."

"What do you think 'KC' stands for if not 'King of the Cards'?"

Matt groaned. "I hope you're kiddin'."

"I'm not. You c'n ask him."

"I don't think I'll bother. I'm goin' to turn in."

"You mean you ain't goin' to listen to the story hour over there?" Dan tipped his head in the direction of KC, Gaines and Red. The gambler, having failed to get up a card game, joined the other two in their animated discussion of a girl Gaines knew in Tuscon. Red wheedled him to bring out his picture of her, and Gaines stalled, egging him on.

"I don't believe I will," Matt said calmly, "but," and his eyes twinkled wickedly, "if you want to, I'm sure they'd welcome you."

"One thing my Mama taught me was that bedtime stories are fairy tales. And everyone knows fairy tales never really happened." A loud guffaw from Red interrupted Dan as Gaines finally brought out his picture. "I think I'll hit the hay, too, if these loverboys'll let a body sleep."

Watching him go, Matt thought about their friendship.

It had just seemed to happen, perhaps because from the first Dan respected Matt's reserve, being a quiet man himself. Over the weeks it grew of its own accord. He was aware the deep respect he felt for Dan was mutual and wished he better deserved the older man's high regard.

Louise Lenahan Wallace

He sighed and tossed his magazine aside. What was he going to do about Christmas? The question had haunted him for days. He told himself again he was right to tell them he couldn't make it home. It was just impossible for him to go.

By exhausting himself with hard, physical labor during the day, he was able to sleep at night. Sometimes. Yet hard as he might work, he found he couldn't keep his mind from going back to scenes he wanted to forget.

Just this morning as he saddled Smoke, unbidden, Eve had come, her delighted laughter drifting back to him on a wave of remembering: The two of them as they rode together on a long ago, sun-drenched morning. She always loved to ride. She galloped her mare, Thistle, across the plains, the horse's black mane and tail streaming in the wind. Eve's red-gold hair loosed from its pins, tumbling behind her. Horse and rider seemed to be one as they streaked over the springtime grasses. She pulled up, flushed and laughing that she and Thistle had beat Matt and Tumbleweed. Matt had been secretly delighted at her joy.

Thus he would remember. And then he fell to working even harder, trying to blot out such memories by sheer force.

When desire and common sense waged such a battle within him, how could he possibly return home for Christmas? He knew they would want him to be there, especially Anne. He could imagine her disappointment as she read his letter. He hadn't even given a good reason for not going, not if he really wanted to see them.

He knew he would be welcome in Anne's eyes, but how about Ben? The blow Ben received had been a bitter one that last night, and he was not a man who forgot easily — much

The Longing of the Day

less forgave. Would he have come to terms with the situation by now?

And Eve. How could he face her again with that farewell between them? What must she have been thinking all these past weeks? Yet, he wanted to see her. Suddenly, in spite of all his doubts and uncertainties, he could no longer evade the truth, nor did he wish to. She was "home" to him.

He would go home.

He topped the last rise and halted Tumbleweed a moment,
gazing at the ranch below. The house was half-buried in
drifted snow, but lamplight spilled cheerfully out the windows,
and smoke curled briskly from the chimney. Even from here he
caught the sound of voices lifted in laughter.

It had been a long, cold, difficult journey. What would be
its end?

He took a deep breath and spoke to his horse. He rode
slowly to the house, his eager glance taking in everything. In
spite of his apprehension, gladness rose in him. It was good
to be back.

He rode around to the barn and unsaddled Tumbleweed.
Outside again, he slowly walked back to the front door. About
to enter, he hesitated. Their voices, raised in merriment, came
clearly to him. Without giving himself time to think further,
he knocked.

At the sound, all talk and laughter abruptly ceased. He
heard heavy footsteps, the door pulled open, and Ben stood
before him.

"Hello, Pa. Merry Christmas!" he said with all the bright

The Longing of the Day

cheerfulness he could muster.

A mixture of emotions flicked across Ben's face — surprise, bitterness, regret — and finally, pain. "Matt." His voice rasped as though the word was hard to push out. He cleared his throat. "Come in."

Matt heard his hesitation, knew for certain now that in spite of the weeks that had passed, in spite of Anne's assurances, Ben was still hurt. All this time he had clung to the belief that Ben would accept his decision. Now, watching him, hope died.

But he had no time to say anything, for the others were crowding around with glad cries of welcome. They were all there: his own sister Catty — blossoming in the joy of new motherhood — and Jason, Luke and their families. And then Anne came forward, her hands outstretched to him.

"Ma!" he exclaimed, putting his arms around her. "It sure is good to see you again, Ma."

She looked up at him, and he saw the brightness of unshed tears in her eyes. "Ma," he said again.

Then Anne laughed and dashed at the tears with her hands. "How foolish it is to cry when I'm so happy! Son, come in and sit down."

He moved forward, the noisy talk and laughter swelling around him, his eyes seeking. His heart pounded as he finally saw her. She stood back from the others, watching but making no move toward him. Now he went to her and, not touching her, said huskily, "Merry Christmas, Eve."

It had long been a special bit of fun between them, his combining the greeting and her name on the night before Christmas. Always before, she had responded with delight.

Now she looked up at him, not speaking, searching.

Finally, she said very softly, "Hello, Matt." And still she searched his face with an expression that was almost pleading. *Why?* he wondered, and his heart gave a sudden leap. *C'n you possibly be hopin'* ...

"Matt, it's good to see you again, friend." Will Braden grabbed his hand and began pumping it enthusiastically. "Say, thanks f'r the job here. I sure owe you a lot."

"I'm glad it's workin' out." He was so wrapped up in joy at the nearness of Eve, he scarcely heard Will. She wore a dress of brown gingham, her bronze hair coiled in its two thick braids around her head. She was beautiful.

"It sure is. Better'n you realize. You know I've always thought a lot of Eve. Since I've been here, we've discovered the feelin' is mutual. As a matter of fact," Will's arm reached out to encircle Eve's waist and draw her close to his side, "we're goin' to be married this spring. Right, honey?" And he smiled happily at her.

Matt's belly jolted as if he had been kicked. Ice-water numbness spread through him as he saw her nod.

"That's right," she said softly.

"I'm goin' to be part of the family!" Will clapped Matt on the shoulder. "Remember how we always wished we were brothers?"

Feeling returned to Matt in a surging wash of agony that threatened to engulf him. *No!* he wanted to cry out. *Dear God, no!*

Wordlessly, his eyes sought Eve's, but when their glances met, she dropped her gaze. He frantically searched her face. Only when Will, somewhat bewildered, spoke

The Longing of the Day

again did he turn away from her. "Congratulations, Will," he said weakly. Will, in his own exuberance, did not heed the lack of enthusiasm but put it aside lightly.

"I was wonderin' if you was goin' to say anythin'," he teased.

"It's just ... you caught me off guard. I wasn't expectin' it. I hope you'll be very happy." His voice caught and he could say no more.

Fortunately, nothing more was necessary, for the rest of the family gathered around, talking excitedly, asking questions, catching him up on all the news.

Catty, rosy with pride, told him of her new daughter, Eden, born Thanksgiving Day. She arrived almost a month early, but without apparent harm except she was so small. "I wish you could see her, but she's sleeping. We just put her back to bed."

Aaron, wise in the ways of fatherhood after having been at the job for a whole month, laughed. "That's somethin' you'll find out when you get one of your own, Matt. Take my word f'r it. If they're sleepin', let 'em be. I woke her the other day, and Cat made me put her back to sleep."

"Served you right, you and your stomping and loud talking," Catty said indignantly.

Aaron's grin told how much he had minded.

Anne told of that first, great blizzard hitting last month. She and Eve were in the garden, gathering the last of the vegetables, when it struck. "We barely made it back to the house. Ben was out with the herd, and we waited hours for him to get back. Each time we were sure the storm couldn't possibly become worse, it'd blast again, and the whole house would shake. Ben finally came back, but he was so frozen he couldn't talk. It was quite a change. For once Eve and I did all the talking, and all he could do was listen. I tell you, we took advantage of the opportunity."

Ben's mouth smiled, but the rest of his expression remained grim. Casting a quick, uncertain glance at Matt, Anne hurried on. "When Ben opened the kitchen door after the storm finally blew itself out, he walked right into a wall of snow. The wind had blown it into a solid bank against the house. You should have seen the look on his face!" Again Ben made no reply to her lighthearted talk, but sat in tight lipped silence.

Over an awkward pause as she searched, obviously flustered, for a new topic, Jason asked if Matt heard the news about Bell's telephone. "It's been so successful in town that folks 'round here are beginnin' to think it would be a good idea f'r them, too."

Luke laughed. "A bunch of poles and wires lousin' up the plains? We need 'em like we need a bunch of sodbuster fences! Give me a good, fast horse any time. I'll get your message delivered a lot surer and prob'ly a lot faster."

Since everyone learned long ago that if something needed to be done surely or speedily, Luke was the last person on the list to ask, his comment was rather ironic, but no one bothered to point out the touch of humor. He wouldn't have seen it.

Cat spoke up. "I bet if you had to ride for the doctor in that storm like Aaron did, you'd think it was a good idea. It took so long to get to town and back, too. If we'd been able to send a message on Mr. Bell's machine, Doc Fergus could

The Longing of the Day

have been there twice as fast."

Luke snorted. "Typical woman doin's, decidin' to have a baby in the middle of a blizzard."

Catty turned red, and Aaron said angrily, "That's enough, Luke. Leave her alone."

Luke sucked in his breath and began to make a furious retort, but Hannah interposed. "Don't, Luke. Please. She's such a sweet baby. Catty's so lucky." This daring opposition to Luke from quiet Hannah startled them all into silence.

"Just forget it, Hannah." Luke had fathered four sons in five years. But in light of the attention this rat-sized rag of Aaron's was receiving, Hannah's failure to give him a daughter suddenly became a glaring omission. They were all laughing at him. He just knew they were. Irritation became burning resentment. How dare they blame him for her lack!

As from a great distance, Matt watched the family circle, feeling himself a part of it, yet not. Time dragged by with agonizing slowness. As Will's words echoed in his mind, one thought stood terribly clear. *No one must know. Eve must never know.* He must play the part of the glad brother. It was all he had left that he could do for her now.

He lay on his cot in the bunkhouse, staring up into blackness. The others finally dropped off to sleep, leaving him alone to face his anguish.

What a mess he had made of everything! He had betrayed Ben, creating a gulf between them that would not soon, perhaps never, be bridged.

And Eve.

The anesthetic of numbness had worn off, leaving his heart raw and bleeding. It was no use telling himself he knew when he left that someday she would marry. Not being blind, he saw plainly enough Chase Aubrey's growing attraction to her. Instinct, his own heart, told him Chase's hopes were futile, that nothing could possibly come of his attentions. But if not Chase, then someone else, obviously. Wasn't that one of the reasons he went away? So she would be free and happy to make her own choice? But, so soon? And to the man he himself had caused to come to her?

Fierce, hot resentment rose chokingly in him. Why should he be punished yet again for something that happened over 20 years earlier and over which he, certainly, had no control? *Why?* He remembered prattling to Eve after the Linderman massacre that if God wanted them to know, He would tell them. That it was so easy for him to accept God's judgments because *he* had total trust in Him. How empty those words were. It was a wonder she hadn't punched him right in the nose.

If that night had never happened, if someone besides Ben had picked him up and taken him home, he would have been free to at least voice his feelings to Eve. But this way ... in his bitterness, he didn't even care that he was being grossly unfair to Anne and Ben.

He never knew such agony of spirit was possible. He had endured physical pain many times, but that was nothing compared to this hurting of the soul.

What was he going to do now? He couldn't stay here. Those two hours at the house told him that. They were like

The Longing of the Day

a black dream from which he couldn't wake, like a gauzy fog from which he couldn't escape.

All evening he forced himself to sit back quietly and watch Will attend Eve. Will was gentle and considerate, and it was obvious he loved her very much.

And that had made it damnably more difficult to endure.

Will, by his open and honest declaration of love, was free to do all the things Matt wanted to do — sit beside her, hold her hand, let his feelings for her show in his every action.

At midnight, Anne had smiled. "Merry Christmas!"

"Merry Christmas and good night," Ben put in brusquely. "Christmas or not, this is still a ranch, and work still has to be done. By somebody." His eyes met Matt's squarely for the first time since the latter's arrival. Then he turned abruptly away to his own room.

Matt understood the look only too clearly, but it seemed the gods even then were not finished dishing out their potions of pain.

Long ago, Ben pointed out it gave Anne such pleasure to have the family all together "just like we used to be," and the families had begun the tradition of spending Christmas Eve night at the ranch — the men taking the bunkhouse, the women and children stacked to the rafters in the house. Home chores were no problem. The winter cowhands took care of everything in exchange for a Christmas dinner of their own, rotating from ranch to ranch each year.

As the general move to retire was made, Matt stopped to say good night to Anne. He happened to look up as Will quietly stepped with Eve into a shadowy corner. He saw Will draw her close and bend his mouth down to hers. The blood rushed into Matt's face as a hot sensation choked in his throat.

Shaken to the depths, unable to hide it, he rushed from the house.

Bolted again, he told himself sarcastically. Why did he always seem to be running from hurtful situations lately? Why couldn't he stay and face facts?

Will, Jason and Aaron caught up with him at the bunkhouse. Will was in an exuberant mood, ready to share his joy with the other men who teased him about soon becoming an old married man. He grinned, not at all abashed, and thumped Matt on the back.

"You do have one fine sister. I can't figure out how I got so lucky."

Matt couldn't find any words of answer. Will, against his silence, said anxiously, "You've been pretty quiet 'bout Eve and me all evenin'. If you're worried 'bout her, you needn't be." His black eyes were direct and honest. "I love her, and I'm not ashamed to tell you that. I'm proud of it. I'll take good care of her. I promise you."

As the two men stood facing each other, Matt knew Will meant every word. But torn as he was between wanting to hate Will and wanting what was right for Eve, it was bitter comfort at best.

Now, lying on his bunk, staring up at the ceiling, he told himself it was true, and he had to accept it for Eve's sake as well as his own. It wasn't surprising she loved Will. Before Will's parents died, the Claytons and the Bradens had been close friends and neighbors. It was only natural the children had been together a lot. More so because Will, an only child,

The Longing of the Day

had found he need never be lonely among the rollicking Clayton youngsters.

For no reason, the wings of memory suddenly bore to Matt an instant out of time: Two dark-haired little boys and one flame-haired little girl, bare-kneed, drenched to the skin, shrieking with laughter as they played in the creek on a long ago, hot summer day.

He rolled over on his belly and buried his face in his arms as though it could drown out the sounds of that innocent childhood happiness.

12

He opened his eyes. The bunkhouse was dark, and except for the resounding snores of the other men, quiet. He turned his head to look out the window. It would soon be time to get up. The fierce, hot resentment of the night before had burned itself out, leaving only a dull, gray dust of ashes in his heart.

The bunkhouse door flew open, and a booming voice filled the room. "All right, ever'body. Up and at 'em! You're burnin' daylight!"

The chorus of snores chokingly broke off as two pairs of feet, Aaron's and Will's, hit the floor in automatic response. Luke's automatic response was to pull the blanket over his head and mumble something about a warmer climate where Jason could take up future residence.

Jason, from long habit, ignored him. "Now I c'n say 'Merry Christmas' without bustin' my lungs to be heard over your sweet music. My Lord, Will, does Eve know you c'n make so much racket? Somebody better warn her!"

"It does keep the wolves away," Will admitted modestly.

Amid a howl of laughter, Aaron put in, "You sure wouldn't

199

be mistaken f'r one of 'em. They're musical!" Will threw his boot at Aaron, who ducked and snickered. "Don't feel bad, Will," he said sympathetically. "One thing this family's noted f'r is snorin'. If you didn't, Eve would prob'ly wake in the quiet and wonder what was wrong."

They roared at Jason's sheepish expression. That final shot hit home because his wife, Becky, had done exactly that. She had sat up in bed and shook him awake before she realized it was his lack of snoring that had caused her alarm. They still teased each other about it.

"You be careful what you say, or I won't tell you breakfast is 'bout ready!" Jason threatened.

A cheer went up, and the men piled out the door. On the way to the house, Matt found himself walking beside Will, who was humming *Silent Night*. He broke off to chuckle, "This is quite a group I'm gettin' into!" And then seriously, "They're really great, Matt. I feel like a part of the family already."

Matt didn't know how to reply. It was bad enough in the bunkhouse, hearing the ribald teasing that painted an all too vivid picture of Eve and Will sleeping together after their marriage. Instinctively his mind shied away from that whole appalling idea, but he could not now evade Will's point-blank truth. Finally he said weakly, "You know you've always seemed like one of us."

"I've always felt that way. I guess it'll just be official pretty soon." He bounded up the back steps, leaving Matt standing bleakly alone.

He was about to follow when the kitchen door opened and Ben strode out. His face hardened at the sight of Matt, and he started to push past without speaking.

Matt reached to stop him. "Pa, I want to explain ..."

Ben thrust out his own hand as if to push the words aside. "You don't have to explain. God, I was 25 once. I know the feelin'. You just picked one hell of a time to be independent. You realize that, don't you?"

Matt nodded slowly. He was also aware of what Ben would not say: It's not easy for a man to watch a lifetime of dreams, plans and work turn to dust before his eyes. He knew how much a part of those plans Ben had considered him. And under any other circumstances he would have given anything to be part of them.

"Pa, I'm sorry."

Again that thrusting gesture. "We been down that trail. Ain't no use to ride it again. I got to go to the barn." He stomped past, down the steps.

Matt felt a chill colder than the morning around him. Ben could understand, but he could not accept. In his eyes the man he raised as his own son had turned his back on him. In his book there was no room for half-way measures. Either a man was loyal and stood by his own, or else he was nothing.

He understood with terrible clarity. Ben had raised him to the code. He had lived with it, seen it in action all his life. But this same code made his dilemma a two-headed coin.

Ben, so unswerving in doing what he believed to be his duty, would not understand any better Matt's feelings for Eve. They were raised as brother and sister. Any other emotion between them would be a violation of all the moral standards he had sought to instill in his children.

He watched Ben, ramrod stiff, stride off. *What would*

The Longing of the Day

you do, if I called you back and said, "I want to marry Eve."
What would you do? You, who so firmly believe black
is black and white is white and every cow has one tail.
What would you do if a she-critter you always depended
on dropped a gray calf with two tails? His shoulders
slumped dejectedly.

What did it matter what Ben thought? It was Eve who
counted, and not for all the gold in Heaven's streets would
he betray her lifelong trust in him by speaking out, to Ben or
anyone, what was in his heart. Far better they think ill of
him than of her! She was innocent of blame.

In the kitchen the women stepped briskly, getting breakfast on the table. Matt's eager eyes sought Eve and found her
at the stove frying bacon. She looked as though she hadn't
slept much either.

He longed to go to her, to speak something as simple as
"Merry Christmas!" But Anne was greeting him happily
and telling him to sit right down and eat before everything
got well-water cold. There was no way he could have gone
to her without causing a stir, and that was the last thing
he wanted.

After breakfast, he still had no chance to talk to her. She
stayed in the kitchen to help with the dishes. Jason, Aaron
and Will drew him into the sitting room to find out how the
northern part of the country was getting through the winter.

He told of the rough time they were having on the LB
because of the unusual cold and how Bardlow was trying to
keep the cattle accounted for instead of letting them wander
over the range. "The coldness of the winter on top of the dryness
of the summer is causin' some hardship on the cattle, feedwise."

That brought up the old argument of free range versus fences, of storing winter feed versus letting the critters wander for forage.

Ben, still sober but no longer grimly silent, put in, "Even if the cattle come through the winter, a strain's goin' to be put on the banks. Come spring, everyone's goin' to need cash money, and they're goin' to find it mighty scarce. I have half a notion to draw out my savin's now, while I still c'n. I sure don't feel like losin' it. It's been too hard to come by."

Luke, ever interested in the subject of money, bent forward in his chair. "You mean if the banks closed you'd lose ever'thin'? You think things are goin' to be all that bad?"

"I've seen it happen before," Ben said flatly. "Ever'thin' goes to hell. I'm not lookin' forward to it, that's f'r sure. I've faced it too many times before."

"That's downright criminal to take a man's savin's! I'd put up one hell of a fight," Luke said belligerently.

"That'd do me a lot of good," Ben said wearily. "I'd end up in jail, and then where would the ranch be? Sometimes I think those men who go in f'r partnerships or run a ranch f'r an absentee owner are a lot smarter'n we give 'em credit f'r. At least they c'n share the headache or put it off on someone else entirely!"

"You sound like you're ready to give up, Pa. That's not like you."

Ben looked over at Jason. "Give up? Get smart might be a better way to put it. God knows, the facts've been starin' me in the face f'r enough years. It's 'bout time I saw 'em f'r what they are. Any man tries to run a ranch without some solid financial backin's playin' a fool's game."

The Longing of the Day

A peculiar look crossed Luke's face. "You might just have somethin' there." He sat back, and in a gesture totally unlike him, had nothing more to say for quite a while.

After an uneasy pause, Aaron commented, "One good thing about the coldness of the winter, it's cut down on cattle stealin'." That brought more discussion.

If only Wyoming could become a state, so many problems would be solved. Then they would have the backing of the law to put an end to the rustling and thievery that were plaguing the territory. But what real difference would being a state make? They'd still have only so many lawmen, and the Lord knew they couldn't be everywhere at once. Vigilantes — that was the answer. But was taking the law into one's own hands ever the answer? It was easy enough to condemn such action until it hit home. Then it was a different story.

After the first few minutes, Matt took little part in all this discussion, for how very unimportant it all seemed against the scope of his personal problems.

They were interrupted by Cat, beaming, who held a blanket-wrapped bundle for Matt's inspection. "I've been waiting to show her to you. Here, you can hold her."

Matt drew back. "I've toted lots of calves, but ..."

Luke snickered.

Catty waited so eagerly, Matt knew he had to take the baby. She handed the bundle into his arms, cautioning him to support the little head. Gingerly, he poked the blanket aside and found two deep-blue eyes staring up at him. He stared back, amazed. She was no bigger than one of his feet! He reached out cautiously to touch the back of one dainty fist and suddenly found that hand gripping his finger tightly. He wiggled his finger gently, and the baby continued to grip it, still staring at him solemnly.

"Aaron's Ma was pleased when we named her Eden. You know that's her name and her Ma's, too."

He kept his eyes on the baby. "Eden," he called experimentally. Whether because of coincidence or gas, she suddenly smiled. "If that ain't a ray of sunshine poppin' through a cloud!" he murmured, delighted. "Just don't start rainin' on me," he warned sternly.

"She wouldn't rain. She'd flood!" Aaron warned with a laugh.

Matt turned red to the roots of his hair. He hadn't meant anyone to hear his foolishness. But he was secretly pleased. When Eden grabbed his finger, she grabbed his heart as well, and already he felt timid affection for the little creature. The realization this mite was of Jamison blood filled him with awed wonder. He and Catty had been two alone all those years. Now they were alone no longer.

He glanced up, right into Eve's eyes. Her face held a strange longing, a deep sadness as she watched him, that he didn't understand. Even as their eyes met, she turned away to speak to Becky. But it had been there; he saw it for one aching moment.

Cat reached down to take Eden, and Anne beckoned to Ben. After they conferred a moment, he turned and called over the noise, "The womenfolks think they can take time off from the kitchen for a few minutes, so now's a good time to have the tree."

Cheers greeted this announcement, and everyone hurried

The Longing of the Day

to find a place to sit.

Matt hesitated, then slipped around the edge of the group. Anne put out her hand in question as he passed. He smiled. "I'll be back in a minute, Ma." He returned a little later with a small bag and sat down at the edge of the crowd to watch the others.

The bad summer and fall had taken their toll of Christmas this year. The presents were simple and almost everything had been made by hand, but each person was soon exclaiming over some small treasure.

Matt waited until they were thus absorbed before he stood. He crossed to Anne and laid a tiny package on her lap. He paused before Cat, Hannah and Becky in turn, giving each of them a little wrapped packet.

He heard their exclamations of delight over the carved figures they found in the wrappings. Heard, but scarcely heeded, for he was approaching Eve. Will sat close beside her, but for once Matt never even saw him. He had awareness only for her, looking up with a shy, questioning smile as he neared.

He reached into his sack and laid the little gift on her lap. "Merry Christmas, Eve," he murmured, and his voice was husky.

She picked it up wonderingly and looked up at him, wide-eyed.

"Go on," he urged. "Open it." And stood waiting while she did so. He watched the expressions on her face — curiosity, pleasure, and finally delight as she opened the box and lifted out the locket.

She gave a little cry of joy. "Matt, it's beautiful! You

remembered I wanted a locket, and it's so much prettier than anything I ever imagined." She stood, her eyes like two great stars. "How can I ever thank you?"

"You already have," he said lightly.

"Put it on me, please." He took it from her, and with trembling fingers, fastened it around her neck.

She touched it in delight. "Where did you find it?"

He grinned. "I c'n exchange it f'r a picket fence if you'd rather."

She looked startled before her own smile turned impish. "Thanks, but I think the fence would be a little heavy to wear."

"I expect so. Besides," he added soberly, "the locket looks much better. It's more your style."

She wrinkled her nose at him, and for an instant she was the Eve of all their growing years. Then her lightness died and she said softly, "Thank you, Matt, with all my heart." She glided away to show her treasure to the others. His gaze followed her, and for the first time in months, the world was right again.

Will, puzzled, spoke from behind him. "I never knew she wanted a locket. She never said anythin' to me 'bout one."

For one magnificent moment, Will didn't even matter to Matt, who just stood, grinning down at his bewilderment. To him, no answer was necessary. Eve's delight spoke plainly for all to see.

He realized that Will, incredibly enough, was actually waiting for an answer. His reply was slow and careful, almost as though Will had trouble understanding English, and his voice held just the faintest trace of pity for one who couldn't see something so obvious.

The Longing of the Day

"Sometimes, knowledge two people have 'bout each other don't have to be put into words. It just is." He turned and strode away, straight and tall, leaving Will staring after him with his mouth open.

Matt's taste of triumph was short-lived, however. He soon found he had no choice but to retreat to the shadows as Will took his place beside Eve once more. He could do nothing but sit quietly and endure the anguish of seeing Will hold her hand, whisper to her, laugh and joke with her in that special way of a young man with his betrothed.

As Matt watched Eve, it struck him that she was oddly quiet and had been so all morning. He remembered how excited she always used to be on Christmas Day, enjoying every minute. Today she seemed to have lost all her former gladness, sitting quietly and not saying much to anyone, even Will. The only time she seemed like her old self was when he had given her the locket.

Memory of her joyous pleasure filled him with rich, warm contentment. She had probably just worked too hard helping Anne get everything ready. She had a perfect right to enjoy some leisure. He looked around at the rest of the family as they sat in little groups, talking. Will was right. They were great. He was ashamed of himself — he didn't appreciate them half enough.

He caught Anne's eye, and she smiled and went over to him. He stood as she reached to hug him.

"I've hardly gotten a chance to look at you, son, let alone have a good talk with you." She smiled. "First things first, let me look." She stood him off a bit and studied him.

Sometime during his absence, she saw, he had dropped

the last vestiges of boyhood. He stood tall and straight, smiling a little at her inspection. There was a maturity about him, a graveness in his gray eyes, that had never been there before.

Anne looked at him, at this man she and Ben had fashioned, and tears came to her eyes. "Our prayers were answered," she said simply.

He looked puzzled. "What do you mean, Ma?"

"It's the same prayer all parents have, to raise their sons or daughters to be fine, upstanding adults. God did indeed hear our prayers with you."

His eyes went to Ben, sitting in earnest discussion with Jason, and a shadow moved over her face. "He needs time, Matt." Her voice was pleading. "Don't ever think he's stopped caring about you. He hasn't."

The shadow became grief, and Matt's heart twisted. "I never meant to hurt you or him. You have to believe that."

"I know, Matt. Sometimes a person gets caught in loyalties. You're an adult. You have the right to decide your own affairs. At 25, you've stayed a lot longer than he had any right to expect. I know that, and he does, too, inside."

She laughed, a little chokingly. "Now, how about telling me how you've gotten along these past months? We got your letter, and we'd given up all hope you'd be able to make it home. And then, in you walk. Just like that! I'm so glad you managed to get here after all." She sat down on the couch, drawing him with her. Her boy was home, and she was very happy.

Because he could say nothing that would help, he accepted the change of subject and told her of the LB and Dan Mackley and their friendship, touching on the lighter details he knew

The Longing of the Day

would amuse her. He was still talking when Becky hurried up to say the turkey was done and should they go ahead and finish up the dinner?

Anne regretfully rose, laying her hand for a second on his arm before she hurried off to the kitchen.

He sat a few moments, and his glance lighted on the gaily decorated Christmas tree. He wandered over to view it more closely. All the old ornaments that graced each tree during the years of his childhood were there. He touched one and then another, recalling the fun they had had making them. Money was scarce at times, but Anne had been long on ingenuity, and she encouraged the children to do their best.

He remembered her own special contribution then, and searched among the branches, half embarrassed at his own eagerness. There it was, a cookie baked in the shape of a bell with his own name on it. She made one for each member of the family every year, even after they were grown and supposedly past such childish pleasures. It was good to know he hadn't been forgotten.

A low voice at his elbow made him jump, and he knew he was turning red. "Ma said she wanted to make one for you even if you weren't going to be here," Eve explained. "She said every member of the family gets one. That way we're all together at least in one way."

His blood warm within him, he answered lightly, "I'm glad. Where's yours?"

She showed him her star, hanging high near the top.

"I guess we'll never be too old f'r her to do it."

"I hope not. When Will and I have a family, I want to do the same thing."

He was spared the necessity of a reply he couldn't even begin to form by Anne's announcement that dinner was ready.

Gathered around the table, heads bowed, they listened as Ben gave thanks for the meal before them. "And bless all our loved ones, both here present and those who are here in spirit and in thought. Guide the work of our hands ..."

Matt suddenly thought of Dan Mackley and wondered, as he had that night in town, whether the older man had family to care about him. Matt hoped so. Christmas was not a day for loneliness.

Although dinner was reduced in variety from years past because of the bad times, the food was plentiful and good. Turkey with sage dressing, potatoes and giblet gravy, home-canned peas and carrots and fresh, hot rolls vanished like snow in sunshine. At the end, Anne, Eve and Becky disappeared into the kitchen, returning in a moment bearing three great pumpkin pies. Applause greeted their arrival, and soon not a crumb was left. Anne and Eve, who planned, schemed and saved from their supplies for weeks, felt amply rewarded when the meal was unanimously voted the best ever.

With groans of repletion, the men retired to the sitting room to lounge in half-asleep contentment before going out to check on the herd. The women tackled the mountains of dishes, teasing one another that they hoped they'd finish before it was time to eat again. With their animated chatter and all the willing pairs of hands, the task was finished in good time and they, too, were free to sit and relax a while.

Cat's suggestion that Eve lead them in singing Christmas carols won enthusiastic approval, for she had a clear, true voice that even Ben, the most plodding singer among them,

The Longing of the Day

could follow. Jason picked up his fiddle to accompany her. Matt retreated to a dusky corner where he could watch her to his heart's delight without fear of being observed. The next minutes were among the happiest of the day for him as her voice blended with the violin's in the poignant *Little Town of Bethlehem* and the joyful *It Came Upon the Midnight Clear*. They sang all the old hymns, for everyone had a favorite that must be included. And finally they reached Eve's special choice, the new song from England.

"What child is this, Who, laid to rest, on Mary's lap is sleeping?" Eve's voice spilled the haunting notes into the room, and they were as soft and clear as a worried mother's tears that fall on her drowsy child's head. One by one, the others stopped singing until she alone was telling the ancient story. "Raise, raise the song on high, the Virgin sings her lullaby."

Anne listened with motherly pride, thinking how becoming was Eve's moss-green dress with the tiny, creamy flowers embroidered over it. Even her knowing eye could find no flaw in the softly draped neckline or the elbow-length sleeves that ended in a fall of lace. The flowing skirt accented her small waist, and the length was right after all that adjusting. They splurged and bought the material over Eve's protests. *She works so hard. She's a good daughter, and if ever anyone deserves a new dress at Christmastime, she does, hard times or no.* The lamplight gleamed on the locket at her throat. *Matt was really perceptive when he chose that particular present. But he's thoughtful like that anyway.* So thinking, Anne turned to where he sat a little apart. Shock slapped her with a cold hand.

Matt was watching Eve, and his face was a mirror of

totally unguarded love and longing.

The cold hand became an icy fist squeezing Anne's heart. *No.* Her thoughts whirled madly, and she wanted to scream, *No! Not Eve, Matt, she's your sister. You can't!* Hands clenching furiously, forcing herself, she looked away from that open testimonial of love and tenderness. But even then another part of her mind was saying calmly, *Why not? He isn't her brother. He never has been except in your heart and in your eyes.* And in rapid memory flicks, it was all before her again, piercing as though it had just happened. Three-year-old Matt standing in front of her, clutching his baby sister. *Will you help me?* The five-months-suppressed arrow of pain slicing her heart for her dead child, for these living children. Tears trickling down Ben's cheeks ...

The murmur of talk swelled around her, returned her to the present. Eve finished singing and returned to her seat. Anne glanced at Matt. His face was quiet and sober. Had it not been for that brief glimpse, she would never have known he was covering such deep feelings. *If Ben knew* ...

A new wave of shock chilled her. That, of course, was the reason Matt had gone away. She saw it so clearly now. He left to protect Eve, to protect all of them. Anne had lived with her husband for 35 years. She knew him far too well to think he would condone such a situation. He was no Bible-thumper, to be sure, but he had an unshakable sense of right and wrong, and to him this would be morally wrong.

Matt knew Ben could not possibly understand. She thought of her own first, unbelieving reaction. And she had worried about Chase Aubrey! How could she be so blind? Why had she not realized?

The Longing of the Day

It had honestly never occurred to her. But it wasn't just the wishful thinking of her own heart. Matt's special way with Eve was always just that — his way. As far back as Anne could remember, he treated Eve with older-brother practicality, sometimes teasing, sometimes exasperated, but always with a strong underlying bond of affection. It was so much a part of life that any other behavior would have seemed strange. Wasn't it only natural that, when they were old enough, a boy's friendship should turn to a man's love?

For Matt, obviously, but for Eve? Anne searched her daughter's face, wondering if she knew how he really felt. Surely not. He had guarded his secret so carefully from all of them. And how did Eve feel about him? Matt, at least, must have been absolutely certain she didn't love him, save as brother, else he would never have gone away.

As Anne knew Ben, she also knew Matt. If Eve had shared his feelings, no power on earth would have kept him from her side. But the little boy who had huddled all night under a bush, protecting his baby sister, would not now, as a man, betray another sister. Instead he went away, after remaining at home much longer than a young man usually did. She knew now why he had no desire to go tearing off, why he had been so content to stay.

The situation must have become unendurable for him to leave like he did. She knew his sense of right and duty was every bit as strong as Ben's. How it must have torn him apart to leave. And then he came back to find Eve and Will ... Dear God, how that must have hurt him! *Lover and friend hast thou put far from me, and mine acquaintance into darkness.*

Bewildered, dazed, Anne rose with the others who were

214

saying good night. She wondered how Eve would react if she knew. She was, after all, Ben's daughter.

Matt said something about leaving in the morning. Everyone protested he had just got here, but he was firm. And Anne, in her new knowledge, could not argue. She could only hold him close as he hugged her and wish him Godspeed. In the face of his courage, she could not be less so. With smiles and laughter and no tears, she must bid him goodbye.

Anne watched as he said good night to Eve, who stood silently back. He took her hand, clasping it strongly in his for a moment.

She looked up at him, her eyes wide and dark. "I'll fix breakfast for you in the morning."

He caught his breath and searched her face for a long moment. "I'd like that." He let go her hand and turned away. A chorus of farewells followed him to the door. Cat clung to him. He held her, then was gone into the night.

Anne said a silent, fervent prayer for him.

Outside, Matt tramped around in the churned snow of the yard for a time, breathing deeply of the lung-chilling air, trying to settle his feelings into some semblance of calm. Detouring dejectedly to the barn, he made sure Tumbleweed was ready for the trip tomorrow.

As he returned past the kitchen, the door opened and two figures emerged onto the porch. Eve and Will. Matt backed into the shadows of Anne's lilac bush so they wouldn't see him. He didn't mean to eavesdrop, but Will's voice, low and

clear, carried to him. "Are you sure nothin's wrong, honey? You haven't seemed like yourself all day. I've been worried. If somethin's troublin' you, I sure wish you'd tell me."

Eve's voice, too, was soft. "It's nothing, Will, really. I'm just tired. But thank you for being concerned."

The anxiety didn't leave Will. "Of course, I'm concerned, honey. I love you and don't want to see you unhappy." He took her in his arms and kissed her. Unable to escape witnessing this exchange, Matt bowed his head, his fists knotted in desperation. He didn't want her to be unhappy either.

Matt was stretched out on his cot when Will, lacking his usual exuberance, flopped onto his own bunk without speaking. Matt sensed his concern and knew it was further proof of how he would treat Eve. When they were married. His mind could go no further with the thought. Instead he concentrated on the knowledge that she was going to fix his breakfast.

The joy of anticipation flooded him.

When Matt woke, he lay a minute, savoring the anticipation of his coming meeting with Eve. He felt incredibly light-hearted. He was going to see her, talk to her, be alone with her — all at her suggestion. The reason for it, and his actual leavetaking of her later, he refused to consider. It was enough, for now, just to know he would soon be with her.

Gathering his gear, he slipped quietly out the door. The first thing he saw was the light in the kitchen and his heart bounded to know she was there, waiting for him.

He went on to the barn, saddled Tumbleweed and led him out. It was too cold to leave him standing outside, even covered, for any length of time. So he led him to the carriage house and left him contentedly munching hay.

Eve was setting the table when he entered the glad warmth of the kitchen. "Matt, come sit down. I'll have your breakfast ready in a minute."

He hung his hat and coat on the peg behind the door, shucked his Colt and holster, and breathed deeply of the mouth-watering odors that filled the air. "You've been busy. It smells good!"

The Longing of the Day

She finished laying out the silverware. As she straightened, she brushed a stray lock of hair back from her cheek. "Hotcakes, sausage and eggs, and lots of coffee. You might as well start out well fed. No telling how you'll end up."

In spite of the warmth of the room, she shivered. "It feels like it's turning colder."

"It is a mite nippy out." He rubbed his hands together. They had chilled even in the short time he had been outside.

A frown creased her forehead. "I just hope you don't run into trouble. You've got such a long way to go."

"I'll be fine," he assured her, touched by her concern. "I've spent a cold day or two in the saddle before."

She started to speak, but stopped. He knew what she was thinking: If a storm hit, he'd be miles from nowhere, with no kind of shelter. "I'll be fine," he repeated. He had to get back, so no use going on about it.

Still concerned but knowing there was nothing more to be said, she told him, "You might as well get warm now. Come over to the stove while I dish up."

He followed her, to rub his chilled hands together over the welcome heat while she flipped hotcakes. Standing close beside her, he felt a warmth that had nothing to do with the nearness of the stove.

She was wearing her blue robe, her hair caught back with a ribbon the same color as her eyes. He glimpsed a bright gleam at her throat and realized she wore the locket.

As if reading his thoughts, she drew it from the neck of her robe. "See, I'm wearing it. Did you think I wouldn't?"

His lips quirked upward. "Just don't lean over any pools of water."

"Dishwater can be mighty treacherous," she agreed solemnly. "I'll try to remember." Then her eyes lit up. "I found the paper you put inside."

He was offhand about that. "I guess you're supposed to put a picture or somethin' inside, but I didn't have one. So I just put our initials and the date. You c'n do whatever you want with it."

"I like your idea. I'm just going to keep it this way."

Her pleasure was obvious, and the realization that he had fulfilled a deep longing of her heart warmed his blood as no fire could. He knew then that this moment — the two of them alone together and her gladness — was a picture he would always carry in his memory. *If only it could go on for-ever!* But a hissing sounded behind them as the coffeepot, untended, boiled over. She gave a small cry and whirled to rescue it.

"C'n I help?" Matt's intentions were sincere, even if his hands were a little clumsy.

With one hand she rescued the spatula as it slid toward the floor and with the other, the pitcher of syrup as it tilted precariously beneath his elbow. Her lashes quivered against her cheeks as, with supreme effort, she choked back her laughter. "Go ahead and sit down," she urged breathlessly. "I'll dish up."

He eyed her suspiciously, but her answering smile was angelic innocence itself.

Acknowledging her supremacy as boss of this range, he obediently pulled out a chair and watched as she finished at the stove. In a few minutes she carried the steaming pot over. As she bent to fill his cup, a lock of her hair brushed his

The Longing of the Day

cheek. Instinctively, he jerked away. Feeling ridiculous, praying she hadn't noticed, he reached for his cup and promptly spilled the hot liquid.

"Matt, did you burn yourself?"

He took a deep breath. "No. Just a little clumsy was all."

"I know that, but be careful. It's hot."

He grimaced. "I found out. Are the hotcakes burnin'?" He looked over her shoulder at the stove. She threw out her hands and hurried over to tend the smoking griddle.

Muttering to herself, she began flipping cakes furiously. Matt, catching a word or two of the one-sided discussion, proceeded, wisely, to soundlessly strangle on his laughter.

In a moment she returned with two full plates. "They weren't burning after all, but I declare, this isn't one of my better meals." As she set the dish in front of him, laughter forgotten, feeling the master fool, he leaned well away to ensure he wouldn't touch her again. He dared not.

When he could eat no more, he sat back, coffee cup in hand, and watched her. He knew he must remember each moment of this time together for it would never, could never, be the same between them again. The next time he saw her she would be another man's wife. Will's wife.

Pain burned in him, and he lowered his eyes so she wouldn't see the tell-tale hurt in them. When she spoke, her words were so close on his own thoughts that he jumped, spilling his coffee again.

"Matt!" Amused exasperation colored her voice. "Today's not one of your better days either, is it?"

He shook his head and swabbed awkwardly at the coffee on the table. "I'll get it." She fetched a cloth, mopped it up efficiently, and poured him another cup. "Dare I trust you with it?" she teased. "All I asked was, will you be coming back for the wedding? You haven't said, you know."

He swallowed hard, grateful that his awkwardness had covered his confusion. "I ... I don't know. It depends on how things go at the LB this spring."

"We sure hope you can. It just wouldn't be the same without you here. I know Will feels the same way. We've all always been so close."

He concentrated on setting his cup into its saucer and started to speak, but she went on. "I'm glad you and Will are such good friends. I wouldn't want to marry anyone you didn't approve of. But you and he are a lot alike in so many ways. I think that's one reason I ... care about him so much."

He looked up quickly, but she was pouring herself more coffee. He asked her the hardest question he had ever had to ask in his life. "You do ... care f'r him, don't you?"

She lowered her lashes, and he saw a sudden flush against her cheeks. "Yes," she murmured, "I do."

He realized he embarrassed her. Seeking to cover his freshest blunder, he said quickly, "We sure had a lot of fun when we were little, didn't we?"

Her smile was in her voice. "That we did. Remember when you roped your first calf and he ran away with you? He went tearing off, and you were holding on to the rope for all you were worth. Pa kept hollering for you to let go. Why didn't you?"

"I really don't know. I guess I just wanted to show him who was boss."

"I think he showed you!"

223

The Longing of the Day

He chuckled. "I sure ate some dust that day. And Ma was so mad at Pa 'cause I ruined my brand new shirt. I ached f'r a week after that."

"Remember skipping rocks down at the creek?"

"Do I! We were goin' to teach you how, and Will, all important like, skipped his four times. Was he ever mad when your first one went eight times, and you, so innocent, asked him if that was the right way to do it." He paused.

"Remember when you gave me the black eye?"

"You know that was an accident," she protested indignantly.

Luke, who didn't have a lot of room to criticize, had teased her about her hair, calling her names of which "bunch of carrots glued together" was the kindest. Matt came up behind him, and Luke had ducked just as she had swung. Her clenched fist, propelled by rage, clobbered Matt right in the eye.

He touched his face gingerly in remembered pain. "You packed quite a punch. I thought the swellin' would never go away. And did I ever have a time explainin' it to my friends. You were quite a scrapper, you know."

"I had to be! Both Cat and I did. With all you older brothers stomping around, it was simple survival."

Memories. The closeness of shared times was a warm bond stretched between them. What they had together could never be taken away.

But at last Matt knew he had to go. There was no excuse for staying longer. He rose slowly and reached for his hat and coat. She stood, too.

"Thanks for the breakfast. It was great." He busied himself with buckling on his holster to avoid her gaze.

"I was glad to do it. I see you still have your scarf."

"You bet. I'm not about to lose it."

"If you do, I can always make you another."

"But not like this one."

At the gravity of his tone, shadow replaced the twinkle in her eyes. His breath came faster as their eyes met and he saw the sadness in hers. With a trembling hand, he reached out and touched the shimmering softness of her hair. She was so dear to him. He wanted her so much the throbbing of the blood in his veins was an unbearable ache.

"Eve," he breathed. "Oh, Eve!" It was a low, despairing groan as the depth of feeling surged up, overpowering him. All his promises to himself, all his resolutions to be casual, slipped into nothing as he took her into his arms.

"Matt." It was a choked whisper. But he could no more heed it than he could the warning that lashed deep within himself. His need now all-consuming, he savagely thrust aside any thought of consequence. "Just one more time, Eve, for something to remember. And then not ever again."

Drawing her tightly to him, feeling the soft pressure of her woman's body as it curved naturally, gently to fit his own hard-muscled length, breathing the sweet fragrance of her hair, his last fragments of willpower and common sense fled. He bent his head down, his mouth seeking hers. As their lips met, the rest of the world faded, vanished, and there was nothing and no one else in the world except Eve and himself. Until he tasted tears.

He raised his head, horror surging through him. "Oh, my God, Eve, don't," he begged. "Don't. Not that."

Her eyes were closed, the anguish she could not conceal

The Longing of the Day

written plain upon her. She wrenched herself from his arms, and turned away, burying her face in her hands.

"Eve," he said in a voice made terrible by fear, "look at me. Look at me!" He started to put his hands on her shoulders to turn her, but froze, barely in time. Dismay flooded him in a sickening rush as he began to fully realize what he had just done.

"Dear God, Eve, I'm sorry. I ... it'll never happen again, I promise." Staring at his still-outstretched hands, he slowly dropped them to his sides. Steeling himself, he turned and stumbled out the door.

He led Tumbleweed out of the carriage house and leaped blindly into the saddle. Twisting, he saw her standing there, her cheeks still wet.

"Goodbye, Eve."

"Matt!" Faintly but clearly, her heartbroken cry drifted to him as Tumbleweed picked up speed.

And in that moment, as his heart shriveled to a meaningless shell, he knew death itself could hold no more pain for him.

The last night of the old year slogged wearily into the first day of the new. Matt, existing in a dull fog since he left the ranch that fate-filled morning, was scarcely aware that 1887 had arrived. He and Dan were with the herd at midnight when the new year was ushered in, and when they returned to the bunkhouse later, he was only vaguely aware of the jocularity of Red and Gaines riding out to replace them on watch. Nothing seemed to have any reality except the terrible aching within him.

Dan knew something was wrong, but even though he left several openings, Matt wouldn't confide in him. His concern deepened as his friend grew thinner daily and more withdrawn. But he well knew he couldn't force a confidence. Matt would have to open up on his own.

By quiet observation, Dan was pretty sure a woman was involved in Matt's trouble. Matt never joined in bunkhouse discussions of women and the fond recollections pertaining to them.

For that matter, Dan never joined in these discussions either, even though, had he so chosen, he could have topped

The Longing of the Day

them all. Since their trip to town he had become even more strongly aware of how much Matt resembled him in his own young days. Although the agony of his youth had passed, the memory of the pain had not. And he remembered he had been unable to talk about it, either.

Matt had never said much about his family. That he had folks at home and had gone to see them at Christmas was about all Dan knew. He realized Matt's deepest agitation surfaced since his trip, but Matt was troubled before that, although certainly not to this present degree.

Dan refused to draw any further conclusions. If Matt wanted him to know, he would tell him. So he waited and wondered and constantly reminded himself he would not pry.

If the days were difficult for Matt to get through, at least with their burden of duties they passed. Yet, with the close of the day came the night, when he must cease work. He hated the night now. While the others slept, he lay wide-eyed, staring up at nothing yet seeing so much. Bad as it was to lie awake, however, it was infinitely preferable to falling asleep. At least while awake he had a measure of control over his thoughts. Asleep, he was totally vulnerable.

As he dozed, Eve slipped into his arms. Once again he tasted the sweetness of her lips and joy overwhelmed him. But always, as he raised his head he saw her tears, and at that moment she vanished from his arms. He would find himself sitting up in his bunk, empty arms reaching out to her, and lie back trembling. She was always so real, so close.

What of his fine faith now, he asked himself bitterly. What of his easy trust in the way things work out? The boot was on the other foot, and the answers weren't so simple.

A chinook ushered in the New Year, a warm wind from the southwest that caused the snow to grow soggy. As the steady weather continued to hold, Bardlow expressed cautious hope that perhaps this winter wouldn't be as bad as the old-timers had predicted. After all, it wasn't much worse so far than many previous ones. A body had to put up with some snow and cold.

Then the blizzard of Jan. 28 hit.

Winds screaming out of the north at 60 miles per hour as the temperature fell to 15 degrees below zero. Sixteen inches of snow fell in 16 hours. Gaines insisted the storm came like a tornado of pure white dust. KC argued it was more like fine-grained sand that stung like a whiplash when it struck. And did Gaines want to bet, double or nothin', on what the others would say?

Across the cattle country, trappers and fur traders — children of the land when it was young, and heirs of lessons they survived to tell about — forewarned of a bad winter when they saw the ducks and geese heading south a full month early. Some cowmen listened; more had not. These dire predictions were now, unfortunately, borne out with a vengeance. Another mild chinook followed that unprecedented blast of winter, but as a reprieve, it was short-lived. The warm southwind lasted just long enough to partially melt the snow and was followed immediately by another chilling blast that turned the slush on the ground to solid ice.

Bardlow's cattle became tormented with hunger and thirst. Even though there was grass, poor as it was, right beneath their hooves, they never figured out how to break through the ice to get to it.

The Longing of the Day

During the entire month of February, snow fell every day but three. It was so cold that when any of the cattle lay down, their legs froze. Temperatures plunged to 44 degrees below zero. Prairie chickens smothered in the deep drifts, and rabbits suffocated in their burrows.

Without choice, the work had to be carried on. Bardlow's men contrived to dress warmly before venturing out of doors by putting on extra pairs of underwear and socks before they donned woolen shirts, pants and overalls. Two pairs of gloves, blanket-lined outer coats and fur caps with ear flaps completed their attire. Canto, before putting on his socks, walked in the snow barefoot, afterwards fiercely rubbing his feet to get them dry. After pulling on socks and riding boots, he stood in a pan of water, then went outside until an air-tight glaze of ice froze to the boots.

The final precaution involved blacking the face and eye sockets with soot to prevent snow-blindness. Even thus well prepared, a man seeing his friend walk out the door, or he himself leaving, could not know whether he would return under his own power or over the saddle of another man's horse.

Facing the unbelievably cruel weather, the men did their best to save the cattle. They went out day after day to push them back from the river into the hills. They chopped through ice and dug through snow to find grass for the starving creatures. They used pitchforks to prod the cattle off the ground to their feet and to keep them moving, for to lie down in that white bed was to die. The feet of the horses became cut and bled from the icy crust of snow. On the cattle, the hair and hide were worn off to the knees.

Perhaps because the bitter weather outside was no worse

than the frozen cold inside Matt, he fared better than the other men. He suffered none of the terrible consequences of working in the sub-zero temperatures. But it was good the instinct for working with cattle was so deeply ingrained in him. So powerless was he to shake loose from the numbness wrapped around him, he carried out his duties almost without conscious thought.

One afternoon in late February, Matt staggered back to the bunkhouse. He peeled off a layer or two of outer clothing and fell back onto his bed. He looked around for Dan before vaguely remembering it was another hour or so before he was due in. He closed his eyes as sheer exhaustion finally caught up with him. He was so tired, for once, he didn't even dream.

The banging of the door woke him. He sat up groggily and ran his hands through his hair, trying to clear his head. He had been asleep at least a couple of hours. Stumbling over to the washbasin, he splashed the icy contents onto his face. KC was crouched in front of the stove, peeling off layers of clothing. His entrance had caused Matt to wake.

"It's pickin' up out there," KC said hoarsely. "I'm afraid we're in f'r a bad one."

Matt became aware of the snow blowing against the windows by the wailing wind, and at the same instant was struck by the quiet emptiness of the room. He spun around. "Where's Dan?"

KC shook his head. "Ain't seen him." He stopped in the act of unbuttoning his outer shirt. "Wasn't he supposed to come in a while ago?"

Matt frowned, uneasiness nudging him. "He was due in

an hour after me. And that was a full hour ago. Maybe he's out back."

The gambler shook his head again. "I just used it. He wasn't there."

"The main house then."

"He wouldn't have no reason to go there, but I'll check. I'm more dressed than you," he interjected over Matt's protest, and started pulling his clothes back on.

As KC left, Matt dressed hurriedly, telling himself that Dan was all right. That nothing happened to him.

He was just starting out the door when KC came back. "Crusty says he ain't seen him all afternoon, not since dinner."

Matt felt something stab, deep in his stomach. "We better check the other buildin's."

Outside, the wind-blown snow lashed at them as they pushed from one building to another. Dan wasn't in any of them, and his horse was gone. As they emerged from the tack room, a blast of snow in their faces almost knocked them backward. Unheeding, Matt turned to the barn. His intention was obvious. KC grabbed him by the arm. "You can't go lookin' for him, Silent. You'd get lost yourself. You can't see more'n a foot or two ahead right now, an' it's gettin' worse!"

Impatiently, Matt shook off his restraining hand. "He's out there someplace. He may be hurt. I've got to find him before it's too late."

He saddled his horse and moved out cautiously. Guided by Buttercup's instinct as much as by his own, he searched all the places between the ranch house and the herd where Dan might have been. The certainty was growing in him that his friend was hurt. He couldn't have gotten lost that easily.

The storm hadn't been that bad up to now.

No tracks were visible, but the way the wind was blowing that wasn't surprising. Any sign would have been wiped away almost at once. His own tracks were already dim behind him.

He found nothing.

The other men were on the way in. As he met up with them, each admitted he hadn't seen anything of Dan for quite a while. They all offered to help search, but such a move was too dangerous. One man was lost already. If they all went off hunting for him, others could find themselves in the same trouble.

"I'll keep lookin'," Matt shouted against the wind. "I know his habits. If I can't find him, I'll head back, but right now we're just wastin' time."

Bardlow hesitated, then nodded reluctantly. Matt nudged his horse on past his boss as Bardlow muttered, "Pray God you find him soon. A body won't last long in this storm. Especially if he is hurt." Uncertainty goaded him as the whipping wind swiftly swallowed Matt's form. He ordered the cowhands in because they could no longer see the cattle to tend them. Now he was allowing a lone man to try to find another who might be God only knew where. Bardlow's decision to leave his cattle to the savage destruction of the blizzard to protect his men had been forced on him. But this choice, to send a man out into that same wildness, even to save another, where was the line drawn? When did a man stop or start playing God?

Matt carefully circled the drifting herd before starting off in the direction he felt Dan would have gone. His mind had

The Longing of the Day

been blurred for days, and all his senses had been dulled by the misery that had enveloped him. Now, miraculously, in this world of whirling white, the daze and dullness were gone. He was deeply grateful, for it was going to be difficult enough to discover any sign of Dan's presence, even sharply alert as he was now.

Trusting his horse to keep its head, he cut across the valley to its upper end. "Dan!" he yelled. But only his own voice slapped back at him in answer. He worked his way back toward the river, stopping every few feet to call.

Slowly, he fought his way to a grove of storm-scarred cottonwoods. Here, at least, was a little protection from the fierce cut of the wind. Hoping against hope, he dismounted and led Buttercup among the scattered trunks.

Dan wasn't there.

He mounted, and once more facing the icy blast, stubbornly continued his search, still heading toward the river. One more idea occurred to him, a slight one, but he would leave no possibility unchecked. Somewhere north and to the west was a wind-blown rock formation. It would not offer much protection but, provided Dan could reach it, it would give a little shelter.

He started in that direction, still stopping every few feet to call. He was beginning to fear he had overshot it in the gloom — the storm now blotted out all objects — when it suddenly loomed, over to the east.

Breathing a prayer of relief — a foot more west and he would never have seen it — he circled the formation until he gained its sheltered side. He dismounted, crouching a moment in its dubious protection, trying to get his breath. His lungs

234

burned, and stopping even those few seconds he felt the cold
bite deeply. He straightened and began to search carefully
among the boulders, all the while calling loudly.

No answer.

Now he hesitated, trying to think what to do next. From
here to the river was an open space of perhaps a mile before
he would hit any of the trees scattered along the bank. Dan
could be anywhere in that open stretch. He could even have
gone as far as the river and be under one of those trees right
now. Matt had no way of knowing. If he was still in the open
space, he could miss him even more easily than he had almost
missed the rocks, and he had expected them, had known their
general direction. Wherever Dan was, a few feet too far west
or east ...

He pulled his hat more firmly down over his face,
wrapped Eve's scarf more securely around his face and
neck, and nudged his horse. But Buttercup was reluctant to
leave the shelter of the rocks, scant as it was. He snorted in
protest and tried to veer south, back toward the ranch. Matt
would have none of it and pulled him back around to the
north. "Come on, Buttercup. Don't let me down now. I got a
feelin' we're gettin' closer. We can't quit yet."

They were in the open stretch, with absolutely no protection from the brutal blast of wind-driven snow. It whirled
dizzyingly about the man and the horse, chewing into them
with cruelly cold teeth. Drifts formed in front of Buttercup's
hooves in a moment's time and in the next instant were
whipped away as though they had never been. The cold
squeezed into Matt's lungs, burned through his chest with ice-
hot fury until each breath was a full-fledged battle of survival.

The Longing of the Day

The hair in his nose had long since frozen. The scarf against his mouth was a solid sheet.

The whole time he peered around for Dan's mount and watched Buttercup's reactions. The feeling grew in him that Dan was somewhere near. He stopped and yelled again. He could see nothing in the white swirl, but his horse's ears suddenly pricked. He let him have his head and shouted, "Dan! Dan, c'n you hear me?"

He waited, then shouted again, straining his eyes and ears as Buttercup moved north.

There! More to the north. He was sure he heard something. He shouted again, the wind whipping his words away. This time the answer was faint but unmistakable. He let Buttercup move cautiously ahead.

The answering call came again, closer now. He could still see nothing through the blinding whiteness, but let the shouts and his horse guide him.

So it was he stumbled upon Dan. By the grace of God and Buttercup's keen senses, he found him.

Dan's mount was down, and he lay in the scant shelter provided by the animal's body. As Matt stiffly dismounted from his saddle to kneel in the snow beside him, Dan managed a faint grin. "Howdy, partner," he whispered. "I sure am glad to see you." He gave a grimace of pain as Matt bent over him. "My leg. I think it's broke."

"Take it easy, Dan. I'll look." His right leg was twisted at an odd angle above the knee. Matt knew the thigh was broken. He glanced at the dead horse. "What happened?"

Dan's voice was tight with pain. "He stumbled over that branch and went down. I knew his leg was broke. I had to shoot him." He looked up at Matt. "You goin' to have to shoot me, too, put me outa my misery? After all, my leg's in the same shape his was."

"Very funny," Matt muttered. "We'll see if we can't come up with a less drastic remedy."

"I'd appreciate that."

"You got any feelin' in your leg?" Matt asked fearfully.

"Not as much as a while ago. I plain feel cold all over."

Matt's heart sank but he only said, "It'll have to be set."

Dan nodded, reading his friend's thought. "I ain't lost it yet. I don't intend to, so we might as well get it over with."

Matt put a stout twig between Dan's teeth and took hold of the leg. After he had pulled it straight and bound it, using his rifle for a crude splint, they were both sweating in spite of the extreme cold. Dan's face was gray as he weakly spat out a mouthful of splinters. Matt's own stomach churned as he dropped, panting, beside the injured man.

Darkness had come, and with it the temperature plunged still further. Dan shook from cold and shock. Matt realized the danger they were in grew every minute. Hurt like he was, Dan couldn't take the cold much longer. It was a wonder he withstood it this long.

Kneeling there in the icy snow with the blizzard blowing harshly around them, Matt knew the decision and the responsibility were his alone.

Dan needed warmth, care and food. Without them, he would surely die. It was a good four miles back to the ranch, dark had fallen, and the blizzard showed no sign of letting up. Remaining still like this, Matt felt the cold biting into him and knew it was even worse for Dan, who had been

The Longing of the Day

forced to lie still in the snow for several hours. Dan had managed to get his blanket under him before Matt came, but that was scant protection against the insidious chill.

He considered making a snow shelter, feeding Dan soup made from the dead horse, but rejected the idea immediately. Such a cave would take too long. There was nothing to build it against, here in the open. He had to get Dan back to the ranch. There was no other choice. He was already succumbing to the hideous cold. Matt had to shake and pound him.

"Dan, you have to stay awake. C'n you hear me?" Matt shook him fiercely until Dan's eyes opened and he mumbled sluggishly. "You have to stay awake! You have to help me get you back to the ranch. Do you hear?"

Dan shuddered. "I hear. So cold," he added chatteringly.

Using his bedroll, cutting lengths of rope from the coil hanging on his saddle, Matt fashioned a crude travois. He got Dan onto it, though how the older man kept from passing out with the pain, Matt didn't know. He wrapped both saddle blankets around the injured man and considered giving him his own coat. But if he froze to death, he wouldn't be much help to Dan. The blankets were a little extra protection anyway.

They started back to the ranch, Dan loosing a reassuring lusty yelp at the jouncing of his hurt leg. On the way, Matt sang every song he had ever heard, over and over, demanding Dan sing, too. It was the only way he had of keeping him awake.

After Matt exhausted every ballad and trail song he could recall, he switched to Christmas carols. Wrenching pain at remembering Eve singing those same songs on Christmas night was, perhaps, inevitable. For the first time, though, he almost welcomed the pain, for it was reality in a world gone mad. Lost to him as she was, she was still with him.

He jerked his head up, staring stupidly at the spinning flakes. Fear cut through him, jogging him to temporary alertness as he realized he had dropped off to sleep. After that he trudged at Buttercup's head to keep himself awake.

He finally lost all sense of time and distance. The world was a mad whirl of snowflakes and never-ending cold. They weren't going to make it. He couldn't help but think he had been a fool to try. He didn't even know where they were any more. Maybe they were miles away from the ranch and heading in the wrong direction.

Despair tormented him. How could he go on? His voice was so hoarse from singing he could barely croak. He looked back. Dan was limp, his arm trailing in the snow. He dragged himself back to the travois, wiped the sleet from Dan's face and shook him with all the strength he could muster. Was it the hundredth or thousandth time? He didn't know, but for the first time, Dan failed to respond.

Matt beat at him, shaking him desperately. "Come on, Dan. Don't quit on me now!"

Finally Dan mumbled something and his eyelids fluttered. Overwhelming relief shook Matt as he continued to beat at his friend. "That's it. Stay awake." To himself he added wearily, "Don't ask me why. Maybe I should just let you go to sleep. And me, too."

Time. Was it passing or was it as frozen as the rest of the world? Matt no longer felt the cold. He stumbled and caught at Buttercup's neck to keep from falling. Clinging there, fighting for breath, he felt the horse's drooping head come up.

The Longing of the Day

He turned his face to peer at the animal and saw, once again, his ears prick forward.

Buttercup heard or sensed something.

Matt squinted through the white, swirling curtain. *Was that a shout?* He tried to answer, but only a harsh grunt came out. The call came again. Was it nearer or farther away? He couldn't tell. He dragged at his gun, but his hands were so numb he fumbled uselessly. Tears came to his eyes. He had to answer before they went away!

Clumsily he pulled at his Colt and finally got it free of the holster. He shook badly but got the barrel pointed up into the air. His fleeting thought was he sure didn't want to shoot Dan, the horse or himself now. With all his strength he pulled the trigger. Again. And again. The gun roared in the roaring wind.

He heard a shout, definitely closer now, and saw figures merge from the white gloom. With a sigh he let go, and the blackness closed around him.

The familiar furnishings of the bunkhouse swam into view. Slowly Matt became aware he lay on his own bed. Turning his head, he saw the storm still hissing against the window.

Dan! The name burst in his brain. He sat up, swung his feet to the floor and stood swaying groggily. At his movement, Red sprang from his chair beside Dan's bunk. "Hey, Silent, take it easy. You're supposed to rest."

"I'm fine," he insisted. Or tried to. His voice croaked like a frog at the bottom of a well. "How's Dan?"

Red gestured to the other bunk. "Still unconscious. Last night, we thought both of you was goners f'r sure."

Matt limped over to Dan's bunk. Every muscle in him yelled in protest at each movement, but he gritted his teeth and bent over his friend. Dan was blue-gray, and each breath was a harsh gasp.

"Mr. Bardlow wanted to know the minute either of you woke up. I'll go tell him 'bout you. He's in Rand's room across the way." Red tugged on his coat as he spoke. He grabbed his hat, then went outside, the door slamming in the wind.

Left alone with Dan, Matt sank into Red's chair. The

The Longing of the Day

happenings of last night, after he started back to the ranch, were a jumbled blur. Perhaps it was just as well. Nightmares are best forgotten.

The door burst open. Bardlow and Rand, followed by the rest of the men, rushed in. Bardlow didn't even glance at Dan, but planted himself squarely in front of Matt. "It was a fool thing you did," he growled, "goin' after him like that. We came damn close to passin' by without seein' you."

Matt, feeling as wrung out as yesterday's rinsed-out socks, let Bardlow's tirade flow over him. "We was only 50 yards off when we found you, but if you hadn't fired those shots, we'd of gone right on. We was headin' away from you when we heard 'em."

Matt had a hazy recollection of fumbling for his gun. That close and he had been ready to give up! But he had no way of knowing ... He turned abruptly to Dan. "Will he come out of it?" Even that much talking hurt his throat.

Bardlow studied the unconscious man. "I don't know. We was sure we'd lost him a couple of times last night, but each time he came back. He's been out of his head, off and on. I don't think he should be left alone."

"I'll stay with him."

"The other boys c'n watch him."

Matt set his jaw. "I'm stayin'."

Bardlow sighed. "You are the bull-headed one, ain't you? I'll have one of the boys bring you somethin' to eat." He turned and strode to the door. Hand on the knob, he paused. "It was still a damn-fool thing to do." He paused in the doorway, his back to the room. "Thanks." The door slammed after him.

For the next three days Matt scarcely left Dan's side. He

242

was delirious much of the time. He kept calling for Jem, and although Matt didn't know who Jem was, it seemed to satisfy and soothe Dan when he answered for him.

But when he called out for Bethany, Matt was helpless. He didn't know who she was, any more than he did Jem, but she was obviously important to Dan. The only way Matt could calm Dan when he called for her was to tell him she had just gone out to the kitchen and would be back in a minute. He accepted this explanation for a while, before he got restless and called out to her again.

Sitting beside Dan, keeping watch in the storm-ravaged nights, Matt had time to do a lot of thinking. He wasn't happy with what he discovered.

That terrible daze he had lived in had been stripped away the night he went out looking for Dan. For the first time in weeks he saw himself and his life with harsh clarity. And he faced up to reality.

He loved Eve. He loved her to the very depths of his soul. She was as much a part of him as his own breath. But she loved Will. Not for one moment did he question that fact. She would never have consented to marry Will if it were not so. And there was no doubt of Will's love for her. Matt, knowing the depth of his own feeling, was able to sense the intensity of Will's.

And why not? Matt and Eve had grown up together, true, but then Will had been around so much that, as he had said, he felt like one of the family. Matt saw now what he would not, could not, admit before.

Will, too, had grown up loving Eve.

Matt could no longer put off the question to which all

The Longing of the Day

these hard facts led. He took a deep breath and faced it squarely. *Did he love Eve enough to put her happiness above his own?*

He buried his face in his hands. He already knew the answer. He had just avoided putting it into irrevocable words.

Yes, he loved her. He loved her enough to see her happy at any cost. He loved her enough to give her up.

If she had loved him, nothing on God's green earth could have kept him from going to her and openly declaring the truth. Neither Ben's objections nor Will's feelings nor prejudice of any kind would have stopped him. If she had loved him. But she didn't.

She had chosen Will as the one to share her future. Much as Matt wanted to hate him, he must not. To do so would only destroy the friendship he now shared with her. It was a poor substitute for love, but it was all he had. To resent Will was to lose her completely, for she would surely end up hating him.

And so he must remain what he had always been — Will's friend and her brother. The memory of those two kisses burned within him. He clenched his fists furiously against the hurt of remembering. He wasn't ashamed of what he had done, only that, by his actions, he had caused her pain. How much had she guessed of his feelings? What had her thoughts been these past weeks? Did she despise him? *She has every right to*, he thought.

The only way he could ensure he would never hurt her again would be to stay away from her. If he could do nothing else for her, he could do this.

He walked wearily to the window and stood gazing out. He wasn't seeing the storm-lashed night but Eve as she had looked on Christmas day, standing before them, singing. Out of a thousand memories, this was the one he would carry with him — her beauty for those few moments untouched by any hint of sadness as she gave herself up to the joy of singing. Singing had always been as much a part of her as her heartbeat, and this was how he would always see her.

Dan muttered, tossing restlessly. Matt went back to him, straightened the blankets and spoke reassuringly, even though he wasn't sure his friend comprehended.

He slumped into the chair beside Dan's bed. This, then, was the way things work out, the final, sure judgment. And this at last must be total acceptance — this feeling of being too weary to fight any longer was something he could not change. Drained physically and emotionally, he closed his eyes for just a few seconds ...

And jumped at sound of Dan's voice, weak but aware. His eyes were open, and he was struggling to sit up.

"Wait a minute, Dan. Take it easy. You just lie still," Matt urged, pushing him down.

Dan sagged back, scowling fiercely. "What's goin' on? How long I been like this?" His intended roar came out a bare sigh.

"You broke your leg, remember? You been sleepin' here all cozy goin' on four days. We wondered 'bout you a time or two, but if your tongue's any indication, we fretted f'r nothin'. I mighta knowed you'd find a way to go sleepin' on the job."

"You oughta knowed it'd take more'n a busted leg and a little snow to keep me outa permanent commission." He glared at Matt. "You must of been grazin' on loco weed,

The Longing of the Day

riskin' your neck like that."

"Yep. And if you'd been in my boots, you old buzzard, what would you've done?"

Dan sputtered and looked sheepish. "Considerin' how close I come to hearin' angel music, I'll never complain 'bout your singin' again. I thought I knew some songs! Where'd you learn some of 'em?"

Matt grinned. " 'Round and about. I had to keep your interest up."

Dan just shook his head.

Matt saw his weariness. "You better get some rest. Don't wear yourself out talkin'." He stood. "I'll go tell Bardlow you've decided to hang around f'r a while longer."

He had his hand on the door when Dan spoke again. "Thanks. For ever'thin'."

As Matt ducked out the door, it flashed through his mind that the thanks should be on the other foot.

Having passed the word on to a deeply relieved Bardlow that Dan was going to make it, Matt stretched out on his own bunk. He fell into exhausted sleep, unaware that his boss had just stumbled through the worst hours of his life. Bardlow had been fighting fear in mortal, hand-to-hand combat, and fear had almost won. Face a striking rattler, shoot a prairie wolf, bargain with a wily Indian who would just as soon have your scalp as your beef cattle — Bardlow had done all these without undue fear, had accepted them as the price that must be paid for the way of life he had chosen.

But this business of sending a man out to die — for that's what it had amounted to if a man were honest with himself, and Bardlow was — made fear an invisible enemy that could not be dealt with by speed and cunning and common sense, but simply must be waited out. Given his choice, he'd rather face the rattlers, the wolves and the Indians any day.

Sunshine streaming through the window woke Matt. *So the storm was over.* He pushed back the too-heavy blankets and went to stand a moment by Dan's bunk. Seeing his friend still slept, he turned to the washbasin, but the water bucket was empty.

Muttering to himself, he picked up the pail and pushed open the door only to have it slam back against the wall as the wind caught it. The breeze was warm, wonderfully, blessedly warm. And so was the sunshine, bathing his face and hands like a benediction. He raised his face to the cloudless blue sky and stood a moment in wordless thanksgiving.

The pounding of hooves caused him to whirl. Gaines, tearing around the corner of the barn, caught sight of him and pulled up so abruptly his horse skidded. "Come out to the herd, fast as you c'n! The river's risin'!" He pulled his mount around, urging him to a gallop even as he finished speaking.

Water bucket forgotten, Matt took off at a hard run for the corrals and his horse.

Arriving at the river, he could see disaster in the making. The warm wind, blowing at close to fifty miles an hour, was rapidly raising the temperature, causing the snow to melt too fast. The river, taking the runoff from the mountains, was rising swiftly in its banks, ready to overflow. If it spilled over, the cattle grazing along the edge and even those far

The Longing of the Day

inland would be trapped.

The men had to get them away from the river, back to the hills. But weakened as the cattle were, not only from the whole long winter but especially from that last, terrible storm, they were in no shape to move quickly. In spite of the men's desperate efforts, hundreds of cows were caught in the fast-flowing waters and drowned.

A weary, muddy group of men made their way back to the bunkhouse hours later. Dan, sitting up on his bed, saw their grim, exhausted faces and sank back silently, his question answered without even having been asked.

As the days passed, the true extent of the disaster made itself plain. The men started on spring roundup with cautious hopes, hopes soon quenched by bitter reality.

Dead cattle lay everywhere. The cowhands found them where they had wandered into ravines and gullies and been trapped by the tremendously deep snow drifts. They found them out on the open plains where they drifted and finally lay down and died. And they found them along the river where they were swept to destruction by the maddened waters.

That last, great blizzard was their undoing. Some losses were inevitable through the winter, but by literally riding herd on them 24 hours a day through bad weather and worse, the cowhands were able to keep those losses to a surprising minimum. Gaunt, weak and exhausted as the cattle were, they had survived. Each passing day brought spring closer when they could recover completely.

But that last storm was too much for them. It had been impossible for the men to ride herd. To have done so would have cost them their lives. Bardlow, gray-faced, forbade it.

Untended, the cattle drifted before the storm, became lost, lay down and died. Even so, complete destruction might have been avoided had those surviving not been trapped and swept away by the angry flood waters.

The stench of death lay everywhere.

The cowhands began the dirty, disagreeable, nauseating task of collecting the cattle and scraping the hides, the only profit Bardlow would make from six years of hard work and high hopes.

Even this small sop was threatened as a new breed of jobless cowhand — rough, dirty, and smelling of his new profession — seeing a profit for himself in the rotting carcasses, descended upon them to steal the hides. They were called hide-hunters and performed their dirty work quickly and stealthily, a knife in one hand and a gun in the other. The cowhands riding out to collect the carcasses went warily, for they never knew when they might stumble upon such a one. Men had been shot for a lot less provocation than discovering one of these at his work.

As the days passed, word trickled in from other drifting cowmen that the rest of the cattle country was suffering the same fate as Bardlow's LB. Rancher after rancher had been ruined. Seventy-five to 90 percent of individual herds had been wiped out. Many were left without a single live cow from herds that had numbered in the tens of thousands.

The severe summer, the terrible winter following on its heels, dumped on them with no adequate hay supplies put by, and the ability of the cattle to wander freely without fences to hold them, all spelled disaster. It had been a long time coming. But it finally arrived. Many of the cattlemen would

The Longing of the Day

never recover from the devastating blow. That winter marked the end of the open range and the huge cattle empires as they had been.

With overwhelming severity, Nature had hammered her lesson home.

Matt received a letter from Anne, telling about the Arrow A.

It was grim, she said. She wouldn't try to hide it from him. Ben estimated they lost close to 70 percent of the herd. Some of the other ranchers fared even worse. Owen Corley's son lost 90 percent; the Brices had nothing left and would have to forfeit their ranch.

Ben assured her they wouldn't lose the Arrow A, but admitted it was going to take a lot of time and hard work before they could consider themselves on steady ground again. He was working hard, too hard she feared, but she couldn't get him to slow down. They had to let the cowhands go. There was no money to pay them. Ben, Jason, Aaron and Luke were doing all the work.

The boys suffered severe losses, too.

Luke had no cattle left, and Jason and Aaron had only a few. They had decided to pool the cows that were left, making one herd from four and share the consequences.

Will stayed, too, she wrote. Ben had told him there was no money for wages, but Will insisted on staying. Will said he figured since he was going to be a part of the family so soon, he might as well take up his responsibilities now. Ben admitted to her he didn't know how they could have managed without him, doing the work of three men as he was. He said for sure Eve picked a mighty fine young man to marry.

As a matter of fact, that was about the only cheerful news they had. The wedding would be Sunday, April 24, at seven o'clock in the evening.

It's going to be very simple. Eve has already decided she'll wear the dress she made for Christmas. I wish there were some way she could have a new wedding gown, but it's just not possible. She says she'd rather do it this way and wear a dress she's been happy in. I can't argue with her.

As I said, it won't be fancy. The neighbors will come in, the ones who are left, and we'll have dancing afterward. At least it gives us something to look forward to and talk about other than the ranch. The Lord knows we all need that.

Hannah dropped by last night. She said Luke'd gone to town so she decided to come over. I know she was upset, but she wouldn't talk about it. Luke's sure got an itch about something. He's been cornering your Pa and asking all kinds of questions about the ranch. Pa can't figure it out, but he's really pleased he's taking an interest in things. Luke's never talked to him like this before. I'm glad he's finally opening up. It's good for both of them.

I have some unhappy news, son. Lass was bit by a rattler. She died this morning. We will miss her sorely. I keep expecting her to come up, tail wagging, every time I go outside.

I must end for now so Will can post this. We pray you are well and that the LB has come through the winter

The Longing of the Day

*without total loss. Pa says Lafe Bardlow is a fine man and
sure hopes he hasn't been ruined like so many others.*
Your loving Mother

Matt put the letter down slowly. It was hard to imagine
Lass dead. He remembered the bright, sun-hot morning Ben
had thrust the wriggling, fuzzy collie pup into Anne's arms,
grumbling that she didn't look like much of a watchdog, but
he guessed she'd grow. In 10 years she had grown to be
more than just a good watchdog.

Abruptly he picked up Anne's letter. Despair twisted in
him as he realized they needed him at home. But he had
already told Mr. Bardlow he would stay on at the LB. He had
thought it over carefully in relation to his determination to
go on with his life. He knew he wanted to work with cattle;
no other occupation held such deep satisfaction for him.
From working another man's cattle to raising his own was a
logical step and one he knew he wanted to take someday. But
if it was logical, it would also take a long time and a lot of
money to accomplish.

In the meantime, he liked working at the LB. Bardlow
was a good man to work for. If the ranch could be pulled out
of its present difficulty, it'd be a top spread one day. A man
could gain a lot of experience, working a place like this one.
So when Bardlow had approached him and asked if he'd
stay on, he agreed. It seemed an ideal situation, until the
arrival of Anne's letter.

What was he to do? On the one side he had given Bardlow
his promise. Once more he heard Ben saying a man was only
as good as his word. On the other side was the knowledge

they needed him at home. He owed them — he owed them his very life. He couldn't evade that fact; it was too clear and simple. Had it not been for the Claytons, he and Catty would have died just as surely as their parents had that long-ago night. That was an obligation not easily dismissed under any circumstances.

But Eve and Will were at the Arrow A. To go home would be to come face to face with them and their future. Matt wasn't at all sure he could do that yet. Dear God, he had surrendered her happiness into Will's keeping. Must he go back and be an onlooker day after day?

He clenched his fists. He just couldn't risk it. He had hurt her enough already by losing control of his emotions, not once but twice. He dared not trust himself not to weaken again. If he did, what would the results be? He could only cause bitterness and unhappiness for all of them.

He weighed one against the other. Which was more important? How could he choose between loyalty and honor?

He picked up Anne's letter. They wouldn't lose the ranch; she said Ben was sure of it. And Ben wasn't one to plant false hopes. When he said something, he meant it. His word, at least, was gold.

So what it came down to was that his return to the Arrow A could make things easier for them, but it could also hurt them deeply. They hadn't asked him to come back. But they wouldn't anyway. They would let him decide for himself since he had gone away once.

On the other hand was his spoken promise to Mr. Bardlow. That could not be lightly set aside.

Matt's final decision was, inevitably, painful, but at last

The Longing of the Day

he knew what he had to do. He would stay away from the Arrow A, from Eve and Will, and would continue at the LB. Mr. Bardlow said his wages wouldn't be much for a while. What Matt did receive he would send on to Ben and Anne. Perhaps the money would help as much as his actual presence. He could hope so, at any rate, and pray they wouldn't think it was just his way of easing his conscience. God knew, it wasn't. It was just the best he could do for all of them.

He debated for several days whether to answer Anne's letter. What could he say? At last he decided not to write until he had some money to send.

He thought he was doing right. He had no way of knowing at the time that his failure to answer her letter was a decision he would regret all the days of his life.

Anne thought carefully for a number of days before she finally wrote to Matt. What could she say to him? It would be unfair to gloss over the troubles at the ranch. Matt should be told, was entitled to know, how things stood at the Arrow A.

But that was not the part of the letter that was so difficult to write. She sighed. Ever since Christmas night she had battled her private torment.

That look on Matt's face! How could she have been so blind not to realize his feelings long before this? The expression had been one of deep and abiding love. She didn't for a moment toss it off as mere infatuation. Matt had clearly loved Eve for a long, long time.

Anne thought of what he must have gone through, hiding his feelings, and her heart ached for him. She knew, of course, why he had done it. She remembered her own first, shocked protest. Even after all these weeks of knowing, it was hard for her to think of him as other than her son, as other than Eve's brother.

She had not said anything to Ben, telling herself it was Matt's secret and she had no right to tell anyone, even Ben.

The Longing of the Day

For she knew, as surely as Matt must have known, what his reaction would be.

She bit her lip as now-familiar uneasiness coiled within her. What she hadn't told Matt was how worried she was about Ben. He looked so gray and tired, and she had seen the flashes of pain on his face when he thought she wasn't watching. But when she tried to talk to him, he snapped at her to leave him alone and quit naggin', that he had enough trouble tryin' to keep the ranch out of the dust without her fussin' at him. He stomped off, and watching him go, she knew more surely than ever that something was wrong. She was determined to get him to the doctor if she had to rope and drag him.

As for Eve, Anne's concern for her intensified daily. She was too sober this spring. Granted it was a grim row they were having to hoe with the ranch, but Eve showed none of the excited anticipation of a bride-to-be. She went about her work dutifully, and she discussed the wedding when her mother brought it up, but she made little mention of it on her own. That bothered Anne deeply.

Was she so quiet because they could do so little for her in the way of a fancy wedding? That wasn't Eve's nature at all. She understood the position her parents were in. She knew they would do the best they could by her. When Ben suggested they put off the wedding for a few months, maybe until fall when they might be able to do a little more for them, both Eve and Will protested. They would rather get married sooner — trappings and frills didn't make people any more married. So Anne knew it wasn't the enforced simplicity of the arrangements that caused Eve to behave this way.

She faced the obvious question squarely: Did Eve know Matt's true feelings? Anne didn't think so. At any rate she wouldn't be marrying Will unless she loved him. Hadn't she agreed with him against Ben's suggestion that they wait? If only Eve would talk about it.

Anne tried to draw her out one afternoon when they sat together sewing. She wondered, casually, whether Matt would be able to make it back for the wedding. Eve drew her needle carefully through the material before she raised her head. Her eyes held a shadow of something. What?

"Eve, what's wrong?" Anne pleaded. "Are you uncertain about marrying Will? Is it ... is there someone else?" She knew she was stumbling, hated herself for it, yet even now she could not name Matt. If he wasn't the problem ... if Eve really didn't know ...

Eve's eyes became wary. "Ma, don't worry. Everything's all right."

"But you don't seem happy!" Anne burst out. "Why can't you tell me?"

"There's nothing to tell. It's all settled. It just seems like such a long time until Will and I can actually be married." She paused. "I feel so impatient. Yet at the same time, I wonder what it's really going to be like. I see Jason and Becky, and they're so right together. Then I see Luke and Hannah, and they're so wrong. I'm sorry, Ma, but it's true," she interjected at the hurt on Anne's face. "They couldn't have started out to be all wrong, but they are now. And it's so permanent. I don't want that for Will and me," she finished in a whisper.

In spite of her pain, Anne felt a wash of relief. She had never known how much Eve understood of Hannah and

The Longing of the Day

Luke's relationship. Enough, obviously, to want to avoid a similar situation for herself. Anne bent her head over the sheet she was hemming and breathed a prayer of thanks. This much good had come, then, of the old sorrow. "Is that really it, daughter?"

Eve's smile was wry. "Yes, that's really it. I wish the time would hurry by, yet I'm a little scared, too." She tried to laugh. "I guess it doesn't sound nice, being impatient."

"It sounds natural, my dear, and so does being a little apprehensive. I think every bride feels the same, but they just don't all admit it. I'm glad you can. You needn't be ashamed."

Eve sewed silently for several moments before she asked hesitantly, "Ma, has being married to Pa been like you expected it would be?"

Anne looked at her lovely daughter and remembered another daughter asking another mother that same question. She had been filled with her youthful love that could see no obstacles looming in the pathway of the next 50 years, and had wondered at the strange, longing expression that had passed fleetingly over her mother's face. Anne understood that look now.

"When your Pa and I were first married, I loved him more than anything else in the world. Now all these years later I realize how small that love was. When you're married to the right person and you go through almost 40 years of good times and bad, you realize that love isn't a single, isolated fact."

Eve listened with the same interest she would have shown if her mother were discussing a broody hen that was trying to set out of season. How could she make her see?

"My daughter, what I'm trying to say is someday you'll

understand. Love is all the successes and failures you go through together — family, home, money, disastrous years and good ones. You can't isolate love, and you can't hide from it or deny it. Just take it as it comes, day by day, and thank God for all of it, the good times and the bad. Sorrow is just as much a gift from Him as joy. If you accept it humbly, and grow from it and learn, you can give back a better part of yourself. One day you can look back on all those years and say, 'Yes, it was good.' " Anne suddenly flashed a tender smile at her daughter.

"It was not what I expected, but it has been good."

Eve's expression was no longer remote. Her eyes became deep and dark as they had ever done in her moments of deepest stress. "Ma, I ..."

"There you are, honey. I've been lookin' f'r you. Are you ready to go ridin' now?"

As Will's voice cut across her words, she froze. The distress was wiped from her expression as though it had never been. Putting aside her sewing, she rose quickly. But before taking Will's outstretched hand, she paused beside Anne and briefly, silently pressed her cheek to her mother's graying hair. "I'll be ready in just a minute, Will."

Anne watched Eve move away and realized with a deep pang that, in spite of all her daughter's assurances, the question was still unanswered. She still didn't know what was troubling Eve.

At almost the same moment, Hannah Clayton was feeling

The Longing of the Day

just as great a bewilderment, but hers was tinged with bitterness. She was in the kitchen, putting the last touches to the early supper she expected to serve in just a few minutes. Luke had been outside, banging around the corral, supposedly replacing rotting rails. She was startled by a sudden drum of hooves and ran to the door just in time to see him charging off in a cloud of dust.

"Luke! Luke, where are you going? Supper's ready!" Whether he failed to hear her over the pounding hooves or whether he chose to ignore her, she couldn't be sure. All she knew was this wasn't the first time he had taken off like this without letting her know. In the last couple of weeks, it had happened almost daily.

She stared after him in bitter frustration, hoping this time he wouldn't come back drunk.

Matt fiercely threw himself into his work as, all around him, the world woke to springtime.

He had always before enjoyed the greening of the earth, had looked forward to the coming of spring after a long, cold siege of winter. Nature had always been to him an unequalled decorator. Now he scarcely heeded the display. He, who gloried in the awakening songs of birds, thrilled to the wonder of topping a rise and discovering anew limitless vistas of earth and sunshine and heady spring air, moved unseeing through those glorious days.

He said little to anyone, attended strictly to his work and found that, in some way, the days and nights did pass.

Louise Lenahan Wallace

Dan, slowly recovering from his broken leg, could see a change had come over Matt. Reflecting, he knew he couldn't actually say Matt was quieter — he had always been reserved. No, more peaceful was closer to it. He was certainly far removed from the white-faced, wild-eyed man who, returning from his trip at Christmas, had flung himself into the bunkhouse with no word to anyone for days afterward. Lately he seemed to have lost the sense of anxiety and urgency that had haunted him since Dan had known him. He kept as busy as ever, but it was not action born of desperation. Rather, it was a busyness of quiet purpose.

So Dan smoked his pipe in the spring sunshine of an April morning and fervently hoped Matt's troubles, whatever they might have been, had ended.

He eased his leg into a more comfortable position and winced. He would sure be glad when it was healed. Matt, riding in, saw him, chair propped against the bunkhouse wall, and turned that way. He hunkered down beside the older man, and Dan grinned wryly. "The first week I would of said I was pretty smart, gettin' a vacation while the rest of you worked. But now I'm downright tired of all this doin' nothin'. I'll sure be glad to get back to work," he confessed.

Matt's smile was sympathetic. "I know what you mean. We'll be glad to have you back." He looked critically at Dan's splinted leg. "It shouldn't be much longer, should it?"

"I hope not. How's it goin' out there?"

"We keep findin' 'em. Seems like it'll never end."

Dan said nothing. What was there to say?

Matt examined his gouged, scuffed knuckles. "A man dreams, and all he c'n do in the end is sell the hides."

261

The Longing of the Day

"What does a man like Bardlow do when he loses his dream?"

Matt's voice was tight, and he gazed unseeing past Dan. "He does what every man has to — he goes on. Somehow, he goes on." He stood abruptly. "I have to get back." He turned toward his horse, and Dan watched him go and wondered.

Slowly, inevitably, April 24, 1887, approached. In spite of all Matt's resolve, the tightness around his heart increased as each passing day brought Eve's marriage closer. All he could do was throw himself into his work and try not to dwell on the unchangeable.

He woke that Sunday to the immediate realization that this was Eve's wedding day, the day she would go away from him forever. Pain seared him. Up until this morning he had not really wanted time to pass quickly, bringing the inevitable closer. Now he prayed the day might go by swiftly, that it might be over and done and in the irrevocable past.

He went fiercely to his work, ignoring Dan's advice to slow down and take it easy. Dan was up and about again, easing himself into the new order of work. His thigh had healed, but he would always walk with a slight limp, the souvenir of that night when, he would chuckle, "Hell froze over."

He kept his eye on Matt, wondering what brought on this fresh attack. They were still gathering hides. It was rough, dirty work, but only Dan's admission that he had to stop and rest his leg caused Matt to cease for a few moments. Even then, his restlessness was evident.

Dan sleeved sweat off his forehead and handed Matt the canteen. "It's a warm one today."

Matt's eyes swept the plains. It was a beautiful day. The blue sky arched overhead with only a few mare's tails drifting across. The plains had greened, and here and there bright clumps of wildflowers in shades of cream, rose and gold added color and fragrance. A faint breeze rustled the grasses. From a nearby willow thicket, a warbler sent out its cheery song.

Matt drew a deep breath. Nature's gift to Eve was a perfect wedding day. He slammed the top back on the canteen, turned abruptly to his work. "Let's get busy."

Dan looked at him and rose heavily to his feet.

In the bunkhouse that evening, KC approached the men with his inevitable suggestion of poker. He got no takers as he worked his way around the room. "How 'bout you, Silent? Wanta play?" He asked without much expectation of agreement, for Matt consistently declined to sit in on any games.

Matt started to shake his head, thought recklessly, "Hell, why not?" It was nearly seven o'clock. He had to do something. He couldn't just sit calmly and let time tick itself away. He couldn't just sit and dwell on what was taking place right now at home.

So, to KC's amazement, he said, "Sure, why not?"

KC blinked and grinned. "Right this way!" He gestured Matt over to the table.

Dan caught Matt's arm. "You sure you want to do this? You know how he plays."

Matt saw the concern in his friend's eyes but shrugged the restraining hand off his arm. "I'm sure," he said flatly and started to follow KC.

"Matt," Dan tried again.

But Matt said fiercely, "Leave me alone. I don't need you tellin' me what to do." He shoved past Dan to the table and sat down opposite the grinning gambler. The other men gathered round. This was a contest no one wanted to miss.

Dan sighed, limped heavily over to the table, and sat down in the chair between KC and Matt.

Matt glared at him. "What do you think you're doin'?"

He said calmly, "It's an open game, ain't it? Any reason I can't join in?"

Matt started to protest, but KC cut in quickly, "No reason at all." He was going to enjoy this.

Matt continued to glare as the cards were dealt. He won the first pot with three queens. KC had two pair, kings and duces. Dan folded. KC acknowledged his triumph with a low chuckle. "Good hand, Silent."

A murmur went round the group of closely watching men. This might be better than they had thought.

In spite of Matt's obvious absentmindedness, and his distracted betting that caused KC to raise his eyebrows more than once, luck fluctuated among the three for quite a while.

Dan took a pot on a straight, then KC took one on two pair — nines over fours.

Only gradually did the money begin to shift to KC's side of the table.

Dan dealt. Matt stared blankly at his two jacks, king, six, and three. When Dan kicked him in the shin, he hastily discarded the six and three. After one glance at his new cards, he folded them into his hand. "One dollar," he told KC.

"Your dollar, and I'll see you two."

Dan groaned and threw in his hand.

Matt looked at his cards and at his last two dollars. "I'll call." He put the money in.

KC smiled and laid down four aces.

Matt stared while the grouped men muttered. He pushed back his chair, letting his own three jacks and two kings fall.

KC gathered in the money and looked up questioningly. "Shall we continue?"

Matt said dully, "That was my last two dollars."

KC looked at Dan, who shook his head. "Well, gentlemen, I guess we c'n call it a night, then, unless anyone else is interested?" The cowhands began to drift away.

Matt stumbled to the door. The night air felt good against his hot face.

"Quite a game, wasn't it?" Dan said behind him.

Matt shrugged and jammed his fists into his pockets.

"That was some last hand," Dan observed.

Matt's temper had been building all day and it suddenly flared as all his bitterness and anger and hurt overflowed. "And you dealt it," he said furiously.

Dan stared at him a long moment. "Yes, I dealt it."

"Four aces!"

"Matt, you been chewin' nails all day. I dealt that hand honest and you know it, but if it'll make you feel better to take a swing at me, go ahead." He braced himself. "Well, go on. What are you waitin' f'r?" he demanded.

All Matt's anger collapsed. "Dan," he said wearily, "I'm sorry. It's just been one hell of a day."

Dan relaxed. "Forget it. You all right now?"

The Longing of the Day

"I guess so. I think I'll turn in." As Dan started to push open the door, Matt asked, "Did you win anything tonight?"

" 'Bout ten dollars over what I started with." He chuckled. "KC ain't the only one c'n win at poker when it comes right down to it." He went in, leaving a staring Matt to follow.

Matt stretched out on his own bunk and closed his eyes. He was so tired. He felt completely drained, yet sleep would not come. He knew the wedding would be over by now. In weary, hopeless despair he realized Eve was lost to him forever.

"Eve," he breathed. "My Eve." But not his Eve, not now, not ever. Tonight had taken her from him, irrevocably.

He buried his face in his arms, trying to blot out the image of Eve and Will together as he knew they must be — as they had a right to be on their wedding night.

Anguish shook him. Unable to endure his own imagination any longer, he sat up and pulled on his boots. The night was moonlit and still, with a thousand stars twinkling overhead. He wandered aimlessly, finally stopping by the corrals. He leaned against the rail, his head bowed in silent despair.

He didn't hear the step, wasn't aware of anyone near.

"Matt."

He whirled. Dan stood behind him, concern stamped on his face. As he glimpsed Matt's expression, he said quickly, "My God, what's wrong?"

All the hopelessness, all the hurt, all the unhappiness in Matt suddenly broke loose. He looked at Dan, knew he could tell him, now that it was too late. "The woman I wanted to marry ..." He swallowed and pushed the words out "... she married someone else today." He had finally put it into words, such a simple statement to encompass so much pain. He

266

turned away from Dan's shock, leaning against the railing once more.

"God, Matt, I'm sorry."

Matt shook his head wordlessly.

"I knew somethin' was eatin' you, but I sure didn't know it was this. Want to tell me 'bout it?" he asked gruffly.

Matt slid slowly down until he sat with his back to the gate post. "I've never told anyone."

"Maybe it's time you did. A man c'n carry a hurt inside him only so long before it comes out, one way or another." Dan hunkered down beside him. "I know what I'm talkin' 'bout, my friend," he said steadily.

Matt let out his breath, and as simply as he could, explained the tangle his life had become.

"That's a hurtin' situation, all right. A man gets caught up in a whole knot of loyalties, and someone's bound to be tromped on, no matter what he does." The bitterness in Dan's voice was unmistakable as he answered Matt's unspoken question. "Oh, yes. I've been there. All the way and back."

He paused for so long Matt wasn't sure he was going to go on. "It was almost 30 years ago. Her name was Bethany, and she was pretty as springtime itself. She was 22. I was 28, and I never knew it was possible for a man to love a woman so much." His voice had dropped, remembering, and the bitterness faded. Matt suddenly knew Dan had never stopped loving her.

He spoke as if to himself. "She never knew how I felt 'bout her. I couldn't tell her because there was only one person in the world to her — my brother Jem. Him and me were always close. We had no other family, so it was only natural he'd ask

The Longing of the Day

me to stand up with him at the weddin'.

"I had to do it. There was no way I could refuse. All durin' the ceremony I just wanted to run away somewhere and hide in a hole. But I couldn't. Everyone would know then. So I stood up there with him and watched them be married.

"I would of gone away after that, but I couldn't. Jem and me was partners on the farm. Times was hard and both of us needed to work it if we was goin' to pull through. Bethany worked right along with us and never complained.

"Christmas was pretty scanty that year. We put together and made do, figurin' as long as we were all together f'r the day, we was luckier'n a lot of people."

Matt's mind flashed back to that night in the livery stable. Dan called him a fool for not going home to be with his family for Christmas when he had the chance. This, then, was what he had been talking about.

"Winter held on hard that year. February was as gray, cold and dreary as any I've seen up to now. Was early in March when Bethany took cold in her chest. She tended it herself, wouldn't hear of sendin' f'r the doctor f'r somethin' so triflin'. But by nighttime she was worse. I knew Jem was worried bad 'bout her, same as I was. She was coughin' so much but still refused the doctor, said we couldn't afford him.

"Jem and me looked at each other, and I could see the fear in him. That's when I hightailed it f'r town. Took less than an hour to get there and back, but even in that time she was worse. Doc did ever'thin' he could, but it just wasn't no use.

"All I could do was just sit there in the kitchen, waitin' and listenin' while she struggled f'r each breath. I couldn't even go to her. I didn't have the right." The bitterness was back in Dan's voice, and Matt glimpsed the anguish that had been his on that terrible night.

"At four o'clock that mornin', her breathin' stopped." His voice was tight with the old pain. "I waited — Jem and Doc was in with her. I stood at the window and waited for her next breath. It didn't come." Dan's voice broke off as, for one long moment, he found himself back in that kitchen of 30 years ago, while all time stopped — holding his breath, willing his beloved to breathe once more. It hadn't happened.

Dan was silent for so long that when he spoke again, Matt jumped. "I thought Jem would go mad. He was never the same after that. But at least he could vent his grief. He had loved her and lost her. But he never knew, and I couldn't tell him or anyone that I had loved her and never had her." Dan spoke steadily and without self-pity.

"Oh, I got mad, all right. I ranted and raged. Cursed God f'r lettin' it happen. But I was just beatin' my head against a wall. All my anger and lashin' out didn't change a thing. She was still dead." He closed his eyes wearily.

"We sold the farm. Neither one of us could bear the sight of it. Jem went south, toward Texas. I never saw him again. I got a letter from him once. When the Civil War came, I heard tell he joined up with the South. Later on, I got word he was killed at Holly Springs." Dan let out his breath in a tired sigh.

"It all seemed so senseless, so useless. Why? I asked over and over again. But I didn't get any answer. I still don't have one. Why? Bethany had never hurt a soul in her life. She wouldn't have known how. And Jem ... I know how I suffered. What must his anguish have been? Three lives

The Longing of the Day

snuffed out, wasted, before they'd even really begun to live." He glanced at Matt and saw his unspoken question.

"Yes, three. Not mine, though I don't know the why of that neither. She was goin' to have a baby. Jem'd told me just a few days before she come down sick. He was so happy and proud." Dan smiled sadly. "You would of thought he'd invented the whole process himself."

Matt said nothing. What could he say about this tragedy that had shaped Dan's life?

Dan stirred. "You know, I feel kind of strange. I've carried that around inside me so long that, lettin' it all out, I feel empty." His eyes were sober as they rested on Matt. "But it's a good kind of emptiness. It won't be easy, God knows. But maybe someday you'll be able to look back and thank Him f'r givin' you the happiness you have had, even with all the hurt mixed in with it."

"You never married?"

Dan shook his head. "Don't get me wrong. It wasn't out of some sick never-love-again feelin'. F'r sure I ain't been no monk. I just never found anyone I thought I couldn't live without.

"I been driftin' all my life since," he went on quietly. "That's all right, mebbe, when a man's young, has lots of time ahead. I been free, it's true. But when you get older, you realize what you've missed not havin' no one and no place permanent in your life. After it's too late, then you know. Freedom may be all it's said. But so is loneliness."

The eyes of the two men met and held while Matt's bruised heart rebelled against reality.

"By Glory!" Dan suddenly slapped his knee. "I know

what you need. I'll be right back." He limped away before Matt could say anything.

Left alone in the coolness of the night, he turned Dan's story over in his mind. Dan had to endure the pain of losing his Bethany twice. At least Eve was still alive.

"Here we are." Dan emerged in the moonlight, and Matt saw he carried something. "Been savin' this f'r an emergency. Can't think of a more needful situation than right now." He held out a bottle.

The average cowman saw hard liquor only once or twice a year on a rare trip to town or at the end of a trail drive when, pockets jingling, he cut loose for an uproarious day or two, which was about as long as his hard-earned cash usually lasted. Whiskey any other time was a rare occasion and one in itself that called for celebration.

Even so, something in Matt drew back from Dan's offering. It was not whiskey he wanted to fill the aching void inside him.

Dan regarded him quietly, waiting. Matt looked from him to the bottle and suddenly thought, *What does it matter?* He grasped the bottle and gulped a long swig. It burned all the way down his throat to his stomach with raw fire. Then the warmth spread through him.

He handed the depleted supply back to Dan, who raised it in a salute. "I propose a toast," Dan said solemnly. "To our women!" He downed a healthy slug.

A dizzying space of time later, Dan helped Matt back to the bunkhouse. He got him onto his bunk and pulled off his boots. Then he covered him with a blanket. He stood looking down at Matt, who was already snoring heavily. "God

knows it's not a solution, friend. But it'll get you through tonight." He swayed, caught himself. "I wasn't given the chance to do it 30 years ago. It might have helped and it might not. I don't know. But, just maybe, the tally's been evened tonight."

For an instant Bethany stood before him with her shimmering black hair and laughing blue eyes. The picture faded, and he realized the hurt he carried so long had faded, too. In its place was peace.

He bowed his head a moment and murmured, "Good night," and with a final glance at Matt, turned to his own bunk.

Dan's insistent voice yammering in Matt's ears dragged him to consciousness the next morning. "Up and at 'em, my friend," he kept repeating. "Daylight's burnin'."

Matt groaned and rolled over. "Go 'way," he mumbled. His head felt like he had been kicked by a span of mules.

"Come on, Matt, you c'n make it," Dan kept urging with nauseating cheerfulness until at last he had to sit up. He promptly tried to dive back under his blanket, but Dan would have none of it.

"Get hold of yourself before the others wake up. Here." He shoved a cup of coffee in Matt's hands. It was scalding hot going down, and his stomach promptly rebelled. He barely made it out the door before he turned wrong side out.

When he dragged himself back inside, Dan had a pan of cold water and another steaming cup of coffee waiting. After burying his throbbing head in the chilly water, Matt dried off with a piece of flour sacking and grumbled, "You and your big ideas. How come you're Sally Sunshine this mornin'?"

Dan only grinned and handed him the fresh coffee. Matt downed it and began to consider staying alive after all. The

The Longing of the Day

other men were stirring, and he felt quick appreciation that Dan got him up and going before the others were awake, thus enabling him to avoid their questions and rawhiding.

The door swung open as Rand entered with orders for the day. When Matt turned back to Dan, the older man had already gone.

They were tallying the live cattle against the skinned hides that day. Matt's head felt as if a whole blacksmith shop had been set up inside and they were using his skull for the anvil. Yet he had to concentrate on what he was doing. If he botched it, they would have to start all over. In a way it was a relief to be forced to focus his attention with such intense care. It left no room or time for other thoughts.

Bardlow's expression became grimmer as the day wore on. It was increasingly evident his losses were much more severe than they had thought at first. A silent group of men drifted to the main house for supper. Bardlow didn't appear at the table and neither did Rand.

All the cowhands knew they were in the other room with the books.

It was a hushed meal, the only talk taking place when a man asked for food he couldn't reach himself. Matt hadn't seen much of Dan all day because the older man rode roundup while he had helped in the count. Now he caught up to walk beside his friend back to the bunkhouse. But the awful solemnity of the day and of the just-eaten meal hung over them. In that heavy mood, triviality and humor were out of the question, and on the subject of the cattle, there was nothing that could be said.

Inside the bunkhouse the portentous silence continued.

Even KC, for perhaps the first and last time in his life, had no heart for cards. He had pulled out his deck automatically, but looked from it to the grim faces around him and quietly put it back.

Matt sat on the edge of his bunk for a few restless minutes. All day he had pushed his personal feelings down. But now, in the vast idle quiet, they rose up to torment him once more. He looked around. Red was stretched out on his bunk; Gaines and Canto were leaning against theirs. KC was pouring a cup of coffee. Dan was slumped on the edge of his bunk, staring at his idle hands.

No one noticed as Matt left. He filled his lungs with the clean night air. The moon was up, casting a silvery radiance over the house and the far-reaching expanse of plains. The faintest breath of a breeze touched his face as his footsteps unconsciously led him to the corral. Always it had been that way with him. Whenever trouble or unhappiness had set upon him, the simple act of watching horses mill in carefree, flowing motion could give him solace.

And so he stood now in the soft moonlight of that April evening and willed himself to be sensible, to stop hurting for that which had been placed beyond the reach of his arms. He got through last night, the worst possible of all nights. Today had passed and he still survived. *So it must be a man didn't die from those things after all*, he told himself sardonically. He'd just have to take it one day, and one night, at a time. Look at the blow Dan survived in losing Bethany to death, that final, unalterable loss from which there is no surcease.

When he walked back to the bunkhouse sometime later, the ache inside him had begun its slow transformation into

The Longing of the Day

acknowledgement of that which could not be altered but must
be accepted if he were to make any kind of life for himself.

He sought out Dan, who was pulling off his boots before
turning in. " 'Bout last night," the words came awkwardly to
Matt, "well, thanks, Dan."

"It's me should be thankin' you."

The hands of the two men met for an instant in a hand-
shake sealing forever the bond of their friendship.

"And now," Dan said briskly, "we'd best be lookin' to
the future in more ways than one. If Bardlow goes under,
what will you do?"

"I've been thinkin' 'bout it. Maybe I'll just drift until I
come across somethin'."

"There's goin' to be a lot of men driftin' this spring,
I'll wager. Thinkin' of headin' any particular direction or
just goin'?"

"I'll prob'ly just be goin'." Matt was carefully casual.
"And you?"

"I'll prob'ly just drift, too. Maybe down Arizona way.
It's supposed to be prime cattle country."

Matt pondered a long moment. "I've heard that, too.
Maybe it is. One thing I know, it could sure never top
Wyomin'." He was now speaking eagerly. "Give Wyomin'
half a chance and she could top 'em all." He saw Dan's smile
and said heatedly, "Go ahead and laugh. One of these days
you'll see. Handled right, there's no limit to her possibilities."

Dan eyed him. "Got some big ideas, have you?"

"Listen, it's no joke. This winter ain't been. All those
ranchers ruined, wiped out. But it didn't need to happen. If
men like Bardlow had stored hay for the winter instead of

dependin' on the open range to feed the herds, think how many cattle could of been saved. And the open ranges themselves ..." He saw Dan raise his hand in protest, but went on rapidly. "I know what you're goin' to say, the same thing cowmen have said all along, fences bring farmers and nesters to tear up good grazin' grounds and cut off water holes. But at the same time those fences will keep cattle from driftin'. Now I'm not sayin' that storin' hay or buildin' fences is the whole answer. It ain't — not by a long shot. But it's a start, and we're sure goin' to have to begin somewhere after what's happened." He stopped for breath, amazed at his own boldness in speaking out so.

Dan stared at him in slack-jawed astonishment. He became aware of the sharp quiet that filled the room as the other cowhands listened. It was a highly unpopular stand he took, and no one knew it better than he. Men had been killed for saying less than he had just now, but he was fiercely glad he had spoken out. *It had needed sayin' f'r a long time!*

Dan shut his mouth, gulped and looked around at the tensely waiting men. His fists tightened instinctively. Right or wrong, if a fight started, he would be on Matt's side.

The tension continued to stretch as they all stood motionless, waiting. It was Dan who finally broke that awful silence. "Well, Matt," he drawled, "I don't know if you're right or wrong on the subject, and I sure hope these fellas don't know neither. 'Cause if they think you're wrong, they're just naturally goin' to lay into you. And I'll just as naturally have to be on your side, and my bones is just too old and too tired tonight to take any pleasure in fightin'. 'Course I will if I have to ..." And he stood up quietly beside

The Longing of the Day

Matt and faced them all, waiting.

There was a muttering and shuffling, and abruptly the tension was gone. The men turned away to their own bunks. Dan grabbed Matt's arm. "F'r God's sake, let's get out of here!" He all but pulled Matt bodily out the door and into the moonlit yard. He continued to pull him along until they were a safe distance from the bunkhouse. Then he let him have it.

"My God, Matt, how could you do that! Those men were ready to tear you apart. And me standin' there on your side when I should of been on theirs!" He spat in sheer disgust.

Matt merely grinned. He still wasn't sure exactly why he chose that time and place to spout off. He agreed with Dan completely. It was a wild, reckless, dumb-fool thing to do. And he was glad he had done it! He'd do it again if he could. A wild exaltation filled him, and looking at Dan's righteously wrathful expression, he began to laugh.

He laughed harder than he had for many a month. He laughed so hard he thought his sides were going to split. And still he couldn't stop. Dan's black scowl changed to amazement, then he, too, suddenly began to whoop with merriment. "The looks on their faces!" he sputtered.

"The look on your face!" Matt gasped. "You looked like you'd swallowed a whole cow sideways. You was even turnin' purple."

Dan pounded him weakly on the back. "I don't know why I'm laughin'," he wheezed. "I coulda got my fool head busted in back there, thanks to you."

Matt, clutching his side, swayed under the assault but caught himself on one knee. "That's right," he agreed cheerfully. "What else are good friends f'r?" and barely managed

280

to duck the swing Dan aimed at his head. But perched precariously as he was, he lost his balance and toppled into the
dust of the yard.

Completely spent with laughter, he rolled onto his back
and stared up to the dizzying height of the stars. A great
weariness and peace filled him.

Dan stood above him a moment, then relaxed his fists.
Unexpectedly, he joined Matt on the ground, lying on his
back with his arms locked behind his head.

Neither spoke as they gazed heavenward, words being
totally unnecessary between them. Tomorrow would bring its
own share of problems; more than likely they would be out of
work after breakfast. But both had been there before, and that
was tomorrow. Each relaxed quietly with his private feelings.

Dan thought of Bethany and knew she was a part of the
stars overhead and the breeze that touched his cheek. Thinking
of her thus, she could never be lost to him.

Matt thought of Eve and of the closeness that was theirs
through all the years. She was and always would be a precious part of him. Nothing and no one could ever take that
away. He would face tomorrow when it came. For tonight,
at least, he had reached a kind of peace with himself. *Set me
as a seal upon thine heart ... for love is strong as death.
Many waters cannot quench love, neither can the floods
drown it.*

In the morning it was as they had figured. After breakfast, instead of giving orders for the day, Bardlow stood gray
faced before them. "Men," he was keeping his voice under
tight control, "I thought I could pull out of this thing, but I
can't. I have no choice but to fold. I can't even pay any of

The Longing of the Day

you what I owe. See Rand anyway. I've made it square as I could." He walked away, a bowed, broken man.

Rand had been standing directly behind him during this speech and when Bardlow turned away, made as if to follow. But he glanced down at the envelopes in his hand, hesitated, and faced the silent men. "Boss gave me your pay to hand out same as always," he said brusquely, and his face was as gray as Bardlow's had been. "Mr. Bardlow," he pronounced the name with fierce pride, "did the best he could. See you remember it."

He handed out the pay to the men who, when they received it, quietly left the room. They had become jobless drifters once more, but this time in the ruins of a world that had crashed around them. When Rand handed Matt his pay, he said quietly, "Boss wants to see you right away." He jerked his head toward the closed door of the office.

Matt looked at Rand questioningly, but the foreman held silent. Catching Dan's eye, he shrugged ever so slightly. He rapped on the closed door and entered when the voice bade him do so.

Bardlow stood, hands clasped behind his back, staring out the window. Over his shoulder Matt caught a glimpse of the men drifting back to the bunkhouse. "Close the door."

He did so and stood waiting.

Bardlow slowly faced him. He was still pale, and his eyes had a lifeless look, not at all like the steely glint of former days. "I had to let them go today. I had no choice. I couldn't begin to feed them, let alone pay them." He was not explaining so much as merely stating facts.

Matt risked a question. "What will you do?"

282

Bardlow drew himself up. His eyes lost a little of their dullness. "Do? The only thing I c'n do. Start again. It'll take time. I'm gettin' on. I don't know how long I'll have. But I know I have to try."

Matt nodded. *Yes, he had to try.*

"I made a lot of mistakes this time around, but I hope to God I learned from 'em. A man's never too old until he can't, or won't, learn. Rand's goin' in with me," he said abruptly. "We'll be partners this time. All of which leads up to what I wanted to say. F'r the first while it'll just be Rand and me, and lucky to make it at that. But later on, we'll be hirin' again. We'll need a foreman. We'd like it to be you."

Matt stared at him, stunned. Foreman! Few cowhands rose to that position.

Bardlow watched him closely. "It wouldn't be f'r a time yet, like I said, but after we get on our feet, all you have to do is come by and the job is yours."

Matt had to ask. "What does Rand say to this?"

"He's all f'r it, same as me. We just wish there was some way we could keep you on now. You're a top cowhand, Matt. One of the best I've come across. It was a good day's work that mornin' I hired you." He paused. "What will you do now?"

"Try to find work, same as ever'one else. See the country while I'm at it."

Bardlow nodded. There wasn't much of any other answer Matt could give.

The door pushed open and Rand entered. He glanced from one to the other. Bardlow said, "I've told him, Delt."

"Good." Rand was never much of one for words, but

The Longing of the Day

now he added, "It's been good workin' with you. I sure as hell hope you'll come back this way and take the job."

He had to answer honestly. "I don't know what'll happen, but if I c'n, I'll be back." He shook hands and strode out.

He found Dan waiting. The older man saw something was up, but figured Matt would tell him when he was ready.

"I got my gear all packed," he said and added apologetically, "you didn't come, so I went ahead and did yours, too. I hope you don't mind."

"Mind?" Matt said absently. "No, thanks, Dan. Let's get our horses. I've got somethin' to tell you."

As they rode in a general southwesterly direction — Arizona was as good a place as any to head for — Matt told Dan of Bardlow's offer.

He was jubilant for his friend. "That's just great. Bardlow's not a man to go back on his word. If he says the job'll be there, it will."

Abruptly, a dark look flashed over Matt's face. Dan saw it, surprised. "You all right?"

Matt's thoughts jumped back to last fall when he had announced he was leaving. The private pain of Ben's anger had been with him all winter. With this new promise of the future before him, Matt wanted to make that hurt right. The fact Ben had refused to forgive him in no way lessened his own responsibility in the matter. But for Eve's sake could he go back? Was he strong enough to face her without giving her hurt? He realized, belatedly, Dan had spoken. "Sure. Just thinkin'."

Louise Lenahan Wallace

He grappled with his problem for several days while they rode southward. As they progressed, they were made ever more aware of how disastrous that winter had been.

Bleaching bones of cattle, picked clean by wolves and buzzards, were strewn everywhere. Time after time they came upon rotting piles of carcasses along the beds of streams and in ravines where the creatures had drifted, become trapped by those following along behind, had piled up and died.

The stench was terrible.

Sickened, they rode on, only to encounter more bones and more carcasses. Yet, as if to atone for her bad temper of the winter, Nature spread springtime with a lavish hand, her own miracle, given birth annually. But this year even her best efforts could not really cover up the unpleasant sights or mask the appalling odors. She had outdone herself, and the joke was on the rancher.

But no one felt like laughing.

During those days Matt became more and more troubled. If everyone else fared so badly, how could Ben have come through any better? He had Anne's letter, but that was no real assurance. Things could take a turn for the worse. They had with Bardlow.

Day after day they passed deserted ranch buildings where the owners had just given up and gone.

What if Ben and Anne had done the same? What if their home was even now standing empty and deserted to the spring winds?

Panic seized him.

Even if they had tried to write, letters had a way of going

285

The Longing of the Day

astray or taking weeks to be delivered. He and Dan had been gone from the LB for over a month. What if the letter came after he had left?

Abruptly he made his decision. He could delay no longer. So suddenly did he know what he was going to do, that they were in the middle of a stream when he pulled up his horse.

Dan's mount, following behind, had to do a quick side-step to avoid hitting him. In shying, his hoof struck a sharp rock and he almost foundered. Dan let out a curse as the animal struggled for footing against the mossy bottom. But just as he got him under control, a brown trout flashed by, almost under Joker's nose. The already spooked horse squealed and reared on his hind legs.

Dan never had a chance. He sailed off over Joker's tail and landed on his backside in the ice-cold water with a splash that would have done credit to a whale and a bellow that would have put a love-sick bull to shame. Joker snorted in protest, shook himself, and trotted to solid ground. He stood waiting as Dan, splashing, flapping and swearing, hauled himself onto dry land. Once out of the stream, coaxing and soothing his still-edgy mount, he got hold of Joker's reins. The horse backed a little, settled down and let Dan inspect his legs.

Matt knelt beside him anxiously. "He all right, Dan?"

Dan couldn't have had a dry inch on him. Water streamed from his hair, oozed from his shirt and jeans, and squelched in his boots. He jerked off his battered old hat and gave it a vicious squeeze. The wringing-out process didn't much help the condition of his headgear, but a cascade of water joined the widening pool at his feet. Ignoring his still-dripping hair, he clapped his hat back on and swiped away the rivulets trickling into his beard stubble.

"Yes, he's all right, no thanks to you. What in blazes made you stop like that?"

"I'm sorry. I'm really sorry, but I've got to go back to the ranch."

Dan was so flabbergasted he forgot to be mad about his unexpected bath. "He decides he wants to go back to the ranch," he explained to Joker. "That's the perfectly good reason he almost breaks my neck and your leg." And to Matt, "Why in the name of all the saints do you have to go back to the ranch? Bardlow can't possibly have made his fortune yet so he c'n hire you!" He was yelling by the time he finished.

Matt shook his head. It was a matter too urgent for humor, even Dan's angry kind. "Not Bardlow's ranch. Back home to the Arrow A."

Dan stared at him as if he had grown another head. "I must be hearin' things," he mumbled to Joker. "After waitin' all winter, he decides in the middle of a fast-flowin' stream he wants to go home." He sat down abruptly. "I must be gettin' old. I would of decided on one side of the stream or the other, not smack in the middle." He looked piteously up at Matt.

But Matt was already tightening the girth on his saddle, preparing to mount.

"Wait." Dan no longer saw anything funny in it. "At least tell me what's goin' on."

"You comin'? I'll explain as we go."

With a loud squelch and a final ooze of water from the

The Longing of the Day

seat of his jeans, Dan mounted and they set off. He listened without comment as Matt explained.

"Maybe you should go. If nothin' else you c'n clear your conscience. But you'll have to take it easy. It's a good 10 days' ride from here. You founder that horse and it'll take a hell of a lot longer than that to make it."

Matt knew he was right and did his best to hold Tumbleweed down to a reasonable pace. He fretted at the hours wasted at night, but again knew they dared not risk the animals in a prairie dog hole or worse.

18

Eve paused outside the carriage house to admire the blood-red sunset before she pushed open the heavy door and stepped inside. Thistle would foal before morning. Since she had had quite a bit of trouble with her last colt, Pa had put her in the carriage house where they could keep an eye on her, like he did sometimes when one of the animals needed closer attention. He and the boys had made an early cutting of plains grass, so there was plenty of hay again. The musty-dried, sun-hot odor of it filled the little room.

Eve's blue skirts fanned around her as she stooped over the mare. Her foot caught in the hem, pitching her forward into a most undignified position. Trapped in the folds of material, floundering awkwardly, she freed herself with more haste than grace. *Long skirts were always getting in the way*, she thought grumpily. *Why couldn't women wear sensible clothes that didn't hamper every movement?*

Still disgusted, she bent over the mare, who raised her head and nickered softly. Impatience abruptly forgotten, Eve stroked Thistle's muzzle and wondered anxiously whether she would have trouble this time, too. Pa said she wouldn't

The Longing of the Day

necessarily, and he ought to know. Thistle had been her gift on her eighth birthday. How proud she had been to have her very own horse, just like the boys! They had ridden a lot of miles together in the years since that day.

Hearing the sudden drum of hoofbeats in the yard, Eve drew her shawl closer around her shoulders and poked her head around the edge of the door. She assumed it would be Jason or Aaron, although that would be unusual at this hour. Luke, on the other hand, had been showing up with pretty fair regularity this time of evening.

Ben, halfway to the carriage house, paused at the sound of the hooves, and his right hand dropped instinctively to the Remington strapped to his hip. For it was not Jason, Aaron or Luke who rounded the corner of the barn, but six strangers.

In the fading light, Eve could see they were rough, unshaven, and dirty. By contrast, their saddle trappings were ornate to the point of gaudiness. The sunset glowed on what even Eve's inexperienced eyes knew to be solid silver, highly polished. The lead horse, a gray, tossed his head and was promptly and ruthlessly brought under control by his rider. All six men sported Colts with use-polished butts protruding from well-worn holsters. At the side of each saddle a late-model Winchester repeating rifle nestled in its scabbard. The leader, having caught sight of Ben, nudged his mount forward with insolent confidence. The other five darted quick looks around the ranch yard, and their expressions were alert, appraising and wary.

"State your business, strangers." Ben's usually hospitable voice was cold as well water. Instinctively, Eve ducked back inside the doorway.

The leader, taller and darker than the others, unshorn hair stringing greasily around his shoulders, scratched his nose with a grimy fingernail. "We're just lookin' for a meal, friend," he said mildly enough.

Ben had already summed them up in that first swift glance, and he didn't like what he saw. These weren't the first out-of-work cowhands to come bumming a meal this spring. He had sent a fair share of others down the road these past weeks, but this group probably took the prize for dirt. Besides, where had men of this caliber dug up saddle trappings like those? Not honestly, he was sure.

All his distrust aroused, Ben told them, "There's nothin' f'r you here. Try the restaurant in town. It's right down that way." With a jerk of his head he indicated the north-south road.

Their response was to dismount swiftly and draw their Colts. Ben, rancher and family man, was no match for such as these in a fast draw. His .44 had not cleared leather before he was looking down the barrels of six cocked revolvers.

"You talk big, Mister, but it don't seem to me you have much to back up your cards," the greasy-haired leader snarled.

His men edged around Ben who, watching them warily, tried not to let them get behind him. But it was hopeless. With a gleeful chortle, one wearing a dirt-encrusted Mexican blanket-coat sprang from in back and chopped viciously with his Colt at Ben's upper arm. It was a short, powerful, bone-deep blow that blazed fire from shoulder to fingernails. As Ben grabbed at his hurt arm, fingers loosing from his gun, Greasy Hair stepped in and coolly jabbed him in the kidneys. Ben's face went green. He doubled over in

The Longing of the Day

pain. Eve, seeing Ben go down, clapped hands to her mouth to stifle her scream of terror. Mexican Blanket calmly plucked the Remington from Ben's holster and made a single, disgusted remark about its quality.

The leader inspected his knuckles for damage and swiped them across the thigh of his filthy jeans. He smiled without humor as he watched Ben fight to keep his balance against the waves of dizziness and nausea that wouldn't let up.

"You ain't so smart, now, are you, Mr. Benjamin Clayton?"

He chuckled at Ben's start of surprise. "What's the matter, Ben-boy?" he drawled. "Sure, we know who you are. We know all kinds of interestin' facts 'bout you. We're goin' to discuss 'em right after that meal we was talkin' 'bout." His smirking affability suddenly vanished. "In the house!" he barked, and gestured with his Colt.

Ben looked at all those weapons pointed straight at him and thought of Anne in the kitchen behind him.

"Move it!" the leader snarled.

"Hold it right there!"

Anne emerged onto the porch. She held the 12-gauge shotgun, and both barrels were aimed directly at the leader's belly. Her voice was shaky, but her hands were steady. "You heard him. Get out!"

They knew she meant it for one, younger than the others, looked quickly at Greasy Hair. "Boss?"

"Shut up!" And to Ben, "You better tell your woman to haul in that widow-maker, 'cause if she don't, we'll let her have it right now."

Ben knew he meant it, just as surely as Anne did. Even if she got the leader, there would still be five determined men, all armed and itching to shoot. And there was Eve, obviously still unnoticed, in the carriage house.

He had no choice. "Anne, put it down."

He saw her unbelieving, fierce protest and said sharply, "Anne, put it down!" For one endless time-tick, he knew she wasn't going to do it, knew with dead certainty that she was going to shoot anyway. But slowly, lips clamped in mute rebellion, she lowered the barrel.

With hoots of triumph, the men pushed Ben up the steps. The youngest one grabbed the shotgun and twisted it out of Anne's hands in a fine display of bravery.

"Anyone else here?" Greasy Hair demanded roughly as Anne reached out to Ben's hurt arm.

Neither one hesitated. She shook her head, and Ben said firmly, "There's just the two of us."

The leader's scowl swept the empty ranch yard. A breeze puff sent an eddy of dust skittering along the ground. At the corrals, Ben's horse snorted, the sound loud in the sharp silence. The scowl deepened. "Go check," he said abruptly to four of his men. "Besides the old folks, there's supposed to be a young gal here. She must be 'round someplace." He and Mexican Blanket shoved Ben and Anne through the kitchen doorway.

The door shut.

Stark terror replaced the dawning fear in Eve as the men spread out and she saw one with a drooping mustache start toward the carriage house.

The Longing of the Day

Matt and Dan doggedly rode toward the Arrow A. The horses were beginning to tire from the steady pace, but Matt figured they should easily make it in two more days.

They were now in country familiar to Matt. Prickles of excitement began to chase through him. *Home! They were almost home.* He no longer dared let himself think they wouldn't be there. Of course they would; they had to be.

That night he had the dream.

Eve came to him, so vividly he reached out to touch her. And woke, to emptiness. *Dear God,* he gritted, *don't let it start all over again!* He hadn't dreamed of her for several nights, had hoped that at last he was getting control of himself. If only she weren't always so real to him.

He lay shivering for a long time before he slept again. And again she came to him.

This time her eyes mirrored horror, her mouth was open in a scream that brought him bolt upright, wide awake and shaking from head to foot.

The first faint gray of dawn lit the eastern sky. Matt's heart pounded so hard it roared in his ears. But over and above it echoed the pure terror of her cry.

Still shaking, he crawled out of his blankets to where Dan lay. Forgetting all else in his desperate need for haste, he took hold and shook him — and promptly received a clout on the jaw for forgetting that in waking a man, you never laid hold of him. Shout at him, cuss him, blast a gun off at his ear, but never touch him.

He scarcely heeded the pain in his jaw as he yelled at the sleeping man, shook him and ducked another flying fist. "Wake up! C'n you hear me, Dan? Wake up!"

Louise Lenahan Wallace

Dan uncoiled, bellowing like an angry bull moose. "I hear you, damn it! Quit shakin' me!" He shoved Matt's hands off his arms and glared at him. "What in hell's name is wrong with you?"

"Listen to me. We gotta go. Right now! Somethin's wrong at home. I know it is!"

"Hey, you ain't jokin'." Dan stared at him, bewildered.

"No. We've got to leave now!"

"Wait a minute, Matt." But Dan could see there was no stopping him this time.

It was a full hundred miles to the ranch. A long ride for fresh horses, and theirs had been ridden steadily for many days. Would they, could they make it? Dan looked at Matt already heading out. "Come on, horse," he said grimly.

Matt would make it or die trying. It was up to Dan to see he made it.

He might not have caught up had Providence not intervened. Matt was far ahead and increasing his lead each moment as Dan set out.

"You blasted fool, you won't even come close that way. Slow down, Matt. Slow down!"

Determinedly he held Joker in, refusing to demand more than the animal could give. He had lost sight of Matt now and concern nagged at him, even as he kept to a steady pace. This patience was rewarded when, rounding a turn, Dan came upon his friend sprawled flat, face to the sky, a rock under his head. Tumbleweed, reins trailing, chomped grass close by.

As Dan dismounted, the horse shied a little but did not spook. He uttered thanks to all the saints in heaven for the

295

The Longing of the Day

inventor of ground-tying horses. Tumbleweed would stay where he was, leaving Dan free to devote all his attention to Matt.

Canteen in hand, Dan knelt beside his friend and thrust a work-callused paw inside Matt's shirt. Relief flooded him at the feel of the strong, regular heartbeat.

Gently raising Matt, he drew the rock aside and heaved a sigh of relief. There was no blood on it. "Prob'ly just a good knot on your head," he muttered, even as his fingers carefully probed the back of Matt's skull.

Matt let out a yell and tried to sit up. *Yep, there it was, and a dandy one at that.* Dan pushed him back. "Lay still, you danged fool," he growled. "You're just lucky your neck ain't broke, or your horse's neither f'r that matter. Tearin' 'round the country like a wild one!"

Even as he was grumbling and scolding, he was wetting a strip of shirt-tail and pressing it to the lump. Matt yelped again at first touch of the chilly water, then accepted the cloth gratefully as Dan thrust it into his hand.

"Here, c'n you sit up? Is anythin' else broke?" Dan helped him sit, watched anxiously as he swayed.

"I'm fine," Matt gasped as the world spun.

"Lady Luck was sure ridin' with you then. Whatever possessed you?" Now he was sure Matt was all right, Dan could express his relief by yelling.

Matt flinched, both at the volume of Dan's tone and because he pressed the lump on his head harder than he intended. But Dan's words cleared the fuzziness from his brain, and he remembered the reason for the headlong flight. "I got to get goin'!" He struggled but Dan pinned him back.

"Nope. Not till you tell me what's wrong."

Matt knew he was trapped. "All right, but we're wastin' time." Rapidly as possible, he explained.

Dan listened soberly, all anger gone. When Matt finished Dan said quietly, "We'll go, friend. But we're goin' sensible, not rushin' off half-cocked. If you want your horse and you to make it, you'll have to slow down."

Matt saw immediately Dan had not discounted his dream. He started to speak, but the older man cut in roughly, "I ain't sayin' there's anythin' wrong. Most likely there ain't. We'll bust ourselves gettin' there and find 'em sittin' all pretty and cozy and surprised to see us. But you won't be satisfied until we do see 'em that way, so we might as well go."

What Dan dared not tell Matt was that he used to have dreams, too.

"We'll go," he repeated roughly, "but we'll do it my way, at my pace. We'll get there faster my way than we will yours."

Dan helped Matt stand. He swayed a moment, but steadied. Moving over to Tumbleweed, he began off-saddling him. Dan watched, then turned to his own mount.

He knew Matt chafed at his insistence the horses be rubbed down, rested and allowed to graze. But a few minutes now would gain them precious time later. He knew Matt knew this and hoped fervently he wouldn't have to argue with him anymore over it.

When they finally set out, Dan held them to a pace that would best conserve the strength of their animals yet allow them to cover a lot of ground rapidly.

All day the uneasiness tore at Matt. The closer they got to the ranch, the more convinced he became that something was

The Longing of the Day

wrong. He didn't want to stop, even when darkness threatened to overtake them. He knew Dan was right about sparing the horses, but at the same time how could he hold back with this terrible fear — this knowing — hanging over him?

Each passing mile strengthened the certainty.

When Dan prepared to pull in for the night, Matt balked. "I've got to go on. I've just got to. They need me. *Somethin's wrong.*"

Dan saw immediately this time there would be no arguing. He supposed he had done well to keep Matt from flying off long before this. He sighed. "We'll go on, but after we've rested the horses. How far out you figure we are?"

" 'Bout thirty miles."

"We'll rest the horses until moonrise. Moonrise," he snapped over Matt's beginning protest. "You just 'bout broke your fool head runnin' in broad daylight. How far you think you'll get in the dark?"

Matt knew he was right, but he also knew that, for himself, he was willing to risk it. Thirty miles! So near and yet so far. Irrationally, Christmas Night, and Catty's talk of Mr. Bell's machine sending messages into the night, flashed into his mind. But that, too, was futile reasoning.

The moon finally rose, a pale, high, silvery gleam. At the first light Matt swung into the saddle and headed out, leaving Dan to follow.

Mile after mile spun out behind them, but the distance ahead seemed scarcely unraveled. Trot. Canter. Gallop. Trot again. The cadence beat upon him, became him until no other motion mattered. The stars wheeled, the moon swung higher, and finally, slowly, tipped into its descent. Tumbleweed's hoofbeats thrummed, their vibrations no louder in Matt's ears than the drumming of his own heart. And the hoofbeats echoed around him, and his heartbeat echoed within him. Together they became one with the chaos of his thoughts, all blended into one wordless, rhythmic prayer of pleading.

Fear, a sneering passenger that weighted every stride the horse took, had clamped onto him so he could no longer hold Tumbleweed to that steady gait the last few miles. The hoofbeats roared, his heartbeat thumped, his thoughts swirled through his brain like dried leaves fleeing before an autumn wind. And his soul was cold, cold as an empty house when the autumn wind wails through it.

The last rise loomed before them. But Tumbleweed had neither breath nor strength for the ascent. Blowing heavily, urged on by Matt's raking spurs, he strained every muscle and sinew in one last, supreme effort, and horse and rider burst over the top of that final slope.

The house still stood.

Even in that first, overwhelming surge of relief — his active imagination all too clearly in those last hours had seen it reduced to cold, drifting ashes — he didn't hesitate. He hallooed with all the breath in his lungs, waited for the answering spark of light at the window, for Ben's deep voice raised in question of his business at that hour.

There was no response.

He hallooed again. His voice slapped back at him from out of the darkness.

Then it struck him. The quiet. Not a sleeping quiet but utter, desolate silence. No breeze moved to rustle the newly leaved cottonwoods. No bellow of frog nor chirp of cricket

The Longing of the Day

nor beat of insect wing disturbed the hush. It was as if the house and the night were locked in a moment of eternal stillness while the silence hovered waiting and listening.

Fear departed to be replaced by terror. Sliding his Sharps from its scabbard, he dismounted in one ungraceful leap. He was running when he hit the ground. But the stone-heaviness of his heart, the weight of his boots sucking at the ground, dragged at him cruelly.

Matt stumbled onto the porch, breath rasping in his ears. The front door was closed and barred. He pounded on it with frantic fists. When there was no answer he leaped the railing, tore around the side of the house, past the newly blooming flower beds, through the passageway between the carriage house and the kitchen, and around the corner to the back porch. He stopped as suddenly as if he had slammed into a wall.

The kitchen door stood wide open to the night.

He saw, and suddenly there was no room left in him for terror. He felt only a deep, overpowering numbness. He had no willpower left in his legs to either carry him forward or to allow him to sink to the ground. He merely stood, holding his rifle, knowing now with deep sureness what had only been aching uncertainty before.

Ben Clayton had reared his family too long under the shadow of Indian attack to be trusting. Never, unless something was horribly wrong, would he allow a door to his house to stand open in the middle of the night.

Matt's brain registered the facts, even while he stood staring in disbelief.

Finally his deadened nerves began to function again. His

feet carried him forward, up the steps, across the porch and through the doorway.

He was not shocked or even surprised to see the kitchen had been ransacked. The moon, casting a silvery glow through the broken window over the sink, showed the usually neat room was in shambles. The contents of the cupboards had been pulled from the shelves and strewn carelessly about. Anne's Wedgwood china, the joy of her housekeeping heart, lay shattered on the floor.

He saw these things, his brain noted them, but his heart refused to acknowledge them. He groped on a shelf behind the door, found the lamp and matches that were always kept there for an emergency. He did feel some surprise, at least, that they were where they should be. Nothing else in the room was.

He lit the wick with trembling hands.

He stopped to straighten an overturned chair in his path, to place it neatly beside the table before he moved toward the doorway to the main room, stepping carefully over the litter in his way.

In the flickering lamplight he could see this room, too, had been wantonly torn up. The furniture was overturned. Anne's whatnot shelf was on the floor, the small treasures she kept on it, smashed.

He saw, but scarcely heeded, because no one was in this room either.

That left the bedrooms and Ben's office.

Anne and Ben's room looked as though a whirlwind had torn through it. Matt paused inside only long enough to make certain they weren't there. The door to the office was

The Longing of the Day

ajar. He put his hand on it with full knowledge of what he would find when he pushed it open.

He drew a breath that was a sob and went in.

But even the terrible foreknowledge he had all those long hours couldn't really prepare him for the bitter actuality. Anne lay in a crumpled heap on the floor between the desk and the window. Ben was near the opened, empty safe, his hand stretched out to her as if he had tried to protect her to the last. The bullet that pierced Anne's heart had been fired at point-blank range. In death her face was serene, revealing none of the anguish that must have been hers in that final terrified, knowing second. Ben had been shot through the back. A smeared trail of blood gave mute evidence that he had not died at once, as Anne had, but that he tried to crawl to her and failed.

With wooden movements, Matt knelt beside each one, the ache in him too great, in this moment, even for rage. They were his parents in heart and soul, if not in actual body and blood, and he loved them deeply.

At the sudden noise behind him, he whirled, Sharps raised, finger on the trigger.

Dan spoke before he stepped into the doorway. "It's me, Matt."

Matt dropped the rifle, bowed his head. He felt Dan's hand on his shoulder, gripping hard, and heard his voice as from a great distance. "My God, Matt, I'm sorry."

He said nothing. The overwhelming senselessness of the act, the complete impossibility of it, coupled with the stark reality before his eyes, made him feel as though he, too, were dead.

"I held you back." Dan's tone was dazed. "All those days. If I'd let you go ahead ..."

If I'd let you go ahead... If I'd let you go ahead. The words thumped through Matt's brain in a meaningless echo.

Slowly, slowly, bitter rage began to seep into the numb, frozen block that was his heart. *Who could have done this and why? Why? In God's name, why?* Anger at Dan for delaying him, anger at himself for not coming sooner, anger at his hands-tied uselessness to help Anne and Ben now, anger so powerful that it exploded through him with actual, physical pain, took possession of him.

And just as suddenly faded as ice-cold fear swamped him. *Eve!*

19

Eve!

Her name burst through him.

Had she been here, too? With the thought he was on his feet and pushing past Dan to get to the door.

"Matt, what ... ?"

"Eve!" he flung back over his shoulder and heard Dan's wordless groan of despair.

She had been here. He was sure of it in every fiber of his being. He thrust open the door to her room and halted on the threshold. This room, too, had been wrecked, her bed pulled apart, her clothes scattered. Someone, something, had smashed the mirror over her dressing table. The contents of the drawers were spilled about.

The toe of his boot caught in the braided rug. He stooped, picked up the object he had almost stepped on. It was the tiny deer he carved for Eve a thousand years ago last fall. His fingers closed around it as, memory flooding him in a sickening rush, he heard her voice saying, *I'll treasure it always.*

He turned so fast he crashed into Dan, standing behind

The Longing of the Day

him with the light.

"She was here, Dan. I know it!"

The older man made no attempt to argue. Forever after he would carry with him the anguish of having persuaded Matt to do differently than his feelings dictated.

The front door had been locked and barred, and for a certainty Eve was not now in the house. Matt seized the lamp from Dan and hurried through the littered kitchen to the back porch where he hesitated, calling with all his strength, "Eve!"

Only his own voice rang back in his ears, but there were any number of places she could be concealed out there. If she were hurt, she might not be able to answer him.

He tried to think where she would creep for refuge if she were able. *The carriage house!* The possibility jolted through him. *It was always her own special retreat.* With that thought, he was down the steps in one long leap, heedless of the peril to the lamp. This door, too, yawned open, something else Ben Clayton would never have permitted.

Please, God, his mind begged. *Please!*

He flung himself inside and halted, appalled.

Thistle, Eve's horse, lay sprawled on her side on a pile of hay. He paused only long enough to make certain the mare was dead before, taking the rungs two at a time, he mounted the ladder to the loft.

The light flicked off the walls in eerie shadow-patterns as he made a complete, swift circle around the room. In front of the window he stopped. The lamp glow picked up a patch of color half-buried in the hay. He bent and pulled Eve's shawl out.

But instead of hope, terrible, stomach-churning fear filled him.

She had been here. But where was she now?

Clutching the shawl, he backed down the ladder to meet Dan's horrified gaze.

"She was here," he whispered as Matt pushed past him. He followed at a limping run from one out-building to another. Barn, sheds and cookhouse had all been ransacked, but there was no sign of Eve.

Gray began to show in the east as they emerged from the bunkhouse. It would be daylight in a few minutes. Already they could see without the aid of the lamp. "Matt, she just ain't here."

"Don't say that." Matt's voice was quiet. His eyes were two pitch-black holes burned in a piece of white paper. And death was in his eyes as he repeated softly, "Don't you dare say that."

Dan looked at him, swallowed hard and shut up.

If she wasn't here, that meant she had been carried off. That possibility, and its consequences, Matt refused to acknowledge, for to admit it even in his own mind was to lose all reason.

"She's here someplace. She just has to be."

He set off toward the creek. She could be hidden among the rocks. There were several large enough to conceal someone as small as she was. He searched with infinite care. Nothing.

Where could she be? In spite of all his efforts, the dread in his heart became a strangling thing.

No! She was here and he'd find her. He would. He had to ...

He stopped at the edge of the water, his eyes searching.

The Longing of the Day

Cupping hands to his mouth, he called with all the breath in him, "Eve!" And again, "Eve!"

Only the sighing of the breeze came back to him. The light grew ever stronger. Rocks and bushes around him were no longer blurred, gray masses but sharp, distinct shapes.

Dan, behind him, spoke. "Matt, I ..."

"Sssh!" Matt cut him off fiercely. "Listen." The dawn breeze rustled through the grasses, whispered through the new leaves of the cottonwoods and willows. Across the creek a lark flew upward toward the sun.

"Eve, where are you?" And his voice echoed back to him in the stillness.

"Did you hear that?"

Dan shook his head reluctantly.

"No, wait." Matt yelled again with all his strength, "Eve!"

This time, very faintly but undeniably, it came, the barest moan borne to them on the breath of the breeze.

"I heard it, Matt!"

But Matt had already plunged into the creek. "Eve, where are you?"

On the other side he stopped and listened, not daring to draw breath lest he miss her faintest answer. There it was again, stronger now, somewhere off to the north among the plains grasses.

"Eve, I'm coming."

He caught a glimpse of a patch of blue in the grass ahead and his heart lurched. "Eve."

And so he found her.

She was sprawled face down in the grass. It was the blue of her dress he had seen. Relief and fear twisted within him as he flung himself beside her. "Eve." His hands trembled as he gently turned her over.

Her red-gold lashes drooped against her cheeks, and her face was white, white as cattle bones bleaching in the springtime grass. In that first, stunned second he clearly noted how the tiny freckles on her nose and cheeks starkly stood out. Her hair had loosed from its pins and spilled over his hands like bronze fire. Her skirt was torn and smeared with grass stains and mud. Sick fear coursed through him. From neck to waist, her dress was drenched with blood.

"Oh, my God! Eve!"

She didn't answer, lying limply in his arms as he searched frantically for the bullet wound that would have caused all that blood. There was none. Not daring to hope, he put his hand to her chest. When he felt her heartbeat, faint but regular, the wash of relief was so intense his stomach heaved.

The blood, then, had come from Anne or Ben.

She moaned and opened her eyes. When she saw him bending close above her, she screamed and began to fight, weakly but desperately.

"No, no," she wailed. "No!" The naked terror in her voice, in her eyes, was like a knife stabbing deep inside him. He had seen anguish like that once before when, after a bad storm, he had come across a pronghorn trapped by a falling tree. Its back was broken, crushed by the trunk as it toppled. The animal's eyes had swum with liquid fear as it had watched him approach, as it waited for death.

And now Eve, not knowing him, looked up at him with that same, heart-wrenching terror, the terror of his dream. He pulled her to him and held her tightly.

The Longing of the Day

"It's all right, my Eve. Can you hear me? It's me, Matt!"

But she didn't understand and kept flailing at him with frantic fists. He called to her again as she continued to struggle. Fear was the taste of brass in his mouth. Her mind ... His arms tightened instinctively as though he could shield her from the damning possibility.

Of all the horrors he imagined for her, this one had not occurred to him.

"Eve, no ..." It was a cry from the depths of his soul, yet it came out the faintest of whispers. He pressed his cheek to the lovely bright flame of her hair and knew in that moment what it is to die, yet live.

She screamed again, and her scream of fear was one with his roar of rage to God Almighty that this could happen. The dawn hush split apart with his bellow and it vibrated back to him, wave on mocking wave.

Sound lapped away into silence, the silence of living death.

Even as it did so she stopped writhing, stared at him wildly. The space of a heartbeat, then two, and she collapsed, weeping bitterly against his chest. And each crying breath was his name, over and over.

With hard male tears trickling down his own cheeks, he held her close, stroked her hair, murmured again and yet again, "My Eve, my sweet Eve. It's all right. I'm here now. It's all right."

Finally she quieted a little, though she still clung to him weakly. He stood up with her in his arms and saw Dan had come across the creek, but halted and stood back, watching anxiously. Now, seeing Matt start forward, he hurried to meet them.

"She's alive, Dan!"

The older man uttered one quick exclamation of thanksgiving, choked it off at the black hatred on his friend's face. A vicious hand squeezed his insides, and his own voice seemed to echo from a long way off. "Was she ... did they ... get to her?"

If Matt had not held Eve so carefully, he would have smashed Dan in the mouth for daring to give voice to the unspeakable. "She's alive," he repeated fiercely. "Do you understand? She's alive."

Dan looked at Matt, looked at the bedraggled burden he carried, and for the second time in his life his heart smashed to bits against a wall of unbearably cruel circumstance. He turned blindly and stumbled back through the creek toward the house.

Matt followed more slowly, cradling Eve against his chest as he waded through the knee-deep water. She was quiet now. Even her sobs had stopped.

So he carried her back through the red blaze of the plains sunrise to the house. So many emotions swirled through him that he felt dizzy. Joy and anguish, pain and grief, bewilderment and relief were all his as he moved up the back steps and through the kitchen. Dan, red-eyed, gestured from Eve's bedroom doorway.

"I've straightened her mattress." His voice came out a rusty croak.

Matt strode past him to the bed and gently laid her down.

Her eyes opened. "Don't leave me, Matt," she pleaded in quick terror.

He bent over her, touching her cheek with gentle fingers.

The Longing of the Day

"Don't worry, my Eve. I'm not goin' to leave you. I promise."

"Pa and Ma ..." she choked. So she knew. She began to cry again, wrenching, heartbroken sobs. All he could do was gather her close in his arms once more.

"It was so awful ..."

"You don't have to talk 'bout it, my Eve. Not now."

"But I have to tell you." The anguish in her voice seared his heart. He looked up bleakly, to meet Dan's own pain-filled glance. She would have to tell it sometime.

"All right, my Eve," he murmured, his cheek pressed against her hair. Cradled in the shelter of his strength, she told her story, sometimes with long pauses so they had to fill in the spaces for themselves.

"Yesterday, when we finished supper and the dishes, I wanted to go out to check on Thistle. Pa had been working on the account books most of the day and had sat down to them again at the kitchen table while Ma and I finished up our work. He told me to go along to the carriage house, that he'd be there in just a minute."

Here she stopped for a long moment and looked back at the bright image she had walked out on ... Anne kneading bread dough for the next day's baking, and Ben raising his head from the books for a moment to say something to her.

Such a commonplace picture that Eve had gone out without really seeing it. Matt held her closer, but there was no shelter for either of them against the stark reality of their shared knowledge that the Artist, having seen fit to paint the picture, had abruptly decided it should be blotted out, forever.

Eve's voice dropped as she picked up the thread of the story and told of the arrival of the strangers.

"When I saw the mustached man heading toward the carriage house, the only thing I could think was to hide as fast as I could, so I ran around Thistle and up the ladder to the loft. When I got there, I burrowed under the straw and stayed as still as I could. I was afraid even to breathe, for fear the hay would move. Down below, I could hear his heavy, clumping footsteps. They hesitated in the doorway, then advanced, slowly. They stopped, and I heard a short, nasty laugh. A gun roared underneath me. I thought maybe he'd seen some hay falling and was shooting up at me through the loft floor. And then, Ma screamed from the kitchen.

"I didn't dare move, not even to cover my ears. I heard somebody shout from outside and the man below shouted back, 'I shot the horse.' He shot my Thistle. I kept hearing the words, but they just didn't make any sense." Her pain-tightened voice told her listeners that those words were making terribly clear sense now.

Only for a moment did the anguish linger in her voice, before it became fierce self-control once more as she told how the footsteps paused near the loft ladder, began a slow, cautious ascent. Too terrified to move, she huddled, waiting. Now he was so close she could hear his harsh breathing as he stood above her. The hay skidded as he aimed a short kick at it, and she heard him grunt. She knew she had been discovered but lay still, the terror holding her powerless to move.

Another kick, so close it actually grazed her arm, and he turned to leave. "I heard him going, but I couldn't believe it. I thought he must be teasing me as a cat does a mouse, waiting for me to run before he pounced on me." But no, the footsteps descended the ladder and shuffled out the door.

313

The Longing of the Day

She wanted to scream with relief, but only for a second. The footsteps were plodding toward the house.

Ma and Pa!

At the horror in her voice, Matt could stand no more. "You don't have to go on, Eve. You don't have to tell us any more." He was pleading with her to stop, to spare both of them the anguish of reliving those moments. One bleak look at Dan, and Matt knew he, too, had already mentally finished the story.

But she had to tell it. The horror was too great to keep stored within herself.

"I could hear them laughing and talking in the house, and I could tell they were eating, but I couldn't hear what they said. I heard Pa every once in a while, but not ever Ma. Then their voices sounded like they were arguing, loud and mean, and I heard dishes smashing." Her words trailed away, and she began to tremble uncontrollably. Long moments passed before she took up the story.

She left the shelter of the hay and crept down the ladder to go for help when Ma screamed again. The first shot came blended with a roar of rage from Pa, drowned out by a second gun blast.

She clung to the ladder, frozen, while the shots echoed and re-echoed around her.

Matt's face was gray. "Don't, Eve," he begged. "Don't."

But she had to go on.

She dropped to the ground and crept to the door in time to see a large group of riders gallop up to the back porch. Fresh terror filling her, she backed away and fled up the ladder once more. Her escape had been cut off. If they searched the carriage house again and found her ...

There was only one thing she could do, and instinctively, in silent fear, she did it. Gaining the shelter of the loft that was a haven no longer, she stumbled over to the window, the window through which she and Matt had climbed many times in their childhood games of hide-and-seek.

"It refused to give at first. It must have warped sometime during the winter. I kept clawing and pushing at it, and it finally lifted." Her dry, controlled voice only accented the terror of those frantic moments.

Choking back a sob of relief, she forced the window the rest of the way open, cringing at the noise. She pulled herself up through the opening, but her skirt caught on a thick splinter hooking out of the sash.

Wild with fear, she tugged at the material, trying to free it. And heard footsteps and loud voices. They were coming to search the carriage house again.

Loud laughter told her they were inside now. Then pause of total silence.

Had they heard her?

"One shot, huh? Not a bad lookin' piece of horseflesh."

"Aw, it was hurtin'. I just put it outa its miseries."

Crude laughter slapped around her and relief flowed through her, giving her the strength she needed to tear her dress free. Keeping as flat as she could to the wall, using the finger and toe holds Matt had taught her so long ago in fun, she crept up to the roof as the footsteps pounded jarringly up the ladder.

Stretched out as flat to the sloping surface as she could get, she lay face down, her head buried between her arms,

The Longing of the Day

and listened over the wild beating of her heart.

"I looked here ... wait a minute!" The voice broke off in an excited chuckle. "Look at this. There was a gal here! It's a shawl-thing, and it sure weren't here before!"

At their yelp of laughter, she huddled closer to the roof, shaking uncontrollably. She heard them tearing through the hay and their frustrated curses when they didn't find her.

"You think she coulda gone out the winder?"

"Mebbe. I don't 'member it bein' open before." The voice was suddenly so clear she knew he was sticking his head outside. A shift of breeze brought to her the odor of horse, whiskey and the sour smell of a long-unwashed body.

"It's a right smart piece to the ground. Break a leg takin' a jump like that."

"Don't know 'bout you, but it don't matter, what I got in mind. Just means she couldn't get very far."

"We better tell the boss."

"And let him in on the fun of findin' her? You crazy?"

"Yeah, and if we didn't find her, he'd string us up sure f'r lettin' her get away."

"Us? You're the one searched here first. I was in the main house."

"Yeah, let's look but not say nothin' lessen we find her."

"And maybe not say nothin' then."

This last was followed by an evil chuckle that told Eve only too clearly what her fate would be if these two men discovered her. Through her terrible fear was one tiny flicker of hope. They weren't going to tell the others. That meant only two would be searching for her instead of close to a dozen.

"What you doin'?"

The voice so startled her that she jumped, then held her breath, paralyzed at making even a small noise.

"Hidin' this shawl under the hay where we found it. See? If we didn't see it, we don't know nothin' 'bout it. Now help me put this hay back."

Silence except for the rustle of straw being piled up. Then, incredibly, she heard, "Come on, before she gets clean away. I sure hope she looks as purty as that shawl smelled." And the footsteps went clattering down the ladder.

She lay pressed to the roof and let her breath out in a slow sigh of relief that was also a prayer of thanksgiving. The noise in the house and the yard continued for a time as the gang ransacked the place. There were shouts of anger and some talk of burning the house when they failed to find Ben's money.

"You said he'd have a roll, comin' through the winter like he did. You said you had it on sure information his money was here, not in the bank. Looks like we come all this way f'r nothin'."

Eve assumed this disgusted complaint was aimed at the boss. She couldn't hear the words of reply, but she did hear the tone they were spoken in. After that there was no more complaining.

Burning the place was vetoed because the flames would attract attention. Listening fearfully, she heard only one revealing comment concerning herself, delivered in the harsh, never-to-be-forgotten voice of the boss. "That little gal must of gone visitin' just like they said. She's sure not 'round here. Damn!" Then, "Mount up."

She heard the words plainly, but for a few seconds they

The Longing of the Day

held no meaning for her. Surely this nightmare was to go on forever. She heard the drum of hoofbeats, loud then fading quickly, but still didn't comprehend.

Several long minutes passed before she realized they were really gone. She wanted to scream with relief but could only lie, trembling violently, for a long time. In her mind was the terrible fear that, for some reason, they would return and find her if she left her hiding place. So she had huddled there for a long, long while before she climbed down.

Her dread for her parents drew her to the house. She knew all the time she lay hiding what she would find, but still she had hoped.

"I went into the office and there ..."

"No, Eve. That's enough."

She buried her face against his chest. "I don't remember anything else, anyway, until you found me. I guess I just ran." Her voice broke and no more words would come.

He cradled her in his arms, trying to soothe away her horror even as the full truth of her story washed over him. Dan stood white and silent, watching them. Suddenly he turned on his heel and strode out.

Finally Eve was able to stop shuddering. "How did you find me?"

"It doesn't matter. What I'm goin' to do now is get some water f'r your face and hands." He eased her gently back onto her bed.

Quick fear leaped into her eyes. "Don't leave me, Matt."

He pressed her hands firmly. "Just f'r a second. I promise." He touched her hair and straightened. At his call, Dan came at once, concern mirrored in his ashen face. When

Matt asked him to bring some water, he hurried off again.

Matt turned back to Eve. Her eyes were closed, but she opened them as he bent over her.

Dan hesitated in the doorway, a pan of water in his hands. He pushed it awkwardly toward Matt and would have retreated again.

"No, stay."

"Matt, I don't think ..."

But Matt was already drawing him toward the bed, saying, "Eve, this is Dan Mackley, a man to go the trail with, f'r sure." And to him, simply, "This is Eve."

Dan looked at her lying there, so white of face, her copper-bronzed hair spilling around her shoulders, her hands clinging to Matt's big ones. Awkwardly he scuffed his feet. And knew he had to say it. "Matt was right, Ma'am," he blurted.

Her eyes were such dark pools that he felt himself drowning in their depths. Another young woman, another time, had eyes that could make him feel like that.

"He said you was one in a million an' not just in looks, neither. Lord, he was right!"

For a moment, wonder overshadowed grief as she gazed at Matt. Her fingers tightened around his hands.

Dan stood clumsily, clutching his hat and wishing fervently he were anywhere else. But in just a moment, Matt carefully released her hands. He bathed her face in the cool water, but hesitated over her dress. She saw his uncertainty and turned even whiter.

"You'll have to change. Think you c'n manage?" he asked anxiously.

The Longing of the Day

Her lips were bloodless. "I can manage."

He helped her sit on the edge of the bed, bent and brushed a kiss against her hair. "I ... we'll be right outside."

While they were waiting for her, one duty had to be taken care of immediately. Refusing Dan's help, Matt carried Anne, then Ben, to their own room and placed them gently on their bed.

"Their limbs," Dan said hoarsely, "they'll have to be straightened."

Matt nodded, scarcely able to see for the blinding tears. Dan found a sheet, and Matt covered them carefully. Only when it was done did he speak, his voice catching painfully. "One of us'll have to go f'r help."

Dan had aged a dozen years in the last hours. "I'll go," he said heavily. "I know you don't want to leave her."

"Go due west four miles. You'll hit Jason's ranch. He'll get the others." Dan would have to walk. Ben's horses had been run off, and neither one of theirs would make it even that short distance.

When Eve opened her door, she was still bleached-bone white, but she had changed her dress and combed her hair. Matt reached out to her. "Why don't you come back and lie down?" *The less she saw of the ruin of the house the better*, he thought. At least the wreck of her bedroom was familiar to her now.

She let him lead her back to the bed. He sat beside her, her still-cold hand clutching his even after she finally fell into exhausted sleep. His head told him there were many things he had to do. His heart said nothing was as important as this. He followed his head once and left her, trying to do what he thought was right for her. This time, he would listen to his heart.

Her question came back to him. How had he known, so many miles away and hours before the terrifying tragedy had actually happened?

The pull of the heart was a strange thing, indeed. How *had* he known and Will hadn't?

With the thought, for the first time in all this terrible nightmare it occurred to him to wonder where Will was. Of a certainty he was nowhere on the ranch. And Eve hadn't mentioned him when she told her story, not once. He frowned, looked at the hand he held in his — her left one. She wasn't wearing a wedding band.

But she wore his locket. It gleamed softly golden against her throat.

He fiercely told himself it didn't mean anything. It had been a terrible winter. Most likely Will had no money with which to buy a ring but planned to get one as soon as he could. As for the locket, Matt had given it to her, as brother to sister. Why shouldn't she wear it?

But where was Will? Matt's anger, grief-damped these past hours, now rekindled by this fresh fuel, writhed to the surface. How could Will have left her this way? He had married her; he had vowed to take care of her. All the frustration and hurt Matt had suppressed for so many weeks boiled up, overflowing in a scalding tide of resentment.

For her sake he had let Will claim her, doing absolutely nothing to stop him. He had done his damnedest to accept the choice she made; he stood meekly aside, trying to content himself with the miserable crumbs of friendship because he thought it was the best way for her. He had trusted Will to take care of her. And this cowardly betrayal was the result.

Rage was a white-hot, consuming flame within him as he swore he would see Will burn in hell before he would allow him to come near her again.

She moaned, and he saw a shadow of terror flicker across her features. He smoothed back her soft hair with a work-roughened hand and silently promised her that never, regardless of the consequences, would he ever leave her again.

His fists clenched. And when he got his hands on Will ...

Over two hours later he heard the pound of hooves and Jason's loud, "Hello the house!"

He pulled open the door as Jason flung himself from his horse and leaped up the porch steps. Over Jason's shoulder he saw they had all come. The men were on horseback and Becky, Hannah, Catty and the children were in the wagons and buggies just careening into the yard. All their faces held a look of pleading hope until they saw Matt's expression. Then they knew all hope was gone.

Jason shoved Matt out of the way and tore into Anne and Ben's bedroom. He stumbled out, his face bloodless. "My God, it's true. He said it happened. All the time of collectin' ever'body, comin' here together just in case ... We couldn't believe him!"

The others rushed into the bedroom, but Matt was scarcely aware of their pushing past him for he had caught sight of Will hurrying toward him. "Eve? Matt, is she all ..." He didn't finish for Matt's fist swung up and caught him squarely under the jaw. He staggered back. "Matt, wait!" he yelled as that clenched fist came up again.

"Stand and fight, you low-down, no-good, son of a ..."

"Matt, will you let me explain ..."

"Explain why you ran off and left her? When you married her, you promised to take care of her. Is that your idea of protection and carin'? I'm waitin'. Let's hear your excuse. Then I'm goin' to lay you in the dirt." His voice was quiet and deadly. Will was a brave man, but the look on Matt's face sent a chill through him.

"She didn't tell you? We're ..."

He was interrupted by a low cry. Matt whirled. Eve stood in her bedroom doorway, clutching the frame for support. He took a swift step toward her as she swayed, but she steadied herself. "We're not married. I ... I just couldn't do it."

He stared at her, not daring to believe what he heard. He reached out, but Jason's voice cut in curtly. "We've no time for that. Cat, you help Eve back to bed. Becky and Hannah, you ... you'd best help Ma." His voice broke a moment, then steeled. "Aaron, you and Luke look after Pa. Matt, I want to talk to you."

At the grim authority in his voice, they obeyed.

Away from the house, Jason faced Matt squarely. "Let's have it. Your friend told us what happened, but didn't give any details. Just told us to come right away. What do you know 'bout it?"

Matt took a deep breath, repeated Eve's story as simply as he could, dazed not only by Eve's just-given news, but by the total unreality of the whole thing, unable to think clearly when it was so necessary. This was Ben and Anne! He realized Jason, too, held himself in check only by the strictest self-control.

"It's obvious they were after money, but why Pa? And

The Longing of the Day

Ma? My God, Pa never kept enough money in the house to cause this."

"I don't know. It just don't make any sense."

Jason spoke through clenched teeth. "We better get the marshal."

"You want me to go?"

"Will c'n. You stay here."

They turned back to the house.

20

Late that afternoon they buried Anne and Ben on the rise of ground to the east of the house, where Elizabeth lay. Word of the tragedy had spread, and neighbors from many miles away came to pay their respects.

It was a softly beautiful June afternoon. The sky arched deeply blue overhead. A slight breeze rustled the drying grasses and brought the fragrance of wildflowers to the group of mourners gathered around the two deep holes in the ground.

"And God shall wipe away all tears from their eyes; and there shall be no more death, neither sorrow nor crying ..."

Matt stood close beside Eve, his arm supporting her. She was pale, and he could feel her trembling, but she didn't cry.

"... for the former things are passed away."

Reverend Wardley's voice sounded above and around them. Matt heard the words, but he was thinking of Anne and Ben as they had been during all the days of his life with them. Loving each other deeply, they had truly shown their children, both those of their blood and those of their hearts, how to live fully and with joy. It was a legacy each child's

The Longing of the Day

heart could carry always.

As for the rift of the last months, the blame was his, not theirs. They tried to teach him, along with the others, to face life fearlessly, to accept full responsibility for his actions no matter what the cost because it was the price of life itself. And now that misunderstanding, too, had become his legacy because the consequences would dwell within him forever, a never-ceasing ache in his heart.

The group was singing now, Anne's favorite hymn, *Abide with Me: fast falls the eventide, the darkness deepens, Lord, with me abide ...*

Matt could hear Eve singing, softly and hesitantly at first, then gradually stronger. *Heav'n's morning breaks, and earth's vain shadows flee! In life, in death, O Lord, abide with me!*

The simple services were mercifully brief. As people came to offer their comfort, Eve — while staying close beside Matt — stood straight and firm on her own. Matt, realizing what this effort to be strong cost her, felt deep pride as he watched her and knew Anne and Ben would have been proud, too, had they been able to see. Somehow he felt they were nearby, watching. It was one small comfort in all that terrible day.

Polly Nigel, Eve's childhood friend, hugged her tight in wordless grief as Phil, Polly's husband, grasped Matt's hand hard. Big Chase Aubrey, his eyes dark with sorrow and yearning, took Eve's hands in his own huge ones. "If ever you need a friend, Eve ..."

"Thank you, Chase," she whispered, knowing he meant it.

Back at the house, Matt wanted Eve to rest. The services had taken a heavy toll of her frail strength, but she refused to lie down. "I couldn't sleep, and I just don't want to be by myself right now."

He saw the misery in her eyes, and his heart ached for her. People were still coming up, offering their sympathy, but gossiping among themselves, too. He knew she could endure no more. Taking her arm, he quietly led her away from the house, the press of people and the sidelong looks. He drew her to a sheltered spot under the cottonwoods, near the house but away from prying eyes. A log stretched under the trees had long served as a bench, and it was here he quietly seated her. She clasped her hands tightly in her lap and looked up at him standing beside her. "Thank you, Matt. I don't think I could have stayed there much longer."

He reached out to put his hand gently on her hair. "You don't have to thank me, Eve. I want to do things f'r you. And I knew you had to get away."

She reached up and pressed his hand. "You're so good to me. You always have been." Her fingers touched her locket, and she saw him follow the movement. "I've worn it every day since you gave it to me. Somehow it brought you close to me even though you were away." She bowed her head. "I guess it sounds strange."

His glance touched the bright flame of her hair, and he silently drew a deep breath. How many times he had seen her in his dreams, both waking and sleeping. "It isn't strange at all. It makes me glad."

She raised her head. He dropped down beside her, taking her hands in his. "Eve, there's so much I want to say to you." As she started to speak, he went on quickly, "I know now isn't the time. I don't want to crowd you or pressure you in any way. That's why I'm goin' to wait."

The Longing of the Day

She looked long into his eyes. "I want to talk to you, too. There's so much I want you to know and understand. But I can't. Not now." She bowed her face into her hands. "I'm so tired and confused right now."

All his being longed to take her in his arms and comfort her as he had earlier. But he couldn't. It wouldn't have been fair to her. He had been able to fill her need of comfort by holding her then. This time, much as his arms cried out to hold her, he knew he must not. He could only stand and clench his fists so tightly the knuckles turned white. He said huskily, "We'd best be gettin' back to the house. They'll be wonderin' where we are."

She raised her head and saw the violet twilight begin to settle around them. She drew her shawl closer and shivered. He glimpsed the fear in her and understood. "It's all right. You c'n bet they're a long ways from here tonight. Let's go back."

She stood and saw the intense look on his face soften. They walked to the house. As he reached to open the door, she put her hand on his arm. "Matt, wait. I just want to say thank you for everything." She raised up on tiptoe and quickly kissed him before she opened the door and slipped in. He followed, the sweet taste of her lips lingering on his.

Becky looked up from tying Patience's apron. "There you are!"

In kaleidoscope fashion, Matt saw Catty's relief, Jason's anxiety, Hannah's bewilderment and Luke's impatience. Even the children had not escaped the horror of the day. Too young to fully understand the reason for the shock and strain and sorrow of their parents, they nevertheless sensed the awful solemnity of their elders and were made uneasy by it. Isaac and Micah tugged at Hannah's skirts, whimpering.

Eden wailed in Cat's arms. Patience looked wistfully up at Becky, reaching up her arms to be held.

Of all the grandchildren, only young Jared, with a terrible knowledge beyond his years, was not fussing. He silently stood between his parents, his arms crossed against his chest. He was so pale his freckles stood out separately. But his head was high, his chin flung up as if in defiance of his red, swollen eyes and tear-stained cheeks. The bitter hatred that held him proudly rigid was chilling to see. He was only 11, but the oldest son of Becky and Jason Clayton would never again be a child.

Eve glanced at Matt. "We were just ... talking." Only he sensed rather than heard the slight hesitation.

"That's right. We didn't mean to worry you."

Becky came forward and took Eve's arm. "Come, let's get your things together. You'll be going home with Jason and me tonight."

Eve turned quickly. "Matt?"

"Don't worry," he said soothingly. "I don't think any of us are goin' to spend the night here."

"He's right," Becky assured her. "We just want to get started because it'll take longer with the team. Jason doesn't want to be on the road after dark if he can help it. Come now, let's get your things." Still speaking soothingly, she led Eve away.

"We'll check the place out before we leave," Jason said. "It won't take long."

They quickly locked the house and all the outbuildings that hadn't had their doors smashed in. They would return tomorrow to begin the sad task of cleaning up, but there was no point in staying tonight.

The Longing of the Day

Dan brought the teams and wagons around, and the women climbed in with all the children. Matt had no time to speak to Eve and could only give her a small, reassuring smile. She lifted her hand slightly in return as the wagon rattled off.

Dusk deepened to dark as they started away. Before they topped the ridge that would cut them off from sight of the house, Matt glanced back for a moment at the two crosses beside the tiny one on the hill. He saw the others doing the same, then they rode silently away.

By unspoken agreement of their need to draw close together and be comforted, they all stayed that night at Jason and Becky's. Once there, they turned immediately to unharnessing the horses and putting the overtired children to bed. Matt was dropping with weariness as they went inside but came sharply alert as Jason said, "We have to talk. It might as well be now while we're all here together."

Dan started to back away. When Matt caught his arm, Dan protested, "It's you as family who'll be talkin'. I don't belong."

Matt's grasp tightened. "Of course you belong, if you'll stay. You're family, too."

Dan's tired eyes rested on his friend. "You really mean it." It was statement rather than question.

They all pulled out chairs at the kitchen table, but Jason remained standing beside his. "We all know pretty much what happened last night. No use ridin' that trail again." His voice cracked and he cleared his throat awkwardly. "What we have to talk 'bout is what we're goin' to do. From what

Eve said and from the looks of the house and the empty safe, it had to of been f'r money."

His words dropped like a rock into the pool of silence. Luke stared at him blankly. Aaron shifted in his chair. "But why?" Aaron protested. "Your Pa didn't have that kind of money."

"What did they mean 'bout Pa havin' his money at home instead of in the bank?" This question had been nagging at Matt for hours. "He never kept enough cash on hand to make a robbery like this worthwhile."

Jason looked uneasy. "Pa did get to considerin' it after the winter got so bad. Said if things went bust this spring the banks'd go down and he'd lose all he'd saved. That happened before, you know. He lost ever'thin', and he had some fool notion he was too old to start over again if it happened this time."

Memory clicked and Matt dimly recalled Ben mentioning something about this at Christmastime. But it was mostly a vague blur. It just hadn't seemed important, then. He felt quick, hot shame that it had been so.

"But he wasn't serious!" Aaron burst out. "Anybody could see that."

"Somebody obviously thought he was." Jason's voice was bitter. "Somebody who knew enough 'bout him to call him by name and to be aware that Eve was supposed to be there, too. But who? He wasn't one to go on 'bout things like that outside the family, and Eve says she's sure Pa didn't know 'em."

"Maybe someone overheard him mention it in town," Aaron suggested. "Maybe one of the cowhands he let go got wind of it. You know how talk gets 'round, and pretty soon

The Longing of the Day

it gets to be fact. 'Specially in a bunkhouse."

"Maybe!" Jason repeated angrily. "We need more than maybes!" He banged his fist furiously on the table, causing the others, nerves already raw-strained, to jump at the unexpected violence of it.

Dan, feeling he shouldn't intrude, had said nothing up to now, but an obvious question had to be asked. He cleared his throat and said apologetically, "Did he actually take the money out of the bank?"

Luke scowled at Dan, whom he plainly considered to be a stranger interfering in family business. Aaron and Matt looked to Jason. He scrubbed the back of his neck before answering heavily, "The marshal's goin' to check. Accordin' to Pa's books, the only money he withdrew recently was just a small amount like he'd done two or three times already this winter. Enough f'r livin' expenses, that's all. He kept his books accurate. Don't seem logical he'd make a big withdrawal and not mark it down. And that makes it all so senseless." He bit off the last words in helpless fury as his hands clenched on the back of his chair. Taking a deep breath, forcing himself to speak calmly, he went on.

"The marshal's goin' to investigate, of course, but he thinks from what Eve said 'bout there bein' so many of 'em, they must of been from Red Canyon." He paused, looking grimly at each grim face.

"You know what that means."

Deep silence answered him. His listeners knew only too well what it meant. If they had come from Red Canyon, there was little hope of catching them. They were a group that struck hard and fast and retreated to the protection of their hideout somewhere in the mountains near the Powder River. None of them had ever been caught in pursuit, but many who had followed them, bent on revenge, had failed to return.

Luke, oddly silent up to now, spoke in protest. "That's a long way from here f'r 'em to come."

"Depends on how desperate they were. Bad as the winter was, pickin's would be slim up where they usually run. They must of figured it'd be worth the chance." Jason's face, already showing all the strain of the last hours, became even more lined and weary. "The question is, what are we goin' to do 'bout it? It's ..."

"I say we go after 'em, make 'em pay f'r what they've done!" Vicious eagerness shone out of Luke's usually sallow face, and his eyes glinted with a strange, frightening intensity.

"Hold on. You didn't let me finish." The new authority in Jason's voice made Luke sit back and clamp his mouth shut, his face almost as red as his beard.

"I was goin' to say," Jason pronounced slowly, "it's rough because Eve's the only one who c'n identify 'em. It could come down hard on her if they found out she was there after all and that she saw 'em. But as a family, each of you has a say in what our final decision will be. What it tallies out is: Do we set out on a most likely useless chase to avenge our parents or do we accept it as hopeless, stay home and let the marshal do what he c'n?"

Luke was again the first to speak. "Hopeless or not, they were our parents," he said bitterly. "I, f'r one, will not sit home and not even try to bring their murderers to justice."

Jason studied him a long moment before he turned to

The Longing of the Day

Aaron and Matt. "You've heard Luke. What do you two think? Remember, what we do will be done *as a family*." The intensity of his voice chilled them.

Aaron stirred. "I vote with Luke. They were as close to me as my own folks, and I can't let what happened to them go unpunished. No matter what the cost."

Jason's eyes rested on him in turn before he spoke to Matt. "You've heard Luke and Aaron. What do you say?"

Matt held silent for a long minute. How to put into words the feeling inside him?

He hesitated so long the others grew impatient.

"Well?" Luke's voice was harsh. "What do you say? Are you with us or not?"

He faced them squarely. "It's easy to say revenge is the right answer. I'm not so sure it is."

Luke cut in with an angry protest, but Matt went on quickly. "Wait. You had your say. It's my turn now." Luke sank back furiously.

"We have to do what's best f'r all of us, as a family. And all of us means Becky and Hannah, Cat and Eve, and the children. Think 'bout them f'r just a minute. What good will it do them f'r us to go tearin' off on a chase that we all know is hopeless? Not *may* be hopeless but is absolutely so. That's been proved time and time again by others that's set off after 'em and couldn't break through to their canyon. But they was like ducks on a fence f'r the guards watchin' f'r 'em. If there was a chance in hell of catchin' 'em I'd say, let's go make 'em pay f'r what they've done. But I ask you, Luke, what good will it do Hannah and those four boys of yours if you come back across your saddle or don't come back at all?"

Luke jumped to his feet, speaking quickly and harshly. "I'm not afraid of the consequences. And Hannah — she'll understand. Even if you don't. 'Course, I am forgettin'," he burst out recklessly, "that Ma and Pa weren't your parents. That slipped my mind f'r a while. I'm sorry. That bein' the way it is, you couldn't possibly understand how we feel since they didn't mean as much to you as they did to us. You proved that by turnin' tail and runnin' out last fall when they needed you ..." His words were choked off by the fury on Matt's face as he came to his feet in a rush.

Luke took a step backward as Matt started around the table toward him.

"Don't ever say anything like that again." Matt's words were quiet and cold. The others froze in their chairs for there was death in his tone.

Jason was the first to react. He stepped quickly between them. "Sit down and shut up, Luke." As Luke, recovering himself, hesitated, he repeated, "I said sit down! You, too, Matt."

Matt stopped, but still faced Luke with deadly intent. "They were my parents in every possible way except by actual blood and in ways you couldn't begin to know or understand."

Jason cut in. "We know how you felt 'bout 'em, Matt, and they knew, too. You were as much their son as either Luke or me, and Luke knows it. It's eaten at him f'r years."

Luke started a furious protest but Jason cut him off. "I said sit down and shut up!"

His mouth a hard, white line, Luke flung himself back into his chair. Matt slowly unclenched his fists, gave him one more cold glance and returned to his seat.

Jason let out his breath. "That's better. Luke, keep your

mouth shut. Matt, go on."

"I wanted to say, how would Pa and Ma themselves feel 'bout it? Would they want us to go off on a wild, hopeless chase f'r blood revenge? Leave all our families open to still more attack and possible danger by our not bein' here? Or would they say there's been hurt and pain and sorrow enough and to just let it be?"

He faced them straight and tall. "I think they'd say just let it alone. Take care of your families because they need you alive more than we need you dead out of revenge." He paused, his eyes holding each one for a long moment, but Luke's the longest. Luke's glance fell first.

"And there's somethin' else maybe none of you have considered. Jason said a while ago that it could come down hard on Eve if they found out she'd been there and could identify 'em. Do you realize just how hard? She's been through hell once. Do you really want to turn her 'round and drag her right back again? They prob'ly don't care if she c'n identify 'em. I'm sure there's lots of people in lots of towns c'n do that. That's not the problem. But if you go up there against 'em, stirrin' em up'd be like poundin' with a stick on a sleepin' hornets' nest, she'll be a threat to 'em then. They proved they weren't playin' games this time, and they damned sure won't be next time."

Absolute quiet followed his final words. Until Aaron finally said slowly, "Maybe you're right, Matt."

"Luke?" Jason prompted. Luke looked everywhere except at the waiting faces in front of him. Suddenly he pushed back his chair and stood. "You said we'd do it as a family, whatever the decision. Looks like I been outvoted, so what difference does my opinion make?" His voice grated. "I f'r one am not goin' to forget this." He leveled a look of pure hatred at Matt. "Any of it." He shoved past Jason, stomped out the door, slamming it after him.

Jason watched him go, turned back to those at the table. "It looks like it's been decided. We let the marshal handle it while we stay with our families, try to go on with our lives. I think that's what Pa and Ma would have wanted."

At the sudden movement near the door, Jason jerked around, his hand going instinctively to his holstered Colt. He stared foolishly as the four women rushed in. "We figured you'd gone to bed," he blurted.

Becky whirled on him. "You said yourself this was a family discussion. If we aren't part of the family, what are we?" She turned to Matt. "Thank you for having the sense to see this thing as Pa and Ma would have."

Hannah hesitated only an instant. "Yes. Thank you, Matt. You *are* right." Her voice broke and she hurried off after Luke.

Becky spoke softly to Jason. "I'm glad you're not going." Some of the anxiety cleared from his face as he gazed down at her.

Catty reached out to Aaron, and Eve slipped over to stand beside Matt. Eve didn't speak, but Matt saw the relief in her eyes. He reached out and lightly touched her cheek.

"Well." Jason cleared his throat. "Now it's been settled by a *family* discussion, let's get some sleep."

Before he lay down, Matt stood a minute gazing out the window at the moon-silvered plains. So much had happened in such a short space of time. Surely he would wake in the

The Longing of the Day

morning and find it had all been a nightmare. But Anne and Ben were dead and it was no dream.

"I'm glad you're not goin', Matt," Dan said behind him. "I think it's the right way."

"Is it?" he asked slowly. "F'r us, person'ly, maybe. But what 'bout the people, families like us, who haven't been hurt yet but will be because of these men? When will it end?"

"You think you was wrong, speakin' up like you did? You sounded pretty sure of yourself, sure enough that you got the others to agree with you."

"I'm sure," he said flatly. "And I'd do it again in a second to protect Eve. That's the trouble. Ever'one's agreed f'r years somethin' needs to be done, but they're all waitin' f'r someone else to do it. And innocent people keep gettin' hurt. How long will it go on?"

Dan heard his bitterness, but how could he answer him? "It'll go on," he said finally, "until a big enough group of people get mad enough to do somethin' 'bout it. It's bigger than you or me or your family. You were right it'd be suicide f'r just a few people to go against that whole group. That's been proved before. But someday somethin' will be done because enough people will be mad enough to see that it is. Until then we'll just have to hang on, not fly off rash and hot-headed."

"I'm afraid Luke's not goin' to forget this," Matt said drearily.

"He's young. To the young, wild revenge seems the only answer." Dan's voice was weary. "He'll learn in the years to come it ain't always the only way."

The next morning they began the pain-filled task of cleaning up the house. In evident anger over their failure to find any money, the raiders performed a thorough job of destruction. Holes were punched in the floors and walls, window panes smashed out and the furniture broken, gouged and hacked apart.

Some furnishings were so completely destroyed there was no hope of repairing them; other articles were carried away so they, too, were irrevocably lost. They worked faithfully, sanding and gluing, doing the best they could with what remained. But no matter how hard they worked, no amount of nailing or patching could repair their shattered lives.

Jason found the package while they straightened Ben's office. He had been sorting out the contents of the desk. The raiders had pawed through it, making a thorough mess of all Ben's papers, even ripping pages out of his ledgers, wadding them up and tossing them around.

Matt was sorting out the pages, trying to put them back in the proper books, when he heard Jason exclaim. He glanced up and saw he held a small box tied with twine. "It's f'r you. It was shoved clear to the back of the pigeon-hole. It's Ma's writin'."

The Longing of the Day

Matt took it slowly. The rush of warmth he felt as he saw Anne's familiar script turned to a chill as he saw it had been delivered to the LB and returned. She had obviously tried, and failed, to mail it before.

He looked up bleakly. Jason's face was gray. "I have to open it by myself," he said slowly. "You understand that." Without waiting for an answer, but feeling Jason's pain-filled gaze following him, he left the room and strode outside.

His footsteps took him over to the corral where Tumbleweed greeted him with a delighted nicker. He stroked the bay's nose absently and walked down to the creek where he sat on a rock and gazed at the unopened box in his hands.

He didn't know exactly what he felt — loneliness, pain, grief and cutting awareness that he would never again receive another letter from Anne. He slowly untied the string and lifted the lid. In the top of the box was a piece of paper, folded many times over to fit into the small space.

Beneath it, nestled in crumpled newspaper, was a gold pocket watch.

Bewildered, he lifted it out. He didn't ever remember seeing it before. Why would Anne ...

He turned it over and stared dumbly.

Amanda to Stephen — 1860

Amanda ... and Stephen ... Remembrance swirled around him — a vague, confused impression of water, bushes and Catty wailing in his arms blending into a terrifying sensation of calls and cries and high-leaping flames — the only association he had with his birth parents.

Louise Lenahan Wallace

Even knowing it for what it was, 22 years later it still had power to chill him to the pit of his stomach.

He passed a shaking hand over his eyes, grimly telling himself to grow up. The box fell off his knee, and Anne's letter with it. In spite of his resolve, his hands shook as he picked up the letter. He unfolded it, the breeze ruffling the edges of the paper.

> *Dear Matt,*
>
> *There is no easy way either for me to write this letter or for you to read it, but you have a right to know about this watch. We found it in your pocket the night Ben brought you home. It should have been given into Catty's and your possession years ago, but somehow the time was never right.*
>
> *Does it seem strange that two wet, cold, hungry babies could give life back to two adults, supposedly years older and wiser? That is exactly what you and Catty did that night you became our children. And we couldn't bear to let anything destroy that. Perhaps we were wrong, but if we erred, it was out of love, never out of intentional deceit.*
>
> *But now, no matter what the consequences, the time has come. Perhaps it will clarify things for you, help you put them in perspective. I pray to God so, because Matt, I know of your true feelings for Eve ...*

His stomach lurched and the page blurred before him, her earlier confession sinking into insignificance beside the enormity of this revelation. She knew — but dear God,

341

The Longing of the Day

how? He gripped the paper tighter, staring at the words she had written.

> *It explains so many things I didn't understand before. I can imagine your shock as you read this. I have to tell you honestly, I was shocked when I found out. I don't know how I could have been so blind except you covered your feelings so carefully. I just never real-ized until you were here at Christmas.*
>
> *No, as nearly as I know, no one else is aware of your secret. If Eve is, she hasn't let on to me but goes ahead with all the plans for her and Will's wedding. She has been very quiet these last weeks but insists nothing is wrong.*
>
> *I'm not the one to tell you, Matt, whether your feel-ings are right or wrong. Only your own heart can do that. I don't know how you will work out a solution, but you have been my son for 22 years, and I know, with deep sureness, that whatever you decide will be because, first, it's the right thing to do for Eve, and only second, because it's the right thing to do for you.*
>
> *Please don't feel I'm prying into your personal business. I have a very good reason for telling you all this so you will know I understand why you went away.*
>
> *Matt, Ben is very sick. He finally went to the doctor today. It's his heart. He admitted he hasn't been feeling well since last fall, but he's been ignoring it, hoping it'll go away. Doc Fergus says he won't get better, though, only worse.*
>
> *That's why he's been so upset this past winter by*

your leaving. It wasn't you he was so angry with. It was his own fears for the future. Do you understand?

Doc says he has about six months left if he takes it easy. I'm not telling all this to make you come running home. I'm only telling you because just as you've been my son all these years, you've been Ben's. You should know. He made me promise not to tell you or the others, but most especially not you. He doesn't know why you left, I'm sure of that. But he says very firmly he won't have you dragged back here because of him.

For the first time in our married life, I'm going against a direct wish of his and I'm deceiving him. As much as it hurts to do it, I think it would be more wrong for you not to be told. I feel under the circumstances you have a right, even more than the others, to know.

Please forgive me for causing even more upheaval for you. I know you are burdened enough. Just know, my son — for you are my son and always will be no matter what — whatever you decide to do, we will accept your decision because it will be made by both your heart and your head and will be what you feel is best for everyone. We can't ask more than that.

Your loving Mother

Long after he finished reading, Matt continued to stare at the paper. The writing was shaky — so unlike Anne's neat, careful script — and here and there a blurred spot where tears had fallen gave mute evidence of how difficult it had been for her to write.

He shook, too, as he tried to comprehend all she had

The Longing of the Day

written. He, who loved Eve enough to give her up for the sake of her own happiness, understood only too well the pain and courage of Anne's freeing him so he might follow his own heart. So she had known, in spite of all his care, how he felt about Eve.

But for that, somehow, he felt only relief. How he had hated deceiving her. It was so like her to tell him about the watch, to give him all the facts upon which to base a decision, and yet offer no judgment of him, only assure him of her love no matter what.

Ben had been dying. All that time, and he, Matt, hadn't known. And if he had? It was useless to ask himself what he would have done. Now Ben was dead, and Anne was dead, and there was no reason to any of it.

He drew a shuddering breath, staring out over the suddenly blurred landscape.

"Matt."

He started and turned. Eve stood a little way off, concern for him overshadowing the grief that had become a part of her these last days. "I don't want to pry, but if I can help ..."

He shook his head, unable to speak over the lump in his throat.

She watched him for a long moment before she turned silently away.

"Eve, wait!" He leaped after her and caught her hand. "I can't talk 'bout it now, but maybe someday." He was pleading with her to understand. "But I do want you to know that you do help, just by bein' here."

She looked deep into his eyes, seeing all his grieving bewilderment. For her, he had always been so steadfast, so dependable, giving her strength and courage so many times when she was unable to find them anyplace else. Now, at last, it was her turn to give back to him.

She opened her arms and reached out to him. "I'm here, Matt," she said softly.

He drew her into his arms and held her close even as she held him. It was a moment too deep for passion as they stood, swaying a little, clinging to each other while her strength flowed into him, renewed him and gave him the courage to go on, to face whatever would come in spite of all that had happened.

With friends and neighbors helping, they worked two more long days repairing and restoring the house and its furnishings to a semblance of the old order. Many willing pairs of hands helped lighten the burden, accomplishing much when there was such an unbelievable amount to be done. By throwing himself into the heartbreaking job, Matt vented some of his grief, anger and frustration.

Dan worked faithfully beside him, saying little except when someone spoke directly to him. Matt knew Dan blamed himself for their delay in reaching the ranch that night, but once past that initial need-to-blame-someone flame of anger Matt had experienced, he held no resentment against Dan and told him so.

Dear Lord, how could he blame his friend when the accountability was his own? When it came to assigning fault, he himself would have to stand in the front rank.

The Longing of the Day

He had little opportunity to be alone with Eve after those first days. She stayed with Jason and Becky while he and Dan moved back to the ranch so it wouldn't sit unoccupied, temptation to any casual passerby.

She came with Becky and Jason whenever they rode over to help with more repairs. The task had stretched out because the damage was so extensive. Aaron and Catty put in many hours, taking turns with the others, but Luke was too busy to help much.

The few moments Matt and Eve had together were to him like the warmth of sunshine in the midst of bitter cold. Yet he felt deep unease. How could he be worthy of her presence, of the sweet light of trust that lay so plainly on her when she was with him, when his soul was so burdened with guilt?

On Friday afternoon they worked in the kitchen. The men were replacing the window over the sink, and Becky and Eve were straightening out the cupboards and taking inventory of the few remaining items, both edible and china. Not only had the raiders had a merry time making destruction, they had also casually carted off whatever had taken their fancy, and they must have considered the supply of foodstuffs a wild delight.

At the sudden drum of hoofbeats, Eve let out a cry and dropped the tin she held. As Becky reached out in questioning alarm, Matt crossed the floor in three long strides to put his arm protectively around her. She was as white as the baking powder she had just spilled and trembling violently.

"Hello the house — it's Abe Coleman!"

"The marshal." Jason hurried out. Relief flooded Eve's face, and she turned scarlet with embarrassment as he and

346

Abe came in.

Coleman took off his hat and courteously greeted Becky and Eve. "Jason, Matt, I'd like to talk to you."

"Have you found out something?" At the shuttered look on his face, Becky's chin came up. "Eve and I are part of this family, too. We have a right to know whatever it is."

The marshal let out his breath. "It's not pretty. You already know your Pa didn't withdraw any big amount from the bank, just what he needed f'r expenses."

Without waiting for an answer, he plunged on. "I've been investigatin' all this time and just now got back. I've talked to a lot of people, includin' a feller who ranches up on the Sweetwater. This man'd been in Laramie on business a few weeks back and stopped at a saloon f'r a quick drink. The feller next to him at the bar was pretty well loaded and was goin' on 'bout his troubles to the barkeep.

"The rancher didn't pay much attention at first until the bartender moved away and this guy started tellin' him all 'bout it. Somethin' 'bout him and his Pa bein' partners on the ranch and how they'd been makin' it through the winter just fine, until that last big storm. Then they'd lost a good portion of their herd, just like ever'one else.

"Now they wanted to buy more cows, but those f'r sale were sky-high f'r quality ones. Reasonable priced ones looked ready to keel over if you spit on 'em too hard. It was frustratin', he griped, to have the money and not be able to get decent cows f'r a decent price.

"The rancher says he made some comment 'bout it bein' such a bad winter, he was surprised anyone had any money.

"The feller bragged how he and his Pa had more money

The Longing of the Day

at home right then than most people had in the bank at any time. They were keepin' it there in case the banks went under; they sure didn't want to lose it all f'r nothin'. If they could just find someone with some quality cows willin' to throw in with them ..."

"Who was the fellow?" Jason cut in. "Did the rancher say?"

"He didn't get his name, didn't think that much 'bout it. Said he seemed like kind of a loser. He did wonder what kind of man would take him on as a partner even if he was his son."

"What's so important 'bout all this? Why're you tellin' us?" Matt broke in impatiently.

The sheriff surveyed his five tense listeners. At his wary expression, Becky took Jason's arm and Matt moved to stand close behind Eve, his hand on her shoulder. Dan stood alone, arms crossed against his chest.

Abe spoke slowly, reluctantly. "Besides havin' kind of a hang-dog look, he said the feller was fairly tall and had a carroty colored beard and curly red hair."

His last words fell into a deep pool of quiet as his listeners stared in shocked disbelief.

"Luke?" Jason's voice exploded the silence.

"But why?" Becky burst out. "What reason could he possibly have?"

"That's just what I'm goin' to find out." Jason was livid with fury. "Come on, Matt."

"Jason, it might be a mistake," Abe warned.

"I don't think so, and you don't neither or else you wouldn't have told us."

"I'll have to go 'long with you."

"That's up to you, but we're wastin' time. You comin', Matt?"

"Dan?" Matt spoke to his friend, but his worried eyes were on Eve.

"Sure, Matt, I'll stay here. You go along."

Becky and Eve followed them to the door, watching in tense silence as they mounted and thundered off. Only then did they reach out to each other in mutual anguish.

Nearly three hours passed before Matt and Jason returned. When they heard the horses, Becky and Eve hurried out to the yard, but seeing the faces of the two men, all their anxious questions died unborn. Dan came out onto the porch, but he, too, said nothing.

As Jason slumped wearily into a chair, his face looked older than its 34 years. "He denied ever'thin'. Ever'thin'. God, I wanted to pound his smirkin' face to a bloody pulp."

"But maybe he really had nothing to do with it," Becky said hopefully.

"That's just it! You could tell by lookin' at him he was lyin'. But he denied it flat out. Even Abe said he could tell."

"But why would he do it? Why?"

How could anyone answer Becky when they were all asking themselves the same question?

"You know how he always talks so big when he's sober. The less he has to brag 'bout, the more talkin' he does. If he was drunk enough, he'd say anythin'," Matt pointed out in furious disgust.

"What about him and Pa being partners? What could he have meant?" Eve was bewildered.

The Longing of the Day

"I guess he felt entitled after we started workin' all the ranches together. It must've made him feel important, like maybe some of Pa's ability would rub off on him." Jason jerked his hand through his dark hair in pent-up frustration.

"What'll happen now?"

Matt's hand tightened on Eve's shoulder. "Nothin'," he said grimly. "Absolutely nothin'. He denies it all, but even if he admitted it, what good would it do? You can't hang a man f'r talkin'. If a fellow from clear up on the Sweetwater could hear such a tale, who knows how many others heard it — or versions of it? It could of traveled all over the territory."

"But to say Pa had a lot of money at home? How could he do such a thing?" Eve asked incredulously.

"To Luke, a little money's a lot, and if he was goin' to tell a story he might as well make it a good one." Jason spoke bitterly. "Ma and Pa paid f'r that one, all right. We all have. And there's not a thing we c'n do 'bout it, not a damned thing ..."

The shadow of gloom and despair hovered low over the family during the next days as Luke continued to vehemently deny ever having spread such a story. Aaron and Catty, shocked at the news, were as much at a loss as the others to understand.

Quiet Aaron voiced all their feelings with remarkable accuracy. As he put it, "I'd like to skin him alive. But it wouldn't do no good. Even his hide's worthless."

On a late afternoon when nearly everything that could be repaired had finally been tended to, Matt wandered out to the corrals to check on Tumbleweed, recovering without apparent harm from the hard ride. While Matt fed him a carrot, Eve appeared to stand silently beside him.

Heart-tearing grief still marked her. Her face was shadowed and her eyes mirrored soul-deep sorrow. But the difference in her was more than that. Some light of youth, of innocent happiness had been snuffed out that night as surely, as heedlessly, as a candle flame pinched by a careless hand.

He knew without words she wasn't sleeping any better at night than he was. How could he find rest when his dreams were made up of horror scenes forever branded on his soul?

Bad as it was for him, how much worse it must be for her. Yet he could not speak of this to her. He was learning that some paths must be walked alone, that no matter how much one person may love another, to enter certain areas of that loved one's heart, no matter how softly it be done, is an intrusion.

So, over the quick rush of gladness at her presence that could not be denied, he greeted her quietly.

"He's really getting his strength back, isn't he?" she asked, stroking Tumbleweed's muzzle.

"He seems to be doin' fine. I want to give him a couple more days rest before I ride him, though."

"I'm glad he's all right," she said softly. He knew she was thinking of Thistle, but there was nothing he could say that would help.

Both were silent for several seconds before she spoke. "Matt, I ... I'd like to talk to you."

The Longing of the Day

He glanced quickly at her and as swiftly away.

"Matt, what's wrong? Between us, I mean?" She put her hand on his arm, and looked up at him pleadingly. "It's like there's a high fence between us, and I don't understand it at all. It's never been like this before."

He looked down at her hand resting so trustingly on his arm. No, it had never been like this between them before. But how could he explain the deep turmoil within him? He started to speak, and looked away in confusion to the far sweep of plains, so peaceful in the late afternoon sunshine. And he knew he had to talk to her, that if anyone could understand, she would.

Putting his hand over hers, he drew her over to the seat under the trees where they previously talked. She sat, but he remained standing until she moved her skirt aside. "There's lots of room for you, too."

He dropped down beside her and put his head in his hands. "Eve, I'm so sorry." The words came out in a bitter rush.

"What do you mean?" she asked, bewildered. He was so lost, so defeated.

"I turned Pa against me. I hurt Ma and you. Now they're dead, and you almost died. My God, if you had ..." His fists knotted in unspeakable anguish. "If I'd been here that night maybe I could have helped. Maybe they'd still be alive. I have to live the rest of my life knowin' that, knowin' they needed me and I wasn't here. After all they'd done f'r me. I don't know how you'll ever be able to forgive me. I know I can't forgive myself."

Her chin lifted indignantly. "How can you say that? You did the best you could. No one could ask more. You have no right to sit in judgment on yourself or to decide how other people should judge you," she said so fiercely that he stared at her. "That's up to God, not you. I don't know why it happened any more than you do. Or why I was allowed to live. But if God wants us to know, He'll tell us. Remember? You've said that so many times. I believe it with all my heart. Besides, have you stopped to think? If you'd been here, I might have lost you, too." Her voice broke.

He raised his head and saw her grief even as the shock of her words jolted him. "I never thought of that. I just felt so wrong 'bout ever'thin'. I never should of gone away like I did."

"Was it because of me you went away?" Her hands gripped each other tightly in her lap.

He nodded wordlessly.

Her cheeks flamed. "I didn't know at first, and then I thought ..." She bit her lip. "Matt, I'd like to explain to you about Will and me."

"Eve, you don't have to explain anythin' to me," he said wearily.

"But I want you to understand how it was." She drew a deep breath. "When you left last fall, when you kissed me before you left, I was shocked." Her hands tightened on each other. "I'd never thought of us that way before. Maybe it seems impossible, but it's true. The way we were raised, the way Ma and Pa treated you — you were my brother. But when you left, you didn't leave much doubt about how you felt." She smiled wryly as he turned red.

"After you left, I was confused and lonely." He started to speak, but she hurried on. "I wasn't used to being without

The Longing of the Day

you. Not like that. Everything was just so empty. I liked Will so much. I always have." She looked out, away across the plains. "I thought what I felt for him must be love. It certainly wasn't the same as what I felt for you — my brother. But I honestly thought it would be all right. I never wanted to hurt Will." Her eyes were back on his, pleading with him to understand.

"When you came back at Christmas, it was as if all the joy and happiness in the world had come back with you. You didn't say much, but you were just you, and that was enough. And when you gave me the locket — oh, Matt, I've treasured it so. It kept you near me all those days when you were so far away. But that morning when you left, I didn't know what ..."

He touched her cheek with gentle fingers. "I made you cry," he said softly. "I hurt you, and I've been so sorry. I didn't mean to. The last thing in the world I would ever want to do is hurt you."

She caught his hand to her cheek. "My dearest, you could never hurt me. It was just that everything was so right and so good, and then I realized it would never be that way again. You were going away, and I knew this time you weren't coming back. It just kind of came over me all at one time. When you hurried away, I called you, but you didn't hear me."

He remembered that moment when he had heard her call his name. If he had turned back then ...

She went on, "All winter I tried to tell myself it would be all right once Will and I married. I tried so hard to believe it. But just before the wedding, I knew I couldn't do it. It wouldn't have been fair to Will.

"But it was more than that. I finally admitted what I'd been denying all those months. I knew I'd rather live unmarried all my life if I couldn't be married to you." Her cheeks were flaming, but her eyes held a look of pleading honesty.

"Why didn't you let me know?" His throat was so tight it hurt to form the words.

"I wrote you. The letter came back. Someone had written on the envelope 'Not here. Return to Sender.' "

He stared at her in dazed dismay as his mind flashed back to the moment when he had told Bardlow he would see the country. He could almost hear the god of chance's mocking laughter.

"Matt?" she asked worriedly.

"I'd have come. You know I would have."

"I knew. I prayed so hard that night that you would come."

The pull of the heart. From his earliest days with the Clayton family, prayer had been offered not as a dreary duty, but as a joyful giving of self to God. As Matt grew older and began, through his work, to live closer to the earth, he also learned to find his God in the ways of nature: wind rippling the spring grass, an eagle soaring high, a she-critter nuzzling her new-dropped calf. God and nature.

The two ideals gradually became so closely joined in his heart that he couldn't have told where either began or ended. As with nature, one did not demand of God, nor wrest from Him. He took and gave at His choosing. But this pull of the heart and of the soul, the bond forged between them in earliest childhood, strengthened by love and faith through the passing years, reached across all the intervening

The Longing of the Day

miles that night, uniting them even in separation.

Wordlessly, he drew her into his arms to hold her close against his chest. "My Eve," he said finally, softly, "my sweet Eve. I love you so much. I've wanted to say those words to you for so long." His voice was suddenly husky as quick joy rushed through him, overwhelming him. "I love you."

He tipped his head down to hers and was caught totally off guard when, instead of meeting his kiss, she swiftly buried her face against his shoulder. "Eve, what's wrong?" A mute shake of her head into his shirt front was his only answer.

Fear jolted through him. He tried to tip her face up to him, but she resisted. "Eve, what is it?" He couldn't keep the panic out of his voice.

"Matt, I'm so afraid." He could barely hear her muffled response.

"Afraid? Of me?" he asked, bewildered.

Her head came up quickly enough at that. "Not of you, Matt. Never of you. But ..." She started to duck her face again, but he slipped his hand under her chin so that she had to look at him.

"But what? Eve, tell me."

"It's just that the two times you've kissed me, right afterward you rushed off like your shirt was on fire. And you stayed away for so long. I don't want that to happen again, and I'm so afraid that it will if I kiss you."

He stared at her, the corners of his mouth bending in the beginnings of a grin, and raised his right hand. "My Eve, I solemnly promise you that won't ever happen again. But ..." and he cupped her face with his hands, all the laughter abruptly gone from his eyes, "... you have to promise me somethin', too."

She searched his face, her own eyes wide and serious. "What?"

"That if I kiss you, you won't cry."

Now her mouth quirked upward. "I promise, with all my heart." Her lips came to his in a soft rush.

He was unprepared for the swiftness of her response, but recovered himself admirably. Finally, reluctantly, he raised his mouth from hers. His gray eyes glowing, he studied her as carefully as she was inspecting him.

She wasn't crying.

He hadn't vanished.

So they kissed again.

Back at the house, Eve hesitated as Matt reached to open the door. "I have a feeling this is going to shock them."

"Prob'ly. But they'll get over it."

Illogically reassured by this complacent reasoning, she let him draw her inside. Jason sat at the kitchen table, going over the books. Becky was folding the clothes they had washed for Dan and Matt that morning.

Eve went over to help her as Jason motioned to Matt. "I want to show you somethin'."

He walked over, but as Jason turned the book so he could see it, Matt shook his head. "I want to talk to you."

Jason frowned. "Now? I'm right in the middle of ..."

"It's important, Jason."

The Longing of the Day

At the sober note in his voice, Jason pushed his books aside resignedly. "What is it?"

"Let's go outside."

Away from the house, Jason faced him. "All right. What's so important?"

"Eve and me are goin' to be married. We'd like to know we have your blessin'."

Jason's jaw dropped. "Married!"

"We love each other. I'll take good care of her. You need have no doubts 'bout that."

Jason closed his mouth enough to sputter, "But you and she ... I never thought ..."

"Why not? If my folks had lived it would of been the most natural thing in the world f'r us to want to marry. Why isn't it right just because the same parents brought both of us up?"

Jason still looked bewildered. "But ..."

"There's no blood tie, no legal reason we shouldn't marry."

Jason finally managed to collect himself. "Wait a minute. Hold on. You caught me clean off guard."

Matt waited.

"It sounds like you intend to get married whether anyone else approves or not."

"Well ..." Matt started to speak.

"No, let me finish. There always was somethin' special between you two. Anyone could see that, even when you was little. But marriage ... did Ma and Pa know?"

Matt forced himself to speak steadily. "Ma did. I didn't know until that last letter. I never talked to them 'bout it. I just left when it all seemed so hopeless. Ma didn't say one way or the other, just that it was a choice I was goin' to have to make on my own. But I have to tell you." He drew himself up straight.

"I haven't asked Eve to marry me just because they're gone and can't do anythin' 'bout it. Even if they were still here, now I know she loves me, we'd still be doin' this. Do you understand?"

"You have to admit," Jason said dryly, "you've thrown me a mighty quick loop. I sure haven't had much chance to chew on all this.

"I know, I know ..." Jason thrust out his hands as if to forestall Matt's protest.

"My opinion don't matter. You made that clear. But the fact is, you did ask me, so I'm goin' to tell you." He rubbed his jaw, searching for words. "The way I see it, Ma and Pa — Ma, anyway — would of understood. All she ever wanted was what was best f'r us. Pa wanted that, too, in his own way." He paused, said slowly, "Hell, she's my little sister, Matt. I know you'll take good care of her."

Matt blinked, belatedly realizing Jason gave his approval. He put his hand out solemnly. "I will. I'll care f'r her always."

"What are your plans? The ranch belongs to you and Eve now, you know."

"It belongs to Eve," Matt said slowly. "It never really was mine, not fairly, anyway. But after all that's happened, she may not want to live here. I wouldn't blame her. So it'll be whatever she decides."

They found Becky and Eve in the kitchen, fixing supper. Eve looked up from slicing a loaf of bread, and he saw the anxious questioning in her eyes. He smiled and held out his

The Longing of the Day

hands. She gave a glad cry and ran to him. He put his arm around her, drawing her close to his side.

Becky, hands on hips, surveyed them as they stood beaming at each other. "Well, anyone could see you two were made for each other. It's about time you finally did something about it!"

Eve woke on an August morning three weeks later and lay quietly, trying to sort out the emotions surging through her. The unceasing ache in her heart for her parents. The futile wish that Ma could be with her today of all days. Awareness that Matt waited for her. Full realization that today was their wedding day.

Becky, Hannah and Catty had protested at first. Such a short space of time between the announcement and the marriage itself simply wasn't done, they said. A proper wedding took time to prepare. Matt hesitated at that. If it was important to Eve ...

She smiled a little now, remembering their reaction when she faced them staunchly. No, she had said. They had waited so long already. Besides, under the circumstances, they just wanted a quiet, simple ceremony, which wouldn't take a lot of planning. They blinked at her in astonishment. How the meek little kitten had learned how to hiss! She had come a long way from that grief-numbed young woman who had fled into the darkness on a night of pain too great to be borne.

The Longing of the Day

Becky shook her head at Eve's innocent reasoning that a simple ceremony would take hardly any planning, but made no further protest.

Matt and Eve married standing before the stone fireplace at the ranch.

Only the family and their closest friends attended the ceremony, for Matt and Eve clung firmly to their decision that, out of respect for Anne and Ben, they would be married with no fuss and no party afterward.

Will, white-faced and silent, stood back in a corner. He simply stood back and watched in silence.

Hannah, even more pale than Will, came with her four little boys. Luke was conspicuously absent. When Hannah woke that morning, she had found his note:

> *Dear Hannah,*
>
> *I've left to find the men responsible for the raid on the ranch. I admit I talked in town that day, but I hadn't meant no harm. I just hoped that by spreadin' the word the Arrow A wasn't broke like every other place else, I'd find somebody interested in helpin' Pa build up the ranch like he'd always dreamed about.*
>
> *I know you never really thought I was much of a man, but when I return with the guilty men, maybe you'll see how unfair you've been all this time and think a little more kindly of me.*
>
> *Luke*

The last of the sparkle in Hannah's green eyes was quenched by humiliation for all the heartache he had heaped so carelessly on all of them. In her shame she, too, stood in the background and uttered no word to anyone.

Eve wore her green Christmas dress with the tiny flowers embroidered on it. Matt's locket was around her throat, and she wore a crown of creamy roses in her shining hair. She had picked the rosebuds at dawn from the bushes Anne had planted around baby Elizabeth's grave.

Becky and Jason stood with them, and Dan escorted Eve to place her hand in Matt's. Eve had asked him, not out of disrespect for her own father, but because in her new-found loneliness, a loneliness not even all Matt's deep love could comfort, Eve had glimpsed a similar ache in Dan. Her woman's heart quickly saw that beneath all his roughness and gruff ways he cared deeply about Matt and her.

She accepted him at first because he was Matt's friend and, in her first grieving days, she was too bewildered to question his presence. But as his gentle concern and caring seeped into the cold loneliness of her heart and warmed it, she understood he was her friend, too.

When she asked him, his eyes grew suspiciously moist. Turning aside, he muttered something about a pesky cold. Now, clean-shaven, hair neatly trimmed, and wearing a new suit — the first one he'd owned in 30 years — he presented Eve to Matt, feeling as if he was taking part in the marriage of his own beloved children.

If any protests lingered over the suddenness or the suitability of the marriage, Eve and Matt were oblivious to them, for in spite of the shadows around them, their love would no longer be denied. As Eve said, the new Eve who learned in the harshest of all schools to value what was important, their

The Longing of the Day

friends would understand and the others didn't matter. *One in mind, one in heart, and one in affection ...*

The little group ate the simple wedding breakfast that was as much of a party as Becky could get Matt and Eve to agree to. Shortly afterward, everyone departed.

Will, white to the lips, took Eve's hand in his, bent and kissed her cheek. Turning to Matt, he said in a low, fierce voice, "You just be damned sure you take good care of her." Then he turned and strode out.

Dan kissed Eve with gentle affection. His eyes were bright as he shook Matt's hand. "You have a real treasure, my friend. The best of ever'thin' to you, always."

Hand in hand, Matt and Eve watched their guests depart. They walked slowly back to the house, deeply aware of the beauty of the day and their own special part in it.

At the front door he paused, turning solemnly to her. "Welcome home, my Eve." He lifted her into his arms. He carried her across the threshold into the sitting room and kissed her long and ardently. Memory of those two earlier kisses, and even more, memory of those dreams when he had kissed her and she had vanished from his embrace, made his arms tighten around her.

He opened his eyes, assuring himself she was truly still there. In sheer exuberance of spirits, he began to twirl her 'round and 'round the room in his arms, until they were laughing breathlessly. Finally he collapsed into a chair and pulled her on his lap.

She nestled her head against his shoulder, reaching her fingers to touch the soft strings of his tie. "Matt."

"Hmmm?" he murmured against her hair.

"I've got something I've been wanting to tell you."

"But you were afraid to 'til we were married?"

"Well, you are stuck with me, now, no matter what, right?"

"I reckon I am at that. Reverend Wardley sealed it up pretty tight, I'd say."

Her fingers continued to smooth his tie. "Remember when you kissed me last fall, before you left?" She felt his sudden intake of breath.

"I remember."

"I told you I was shocked, that I'd never thought of us that way before. That part was true." He became totally still, his breath scarcely stirring against her hair. She swallowed. "It was supposed to be wrong. You, my brother, shouldn't do something like that. I shouldn't let you. Ma and Pa — I knew what Pa would say. The whole idea was so unbelievable, so totally impossible. I hadn't lived with it like you had. And you were going away. It seemed the best way all around, just to let you go like you'd already decided.

"After you left and I went over and over it, it still seemed best. Will was here ..." She felt a tremor in the arms still holding her tightly. "I thought I was in love with him. How could I not be when he's so much like you? But it was never even close to the same." Her voice trailed away.

Silence above her head, his heart beating under her ear.

"I thought you hated me f'r what I did to you," he said softly.

She shook her head and her fingers gripped his tie. "The second time, at Christmas when I fixed breakfast for you, I *wanted* you to kiss me again, whether it was wrong or not."

Only then, and very slowly, he moved her away from

The Longing of the Day

his chest so he could look directly into her eyes. "And you liked it?"

She nodded, her cheeks crimson.

"Both times?"

Again her agreement.

The grin began in his eyes, rapidly working its way to his mouth. "Any time you want to make a confession like that, my shoulder, my lap — and my tie ..." he gently unclenched her fingers from the crumpled strings, "... are available. No appointment necessary."

"Matt, I'm being serious."

"So am I." His mouth against hers effectively stilled any further protest. "And just to show how understandin' I am, there's somethin' I'd like to ask you to do with me."

Her eyes glowing, she turned her head toward the closed bedroom door. "Now?" she asked with wide-eyed innocence.

"Coppertop, you shock me!"

"I imagine I'm going to shock you quite a bit in the very near future," she said demurely, "but I wasn't expecting to until tonight."

"Such talk, Mrs. Jamison! What am I goin' to do with you?"

"Are you asking for suggestions?"

"No," he said hastily. "I rather do have a few ideas of my own. And I think I better get you out of here before you lead me astray. As I was goin' to suggest, we are goin' f'r a buggy ride. Now," he added sternly as he felt laughter bubble up within her.

Louise Lenahan Wallace

Buggy top up, they rode through the yellow-green countryside, the beauty of the earth intensified. Never had the sky been so blue, the trees so green, the flowers so fragrant. They stopped beside a rippling little creek, and Matt lifted her down, holding her close for a moment before, hand in hand, they strolled down to the water's edge. She challenged him to a rock-skipping contest, but he promptly shook his head, telling her with lofty dignity that married men with family responsibilities didn't engage in such pursuits. Besides, he was smart enough to know when he was whipped before he started. If a little frail thing like her beat big strong him, whatever would folks say? After all, they had to be careful of gossip like that. Because they were young, and very much in love, and this was their wedding day, they laughed themselves breathless.

Eventually wandering over to a huge cottonwood, they settled beneath it in leaf-and-shadow dappled coolness, just enjoying the peace of being alone together and married. He reached for her hand, the one with the slender gold band circling her finger. He didn't say anything in words, but he didn't have to. As he put her hand gently back in her lap and stood, she looked up questioningly and saw his eyes were twinkling. "Close your eyes," he commanded. She looked puzzled. "Come on, close your eyes."

"Why?"

"Never mind, Eve Jamison," he said authoritatively. "Remember, you promised just this mornin' to obey me in all things. Am I goin' to start havin' trouble with you already?"

"No, my dearest," she said with becoming wifely meekness, but promptly spoiled it by laughing delightedly. "I

The Longing of the Day

surely do like my new name."

"So do I."

Making sure she wasn't peeking, he moved swiftly and in just a few minutes bade her open her eyes.

She caught her breath in pleasure. "A picnic! How wonderful. I hardly ate anything this morning," she confessed, "and I'm starved. But how did you ... ?"

He grinned. "I had a slight problem myself this mornin' with eatin'. Becky helped a little, fryin' the chicken and stuff," he admitted, "but it was my idea."

He knelt beside her, taking her hands. "I'm sorry we can't afford a real weddin' trip. Maybe someday we'll be able to go ..."

She put her fingers gently over his lips. "This means more to me than any other trip possibly could. Besides, a wedding journey isn't important to me. Being with you is all that matters."

"You aren't afraid?"

She shook her head. "Remember when we were talking once and I said I'd be scared to get married?"

He remembered very well.

"You said I wouldn't be afraid if it was the right man to love and care about me as much as I did him. And my dearest," she laid her head against his chest in a glad little rush, "you are so right."

It was late afternoon before they started home, and the sun was setting as they reached the house.

They had carefully discussed whether they should live at the ranch. It was Eve who finally said she thought Ma and Pa would want them to. They had been happy there during the years of their own marriage, and somehow she felt they would have wanted Matt and Eve to live there and continue that happiness.

"Will you be able to be happy there, Eve?" he had asked, concerned, knowing she was haunted, even as he was, by the family tragedy.

She had gazed past his shoulder at a picture he could not see. "The past is going to be with us," she whispered, her voice trailing into a silence so long a horseshoe-heavy lump of fear settled in the pit of his stomach.

"Eve ..."

Even as he spoke, she raised her eyes to meet his directly. "Wherever we go, whatever we do, we can never erase it from our lives. But as long as you are with me, I can be happy."

"You're sure?" he asked gently.

"I'm sure."

That settled it once and for all.

In the deepening dusk they returned to their home. Matt pulled the buggy to a halt near the back door and turned to Eve. But his light words of welcome were never spoken for he saw her eyes were dark with grief. His own pain-filled glance followed hers around the too-quiet ranch yard.

"It seems to hurt even more at this hour of the day." Her voice broke.

"I know," he managed over the lump in his throat. "Seems like Pa should be comin' from the corrals, and Ma should be hurryin' down the steps, all smiles, so happy because he's home."

" 'Abide with Me: fast falls the eventide.' Will we ever be done missing them?"

The Longing of the Day

He shook his head, unable to speak as his throat closed completely. Only with great effort, he said huskily, "Pa said once that when he and Ma built this place, they had a dream of makin' it the finest cattle ranch in Wyomin'. Said they'd done the best they could with what they had and that one day it'd be up to us younger ones to carry on that dream. Seems like he knew even then.

"But I just didn't understand. Now I think maybe he was sayin' that as long as we keep their dream alive, they'll live, too." His voice trailed off and his vision blurred for a moment so that he was awkward stepping from the buggy.

"We have to do the best we can, don't we?" she said softly. "Just like they did. For them and for us."

As he reached to lift her down, he saw some of her deep hurt had eased. He held her close for a long moment. " 'Abide with me,' my Eve."

Hand in hand, they turned up the steps to the kitchen.

Epilogue
1946

Matt Jamison carefully latched the gate of the white picket
fence. Gnarled hands gripping his cane, he stood a long
moment and gazed down at Eve's grave. With some difficulty, he knelt and placed a single spray of flowers beside
the white cross. Lilacs — how she had loved them! And how
she would have delighted in a day such as this with the wind
blowing over the newly green grasses, bringing the scent of
a thousand springtime fragrances, blending them into the
sweetest perfume of all.

He probably should be getting on down the hill.
According to his pocket watch he had been gone most of an
hour and they would be wondering, back at the house, where
he was. They fretted about him so! He knew he should be
grateful, but sometimes ...

His glance fell once more upon the watch hands that had
calmly ticked away the seconds and minutes of his lifetime.
The night before he and Eve were married, he had offered
the watch to Catty, knowing she had as much a right to it
as him.

She had taken it carefully from him, turning it over

wonderingly. *"Amanda and Stephen.* It's such a strange feeling, knowing that this is probably one of the few things left on the earth, besides you and me, that they touched."

She had put the watch gently back into his hand. "No, Matt. You keep it. Ma and Pa — that's just who they were, Ma and Pa. I've never known or needed anything else. But with you, it's different. You remember bits and pieces of what happened. All I know about that night is that if it weren't for you, I wouldn't be here now." She had blinked back the sudden tears and curled his fingers around the watch so it lay protected in his palm. "As long as I know it's safe with you, I'll be content."

Now, six decades later, he peered at the hands of the watch that had, like himself, survived the years. A little battered and worn, but still ticking.

Lingering under the cottonwood that shaded Eve's grave, his thoughts touched on the 52 years of married life that had been theirs. They had been good years, for the most part.

They had prospered, and Ben and Anne's dream had come true.

Children had come along, bringing with them the wondrous joys and the deep responsibilities of parenthood. The terrible, aching sorrow that comes with the loss of a child had been theirs, too.

Even the deepest faith can shudder under one too many such blows. How well he understood, now it was too late, that only a strong soul can emerge unscarred from such anguish, be strengthened, not defeated by it. But where did such a philosophy fit in with the thinking he had witnessed all his life? Who had had the right way of it all those years and who the wrong? Ben — with his dogged determination that he knew best? Anne — so deeply certain that sorrow, as well as joy, was a gift from God, and given out of love, not vengeance? Eve — trusting everything would work out all right because whatever happened, God willed it so? Dan — grateful for happiness given even in the midst of pain? Was there a right or a wrong? They had all been working toward the same goal the best way they could.

And what about himself? Where did he really fit in? So much of his life had been molded out of tragedy. Why had events worked out the way they did?

Why did his birth parents have to die so horribly? And why Ben and Anne so senselessly when he, by unwitting choice, was not there to help them? Why had Dan's Bethany and her child been taken, for that matter? Lives young, innocent, vital — snuffed out before they could be said to be fully completed. So much suffering.

Was it all part of a greater plan that their eyes had not been meant to see, a testing of the strength of their trust in Him, their acceptance of His will? Matt supposed that summed up his own feelings, as well as they could be put into words. Of one thing he was certain. After 80 years of wondering, he was finally going to be given some answers. Soon now, probably.

Did he fear death? Why should he? After all, it would only be a completion of the cycle begun by his parents at his conception. How could he fear death when the culmination would result in once again being with those who had been — and given him — life itself?

Eve had not been afraid.

The Longing of the Day

She had been ill. Her heart, the doctor said after all his new-fangled tests and fussing, was simply worn out. She had died in her sleep with no fretting, no final farewell, only her lips curving a little at the last. But what had pleased or amused her, they did not know.

Seven Octobers ago now ...

Matt fumbled in his pocket, drew out Eve's locket. The gleaming bit of gold seemed lost in his wrinkled old palm. He pressed the catch and the halves parted. The paper, so crisp and clean and new when he had painstakingly cut it to the shape of the locket, was brown and delicate from time that had passed. The letters, so bold and black when he had penned them, were faded from years that had spun away.

EC

1886

MJ

That time — where had it gone? Those years — into what shadowed vastness had they slipped?

He knew he really ought to be getting back. They'd be worried, his being gone so long. But he was so tired, and it was so pleasant on the slope. Only here did he ever really feel complete anymore. Here ... under the tree ... in the shade ... beside Eve ...

He dozed. And dozing, dreamed.

Scraps of time before remembrance, and pieces that were memory wove themselves in and out, forming a whole — yet not. He, so young, strong and unaware, riding across the sun-drenched, springtime-green plains into all the tomorrows that were so swiftly to become all the yesterdays. A terrified 3-year-old, huddled in a patch of weeds, not understanding why he had been abandoned. Ben striding to the house from the corrals, and Anne, with outstretched arms, flying to meet him. Two dark-haired little boys and one flame-haired little girl playing in a creek on a hot summer day, their laughter echoing across all the years. A young woman with wheat-colored hair, laughing up at a man with eyes the same camp-fire-smoke gray as Matt's so that after 80 years he could say to his parents, wonderingly, *This is how you looked*. Bowlegged, stoop-shouldered Dan hunkered beside him, their backs to a corral gate on a moonlit night in the springtime, when past and present had collided and there had been no future.

The people were so real in those dream-moments that Matt felt a rush of gladness and a strange urgency. Where ... ?

"Matt?"

Hearing Eve call him, forgetting for the moment that she could never do so again, he jerked his head up. And, still caught in the fragments of his dream, blinked because she was coming toward him. At first, he thought her dress was green, patterned with tiny flowers, but saw immediately it was only sunlight flickering through the cottonwood leaves.

"Matt." She was laughing, calling to him in the old way. "It's time to come home now."

He tried to speak, to tell her of the rush of gladness he felt at her presence. But all his young awkwardness at expressing his deepest emotions closed his throat. Mutely, he looked up into her beloved face as she stopped a little way off, reaching her hands to him.

From the long-gone past, a fragment of time quivered,

The Longing of the Day

hung illumined. Azure skies and cotton clouds. Deep green Douglas fir and red-brown, drought-battered earth.

He was striding toward her after that wretched summer spent at Wildcat Creek. And he was young and strong, with 60 years of his life not yet lived. He took off his hat, revealing the pale stripe on his forehead in sharp contrast to the rest of his dark-tanned face, the stripe that every year amused her at first glance.

But this time he beat her to it. He grinned. "Hello, Coppertop."

"Matt." All the joy of the world was held in that moment.

Sun-glints were kindling flame deep within the copper-bronze braids wound around her head, were suffusing her face, her entire figure, in shimmering radiance.

This time ... This time he stretched out his hands to her waiting ones.

The watch he had been clutching slipped, unheeded, from his fingers and fell with a soft *thunk* to the grass beside Eve's grave. It ticked once.

And was silent.

About the Author

Biography

In her hometown of Port Angeles, Wash., Louise Lenahan Wallace edits *Footnotes*, her state square dance magazine. Her other publishing credits include two stories in GRIT, *Eight Letters* (July 14, 1996) and *The Ten-Cent Christmas* (Dec. 26, 1999); and one in *Chicken Soup for the Single's Soul*. Louise earned a bachelor's degree from Western Washington University in 1992.

Louise Lenahan Wallace

The Longing of the Day received a fourth place award in the Pacific Northwest Writers Competition in 1994.

Watch for *The Longing of the Day*'s sequel, *Until the Day Break*, to be published in GRIT's Fireside Library January 2001.

Publishers acknowledgment

Published by Ogden Publications
1503 SW 42nd St., Topeka, Kansas 66609

Edited by Angela Moerlien, lead editor, and Andrew Perkins, associate editor. Cover design by Carolyn Lang

Photography by Miller's Photography, Colby, Kan., and Angela Moerlien. Cover photo from *GRIT* Photo Library

Publishing Credits:

Songs from *Christmas Carols* © 1969, 1942 by Western Publishing Company, Inc. Used with permission.

Lines from *Longing* by Matthew Arnold, public domain, Doubleday.

"Bury Me Not on the Lone Prairie," "I Ride an Old Paint" and "Little Joe, the Wrangler" appear in *Songs of the Great American West*, compiled by Irwin Silber (New York: Macmillan, 1967).

Lines from "Lord Lovel," "Mollie Bond" and "In the Summer of Sixty" are reprinted from *American Ballads and Songs*, edited by Louise Pound, with Introduction by Kenneth S. Goldstein, with the permission of Charles Scribner's Sons. Copyright 1922 Charles Scribner's Sons; copyright renewed 1950 Louise Pound; copyright © 1972 Charles Scribner's Sons.